K<small>THE</small>INGFISHER'S CALL

THE KINGFISHER'S CALL

A NOVEL OF ESPIONAGE

JOHN REED

SOURCEBOOKS LANDMARK™
AN IMPRINT OF SOURCEBOOKS, INC.®
NAPERVILLE, ILLINOIS

Published by Sourcebooks, Inc.
P.O. Box 4410, Naperville, Illinois 60567-4410
(630) 961-3900
FAX: (630) 961-2168
www.sourcebooks.com

Library of Congress Cataloging-in-Publication Data

Reed, John Robert, 1938-
   The Kingfisher's call / by John Reed.
      p.cm.
   ISBN 1-57071-796-6 (alk. paper)
1. Intelligence officers—Fiction. 2. Americans—China—Fiction. 3. Moles (Spies)—Fiction. 4. China—Fiction. I. Title.

PS3568.E36645 K56 2002
813'.54—dc21

                                                                    2001054284

Printed and bound in the United States of America
         PX   10 9 8 7 6 5 4 3 2 1

This book is for Fred and Donald, whose passing I note with sorrow. Their advice and counsel helped guide my course—especially through Burma and China. And for the other intelligence officers who helped, as always, from behind the scenes. And most of all for Jodi who believed, and still believes.

PROLOGUE

Baghdad, Iraq, 1990

The only sound in the stifling blackness was the breathing of two men, the American and the Iraqi. Sweat, mingled with tears, trickled down Tuck Nyland's face. Had he cried out in his sleep? The man beside him grunted and shifted his body slightly. But there was little room to move. The spider hole had been built for two people—now there were three.

The girl had been dead almost nine hours. Her body, lying between the two men, had begun to stiffen. Nyland's shirt was caked with her blood. He closed his eyes and tried not to think about the man who had killed her.

The official line in the Gulf War was that the U.S. had no intelligence sources inside Saddam Hussein's inner circle. The system is too closed, the briefing officers said. Most people believed it was true. But the stories were disinformation designed to protect the CIA's most sensitive asset, Aziz Mohammed al-nuri, a member of Saddam's General Intelligence Directorate. His code name was Jasper.

The night before Operation Desert Storm was to begin, the Agency, with support from units of the U.S. Air Force First Special Operations Wing, had inserted one man, a former Navy SEAL, into the desert outside Baghdad to bring Jasper back. The first wave of air attacks was only hours away. If they were ever going to get him out, it would have to be now.

Nyland's boss, a senior officer in the CIA's Directorate of Operations named Jon Cross, had briefed Nyland in Riyadh just before the insertion: Nyland was to keep Jasper hidden in the spider hole until nightfall when the BlackHawk could return. What if they were discovered, Nyland had asked. Kill him, Cross had said. It would be the kindest thing to do.

The drop had been picture-perfect. The MH-60 BlackHawk helicopter, flying just above the sand, had dodged up narrow wadis, swerved to avoid Bedouin camps, and arrived at the drop point within twenty seconds of the designated time.

Nyland had rappelled from the BlackHawk and dropped onto the hot sand, clutching his silenced Uzi. As the dust from the helicopter cleared, he could see before him, outlined against the desert stars, the dark, angular shapes of the Baghdad skyline.

The hole he dug was six feet by three, barely three feet deep, covered by a lightweight plastic panel with built-in trapdoor. He had shoveled sand over the panel, leaving only a thin viewing slit. After the wind smoothed and leveled the sand, the slit was unnoticeable even a few feet away. A spider hole—a technique the Green Berets had borrowed from the Vietcong.

Jasper arrived at the hole just before noon on January sixteenth. Nyland immediately contacted the CIA on a satellite radio link. The reply came five minutes later: pick-up at 0100 hours, seventeen January. Two hours before the Allied bombing was to begin. Cutting it close.

Thirteen hours to wait. The two men had lain side-by-side in the darkness, each lost in his own thoughts. They had shared Nyland's rations, and taken turns watching through the small viewing slit. A road, nothing more than two narrow ruts in the sand, curved along a gentle rise before them and disappeared up a wadi. Nyland had been dozing when Jasper shook him awake and pointed toward the viewing slit. A young girl wearing a ragged, brown dress had wandered up from the dirt track and was walking toward the spider hole. Nyland held his breath.

She paused a moment, staring at the viewing slit, then squatted and pulled open the trapdoor. Her eyes widened at the sight of the two men. She opened her mouth to scream. Jasper shot her through the heart. The "chuff" of his silenced pistol was lost on the wind.

As he dragged the girl's body into the hole, he had laughed at Nyland's stunned reaction. "What do you think war is? You do what you must do, and you trust Allah. Here we do not let machines fight for us—we kill face to face." He had grasped the dead girl's hair and jerked her head back. "This is what war looks like. Get used to it, CIA man."

But, in the hours that followed, Nyland had not gotten used to it. Darkness had crept across the desert and soon Jasper fell asleep. Finally, exhausted, Nyland dozed off. As usual, the nightmare was waiting: an image from his childhood. His sister, Lynn, lying dead on the rocks beside the ocean, her head smashed. Blood soaking into the sand.

★ ★ ★

It was midnight. Nyland lay staring at the darkness, his breathing ragged. Beside him, the Iraqi agent chuckled. "You cry in your sleep, CIA man. You are not suited for this kind of work."

"You didn't have to kill her."

"What choice? Her or us. You don't know what Saddam does to his enemies. Believe me, I have seen firsthand."

"We can't just lie here with her...body."

"You want to do something else?" Jasper chuckled.

Nyland's voice was barely a whisper: "You're getting close, friend."

"Save your schoolyard bravado. I am doing your country a great favor. Show some appreciation."

Think about the mission. Maybe Jasper was right, what did one more death matter—even the death of a child? Slow breaths. Relax. The helicopter would come in less than an hour and the nightmare of the spider hole would be over.

"You are a man who follows orders," Jasper said. "Yours are very clear. You will bring me out of here safely. Forget the girl; she is a casualty of war. Say a prayer to your god if it makes you feel better. I'm going to sleep." The Iraqi rolled over, facing Nyland. As he shifted position, the girl's body rolled against him. He chuckled in the darkness. "I think she likes me."

Nyland drove his fist into Jasper's face.

★ ★ ★

The BlackHawk hovered above the spider hole, again precisely on schedule. The crew winched its passengers on board and the helicopter raced away toward the Iraqi border.

An hour later, to the south, choppers from Task Force Normandy swept in over the desert. Two Pave Low helicopters, crammed with exotic navigation gear led the way followed by four heavily armed Apaches. Eight miles from the target, the Pave Lows dropped glowing chemical sticks to position the Apaches. The Apache's laser-guided Hellfire missiles were dead on target, ripping apart two Iraqi radar stations in a string of fiery explosions, punching a hole in Saddam's defenses.

Hundreds of allied planes streamed through the gap, headed for Baghdad. It was 3:00 A.M., Iraqi time. Operation Desert Storm had begun.

★ ★ ★

Langley, Virginia

Robert Jaynes, the CIA's Deputy Director of Operations, was a man of order and precision. He arranged the papers before him in a neat stack, squaring their edges, and laid his red pen on the polished walnut table. The DDO stared for a long moment at the man seated before him.

The man sat rigidly upright in the armless chair. He wore his black hair in a military buzz cut; there was an insolent look in his pale blue eyes. His face was deeply tanned, highlighting the four white scars down his cheek. "You understand, Mister Nyland, that this is an administrative hearing and not a trial."

Tuck shrugged his shoulders but said nothing.

A hard case, Jaynes thought. Another one of Jon Cross's god-damn cowboys. It was going to be a pleasure to take this one out of action. "These gentlemen and I will be asking you some questions about your operation in Iraq. For the record, Mister Craig is representing the general counsel's office, and Mister Phillips is from the director's office. Miss Hamilton will be recording."

A stenographer in the corner keyed her machine and paper spooled from it, a permanent record of the hearing, formal and proper.

Craig from the general counsel's office said, "This is not a legal proceeding, per se, but is there anyone you wish to have present?"

"Jon Cross."

Nyland's voice was surprisingly deep, an actor's voice, Jaynes thought. "Mister Cross has been—reassigned," he said.

"You can't punish him for what I did." There was an edge to Nyland's voice.

"He is not being punished."

"I want him here."

"That's impossible. This hearing is not about Mister Cross. True, he was your control, but he wasn't *there*, was he?"

No, Nyland thought. Jon Cross had not been there. But he understood in a way these REMFs never could.

A faint smile crossed Nyland's face at the thought. "Rear Echelon Mother Fuckers," he muttered.

Jaynes looked up. "What did you say?"

Nyland shook his head.

"You find these proceedings amusing?"

"No sir."

Craig said, "You beat Aziz Mohammed al-nuri to death. Do you dispute that fact?"

"It wasn't my intention—"

"Not your intention?" Jaynes threw up his hands. "You killed our most valuable intelligence asset in the Persian Gulf, whose information could no doubt have saved hundreds of lives and a few million dollars worth of equipment, and you say it was not your intention?"

Phillips, the DCI's man, looked up from his notes. "Jasper was unconscious when they pulled him onto the helicopter. The Air Force medics said his face was beaten beyond recognition. He died an hour later. Are you trying to tell us this was an accident?"

Nyland said quietly, "It wasn't an accident."

"Your orders were to kill this agent if there was any possibility of his being captured by the Iraqis. Was there any such possibility?"

"In war there's always that possibility."

Phillips shook his head slowly. "There were no Iraqi soldiers in the area; you were hidden in the spider hole. The truth is, Mr. Nyland, all you had to do was stay put and keep quiet and Jasper would have gotten out safely. You're not some rookie; you've been in combat. Your record up to now is damned impressive. What the hell happened in that spider hole? If you think there are mitigating circumstances..."

Nyland looked at the three men across the table. It was difficult to explain his attack on Jasper, even to himself. What kind of man jeopardizes the lives of his comrades over personal feelings? At the time, his fists had almost seemed to move on their own, pounding the man's face again and again. In the pitch black spider hole, Nyland had felt the man's fingernails ripping his face, heard his guttural screams of pain. Blood had flowed down Nyland's arms, soaked into his shirt. And he *had* meant to kill the man, he thought. These three men, his judges, couldn't possibly understand.

"The little girl—" Nyland's voice broke.

"Yes," Jaynes said. "The little girl Jasper allegedly killed. We really have only your word on that, don't we?"

But the little girl had been there. For the past three months, the image of her face had appeared more and more in his dreams. In the dreams, the little Iraqi girl became Lynn, his sister. An endless replay of the scene: his sister attacked, molested by high school bullies while Tuck was forced to watch. She had broken free, tried to escape. Pursued by her tormenters, she had fallen off a cliff onto the rocks. Her brother, powerless against the bigger boys, could only cradle her broken body in his arms as the cold Pacific surf washed around his legs, mingling with the blood from the terrible gash in her forehead.

On the beach in Fort Bragg, California, he had sworn to himself he would never let anything like that happen again. But it had.

"I take it from your silence that you have nothing to say in your defense," Jaynes said.

"No, sir." Nyland's gaze was steady.

Jaynes coughed nervously and looked away. Nyland's muscles tensed, tightening the fabric of his coat across his shoulders. Hastily, Jaynes went on, "If you have nothing further, we're adjourned for one hour." The three men in suits rose as one. The hearing was over.

An hour later, Tuck was called back into the hearing room. Jaynes turned to the stenographer. "This is off the record, Ms. Hamilton."

She rested her hands in her lap.

Jaynes said, "My recommendation was that you be charged with treason for the damage you have done to this country. That offense is punishable by death. But apparently, someone up there likes you, though I can't imagine why."

Jaynes frowned as he pulled a single sheet of paper from his jacket pocket. "Mr. Nyland, would you please rise?"

Tuck stood up.

"Daniel T. Nyland, by order of the Director of Central Intelligence, you are hereby released from employment by the Central Intelligence Agency, and permanently enjoined from rehire."

◀1▶

Xinjiang Uygur Autonomous Region, China

The razor wire around the cluster of squat, gray buildings was rusted, the warning signs on the gate faded and hard to read, but still the locals stayed away. The soldiers shot trespassers without warning, they said, and the Alsatians prowling between the double chain-link fences had been specially trained to rip off a man's genitals.

The complex, halfway up the icy slopes of Bogda Mountain, above the town of Qitai, had gone into operation in 1980 and was run by the People's Liberation Army, that much the locals knew. It was rumored that westerners sometimes visited the compound. The villagers would have been surprised to learn that the facility was a listening post built by the American Central Intelligence Agency.

It was one of the few joint undertakings between Chinese Intelligence and the CIA. It had been built to intercept telemetry from Soviet missile and space shots. It was overseen by the Third Department of the PLA general staff in Beijing, the organization responsible for monitoring telecommunications of foreign armies. Kazachskja, part of the former Soviet Union, was less than three hundred miles away across the deserts of the Junggar Basin. The phased array radar concealed in the low, windowless buildings could detect and track an object the size of a basketball over a distance of two thousand miles. Its powerful antennas intercepted radio and telephone conversations across the border with ease.

The compound had been built with little concession to comfort. The floors were bare concrete, crisscrossed with cables and wires running to racks of equipment along the walls. The rooms were connected by narrow corridors lit by naked lightbulbs, half of which were usually burned out. Technicians on the morning watch sat at their consoles, faces bathed in the blue-green light of the radar scopes.

They paid little attention as the American CIA officer, Anne Hammersmith, slipped a test meter into her pocket and walked down a dimly lit corridor toward the rear entrance. It was just past seven o'clock. The morning briefing had begun; her Chinese counterparts would be occupied for at least an hour. She leaned against the heavy steel door listening to the wind outside.

Anne squeezed her eyes shut and pushed the door open. The wind nearly ripped it from her grasp, and a cloud of dust swirled around her. Spring and fall meant frequent gales in the high mountains, she knew, and this had been a particularly nasty spring. You didn't want to think about winter. She closed the door and started up the hill on her inspection tour.

Walk slowly, she told herself. No hurry. Don't want Ruilin suspicious. Her Chinese counterpart, a PLA captain, viewed her with a mixture of suspicion and lust. Fuck him, she thought—she had handled worse.

She climbed the gravel path, surveying the clusters of concrete buildings. The insulation on one of the cables leading to the main antenna array was deteriorating under the endless assault of the wind and snow. She made a point of moving her test meter over the cable, then, for appearances, wrote on her pad with a thin, black pen, a series of fluid Chinese ideographs.

It had been her fluency in Mandarin as well as her computer skills that had gotten her this posting. Once a month, she traveled the fifteen hundred miles from the American embassy in Beijing to inspect and repair the computers and communications equipment in the listening post. It was not a bad assignment, but career limiting. Not much data of any real use was relayed from the station these days. The Soviet side of the border was mostly quiet. Still, the post stayed in operation. No one believed the Russian bear was permanently silent. Too many nukes in the hands of too many crazies.

She sat on a rock near the fence and tilted her face to the sun. The three Alsatians patrolling the double fences loped silently toward her and stood, tongues lolling, behind the wire. "Good dogs," she said. Ruilin, she knew, feared and hated the huge animals.

It was her favorite time of day. The sun, newly risen over the mountains, threw sheets of gold across the basin. Its light sparkled on several small lakes below, sewn like jewels into the endless tapestry of brown and tan. The stark beauty of the scene overwhelmed her. Three hundred and twenty thousand acres of nothing. It seemed like the end of the earth, the vista unbroken for nearly two hundred miles. The savage isolation of it seemed to match her own spirit. Here, she felt alone—and alive.

She had few friends outside the Agency; her mother and father were dead. No serious relationship. She thought of Marty Hausler, the man she had been seeing for the past six months. No real future there. Marty was a nice guy, but he was not "the man in the mask."

She always saw the words in quotes, a bad title for a bad movie. Silly as it was, she could not get the fantasy out of her mind. She had been jogging through an isolated patch of woods on the outskirts of Camp Peary, the CIA training camp in rural Virginia, when a man, dressed all in black, had stepped from behind a tree, blocking her path.

"Restricted area," he said. His voice was deep and resonant. His face was covered with a black ski mask, revealing only his pale, piercing blue eyes. It was the eyes that held her attention.

She stared at him, unable to move. He stepped closer. Later, she would remember his feet made no sound on the leaves. "Go back," he said quietly. He carried no weapons, but there was a feral intensity in him that frightened her.

She had reacted instinctively, as her Tae Kwan Do instructor had taught her, sending a roundhouse kick at the man's head. There was no other way to describe what happened next: the man simply disappeared. An instant later, he was behind her, his hand on her wrist. She struggled against it and felt his grip tighten.

"Don't." His fingers felt like steel.

"I'm CIA," she said weakly.

"I know."

He released her wrist. She spun around, but he was gone. The forest around her looked deserted, but she could still feel his eyes on her. She turned and ran. The encounter had lasted perhaps twenty seconds, but she remembered the man, the feel of his hand on her wrist, and, most of all, the sadness in his pale eyes.

She had never seen him again. Her instructors had only smiled when she related her encounter. There was no training exercise scheduled in that part of the camp, they said. Maybe you dreamed it.

Over time—it had been eight years since Camp Peary—the man had become a mythical standard against which other men were measured. And the others, including Marty, had always been found wanting. It was a silly defense mechanism to protect herself from getting hurt, she told herself. Set yourself an unreachable goal, and you never have to worry about meeting it. Anne and her imaginary boyfriend.

Anne Hammersmith had turned thirty the week before. The embassy staff in Beijing had given her a party and a cake with "Over-the-Hill-Hammer" scrolled in chocolate frosting. A lot of laughs. Later in her room, she stared into her glass of Wild Turkey and tried not to think of the loneliness inside. She consoled herself with one thought: she had her career—that would have to be enough.

A woman in the Central Intelligence Agency had an uphill battle, she thought. The newspapers were full of sexual harassment stories, job favoritism, men promoted over women. To be equal to a man, the saying went, a woman must be twice as good.

She was more than twice as good, dammit. A master's in computer science from Berkeley, fluent in Mandarin, top of her class in unarmed combat. And her service record was impeccable: devoted to the job, willing to go the extra mile, her supervisors had been effusive in their praise. And though she had not been promoted, she had gotten three commendations in the past five years.

And she had finally caught Jon Cross's attention. Cross was a senior operations officer, a legend in the clandestine services. He had served in every country in the Far East, and was one of the Agency's top China experts. She was surprised and flattered when he offered her a position on his new, super-secret task force. He had flown all the way to Hong Kong to make the offer in person.

She would have two jobs, he told her. As a technician in the Science and Technology Directorate, she would play the role of a colorless computer nerd. "You are absolutely uninteresting," Jon Cross explained to her. "You are invisible."

"I've been practicing that," she told him.

Her real job, Cross said, was to gather intelligence about specific targets in the Far East and report the findings directly to him. Cross told her little about his new task force except that it had been formed by presidential order. Only a handful of people knew of its existence. The president of the United States, the secretary of state, and the top echelon of the CIA. Even its name, "Task Force Seven," was classified top secret.

Her new assignment had changed her life. She had been, before Jon Cross's recruitment, just the kind of techno-drone he had described, laboring diligently in the trenches. Career stagnated, a woman in a man's world. Now she was somebody, she thought; but, there was no one she could tell.

She had been taught at Camp Peary that a good intelligence officer knows when to take risks, and no one rewarded a risk-taker more than Jon Cross. During last month's visit to the Qitai station, she had taken one hell of a risk. Now it was time to see if it had paid off. She glanced down at the compound. The gravel paths between the windowless buildings were deserted.

She slid the test meter from her pocket and opened the cover. The meter was actually a powerful computer with an infrared linking device built in. An hour before, she had placed the device on a computer console in the communications room and pressed two buttons. In an instant, a series of files were downloaded over the infrared link. No connection to the central computer, no alarm.

In the files, if she was lucky, would be copies of any messages transmitted on the frequency she had programmed into the master computer a month before. And, if she was really lucky, none of the Chinese intelligence officers staffing the post had stumbled onto her reprogramming.

Her target was General Xing Wanpo, a man Jon Cross wanted watched. Xing was a ruthless hard-liner recently promoted to the PLA general staff. He was conducting a field training exercise near Qitai, unusual for someone of his rank. The Agency was most eager to learn what he was up to. He had commanded the 27th Army, most noted for the Tieneman Square massacre of 1989, then been promoted to western regional commander. Some months ago, he had been given his fourth star and his general staff assignment. Xing was headed for bigger things. Find out what he's up to, Cross had said—be creative.

Anne had gotten Xing's radio frequency from the NSA liaison. It was for short-range communications, usually between vehicles or small field outposts. The signals were too faint to be heard by the satellites. She had added several lines of code to the computer's program that would, in effect, turn the "ears" of the Qitai listening post around, and use the PLA's own installation to eavesdrop on the general's secret conversations.

Had her dangerous plan worked?

She tucked a small earpiece in her ear and tapped the keypad. A list of dates and times appeared on the test meter's screen. Twelve messages intercepted, the latest only two days ago. She highlighted the date and pressed another key. There was static for a moment, then a voice speaking Mandarin: "Panther Seven, go ahead."

Hammersmith turned up the volume. 'Panther Seven,' she knew, was the general's call sign. Xing Wanpo's voice, even filtered through her tiny earphone, had the unmistakable ring of command. He was talking to someone in another vehicle: "...last link is forged, we are ready to move. Our friend in Washington has seen to it."

An older man's voice, curt and heavy with authority: "The question is, when?"

"Tell them I will be..." The general's voice faded, leaving only the sound of static in Anne's ear. She sat back stunned. "We are ready to move," what the hell did that mean? Who was the "friend in Washington?" If it meant what she thought it did, and she was the first to bring it back to Langley, her career would take a major step forward.

Behind her, near the fence, one of the guard dogs growled, a low rumble, deep in his throat. She snatched the earphone from her ear. Ruilin was walking toward her.

"You are enjoying the sun?" he said.

"The view up here is wonderful," she said. Her Mandarin carried the short, brisk accent of Beijing, where her instructor had grown up.

"There is nothing to measure up here." Ruilin pointed to her test meter.

She slid the instrument in her pocket. "I was reviewing some data—"

"You were reviewing what you should not, I think. The instrument, please." He held out his hand.

She stepped back toward the fence. The dogs, alerted by the tension in her stance, growled softly. "This device is U. S. Government property."

"Give it to me."

"Step away from me, Ruilin," she said. One of the dogs stood on his hind legs, forepaws clawing at the wire. She could feel the animal's breath on her neck. "You're upsetting the dogs."

"They are behind the fence, they cannot help you. No one can help you." He turned to look down at the cluster of buildings below. "And you are a long way from home." He ran his hand up her arm and squeezed her shoulder.

She jerked away and stumbled against the wire. "I won't tell you again."

"You are in no position to make threats. But perhaps we can reach some kind of agreement. Give me your test meter, which I suspect is something more, and show a little friendliness." His hands slid down the front of her parka. She stood stiffly as he cupped his hands around her breasts.

"You fucking pig," she said in English.

He reached between her legs. "English, Chinese, all the same here."

She trapped his hand in a painful wrist lock and bent him forward. His face was inches from the wire.

"Bitch. You are guilty of espionage; you changed the frequencies. I can prove it."

"Who else did you tell?" Anne pulled his arm higher behind his back, forcing him onto his toes.

"The honor will be all mine," Ruilin said. "I will tell my superiors in due time, after I have had the pleasure of—" He reversed his stance, pivoted, and threw her over his hip. She crashed to the ground, stunned. He reached in her pocket and pulled out the test meter.

Anne opened her eyes. Ruilin was unfastening her belt. She let herself go limp. Her head lolled to the side, her eyes closed. She felt his hands on her again, tugging down her panties. Her open-handed strike caught him on the bridge of the nose, split the cartilage, and he fell backward against the fence. The dogs, excited by the blood, began to bay and throw themselves against the wire. Ruilin scrambled back, mesmerized by the huge animals. Anne's boot caught him in the temple and he fell face first into the dirt. The rock she smashed against his skull finished the job.

The dogs' howling would bring someone in a moment. She retrieved the test meter, pulled out a small circuit board, and slipped it in her pocket. The messages she had recorded would be safe now. The test meter was again just a harmless instrument. Deliberately, she grasped the front of her bra and ripped the silky fabric. She was on her knees in the dust crying when the guards found her.

The commander of the Qitai listening post was beside himself with apologies. The actions of Ruilin did not represent the PLA or any of the men under his command, he assured her. He believed her story. During their scuffle, Ruilin had fallen and hit his head on a rock. It would be listed as an accident. Surely, there was no need to mention this—unfortunate incident—to Beijing?

Anne shook her head. It was a tragic accident, perhaps Ruilin had been frightened of the dogs, slipped and fallen. There was no reason to file a complaint. The incident need never go beyond this room.

The circuit board was hidden safely in the sole of her hiking boot. Its contents would be transmitted to Langley in twenty-four hours. She stood and bowed formally. Let the matter be forgotten.

The commander drove her to the airport in his personal car. As she settled back in the seat of the small military jet, she smiled. Jon Cross would be pleased.

◄2►

The rain stopped just after 2:00 A.M. By then, the SEAL team had crept out of the surf and crossed the beach. A few faint stars appeared, revealing a pale crescent of sand and a line of trees beyond. The surf washed against the trunk of a eucalyptus tree lying half-buried in the sand. In the log's shadow crouched the figure of a man in a wet suit.

The SEAL team leader, Chief Petty Officer Thompson, could feel it in his gut: something was wrong.

His night vision goggles showed an open stretch of beach leading to the rocky outcropping that was the team's objective. They should have been there by now. The five SEALS were nowhere to be seen. He whispered into his microphone, "Sparrow Five, this is Hawk. What is your location?"

A flicker of movement to his left.

He lifted the Sig Sauer 9mm. A man, walking toward him down the beach. What the hell? Though this was supposed to be a training exercise, he knew his team would not permit an aggressor to stroll calmly down the beach. Especially not in the middle of a critical operation like this, the final qualifying trial. "Sparrow team, come in," he whispered. "Aggressor headed my direction, over."

Silence in his headphone.

It was as if the entire five-man team had disappeared. The exercise was turning into a fiasco. And to be beaten by a bunch of CIA creeps—the humiliation burned his cheeks. The CO had arranged for a special group of aggressors to test his best SEAL team. It looked as if the CIA had won.

Chief Thompson began mentally adding up the years to

retirement. There would be no forgiving an operation like this. Should drop the son-of-a-bitch now, he thought. His finger tightened on the trigger. The figure on the beach stopped and Chief Thompson heard a low chuckle. "Before you kill me, Tommy, don't you want to know what happened?"

Thompson lowered his pistol. "Tucker Nyland. You miserable, low-life, bottom-feeding mother fucker."

"They told me you'd mellowed out, Chief," Nyland said.

"It had to be you. Who else has the balls to take on the SEALS on their own turf?" Thompson holstered the pistol. "Where the hell is my team?"

"Three resting comfortably about twenty meters back in the trees, one behind the rocks there." Nyland pointed up the beach.

"That's four." Thompson said.

"Oh, yeah. I think your point man must have tripped in the sand."

"—the fuck?"

Nyland grasped the outstretched hand of a SEAL who had been lying just on the other side of the tree trunk, and pulled him to his feet. He had been less than three feet from Chief Thompson. "You OK, point man?" Nyland said.

"Yes sir." The young SEAL looked sheepishly at his team leader. "Got me fair and square, Chief." He pointed to the smear of orange paint on his wet suit. "Never saw him. Sorry."

Thompson glowered at the man. "Are you laughing, Rico? Because if you are—"

"Sir. No sir!" The young SEAL's lips were tightly pursed.

"Nyland, where's the rest of *your* people?" Thompson asked.

"Just me," Nyland shrugged. "Only one SEAL team, only sent one guy."

"That was the Texas Rangers, asshole." He turned to the point man. "Rico, round up the rest of your buddies. We have some serious debriefing to do before the brass get here."

The man trotted up the beach.

"Surprised you're still alive, Tuck. Heard you joined the CIA, then you kind of disappeared. I won't ask what you've been up to."

Nyland pulled off his black hood. "Little of this, little of that."

And a lot of nothing, he thought. He hadn't realized how much of his life was wrapped up in his CIA career until it was taken from him. He had returned to California and taken a job on a fishing boat in Fort Bragg, his boyhood home. It was tedious, backbreaking work, without respite, without a future. Occasionally, out of boredom, he joined the crew in a dockside tavern. One night, after several whiskeys, the fishing boat's captain had risen unsteadily and announced, "I told myself when I was eighteen, I wasn't gonna spend my life on a damn boat. But, by God, that's exactly what I've gone and done."

Nyland had quit soon after that, taken a job as a security guard at Wal-Mart. They had given him a badge and a cheap .38 revolver.

Then, late one Saturday night, he had had a visitor.

He had been sitting in his rented trailer, turning the revolver over and over in his hand. Hell of a comedown from the high-tech MP5 submachine gun he had carried as a CIA officer. And no longer could he call in multi-million dollar attack helicopters as he had done in Bosnia and the Persian Gulf. His back-up now was an aging rent-a-cop in a green Ford sedan.

The man who had knocked on his apartment door that night had been in civilian clothes, sport jacket and slacks, but his bearing was military. He sat stiffly in the chair Nyland offered, opened his briefcase, and made his pitch. The SEALs were looking for people to act as aggressors during training exercises. Nyland would be a civilian contractor, the man told him. It paid well, but the SEALs demanded top performance. The man looked Nyland up and down. The job would start in one month. He might want to use that time to get in shape—and lose the beard.

Nyland read the contract, but hesitated when the man handed him a pen. "A lot of people remember you, Tuck," the man said. Nyland signed his name.

He had shaved his beard and gone to work. He ran along the beach for hours at a stretch, ground through the PT exercises, straining his muscles to the point of collapse, then plunged into the icy surf, and swam until exhaustion overtook him. He hadn't trained so hard since the BUD/s course. The grueling six-month program, "Basic Underwater Demolition/SEALs," was said to be the most difficult in the world.

Though he was a civilian, an outsider, his new job at the Naval Special Warfare Center in Coronado had been a welcome challenge. The SEALs tended to attract a particularly aggressive type. They hated to lose, especially to a civilian. But Nyland had more than kept up, infiltrating their night exercises, approaching their boats underwater, scoring "kills" with his paint gun. The old instincts got sharper; he moved silently through the darkness, appearing almost magically where the SEALs least expected him. Finally, he had been given an assignment to infiltrate Chief Thompson's team.

Thompson had been Nyland's instructor in the BUD/s course. Nyland had finished at the top of the class. He owed that success, he knew, to Thompson's driving him—harder and harder—until he was sure he could go no farther, then showing him he could.

As Chief Thompson shook Nyland's hand on the dark beach, he noted the four white scars along his cheek, the haunted light in his eyes. The CIA had used him roughly, Thompson thought. "You miss the SEALs?"

"Yeah. Just that I don't always like playing by the book. But that's how I got you tonight. I read the same book—changed a few of the pages."

"Wrote a few from what I hear. They're still talking about you at the BUD/s course. How you gonna write this exercise up?"

"Off the record, I'd recommend that you not rely on that nightscope technology so much. Those goggles cut your peripheral vision down. Makes you a little easier to sneak up on. And a couple of your people need to brush up on their noise discipline. Officially, I can't write up anything." Nyland pulled a pistol from his belt, pointed it at his chest, and pulled the trigger. A splotch of orange paint spread across the black rubber of his wet suit. "You killed me in the first five minutes."

"I owe you, my ass was hanging on this."

"What happens now?"

"Classified. But, thanks to you, it looks like we'll be joining

SEAL Team One."

It was the team, Nyland knew, that operated in South East Asia. "Wish I could join you."

"If it was up to me..." Thompson shrugged. "You can always get in touch through Special Operations Command."

"See you sometime, Tommy," Nyland shook his hand. "Maybe—"

The sound of a helicopter interrupted the conversation. A chopper moved in off of the ocean, its searchlight playing on the water. Thompson raised his voice over the sound of the rotors, "Little surprise for you, Tuck. Like to stick around, but we're not authorized."

Nyland looked up at the approaching light. The chopper settled onto the beach a hundred yards away, rotors still turning. A solitary figure climbed down and started toward him.

When Nyland glanced around, Thompson was gone.

The rain had started again, the drops throwing up miniature geysers of sand. Jon Cross pulled his overcoat closer around him as he walked. Salt mist coated his glasses, giving the scene before him a watery, surreal appearance. He fought the urge to take them off and wipe them. A trickle of cold water ran down his neck and he shivered inside his coat.

Nyland stood watching Cross's approach, making no move to come forward. Bad sign. His black-clad form was only faintly outlined against the pale sand. As Cross approached, Nyland said, "Surprised to see you standing out here in the rain. I thought you would be DDO by now."

"Robert Jaynes has that job and welcome to it."

"What do you want?"

"Your help," Cross said.

"You're the one who arranged this training contract with the SEALs?"

"They jumped at it. You're one of the best."

"Not according to Robert Jaynes." Nyland smiled crookedly.

"A lot of things have changed since—"

"Since they threw me out? I failed you, let's leave it at that."

"Hear me out," Cross said.

"If you're feeling sorry—"

Cross moved closer to the tall man and looked up at his face. "You acted with honor and principal in Iraq. I'm not sorry for you. And I won't have you feeling sorry for yourself. You have a very special set of skills, and a particular kind of loyalty that I am in need of."

"I can't work for the CIA again. I wouldn't, even if you could pull it off." Nyland said. He turned and looked out across the water, his profile faintly lit by the helicopter's light. Cross studied the face. Pride there, bitterness. It was going to be a hard sell. Cross took off his gold-rimmed glasses and wiped them on a handkerchief. "Would you work for me?" he asked.

"Why would you want me to do that?"

Angry but interested. Cross took the small opening. "I was out of the game for a while, but I've been given an opportunity to, shall we say, restore my career. I can't tell you more than that, except that if you agree to my proposal, you report only to me. No one, not Jaynes or anyone in the operations directorate, will know you're back in."

"Back into what?"

"A special task force. Far as I can go."

The first meeting of Task Force Seven had been in the Oval Office. Cross would be in charge, the president had told him, allowed to hand-pick his team, authorized to expend whatever funds he deemed necessary. The task force was charged with gathering intelligence related to the Chinese Ministry of State Security, the Chinese equivalent of the American CIA. To get an agent inside, if possible.

The only man he hadn't been allowed to pick was Tuck Nyland. Jaynes had made that clear. But there were ways. No one at CIA knew he was standing on this rain-soaked California beach. The SEAL team had been ordered to leave the area, and Cross's helicopter pilot was a civilian, a loyal, personal friend. He was breaking a lot of rules, he knew. But there was no choice now; he had Kingfisher to think about. Cross stuffed his hands deeper in his pockets, hunching his shoulders against the chill. "I have a job for you."

Nyland stood looking out to sea and said nothing.

"Overseas," Cross said.

Nyland turned back toward the older man, rain dripping down his face. In the dim light off the water, Cross could see the scars on Nyland's cheeks. Fingernails. The agent, Jasper, in a last desperate effort to save his life, had raked Nyland's face, flaying off pieces of skin. The wounds had become infected in the desert heat. The scars were permanent.

Nyland was on edge, Cross could see, ready to withdraw if the proposition was wrong. Ready to strike out in anger if provoked. A dangerous man, on edge. Perfect. But Cross could sense he hadn't made up his mind. There was something else.

Nyland let out a long breath. "Where were you?"

Cross knew exactly what he meant. Being banned from the dismissal hearing had brought Jon Cross as close as he had ever been to insubordination. There was a cardinal rule in his life: stand by your people. He had been responsible for Tuck Nyland, for his being in Iraq. And he had been ordered not to attend the hearing, leaving Tuck thinking his boss had deserted him.

A difficult order to follow, but there was no choice. It had come directly from the DCI. Jon Cross was being placed on a temporary leave of absence for the "greater good," Robert Jaynes had said. What greater good was there, Cross wondered, than loyalty to your people?

"I was ordered out to pasture. They pulled my clearances, and if Robert Jaynes could have had his way, I would have joined you out in the cold."

"I didn't know that," Nyland said.

"Didn't get to tell my story until after the fact. Jaynes got my side of it—straight up his ass. He just laughed. But since the operation was my responsibility..." Cross shrugged his shoulders. "That's history now. My situation has changed; I have a little more—leeway in my operations."

"So I see."

"Not everyone likes that, and first among them is Robert Jaynes. He wants me under his control." Cross smiled faintly. "Movie I saw on television the other night, Clint Eastwood says to the bad guy, 'That's not gonna happen.'"

"Whose control are you under?"

"That's not your concern."

"If I were going to work for you," Nyland said. "When would I—"

"Are you in or out?"

Nyland looked down at the sand. "I don't know."

"Bullshit. You were about to ask when would you start."

"Well—"

Cross nodded toward the chopper. "How about right now?"

The SEAL team gathered around Chief Thompson on the beach as the helicopter moved away across the water. After the noise faded, Rico said, "So that was Tuck Nyland?"

The chief's voice dropped to an ominous whisper: "He was never here, understood?"

"I sure as hell never saw him." Rico said.

Thompson studied the circle of faces around him. "Would one of you SEALs like to tell me what the fuck happened here tonight?"

◄3►

The White House, Washington D.C.

President Jack Gardner and his cabinet were discussing the CIA. There was no question in their minds that the Agency was in trouble. It was seen now by many as an outmoded relic of the Cold War. Wracked by scandals and intelligence gaffs, employee morale in the toilet.

Everyone agreed there was a problem. Not everyone agreed on the solution. Secretary of Defense Charles Blanchard was President Gardner's long-time friend and ally, but today, the tension was strong in the room as Blanchard rose to speak.

"Mr. President, with all due respect, we're trying to put a Band-Aid on a cancer here." Several strands of white hair fell across Blanchard's forehead. He brushed them back in place. The man had been a hero, had won a Medal of Honor in Vietnam, but, lately, his military bearing seemed to be slipping a bit, the president thought.

"And the cancer is spreading," Blanchard said. "Spreading."

Blanchard was wound up tight; the secretary's voice was a pitch higher than normal. Building a head of steam. "Charles, change has to come incrementally. We have to alter the whole culture of the place, but we mustn't destroy it in the process."

"And my point is, that is exactly what we must do. Tear it down and rebuild it."

"Yes, starting with the Directorate of Operations." The DO was often called Clandestine Services, the branch people thought of when they thought of spies. "We've had this conversation before, Secretary Blanchard."

No more "Charles." The president was digging in his heels. Still, Blanchard pushed on. "A culture built on contempt for accountability, a cult of secrecy, serves no one—certainly not the policy makers."

"Such as yourself?"

"And you, Mr. President." Blanchard smiled a practiced smile and spread his hands in a gesture of conciliation. "We must simply make it easier for policy makers to use what intelligence has to offer. Diplomacy cannot be the tail of intelligence—"

"Charles, before we get into your dog metaphor, let me say that I understand your agenda here." The president motioned Blanchard to sit down. He sat. "You want the CIA broken up, you want the Directorate of Operations under control of the Defense Department."

Blanchard said, "Defense Department could handle the paramilitary aspects, the National Reconnaissance Office could take over the satellite operations, they do most of it already. State is the best at working open sources. It all—"

"I've read your briefing paper, Charles. It has merit, I agree, but I'm not ready to hand you the CIA just yet." The president snapped closed his leather portfolio and stood up. Meeting adjourned.

Blanchard's voice was cold, formal. "Thank you, Mr. President."

★   ★   ★

San Francisco, California

While Cross was making coffee in the kitchen, Nyland explored the safe house, walking the dark hallway, peering in the bedrooms. God damn, the place was depressing, cheaply furnished with tweed sofas, Formica tables, and green shag carpet. A few cheaply framed prints hung on the walls, mountains and seascapes. Blue and yellow ducks adorned the bathroom wallpaper.

As with all safe houses, there was a desolate air about it. A vase of dried weeds and flowers sat on a dresser in the back bedroom, beside it a copy of *Leaves of Grass*. He picked up the book and ruffled through the pages, then, out of habit, wiped it clean with the tail of his shirt. A ghost of a house, with no trace of its inhabitants. Had normal people ever lived here?

As Nyland walked into the kitchen, Cross was pouring boiling water into a glass carafe. He sat the French press aside and said,

"Four minutes." While the coffee brewed, the two helped themselves to sandwiches from a paper bag on the counter. Cross said, "I'd better put you in the picture."

Nyland smiled. How many times had he heard that phrase? Somehow, the words seemed comforting.

Cross's helicopter had taken them to a small civilian airport north of San Diego, where a chartered Cessna was waiting. Nyland would be traveling alone, Cross said. The less they were seen together, the better. His helicopter was already in the air as Nyland boarded the small plane.

He had flown directly to San Francisco and had been met by a young black man driving a nondescript van with heavily tinted windows. The driver said nothing as Nyland climbed in. The trip to the Agency safe house took almost an hour as the van wound its way around San Francisco. Cross had been waiting when Nyland arrived.

Cross poured two cups of coffee. "The story starts about seven months ago, when a software designer named Jennifer Chin met the bad guy in the piece, Tommy Lin," Cross said.

"A chance meeting?"

"Correct."

"What do we know about this bad guy?" Nyland asked.

"He owns an export company that procures high-tech equipment for the Chinese government. We traced him to a company in Hong Kong that is owned by the People's Liberation Army." He sipped his coffee. Lin was a San Francisco businessman, Cross explained, dealing in computer software. He wasn't too particular about the legalities of his transactions.

It had been the classic espionage recruitment: a supposedly chance encounter with Jennifer at a restaurant near her office. Two people sharing their ethnic heritage, both in the computer business. May I share your table? He had been personable, charming. The two had chatted for nearly an hour.

Jennifer worked for Omega Data Systems, a software design firm in Palo Alto. She had not told Tommy Lin that the company existed on secret government contracts, mostly with the CIA and the State Department. The two arranged to meet again. Jennifer Chin reported the contact to her superiors. The FBI had been watching him, noted his approach to Jennifer Chin, and called the CIA liaison office. The report was forwarded to Jon Cross. Cross passed a message back through channels: play along with him.

They went out to dinner. Lin asked her for a small favor. Could she get him a copy of the confidential employee telephone book? To help him develop contacts, he had explained. She had done so, though it was technically against the law. As the weeks went by, it became evident that he was looking for something more. That was when Jon Cross arrived on the scene and had become her case officer.

Nyland took a bite of his sandwich. "Not usually the kind of thing a senior officer gets involved in."

"Let me finish the story," Cross said.

Nyland nodded and took another bite. Cross was holding something back.

Jenny had given Tommy Lin a hard-luck story about drug habits and car payments. Perhaps he could help, Tommy said. Did she have access to any C4I software?

The acronym, Cross explained, stood for, "Command Control Communications Computers and Intelligence." Modern warfare involved molding a collection of technologies into a coherent whole. The C4I system tied everything together, he said, the vast network of computers, space-based weapons, missiles, and conventional weapons, setting up the link through which targeting information was passed to weapons. The sensor-to-shooter link. It had become the eyes and ears of the commander moving onto the twenty-first century battlefield.

It just happened that Jenny had access to C4I; in fact, she had written most of the computer code.

Jon Cross paced back and forth in the safe house's tiny kitchen, pausing occasionally to lift the blind and stare out at the darkened street. "Tommy Lin was very excited about the C4I package. It's the technology, after all, that will probably win the next war."

Nyland ate the last of his sandwich and crumpled the wax paper wrapper into a ball. "And Jennifer Chin told him it might be for sale?"

Cross nodded. "He didn't blink when she mentioned her price: a quarter-of-a-million dollars."

"He's either very eager or very dumb."

"Probably both. Anyway, the drop has been set up," Cross said. "Tommy Lin contacted Jenny a few hours ago. They meet at two o'clock tomorrow morning. She hands over the C4I software, he gives her a briefcase full of money. Jenny's C4I software is headed for General Xing Wanpo. You may remember him as the man whose troops massacred all those students in Tieneman Square. He got promoted. He's been stockpiling American technology. He's the hardest of the hard-liners in the PLA, and he's now been promoted to the PLA general staff. If trouble starts, he will be the one to start it."

"Trouble?"

Cross said, "The People's Liberation Army is getting bigger and more powerful every day. They operate twenty or thirty thousand different companies around the world. They pour billions in profits back into their defense budget every year. That kind of power sometimes makes men like Xing Wanpo hungry for even more.

"Are we talking about the PLA trying to take over the country?"

"Xing would not be too unhappy at that eventuality," Cross said.

"We're *giving* him this software?"

Cross motioned with a tilt of his head: outside.

The rain had stopped, but the lawn was soggy underfoot as the two men walked behind the house. Nyland could smell the ocean on the damp night air. "The house bugged?" Nyland asked.

"We're getting into a very sensitive area here. The FBI and most of the Agency are being kept in the dark."

"Why? How legal is that?"

Cross looked at him sharply. "Not your concern at this point. What I'm going to tell you goes no farther: there's a trapdoor in the software."

"A bug."

"Not exactly. Know anything about nonsinusoidal waveforms? That's what makes the trapdoor work. I got a four-hour briefing from Science and Technology, of which I understood about 1 percent. But I gather that any data the Chinese put into the C4I package is directly transmitted to our satellites: all their message traffic, the location of their weapons systems, all their forces in the field. We receive it in real time. It's an incredible asset, too sensitive to share with the FBI just yet."

They had stopped in the farthest corner of the lawn. "There's something else," Cross said. "The software contains a virus that kicks in sixty days after they activate the C4I package. This gives us time to get a complete picture of their operations before—"

"It crashes."

"And takes their whole computer system with it, if things go according to plan. They call it softwar."

Nyland could feel the dampness of the lawn soaking into his shoes. He said, "Even if this C4I stuff gives us a window on the PLA, what if this virus thing doesn't kick in? Aren't we handing the Chinese a hell of a weapon to use against us?"

"Calculated risk."

"You must have had a bitch of a time getting an operation like this approved."

Cross stared at him, his face barely visible in the darkness.

"Christ," Nyland said. "You did it on your own. Who else knows about this operation?"

"Five people, including me. The DCI, two deputy directors, and the computer programmer who wrote the software."

"Jennifer Chin?"

Cross nodded. "We have to make the handoff, and make the FBI's attempt to stop it look real."

"I can see that, but to tell nobody else in CIA...?"

"Again, this goes no farther. I believe we have a mole somewhere—top level, maybe even the White House. The Chinese can't know that the software is booby trapped or they'll never use it."

"If the FBI is watching Jenny, what's to keep them from following her when she makes the drop, rolling up this Tommy Lin, and scuttling your operation?"

"You."

"You better put me in the picture." Nyland said.

Cross glanced at him but said nothing.

As they walked, the wet grass squished under their feet. "Jenny will make the drop at 2:00 A.M. in a park up in the Santa Cruz mountains," Cross said. "The FBI will receive an anonymous tip at about one-thirty. They will haul ass out there in their snazzy blue wind breakers and bulletproof vests, but they will not be successful in capturing Tommy Lin."

"Why is that?"

"Because you will fuck them up. Jennifer will be arrested, but Tommy Lin will escape. They'll put on a great show for Mr. Lin and he will be convinced he has gotten away with the real thing. When the FBI finds out that we kept them in the dark, there will be outrages and denunciations, but by then the software will be on its way to General Xing Wanpo, trapdoor, virus, and all."

Cross handed Nyland a black-and-white photograph. A smiling, Chinese man getting out of a car. "Tommy Lin is a merchant, basically, buying and selling. There shouldn't be any violence, but I want you ready. Nothing must happen to Jenny."

"You said something about a job overseas."

"This comes first," Cross said.

"You're pretty fond of Jenny."

"Let's say I've known her family for a long time. I promised them I would look after her." There was a softness in Jon Cross's voice that Nyland had not heard before.

"Don't worry. I'll watch out for her, but my track record's not—"

"Leave the self-pity behind, there's work to do."

Nyland nodded. "Tell me how I'm supposed to fuck up the FBI."

◄4►

Karley State Park, California

Fog swirled across the Santa Cruz Mountains, drifting amongst the eucalyptus and scrub pine, coating every surface with a film of moisture. Nyland wiped the lens of his nightvision scope and tugged at the head straps, tightening their fit. When it was time to move, he would be ready.

The scene before him had remained unchanged for the past several hours: a single streetlight at the edge of the parking lot, shining on the cinder-block restrooms, a bark path edged with stones winding up the hillside, a picnic table at the edge of the trees.

His night scope revealed two racoons pawing at the lid of a garbage can near the picnic table. This was where Jennifer would meet Tommy Lin. At 2:00 A.M., Cross had said. Ten minutes from now.

The park was less than a mile off of the main highway, connected by a narrow, two-lane road. Earlier in the evening, Nyland had walked the road making note of escape routes. Why had Tommy Lin chosen a spot with only one way in and out? True, he would not be expecting trouble, but no trained agent would put himself in such an obvious trap. There had to be a fall-back plan, another way out.

As Nyland had scouted the woods around the parking lot, he had found it. Faint tire tracks in the carpet of pine needles lead him to an unused forest road. It intersected the highway near the park entrance, a pile of brush concealing the entrance. Nyland had studied the ground nearby. A few faint scuff marks near the brush pile. Someone else had come to check out this obscure dirt track. He had found Tommy Lin's escape route.

It was almost two. Nyland swept the area again with the night scope. Lin's escape route was hidden around the shoulder of a hill. A car parked there could easily slip down to the highway undetected.

Nyland heard the soft clink of the garbage can lid, but when he looked, the racoons had disappeared. The staccato bark of the motorcycle carried well in the silence of the forest. Nyland could follow the machine's progress as it turned off the highway and climbed to the park.

Jennifer Chin wore black motorcycle leathers and a full-cover helmet. She rode the Suzuki straight across the parking lot, up the bark path, and into the trees.

She walked back down the path, an aluminum case in her hand. The street light shone on her long, black hair. She was slender, and looked to be in her early thirties. She glanced at her watch, then turned to stare directly at Nyland's hiding place twenty yards back in the trees.

He froze, gloved hand over the nightvision scope, masking any glare from the lens. He had constructed a blind out of dead brush and limbs at the base of a eucalyptus tree. There, in a black jersey and trousers, he became part of the night. He knew she could not see him. Had she sensed his presence?

She looked toward the highway, head cocked, listening. Nyland, too, heard the sound of a car engine. Tommy was on time. A gray Toyota sedan rolled slowly through the cone of light from the street lamp and disappeared around the edge of the hill. Going for the dirt road. Nyland had been right. A moment later, a man appeared, moving through the trees toward Jennifer. The man wore a long, dark overcoat; a soft-brimmed hat obscured his face.

Jennifer stood up, and wrapped her arms around herself as if warding off a chill.

The man came steadily forward, a purposeful stride. He was carrying a black leather briefcase that bounced against his leg as he walked. He looked up at Jennifer as he passed under the streetlight and Nyland got a glimpse of his face. A Chinese man, mid-thirties. It wasn't Tommy Lin.

The man sat his briefcase on the picnic table and bowed to Jennifer. She backed away. Nyland caught a word or two of their conversation: "...works with me." Trying to convince her to hand over the aluminum case. She passed it to him.

He flipped open the case and pulled out a small package wrapped in white plastic, glanced at it, then put it back in the case.

"I know who you are!" Jenny said.

"Very unfortunate..." The man's words were lost in the sharp crack of a pistol. The man fired point-blank into Jennifer's chest. The grainy, green image in Nyland's scope was almost surreal. Her mouth flew open in an expression of surprise and pain. Her knees buckled slowly and as she fell, her head turned toward the spot where Nyland was hiding, almost as if she were begging him for help. She fell across the picnic table, knocking the black briefcase to the ground.

Nyland exploded out of his blind on the run. The Chinese man fired once toward the sound, but jerked his head around as three cars rolled into the parking lot and slid to a stop, red lights flashing. He snatched the aluminum case and faded back into the trees.

Nyland ran toward Jenny. As he lifted her head and brushed pine needles off of her face, she opened her eyes.

"Tell Uncle Jon...I'm sorry." The corner of her mouth twitched in what might have been a smile, then her head fell back and Nyland felt her body go limp.

"Keep an eye on her!" The words echoed in his head. Lynn, his baby sister, lying on the sand, lifeless eyes staring up at the sky.

As he cradled Jenny in his arms and felt the warmth of her blood soaking into his shirt, he remembered the little girl in Baghdad. She, like Jenny, had been guilty only of being in the wrong place at the wrong time.

He stared into the darkness where the Chinese man had disappeared. Even though Tommy Lin had not appeared, the newcomer, whoever he was, now had the package Jenny had given her life to deliver. The bugged C4I software it contained was now on the way to Beijing. Or was it? Who had sent this stranger to intercept Tommy Lin's pickup? A terrorist group? The Russians? It was too late to help Jenny, but it was not too late to get the man who had killed her—and ask him some questions. Nyland laid her down gently on the carpet of leaves and slipped into the forest.

The FBI men crept up the bark path. "Somebody down," one of them called. "A woman."

Two agents approached Jennifer; the others were fanning out around the parking lot, guns drawn.

Nyland ran silently through the woods back toward the entrance road. The urge to catch her killer was strong, but the training had taken over. The gravel truck he had hidden in the woods beside the road loomed before him like a prehistoric beast. He climbed inside, released the brake, and let it roll into the road. He jumped out and jabbed his K-bar into the left front tire. The truck listed like a ship run aground. The road out of the park was blocked. Now the FBI would never catch the Chinese man. But, Nyland thought grimly, he would do the job for them.

Nyland crouched behind Jenny's motorcycle, watching as two agents carried her body down to the parking lot. Another followed, carrying the Chinese man's briefcase. The agents laid Jenny's body on the back seat and covered it with a blanket.

In the parking lot, someone yelled, "Car down on the main road! Bastard got around us!" The agents ran for their cars.

Nyland walked Jenny's motorcycle quickly through the trees, leaving the chaotic scene in the parking lot behind him. The agents spun their cars around and roared out of the parking lot. The FBI was in for a surprise.

With a gloved fist, he smashed the motorcycle's headlight then jabbed the electric starter. The motorcycle roared to life. In his night scope, the dirt road appeared as a greenish slash through the woods. He forced the image of Jennifer's face out of his mind and twisted the throttle open, throwing a plume of dirt and pine needles into the air. The highway was half-a-mile away. Her killer had a good head start.

As he gunned the motorcycle along the narrow dirt track, Tuck was remembering his morning reconnaissance. The main road turned sharply left just ahead, following the course of a small stream along the hillside.

A flash of brake lights on the highway below.

Nyland wheeled the motorcycle off of the dirt track and crashed down the hillside, brush tearing at his clothes. The ground leveled slightly and he caught the glint of the creek water. The highway was less than fifty yards away.

Near the creek bank, the trees grew thicker. Suddenly, two tall pine trees loomed before him. Not room enough for the handlebars to pass. No way around, no time to stop. Almost without thinking, Nyland slammed the throttle open. The bike stood up on its back wheel and he wrenched the handlebars to the side just as they flew between the two trees. The bike hit the water and skittered on the rocks. Nyland let its momentum carry him up the bank onto the highway.

He leaned into a sharp turn, still navigating with the night goggles, and raced down the road. He saw the car's lights finally, negotiating a turn below him. On a winding road like this, he knew, a motorcycle had every advantage. His tailpipe scraped the pavement, sending off a fountain of sparks as he leaned hard into a turn. The car's taillights were a hundred yards ahead. He opened the throttle, urging the big bike forward.

The first sign the Chinese man had of pursuit was a shower of glass and blast of air as the Toyota's window exploded beside him. The roar of the motorcycle engine drummed against his ears and he stared in horror at the figure of a man reaching for him through the shattered glass. He raised the pistol and fired. The figure disappeared. He glanced in his rearview mirror. The motorcycle was on his bumper, running with no lights. Who was this maniac?

He pointed the pistol awkwardly over his shoulder and fired twice. The motorcycle dropped back for a moment, then sped up and moved alongside the car.

As he raced beside the Toyota, Nyland rode cross-handed, reaching to grip the throttle with his left hand, leaving the right free. The driver raised his pistol again, but Nyland batted it away. The car and the motorcycle slid around a turn side by side, both drivers fighting for control. Nyland grabbed for the man again and heard a scream as his fingers closed on the man's ear. The car was weaving from side to side as the driver struggled to free himself. Nyland felt the motorcycle slide beneath him and shifted his weight, riding almost by instinct.

A red flashing light ahead. A main intersection. The man clawed at Nyland's fingers, desperate to break his grip. The car raced through the red light, the driver screaming as Nyland's fingers bit deeper into his flesh. He swerved hard to the left, forcing the motorcycle into the oncoming lane.

The milk truck driver's air horn roared a warning and he saw a flash of red as the motorcycle flew across the highway in front of him. He slowed his truck and peered in his rearview mirror. A car was just disappearing over a hill behind him. The motorcycle was nowhere in sight. The driver cursed softly. His first pickup was in half an hour. What a way to start the day.

Nyland stumbled to his feet in the brush beside the road. The machine was still running, but the front wheel was crumpled, handlebars bent against the tank. The Chinese man had gotten away. But he would remember Tuck Nyland.

Nyland's last image of Jenny's killer was the Chinese man's face, crazed with fear, blood coursing down his cheek. He had screamed incoherently, staring at a scrap of bloody skin still clutched in the CIA man's hand.

A piece of his left ear.

San Francisco

The milk truck driver had dropped Nyland at a mini-mart beside the highway just before 3:30, glad to be back on his route. The fifty dollars Nyland had given him was more than enough incentive to forget the whole incident. Let the motorcycle man call the cops if he wanted to.

A phone booth stood at the corner of the darkened building. Nyland stepped inside, sat down, and rested his forehead against the glass. Everything had gone wrong. His job had been to protect Jennifer. But he had stood helplessly by while she was murdered. With her dying words, she had called Cross, "Uncle Jon." Cross had depended on him, trusted him with the woman's life. Nyland's hand shook as he reached for the phone.

It was nearly 3:30, but Cross answered on the first ring.

"Jenny's dead." Nyland said.

"Wait." A faint click on the line as Cross activated the scrambler. "Go ahead."

Nyland recounted the scene in the park, repeating Jenny's last words in a flat, emotionless voice.

"But he did take the package?" Cross asked.

"She handed it to him. He shot her."

"It was not Tommy Lin?"

"Older, stockier. Who was it, Jon?"

"We'll find out. Meet me at Hidalgo's Cafe, block up from the ferry terminal."

"She called you, 'Uncle Jon,'" Nyland said.

"Be there in an hour." Cross hung up.

★ ★ ★

Jon Cross slid into a back booth in Hidalgo's Cafe.

Nyland sat across from him, staring out the window at the early morning traffic. "Bastard just pulled out his gun and shot her," he said. "There was nothing I could do."

Cross studied Nyland in the diner's flat flourescent light. His short black hair was pasted to his forehead with sweat. His jacket was smeared with dirt, the sleeve ripped. A waitress wiped the counter, eyeing him nervously.

Nyland's voice was just above a whisper. "She was counting on me."

"She didn't even know you were there."

"She knew. She looked..." His words choked off.

"If it's anybody's fault, its mine. I missed you by ten minutes. You were already on your way up to the park when I got word the FBI had Tommy Lin in custody. Apparently, he took off and tried to shake their tail. Of course, that pissed them off, so they chased him. There was a little fender bender, and they brought him in.

"I thought that Tommy being unable to make the pickup meant the deal was off. But somebody sure put it back on in a hurry. And that somebody murdered Jenny and grabbed the C4I software. We have to know who that man is. Tuck, are you listening?"

Nyland wiped his hand across his eyes. The scars on his cheeks stood out against his flushed skin. "She said, 'I know who you are.' She recognized him."

"Somebody well known?" Cross asked. "Who couldn't risk being recognized?"

"Maybe he planned to kill her all along." Nyland looked up as the waitress sat a plate of bacon and eggs before him. When she had gone, he said, "The son of a bitch will be easy to recognize now." He recounted the motorcycle chase and his attack on the Chinese man.

Cross sat down his coffee cup. "You tore off his ear?"

"Part of it."

"Christ, Tucker."

"What would you have done?"

"Probably something worse." Cross sipped his coffee, wrinkled his nose at the bitter taste, and put it down.

"I'm gonna find that son of a bitch," Nyland said. "He's going to pay with a hell of a lot more than his ear. But after that, I disappear. Out of your life for good. You don't need—"

"Don't tell me what I need," Cross said. "The FBI knows somebody deliberately sabotaged their operation. If their forensic people can put you at the scene, then they've got you as an accomplice to murder. And the only reason you could have been up there was to be part of the software drop. If this thing goes wrong, as it seems to be doing, they will certainly charge you with espionage. We can't let that happen. So I agree that you're going to disappear—but on my terms."

"That makes us both guilty—aiding and abetting."

"Let's call it 'independent action.'"

"What are your terms?" Nyland asked.

"There's another life that needs saving. I can't talk about it here."

"What you were talking about on the beach?"

Cross looked around at the other diners. Finally, he nodded.

"Is all this connected?" Nyland asked.

"I don't know." Cross scribbled on a napkin and handed it to Nyland. "Tommy Lin's address. See what you can find out."

Tommy Lin's house was pink stucco with little else to distinguish it from its neighbors, except for the gray Toyota with the broken window parked outside. As Nyland walked past the car, he could see blood on the door, a trail of droplets leading up the sidewalk.

Nyland crouched in the alley behind Lin's house. Light from a downstairs window spilled onto the dusty asphalt. Nyland crept up the back stairs and peered in the window. Standing beside the kitchen sink, a bloody towel wrapped around his head, was the man who had shot Jenny. The aluminum case sat on the counter. Nyland had his hand on the doorknob when the man lifted his head, listening. Then Nyland heard the sound. The front doorbell. The man stumbled toward the door.

Nyland raced down the alley in time to see the man climb into a black limousine. He crouched behind a dumpster as the car rolled by. Beneath the streetlight, he got a glimpse of the license: the letters DPL.

Diplomatic plates.

Nyland was halfway back down the alley when he heard footsteps behind him. "Police! Freeze!"

He turned slowly. Two uniformed officers moved toward him, pistols drawn. The one who had shouted aimed his flashlight at Nyland's face. The officers stood fifteen feet apart, well back out of reach.

"On the ground, asshole," the other officer growled.

Blinded by the light, Nyland dropped onto his knees in the gravel. The handcuffs bit into his wrists, the steel cold against his flesh.

◄5►

Karley State Park

Special Agent Ed Dwyer was getting mad. His shoes were soaked, rain dripped down his collar, and there was a banana slug on his briefcase. He flicked the creature onto the ground. An hour of sleep on the plane from Washington, airline coffee and pretzels for breakfast. Shit.

Fatigue blurred his eyes. Get it together, Dwyer. Up to you to figure this out. Agent Prober had called him from San Francisco just after 5:00 A.M., Washington time. A major espionage operation had gone wrong. A woman dead—you said to keep you informed, boss. Prober was enjoying this.

Dwyer picked up his briefcase and slogged down the muddy service road. Fog still enveloped the park, and evidence technicians moved like ghosts through the forest around him. He shivered inside his coat as he knelt beside the narrow dirt track and examined the moss and pine needles on the ground. There had been at least two of the bastards.

A motorcycle had followed the car, its tracks overlaid for a quarter of a mile, then veered off down the hill. The motorcycle was most likely Jennifer Chin's. But who was the driver? The same man who had disabled the truck in the middle of the access road?

Dwyer flipped open his cellular phone and cursed as drops of water fell on the keypad. He punched Redial, and Special Agent Al Prober came on the line.

"Prober." The man sounded tired.

Dwyer growled into the mouthpiece, "This is the most colossal fuck-up I have seen in my twenty-two years with the bureau. This was your operation, Prober. What happened?"

At his desk in the San Francisco office, Al Prober snuffed out a cigarette, lit another, and blew out a long stream of smoke. "We put Jennifer Chin to bed about midnight. Stayed another hour, it looked like everything was quiet. There was no reason to expect—"

"Has Tommy Lin given you anything?"

"Nothing. How long do we hold him?"

"He suckered you, lead you off in the wrong direction. Sweat that son of a bitch. He knows who was up here. I want these slimeballs, especially the guy who parked that truck in the middle of the road."

"Prober, this thing has stink all over it. And I smell CIA. There was at least one extra man up here last night, who just happened to know the exact time and location of the drop. Either the Agency planned this or they've got a rogue officer in their ranks who's selling secrets to the enemy. It wouldn't be the first. You get your CIA buddy on the phone, rack his ass. I'll be back in an hour and I want progress in this case. I have to tell the director something."

The phone clicked and Dwyer was gone. What a moron, Prober thought. Career goal number one, protecting his ass. He chuckled as he hung up the phone. It was one thing he and Dwyer had in common.

"Your operation, Prober." Meaning your ass when it goes south. And that was definitely the direction it was headed. He dialed a Washington D.C. number.

"Carter."

Prober sighed. This was the third 'Carter' he had talked to in the CIA's liaison office this month. "Can you shed any light on an operation involving Omega Data Systems, any Agency involvement we ought to know about?"

"Defense contractor in Palo Alto, software design. That's a domestic company. Out of our jurisdiction."

"Right, and you're never out of your jurisdiction. You've been getting our reports on Tommy Lin? We've been on him for over a month."

Carter paused for a moment. "We're following up on that."

"Your follow-up have anything to do with the murder of Jennifer Chin?"

"Murder? Under what circumstances?" Carter asked.

"Shot to death. We believe she was supposed to meet Tommy Lin, maybe sell him some information. The only problem was, he was sitting here in our holding cell at the time of her murder."

"I'll—have to get back to you." Carter hung up.

Yeah, sometime around the turn of the century. So much for liaison. But "Carter" was definitely nervous about Jennifer Chin. The spooks had an interest, that was for sure. But they were probably doing what they did best: lying. They had to be. Jennifer Chin had worked for Omega Data Systems for nearly three years. The company's principal client was the CIA.

The FBI man lit a cigarette and began jotting notes on his pad. Very odd that the Agency had no information on Jennifer, who was apparently involved in a number of top-secret software projects. Ed Dwyer was right, it was beginning to smell like CIA. But smelling the stink and finding the source were two different things.

The night before, Tommy Lin had left his house around midnight and lead the FBI agents on a meandering trip through the streets of San Francisco. And for the first time, he had tried to shake them. The agents were immediately suspicious. Tommy was going somewhere he didn't want the FBI to know about.

His clumsy tricks of exiting and entering the freeway didn't work against three pursuit vehicles, all equipped with radios. Suddenly, he shut off his lights and roared away down a one-way street. The agents, panicked at the thought of losing him, took off in hot pursuit. The two cars collided. The agents found a suitcase full of money in his car. Money for secrets.

Should they bring him in, the agents wanted to know. Charge him with what—reckless driving? Prober had called his boss in Washington. Dwyer was furious. Now they would never know who he had been going to meet. Roust the bastard, Dwyer had said, push him into making a mistake. Prober had been against it, but Dwyer, apparently feeling the unrelenting pressure from Washington, had demanded results. Well, he had certainly gotten some. And he was right, serious mistakes had been made in Karley Park, but Tommy Lin hadn't made them. And the goddamn FBI had been set up.

Then who had killed Jennifer Chin and why? Maybe he would get an answer when "Carter" got back to him. And maybe Elvis was alive and well in Tupelo.

The phone jangled on his desk. "Prober."

"This is Sergeant Lakeland, San Francisco P.D. Hate to admit it, but I think we may have fucked up here."

"Lakeland, you're a breath of fresh air."

"We detained a suspect about four o'clock this morning outside a house on Clark Street, off Divisidaro. He wouldn't tell us his name, anything. We put him in the tank overnight. The day shift guys just told me there's an FBI priority watch order on the house."

"Don't tell me the owner is Tommy Lin?"

"Sure is. Hope we didn't jam you up. We don't really have much on our mystery man, are you interested?"

"You'll never know. We'll pick him up in twenty minutes."

★　★　★

"What have we got, Prober?" Ed Dwyer, coat still dripping from his visit to the park, looked at the tall man in handcuffs in the FBI holding cell.

"The guy they picked up at Tommy Lin's house. Driver's license says Kenneth Carlyle. Stanford grad student."

"You believe him?"

"In a word, no. I'm taking him up to interrogation."

Dwyer nodded. "We're going to have to let Tommy Lin go. He hasn't given us squat."

Prober shrugged. "I told you there was nothing to hold him on."

"Don't second-guess me," Dwyer growled. "I want more people on this Jennifer Chin thing, and put the heat on Mr. Carlyle. Results, Prober." He walked down the hall.

Prober unlocked the holding cell door. "Been thinking about your story?"

"I told you my story," Nyland said.

"Let's take a walk."

The interrogation room was one flight up. Nyland climbed the stairs with Prober close behind, hand on his elbow. "I wasn't hurting anybody. I just got lost. Don't get up into the city much," Tuck said. Playing the role.

A Chinese man leaned wearily against the wall on the first landing, back pressed against the painted cinder blocks. His white shirt was rumpled, hair mussed. He was staring at Tuck Nyland. Nyland glanced at him, fighting to keep his face expressionless. He remembered the picture Cross had shown him: Tommy Lin.

Lin stumbled past them down the stairs. "Stay in touch, Tommy," Prober called after him. But Lin was already out the door.

★ ★ ★

Agent Prober was not a good interrogator, Nyland thought. He had neither the attitude nor the timing. His questions were predictable and plodding. Nyland played the role of indignant grad student. A night on the town, couple of beers, took the wrong bus. Jesus, do we have to make a federal case out of it?

But, when another agent stepped into the interrogation room and handed him a slip of paper, Prober's attitude changed. He glanced at the paper, then crumpled it. "My friend, you are a lying piece of shit. Doesn't seem to be any record of Kenneth Carlyle."

Nyland shrugged. "I'm a grad student, I don't have a record."

"Don't smart-ass me, you son of a bitch. Your driver's license is legitimate, the DMV issued it. Beyond that, according to our computers, you just don't exist. There aren't many people carrying this kind of paper, Mr. Carlyle, and most of them have the initials C. I. A.

"You were in Karley Park last night. You blocked the road with that truck, and interfered with an FBI operation."

"You're crazy," Nyland said. "I want a lawyer."

"Do you know what's at stake here?" The FBI man bent forward, his face an inch from Nyland's. "I want you to get on the line to whatever faceless bastard you report to at Langley and tell him his little game is coming undone. The CIA has no authority to operate on domestic soil. The attorney general is going to hear about this; the president is going to hear about this."

Though he tried for another hour, Prober got nothing from his suspect. "Carlyle" refused to confirm or deny his involvement with Jennifer Chin's death, or his affiliation with CIA. Finally, Prober returned him to the holding cell and went to face Ed Dwyer. Dwyer would not be pleased.

★ ★ ★

Song Zhenyo had parked in an underground garage near the Federal courthouse in downtown San Francisco—a long way from his comfortable office in Washington, D.C. His mutilated ear throbbed with every heartbeat as he sat in the darkness of his rented van.

Song was a fund-raiser for the president of the United States. He had served unofficially in that capacity under two administrations, channeling millions into party coffers from a variety of donors at home and abroad. There had been a few minor scandals in the previous administration, but little proof was forthcoming, and the public's attention span was short.

He had become a regular at private White House meetings with the president's top advisors, members of the cabinet—even the Man himself. There was no official title, no White House office, and very little publicity. The perks were power and access. And that was all his real bosses were interested in. No one in Washington's inner political circles suspected who those bosses really were.

Song Zhenyo, frequent White House guest, Washington insider, and fund-raiser *par excellence*, was a spy, an officer in China's Ministry of State Security, the Chinese equivalent of the CIA.

A quick call to the Chinese consulate the night before had brought the limousine to Tommy Lin's house. The consulate had bucked his request to the intelligence resident at the Chinese embassy in Washington, D.C. He was not pleased, but he gave his approval. The limo had taken Song directly to the hospital and an emergency room doctor had called the San Francisco police. Two officers had questioned Song as the doctor stitched up his damaged ear, dutifully writing his made-up assault story in their notebooks.

There must be absolutely no publicity, he had told them. You can imagine what the press would do with a story like this. He was in town on political business, and any word of his assault would embarrass the president, not to mention the city of San Francisco. The detectives understood, said they would look into it. Their tone said file and forget.

That was fine with Song Zhenyo. The police would be no help in finding the man who had torn off his ear. He would have the exquisite pleasure of doing that himself.

Now, in the darkness of the underground garage, a chill came over him as he remembered the horrible strength in the man's hand, a steel claw crushing his brain. Gingerly, Zhenyo touched the bandage on his head. The pain was getting worse. He slipped a pill in his mouth and studied his bandaged ear in the rearview mirror. A small spot of blood had seeped through the gauze. His vision blurred and his head sagged. Must get some rest.

How long would he have to wait for that idiot Tommy Lin? The man was half an hour late. A red Miata convertible with a crumpled fender wound its way down the ramp and slid into a parking space several cars away from Song's van. Tommy Lin trotted to the van and slipped into the back seat.

"What happened to your ear?"

Zhenyo spoke sharply in Mandarin: "I was attacked by a maniac. I managed to get away with the merchandise. I am taking it to Washington tonight. But I was seen last night by the man who did this." Song gestured to the bandage on his head. "He was at the park. He saw me shoot the girl."

"You killed Jennifer?"

"Of course. She recognized me. You were supposed to meet her, remember, until you decided to play hide-and-seek with the FBI."

"I wasn't sure they were following me last night, but just to be sure, I doubled back several times, got off the freeway, and then back on."

"Techniques you learned from television. You shut off your lights, took off down a one way street, of course they came after you."

"They rammed me with their bumper. My tire blew out."

"It was very fortunate you had time to call me on your cell phone. You're lucky that I was able to take your place in Karley Park.

Your stupidity, however, has put me in an extremely dangerous situation."

"You shot her. Now you're going to shoot me." Lin cowered against the passenger door.

Zhenyo grabbed Tommy Lin's coat and yanked him back. "Pay attention! This madman who came after me on a motorcycle, he can identify me."

"Who is he? How did he know about the drop?"

"Maybe Jennifer Chin was not as reliable as you lead me to believe. You have bungled every step of this operation. You almost got me killed."

"The FBI followed me, I had to get away." There was a pleading tone in Tommy's voice. "It was an accident. They got the money—"

"Which you will pay back to the Ministry of State Security. Three carloads of agents came roaring into Karley Park just as I was making the pickup. The timing is extremely suspicious."

"You don't think I tipped them off? I swear—" Lin held up his hand.

"Save your swearing. Find the man who did this to me."

"I may know where he is," Lin said. "Is he tall, about thirty, big shoulders like a boxer?"

Song leaned closer to the man. "Black hair, cut short?"

Tommy Lin nodded. "Like military."

"Where is he?"

"I saw him two hours ago." Lin explained his chance encounter on the stairway at the downtown FBI office.

"He was in handcuffs?" Song asked.

"They were taking him up to the interrogation room."

"I want you outside the FBI office in case they release him. He is the only loose end in this disaster. We have to find out who he works for, what he was doing up there," Song said. "Then we have to kill him."

6

Hong Kong

The man on the indoor jogging track wore only a pair of blue nylon shorts. Sweat poured down his back and chest, a testament to his effort and the unrelenting humidity. The track was a perk for the employees of Global Links, Inc. The runner, who was learning to think of himself as Lester Craine, was an account executive with the giant communications consortium. A marketing manager who split his time between Beijing and Hong Kong. "Craine" was a regular employee who kept to himself, did his job well, and paid his taxes. Only the president of Global Links and a few people in Washington knew he was paid a second salary. It was deposited under his real name, Martin Hausler, in a bank in Falls Church, Virginia. The money came from the Central Intelligence Agency. Marty Hausler worked for Task Force Seven. His boss was Jon Cross.

Hausler was NOC. The letters stood for "non-official cover." Gone were the days of "official" cover, when intelligence officers worked as "cultural attaches" or other innocuous titles in American embassies. The kind of people who were of interest now, drug dealers, arms merchants, white-collar thieves, seldom appeared at embassy receptions.

It was almost six o'clock, and Hausler had the track to himself, the way he liked it. Most of the Global employees would have left the building by now, headed for the trendy Hong Kong watering holes. Hausler had run five miles in the last half-hour, but showed no signs of slowing down.

On his final two laps, he picked up the pace. Breathing harder now, maximum training effect kicking in. As he sprinted around the cavernous room, his footsteps made only a whisper on the blue composition track.

Fifteen years before, in Afghanistan, his training had saved his life. He had been nearly twenty miles inside the Afghani-Pakistan border, traveling with a colonel from the Chinese People's Liberation Army who had demanded to see the Russian Bear up close. He had more than gotten his wish. Soviet Hind helicopters had nearly destroyed a rebel village, killing most of the Mujahaddin hiding in the mud huts.

The Chinese colonel had been slightly wounded. Marty Hausler had hidden him in a cave near the village and gone for help. It took him most of the night to cross the mountains into Pakistan. He ran blindly along narrow, rocky trails, stumbling often in the dark, but reached the border just before daylight. The Chinese officer's life was saved, a major international incident prevented, and Colonel Liu Yin became Hausler's friend for life. "Always, I will be in your debt," he told Marty.

When Colonel Liu returned to Beijing, Marty Hausler had followed. He kept the friendship alive. A year later, Liu Yin repaid his debt: he became an agent for the CIA.

Hausler toweled sweat off his face as he walked to the locker room. He glanced at his watch. Anne's flight from Beijing would be on the ground by now. But it would take at least an hour by taxi to get to the restaurant. He smiled at his mental image of Anne striding toward him wearing her Chinese silk dress. Of course, no one would mistake the long-legged redhead for Chinese. She would look more at home on the beach at Malibu, Hausler thought, in a tiny white bikini.

Anne Hammersmith, based at the U. S. Embassy in Beijing, was known to the Chinese government as a CIA employee and operated openly with her technical counterparts in the PLA, but Hausler was undercover, supposedly with no intelligence connections at all. The two played a dangerous game, meeting in public, but that made it all the more exciting. On each of her monthly trips to Hong Kong, they chose a different restaurant and rented a hotel room under a fictitious name.

Tonight was an anniversary of sorts, and Marty had rented a penthouse suite for the occasion. It had been two years since their first meeting, a comedy of errors at a cafeteria in Langley. He had bumped her with his tray, splashing coffee on her skirt, spilling clam chowder on her shoes. He had taken her out to dinner, had her skirt cleaned, and bought her new shoes. They laughed together easily; the lovemaking had been great; but, she resisted his attempts to get more serious. It had been two years. Tonight, maybe he could change her mind.

★   ★   ★

"The lady in red." Hausler bent to kiss Anne Hammersmith's outstretched hand, then pulled her against him. He could feel the warmth of her body through the thin silk dress.

She kissed him softly on the lips. "You're late. I ordered wine."

"Backtracked a couple of times. Nobody following me. You clear?"

"Changed cabs twice, walked the last few blocks. No problem, at least not with being followed."

"Different problem?" Marty asked.

They sat at a corner table. The lighted windows of Hong Kong's countless high-rises glowed steadily against the black sky. "I either just made my career, or just blew it." She told him the story of the intercepted radio transmission at the Quito listening post, and the assault by her Chinese counterpart.

"Did he hurt you?" Marty asked.

Anne sipped her wine. "I killed the sorry fuck," she said. "The tape went by pouch to Langley. Either they promote me or fire me. I'm thinking maybe my listening caper was a little too risky for comfort."

"Unauthorized, but pretty damn lucky. It ties in with a couple of rumors I've picked up."

"Should we be talking out of school like this?" Anne looked around her at the crowd of mostly Chinese diners. A waiter brought a steaming plate of fish and rice. She thanked him in Mandarin, and ordered two more glasses of Chardonnay. He bowed and walked away.

Marty said, "I think the guy you heard talking on his radio has some bigger plans. An old friend of mine from Afghanistan tells me the general has been making surreptitious visits to a certain member of the Central Committee. He says he would put his money on some kind of military reorganization at the top. The general isn't too happy with what he sees as his country falling into bed with the West. If we can put that together, so can Langley."

"I'm sure Jon Cross already has. With the help of we peons."

Hausler paused, his glass halfway to his lips. "You know Jon Cross?"

"I didn't say that, did I?"

"You never told me. I'm impressed." He refilled their wine glasses. "Here's to we peons—and to getting in bed with the West."

She smiled and raised an eyebrow. "Who would the 'West' be in this hypothetical getting-into-bed scenario?"

"Do you know what day this is?" Marty asked.

She thought a moment. "Saturday?"

"Two years—it's been two years since the great clam chowder incident."

"Right, right. Of course. Happy anniversary."

"Anne, have you thought about what I asked you, about when we get back? We're not going to be in China forever. I mean, that condo of mine in Washington has more room than I need, maybe you would consider—" He felt his face flush. This was not how he had rehearsed it.

She looked down at her plate. "I like you very much Marty, but I—"

"Hey, no pressure. We have all the time in the world. I would just like us to be closer, that's all."

Anne nodded and looked away.

"You look beautiful in that dress," Marty said. He laid his hand gently on her knee. "I got us a penthouse suite, champagne, and the whole bit."

"Sounds like you have big plans."

"Could be."

They raised their glasses in a toast. "To being closer," Marty said.

She brushed her fingers across the back of his hand. "Einstein said, 'I never think about the future. It happens soon enough.'"

★ ★ ★

Washington, D.C.

The president of the United States sat behind his desk in a blue cardigan sweater and a baggy pair of chinos, a bit casual for the Oval Office, but the official business of the day had long been concluded; most of the staff had gone home. A bronze bust of Lincoln gleamed softly in the dim light from a banker's lamp on the leather-trimmed blotter. President Gardner ran his hand tiredly through his white hair, rose, and paced around his desk.

His chief-of-staff, Fred Stevens, sat on a brocade sofa sipping a cup of coffee. The boss was in worry mode again; it was going to be a long night. "You'll wear out your rug, Mr. President."

President Gardner stopped and leaned against the corner of his desk. "It's the people's rug, Fred. The people's room."

Stevens nodded. "And the people's business needs doing—but not twenty-four hours a day. It's almost midnight, Mr. President."

"Without and within," the president said.

"Sir?"

"Where the danger lies. Tennyson said something like that. He never had to deal with China. I don't trust one word they say."

"You've got Task Force Seven, Mr. President. The best people in the country watching China. Is there—?"

Gardner resumed his pacing. "Ah, yes, the CIA boys. Do you trust those people?"

"Personally, they're not my kind of folks, but keeping secrets is their business."

"My staff, my cabinet doesn't seem to think very highly of the Agency."

"Looking to chop them up and divide the pieces."

"These goddamn turf wars. I wished we could just get on with the business of running the country."

"And the business of raising money."

"Yes, that's what it comes down to. You worry too much about money, Fred. Our coffers are in pretty good shape, aren't they?"

"For the moment, but there are a lot of congresspersons up for reelection this year. We're going to have to help them."

"Congresspersons, right. Which means we make another call to Mr. Song Zhenyo?"

"Whatever else you might think of him, Mr. President, he's damn good at what he does."

"I'm sure he is." The president sat down behind his desk and absently fondled the Lincoln bronze. "But I need a minute here—a minute's respite from thinking about what Song Zhenyo does—and how well he does it."

"Mr. President?"

"Then we'll make the call."

San Francisco

They had sent a child, for chrissake. Was the FBI hiring them young, or was he getting old? Nyland glanced at the man walking beside him down the steps of the Federal Building. Mid-twenties maybe, with the look of an accountant. A few moments before, in the holding cell, Special Agent Prober had introduced him as "Agent Jacobs," and informed Nyland that the FBI was moving him to another facility. Prober did not look happy. Jacobs had handcuffed him, signed a release, and the two had walked out into a rare morning of San Francisco sunshine. As easy as that.

"My car is down this way," Jacobs said.

"Where are we going?"

Jacobs slipped a key from his pocket and unlocked Nyland's handcuffs. Nyland stared at the young man. "You're either the dumbest FBI agent in the world, or—"

Jacobs handed him an envelope. "Plane leaves at zero-nine-fifty. Call Mr. Cross at this number when you get there." He handed Nyland a slip of paper.

Nyland glanced at it, memorized it, and handed it back. "*Huevos de acero*," he said.

"Excuse me?" Jacobs said.

"Steel balls. Strolling right in under their nose."

"Mr. Cross said I looked the part."

"Baby face, steel balls." Nyland held out his hand and the young man shook it, a faint blush on his cheeks.

Market Street swarmed with people on this bright spring day, some hurrying by with briefcases, others shuffling aimlessly along the sidewalk, hands in their pockets, eyes downcast. Nyland glanced around as he and Jacobs passed the Greyhound bus depot. Three men, clad in the tattered street garb common in this seedy, south-of-Market neighborhood, were moving up behind them.

"Heads up," Nyland said. He slipped his hands out of his pockets and moved closer to the side of the building. The three men were walking faster now, spreading out as they approached.

Jacobs glanced back at the three men. "What do we do?"

"Run," Nyland said.

"But there are three of them. I can—"

Nyland looked back at the men, now only a few yards behind. A rusted-out white panel truck pulled to the curb half a block ahead and the side door slid open, closing the trap. "Get your ass out of here," he said. "Tell Cross I'll see him in Washington."

Jacobs did as he was told. The three men ignored him, their attention focused on Nyland. The leader, a thick-set black man with long dread locks, circled in front of Nyland, hands in the pockets of a filthy, khaki overcoat. The two beside him were younger, affecting a punk look—leather jackets and pants, heavy motorcycle boots. One was tall and slender with an acne-scarred face. He clenched and unclenched his fists as he moved toward Nyland. Street fighters. Nyland caught the glint of a knife in the shorter one's hand. The three men formed a loose circle around him, backing him toward the wall of the bus depot.

"Spare change, man?" The black man leered. The two in leather jackets flanked him, staying just out of reach. Nyland felt the rough surface of the wall against his back. He made himself relax.

Knife man on his left, inching closer.

Nyland could see the outline of a gun in the black man's pocket, but he wouldn't use it if he didn't have to, confident the two leather jackets were more than enough to handle one man.

"Gonna go for a little ride," the black man said, motioning with his head toward the panel truck.

The knife man held his weapon low, weaving the blade back and forth. "Move it, asshole," he said.

Nyland spun on his heel and kicked him in the throat. The man collapsed backward, knife skittering across the sidewalk. A woman screamed. The tall man swung his fist at Nyland's face, but Nyland slipped inside the blow, grabbed the man's jacket, and slammed him face-first against the wall. Blood gushed from his nose and he slid down to the sidewalk. As the tall man fell, Nyland's foot lashed behind him, slamming into the black man's groin.

The black man toppled forward, moaning in pain. Nyland glanced at the van. It lurched away from the curb, fender scraping a passing taxi. He had seen the driver's face briefly in profile. It could have been Tommy Lin. Nyland's three assailants were sprawled on the sidewalk. The two leather jackets were unconscious, the black man was fumbling in his overcoat for the gun. Nyland kicked his elbow savagely, and the man screamed in agony. "Broke my fuckin' arm," he shouted.

Nyland knelt beside him, jabbed a thumb into the hollow of the man's throat, and squeezed. The man convulsed with pain, eyes rolling back in his head. "Ten seconds and you're dead," Nyland whispered. "Who hired you?"

"Some Chinese guy. He drivin' the van. Say pick you up, toss you in—Christ, let go of me!"

Nyland tightened his grip and the man's head flopped back onto the pavement. A police siren rose and fell and Nyland could see the cruiser turning the corner at Market Street, lights flashing, caught in traffic. He ran, pushing his way through the crowd.

Two scruffy teenage boys stood staring down at the three figures sprawled on the sidewalk. "You see that shit? Streets definitely *ain't* safe around here anymore," one said.

★ ★ ★

Nyland, among the first to board the plane, took an aisle seat in the next-to-last row. The seat assignment was a Jon Cross touch, putting him in position to watch the other passengers. At the moment, however, the passengers searching for seats and jamming luggage in the overhead racks blocked his view.

Twenty minutes later, the plane still hadn't taken off. Nyland glanced up as the cabin TV sets came to life and the CNN logo flashed on the screen. The woman sitting next to Nyland slipped on her headset and stared up at the screen. Three men in overcoats were getting into a limousine. The camera moved closer. One of the men turned, waving it away.

Nyland stared at the screen. He was looking at the face of Jennifer Chin's killer. He touched the woman's arm. "Who was that?"

She slipped off her earphones. "Name is Song Zhenyo. Some kind of money man for the president. Bag man is probably more like it. They're all crooks, if you ask me."

Nyland said, almost to himself, "That one is."

After the plane was airborne, the pilot's voice announced that passengers were free to move around the cabin, then droned on about cruising altitude and the sights visible along the way. Nyland unfastened his seat belt and walked forward to the galley.

A flight attendant smiled at him. "Restrooms are in the rear of the aircraft." He thanked her and walked slowly down the aisle, glancing casually at the other passengers. Seat 27A: a Chinese man staring out the window studying the flat, brown landscape below.

Tommy Lin.

Nyland settled back in his seat, accepted a cup of coffee from the flight attendant. Lin had moved quickly, managing somehow to set up a kidnap attempt outside the FBI headquarters, then to get a ticket and make the same plane. He likely had help, Nyland thought, from his powerful ally, Song Zhenyo. Nyland remembered the scene from the TV newscast: behind Song's limousine stood the imposing facade of the White House. And now Song knew Nyland had been in Karley Park, and that he had seen him kill Jennifer

Chin. Couldn't leave a witness like that alive.

But Lin wouldn't try anything on the plane, there was no way of escape. He would probably have backup waiting at the airport. There, Nyland was certain, they would try again.

◄7►

Culpeper, Virginia

John Cross wore faded blue shorts and a cotton shirt unbuttoned to the waist, his Culpeper uniform. He slipped off his platinum Rolex and laid it on the dresser. He never wore a watch at his country house, his reminder that here in the Virginia countryside time mattered much less than it did in Washington. His face was deeply tanned from his blue-water fishing expeditions on the Chesapeake, his body still trim and fit from a lifetime of exercise. The afternoon breeze from the open French doors was cool on his skin. It ruffled his white hair as he stepped onto the deck.

He let his eyes wander across the green hills. In the distance, the Smokey Mountains were bathed in a soft blue haze. Though the Capitol was an hour's drive away, it seemed part of another world.

But the world was connected now, he thought, and there was no way to calculate the effect of a small strand pulled loose, a tiny link severed. A link like Jennifer Chin.

On the flight back from San Francisco the night before, he had tried to make sense of the C4I operation. Why had Jennifer been killed? Had Beijing found out about the trapdoor? If so, her death had been for nothing. Was someone in the U.S. Government involved, the White House? All connected—but how? The man who killed Jennifer Chin was the key, but he had disappeared.

"Mr. Cross?" Doug Smith, Cross's young assistant, still wore his white shirt and red-striped necktie, knot snug at his collar. He stepped onto the deck, an apologetic smile on his face. "We're all set up."

His blonde hair, moussed and roughly combed in the current style, gave him the look of a college freshman, but he was one of the CIA's top computer experts. The Agency had snapped him up soon after his doctoral dissertation on cryptography had been published by MIT. Though he held three advanced degrees and had two years of hands-on experience with the CIA's communications security systems, Smith was barely twenty-five when Cross recruited him for Task Force Seven.

"Back to the dungeon?"

"We've established three blind links, and the satellite—"

"Any word from San Francisco?"

"Mr. Nyland's plane is in the air. ETA seventeen-thirty. Jacobs says they were attacked by a bunch of street punks. Apparently Nyland handled things."

"I imagine. This was a random attack?"

"Jacobs thinks it was a kidnap attempt."

Cross said, "Somebody's a step ahead of us."

The "dungeon" was a windowless strong room concealed in the center of the house where a portion of the hillside had been dug away. The walls were soundproof, the door tensile steel protected by electronic sensors. It was Jon Cross's communication center, the heart of Task Force Seven. A fiber optic link connected it directly to Langley, two satellite dishes on the roof put him in instant touch with CIA stations anywhere in the world. The Agency, however, didn't know about the special digital line Doug Smith had just installed. It was what he called a phantom line. It sent out false signals, he told Cross, disguising its location.

Smith sat down at his computer. "There's flash traffic from the director, want to take it?"

"Not really, but—" Cross typed his password and watched lines of random characters scroll up the screen. He tapped another series of keys, and the plain text message appeared: CONCERNS RE ECLIPSE INTERCEPT HATCHET. DEBRIEF 1600 HRS. VAIL

Mentally, Cross deciphered the cryptic shorthand: Eclipse was Anne Hammersmith, Hatchet was General Xing Wanpo. Vail was Billy Vail, the Director of Central Intelligence, a man jealous of his domain.

Cross had forwarded Anne's report to him, along with the text of General Xing's radio calls. The president himself had directed

Cross to penetrate Chinese intelligence by "any means possible." Exactly what Anne had done. But, as a member of Task Force Seven, she reported first to Jon Cross. And now, it seemed, the DCI had "concerns." His real concern, Cross thought, was that the president had given Cross and his task force too much power.

The DCI wanted to meet at four o'clock. Cross sighed inwardly. Back into the pinstripes in two hours. But there was work to do first. He cleared the screen and turned to Smith. "I'm ready for your famous phantom line," he said.

"I have to say this again, Mr. Cross. I can't recommend this civilian tie-in. I can't guarantee you'll be secure. If there's any other way—"

"No," Cross said. "There's no other way, not now."

Smith moved to a nearby equipment rack and threw a switch. A series of lights glowed green and the screen of a small laptop computer on the desk came to life. Without a word, Smith walked out the door.

Cross unlocked his desk drawer and took out a leather-bound volume, the collected works of Robert Browning, and opened it to the poem, "Love among the Ruins." He moved his finger down the page, counting the lines as he went. He would convert the words into a series of numbers, undecipherable to anyone without an identical volume—what cryptographers called a "Shakespeare code."

His eyes fell on a line near the bottom of the page: "Where the domed and daring palace shot its spires/Up like fires." He needed the seventh word. The line and page number completed the first number group. It took nearly twenty minutes to compose the message. He typed a password on the laptop's screen. The Internet provider flashed the message: "Welcome JenChn." Jennifer Chin's email address.

He typed quickly, inserting the numbers he had written into an innocuous letter about the rent going up, the difficulty of finding good Chinese produce, and the rising price of clothes. He rechecked the string of numbers and then, feeling the tears smart in his eyes, typed, "Love, Jennifer."

The computer's on-screen clock blinked in the dim light of

the strong room: 6:07 P.M. The sun had been up almost an hour in Beijing.

★ ★ ★

Dulles Airport, Washington, D.C.

The flight from San Francisco was half an hour late. The passengers, mostly business travelers from the look of their clothes, were grumbling to each other about traffic jams and missed appointments, ignoring the flight attendant's mechanical good-byes as they shuffled off of the plane. It was almost 6:00 P.M. Beltway traffic would be at its peak. Welcome to Washington.

Nyland was last off of the plane. As he pushed his way through the crowd of passengers, he spotted Tommy Lin standing by a drinking fountain pretending to study flight schedules on an overhead monitor. Nyland stopped at a phone kiosk near the gate. Tommy Lin strolled past.

Nyland dialed the number Jacobs had given him. When Jon Cross answered, Tuck said without preamble. "I know who it was—in the park. I saw the bastard on CNN. He's some kind of fund-raiser for the president."

"No names," Cross said.

"And I acquired a tail."

"The man who missed his appointment in the park?"

"Affirmative."

Cross said, "He have friends?"

"I wouldn't be surprised. Haven't spotted them yet."

"The FBI has your description, maybe even your picture by now. I want you out of there. My man's in the short-term parking lot in a green Toyota pickup. Blonde hair. He's got a cell phone. I'll tell him you're coming."

"Tell him to keep the engine running." Nyland hung up.

As Nyland left the terminal, he saw Tommy Lin again, standing near a shuttle bus stop. Out in the open, not caring if he was seen. Why was Lin suddenly so confident? He gave the answer away by glancing down the street at an approaching car, a black Saab moving slowly along the curb toward Nyland. Tommy's backup team was in place; it would be a repeat of the attempt in San Francisco. But this time it would not be street toughs; the four men in the Saab had the look of professionals.

Nyland stepped aboard the parking shuttle and grabbed the overhead rail as the bus moved into traffic. He glanced out the back window. The Saab was several cars back. Tommy Lin sat in the front seat talking on a cell phone. Was there another team nearby? They would probably make their move in the parking lot, away from the crowds and the airport police.

The short-term parking lot was nearly full, but Nyland spotted the green Toyota pickup immediately. It moved slowly along the rows of parked cars toward the shuttle bus. Cross's man would have no way of knowing which shuttle Nyland was on, so he was roaming, checking each one as it entered the lot. At the first stop, Nyland jumped off and ran toward the pickup.

"Black Saab behind you," he said as he climbed in.

"Gotcha. Hello, Mr. Nyland," Doug Smith said.

"Yeah."

The Saab was fifty feet behind. A station wagon backed out of a parking space, nearly clipping the Saab's front fender. The driver honked her horn angrily. The Saab reversed itself with a squeal of tires.

"Are you a good driver, kid?" Nyland asked.

"Sprint cars, the summer before I went to college." Smith floored the accelerator and the pickup raced along the rows of parked cars. A fat man in a brown suit dropped his suitcase and dove out of the way. "You might want to fasten your seat belt." Smith laughed as the pickup drifted around a corner, tires smoking, and shot through the exit gate, splintering the wooden arm.

"I've always wanted to do that," Smith said.

As the green Toyota roared along the access road toward the highway, Smith flipped a switch on a small metal case on the seat beside him. A series of red lights flashed, then turned to steady green. "Got their cell phone," Smith said.

He punched a button and Tommy Lin's voice came on the speaker: "...going west, getting on the toll road."

Another voice: "I want him alive, understand? He's going to tell me how he came to be in that park, who he works for, and then he's going to disappear."

"We'll get them as soon as they leave the freeway—no mistakes this time, Mr. Song." Tommy Lin sounded frightened.

"No names. And let my team do their job; you've fucked things up enough."

The lights on Smith's receiver turned back to flashing red. He turned off the speaker. "Bad communications security," Smith said. "Do you know these guys?"

"I do," Nyland said. He was certain now that Song was Jennifer Chin's killer, but what good would the information do? He was the only witness, and there would never be a trial.

Traffic thinned as they moved away from the airport and now only a few cars shared the westbound lanes of the Dulles toll road. The countryside was open, rolling hills, a few farm houses, the occasional row of newly constructed town houses near the freeway. Suburban sprawl. The Saab was several car lengths back. Waiting for the end of the freeway.

"What do we do?" Smith asked.

"I don't suppose you have a gun?" Nyland asked.

"I'm a computer guy. Mr. Cross doesn't put me out in the field much."

Nyland studied Smith's boyish face. "You're enjoying this."

Smith glanced in his mirror and shrugged.

"You'll get over it," Nyland said. Another young one raised on TV violence. Bang—cut to commercial. The men in the Saab were professional killers, Nyland thought, probably good at what they did. There would be no cutting to commercial, only blood, torture, and a slow death if they were caught.

The freeway's paved shoulder gave way to tall grass. Beyond that, across a ditch, a chain-link fence paralleled the roadway, set back twenty yards on a gently rising slope. There was open farmland beyond.

"Can you get through that fence?"

"One way to find out." Smith downshifted and veered off the

pavement. The truck bounced through the ditch and up the slope. Smith hit the gas, and dirt plumed from all four tires. The Toyota rammed the fence, bucking like an angry horse, but the wire held. The Saab had pulled off the road, and was nosing cautiously down into the ditch.

"Back up, ram the bastards!" Nyland shouted.

The pickup raced back down the slope. The Saab's driver had the car in reverse, tires spinning, when the pickup's bumper slammed into his grill. The pickup rode up on the Saab's hood, caving it in. Smith shifted into low and jammed his foot on the accelerator. The pickup lurched forward off of the Saab's hood. Nyland heard the dry chatter of an automatic weapon and the Toyota's rear window exploded in a shower of glass.

Smith spun the wheel and the pickup fishtailed along the shoulder, finally lurching back onto the freeway. Behind them, the Saab was in flames. Nyland caught a glimpse of the driver, crouched beside the car, still firing, but the shots went wild. The Toyota was out of range.

Wind howled through the demolished window as the green pickup sped down the highway. Nyland shouted over the noise, "Cross ought to put you in the field more often."

★ ★ ★

Beijing, China

The Ministry of State Security was a sprawling bureaucracy occupying several downtown buildings. The cryptography section occupied the top two floors of a nondescript, gray tower near the fourteenth-century walls of the Forbidden City. The senior cryptologists were assigned the top floor in recognition of their long service to "the people." Here, ten floors above the street, the air was supposedly better, but, for the workers, it seemed to make little difference in a city where the air quality was said to be five times as bad as Los Angeles.

As she had done every day for the past twenty years, Bao Qing, the department's senior cryptographer, had ridden her bike to work, mingling with hundreds of other riders, tires swishing quietly along the special bicycle lanes. Like most of Beijing's morning commuters, she wore a gauze mask against the pollution and the sandy winds.

She climbed stiffly off of her bike in the basement of the building. This morning she was feeling every one of her sixty-nine years. Another year and she would retire. How many years had it been since she had stopped believing in her country's causes? She removed her mask. A film of grayish-brown residue coated the gauze. She tossed it in a trash bin with a dozen similar ones and stepped into the elevator, forcing her mind onto the tasks for the day.

There would be a batch of intercepted cables from the Japanese Embassy that might provide enough text to crack their new diplomatic code. Perhaps the results of field testing for General Xing Wanpo's new crypto system would be available. Bao Qing hoped so. The general had called several times already this week and was threatening to complain to her section leader. He was a vindictive, demanding client, one the section would be better off without. But it was not in their power to pick and choose. And Xing was an up-and-coming figure in the People's Liberation Army.

As she sat down at her computer, she noticed a small message blinking at the top of the screen: MAIL WAITING. This was Tuesday, there should be no mail until Friday. Had something gone wrong? She typed in her password and brought the screen to life.

One of the perks of her office was email service, routine in most of the world, but viewed by suspicion in the State Security apparatus in Beijing. All email traffic was carefully screened. Bao Qing used the service for one purpose, approved by the Director of MSS, to keep in touch with her granddaughter in the United States. The two had established a regular weekly schedule. Why had her granddaughter changed it?

Out of long habit, Bao closed her office door before bringing up the message. Her granddaughter talked about her rent going up, the price of clothes in San Francisco. Routine comments about the cost of Chinese vegetables in the market. There was a brief reference to their ongoing discussions about her getting older, still with no husband. She would be thirty-one in June. Her mother had been twenty-two when she was born, the message said. Nine years behind schedule, she wrote.

Bao read the message again. The tone was right; it was all the numbers that sounded the alarm. It was something only a cryptographer would notice. She frowned at the screen. If the message was not from her granddaughter, it could only have come from—she could not allow herself even to *think* the man's name in this inner chamber of Chinese Intelligence. As if the security people could read her thoughts.

It must be his response to the message she had sent.

She struck a key and sent the message to her printer. She routinely saved the messages and, after the counterintelligence branch had cleared them, kept them at home in a green cloth notebook. No doubt the watchers had already read this message, but since it was similar to the dozens of others she had received from her granddaughter over the past three years, there should be no cause for suspicion. She folded the message and put it in her pocket

She sent a brief reply, thanking Jennifer for being so thoughtful of her aging grandmother, and chiding her to be careful with her money, even if she did have a better job and better salary. And be patient, the right man would come along. You must believe always in love.

Her day dragged on. The Japanese diplomatic code remained unbreakable, but General Xing's new field encryption equipment seemed to be performing perfectly. She would have something positive to report. Finally, just after six, she shut down her workstation and put on her coat.

The security officer at the door studied the message she handed him. "Your granddaughter sends many numbers this time," he said.

"She is concerned that I will think she is spending too much money," Bao Qing replied. "She is a very thoughtful child."

"She works for Stanford University. Very important job."

Bao nodded, smiling. Was the man suspicious? "I know nothing about her work, only that it is with computers, as is mine."

"She is in intelligence work?"

"She is a programmer, nothing to do with the government."

The security man stared at her for a moment and then handed back the message.

The late afternoon air was cool as she pedaled home. Clusters of fanciful, bird-shaped kites darted across the sky above Tieneman Square. At this distance, they seemed to fly free—the lines that held them, invisible.

Bao was sweating when she parked her bike outside her apartment, not entirely from the exercise of peddling home. She threw off her coat and reached for a book from the meager collection on her shelf. The government still harbored suspicions about books from the decadent West. Robert Browning was probably not on the approved list.

She laid the email message beside the poetry book and began the translation. Her fingers shook as they traced the poet's words across the pages.

She did not bother to write the decryption down. The message was short, but the meaning burned itself into her mind. As her finger found the sixth word of the tenth line, tears began to fall on the faded page. The word glared at her with a terrible finality: shot. Her granddaughter was dead. There was no mention of the message she had sent, the message on which her life depended.

She closed the book and rested her hand on the smooth, worn leather. How long ago a young woman and a young man had sat together in the Strawberry Market, holding this book in their hands, laughing together as only young lovers laugh. "No, Jon," she whispered, "*Ano.*"

◄8►

DCI Vail's four o'clock meeting took place in a basement room at CIA headquarters reserved for just such sensitive gatherings. Three men had come down the private elevator from the seventh floor director's office, the fourth had slipped in unseen from an underground garage. The director's Task Force Seven committee was in session.

The walls of the windowless room were decorated with seals of the twelve agencies in the so-called intelligence community. All twelve, civilian and military, were overseen by the director of Central Intelligence. At least in theory.

Jon Cross smiled at the thought. On the wall across from him hung the seal of the State Department's Bureau of Intelligence and Research. If the secretary of state had his way, the DCI would report to him.

"Eclipse overstepped her authority a bit," Director Vail was saying. He looked at the faces of the three men around the oak table, searching for their reactions. Ray DeLong, the deputy director for Science and Technology, looked away uneasily; Anne Hammersmith, the officer code named Eclipse, worked for him—at least on paper.

Vail could read nothing in Robert Jaynes's face, but the deputy director for operations was good at hiding his feelings. Jon Cross seemed distracted, glancing around the room as if wishing he were somewhere else. The director had handpicked these men to advise him on Task Force Seven. Had his choices been wise? he wondered.

"We are willing to overlook, even to reward, a bit of initiative from time to time, in spite of what you might have heard," Vail said. "Bottom line, she got results. A transcript of her intercept is in front of you. Comments? Jon, are you with us?"

Cross picked up the sheet of paper. "It ties with the information I have from Marty Hausler. According to his man in the PLA, there are rumblings that Xing has acquired a command and control vehicle that sounds a lot like one they're working on down in New Mexico. It's a field platform for our C4I software. This is the age of computerized warfare. In the field, everything depends on split-second coordination, and the ability to feed targeting information to all these computerized weapons systems. Without C4I, the instantaneous coordination it provides, all of Xing's high-tech weapons are just scrap metal."

"Satellite images have just confirmed that," DeLong said. "What does this mean, Xing Wanpo is going into the field?"

"Or going to war," Jaynes said. "Our people are looking at the idea that Xing is putting together some kind of alliance, possibly with someone on the Central Committee. He's getting a bigger taste of power these days. Just how he'll exercise it isn't clear, but it will be soon. He's not a patient man."

"You're the China expert, Jon, what do you see happening?" Director Vail asked.

"Hatchet is amassing a lot power in the PLA, possibly elsewhere in the government. He has allies on the Central Committee, in the intelligence community, and with the army behind him..."

"Are we talking palace coup?" Jaynes asked.

Cross said, "Not my choice of words, but the signs are there. His acquiring this command and control vehicle, the field platform for C4I is a logical step along that path."

"How imminent is the threat?" Vail asked.

"Depends on what he's planning. You don't overthrow a country like China in a week."

DeLong said, "The internal threat is serious enough, but it's the externals I'm worried about—Taiwan, the whole goddam Pacific Rim."

"China can't conduct a large-scale assault on Taiwan or anyone without the next-generation C4I software. When you're talking about the modern battlefield, you're talking about coordinating AWACS, space-based weapons, computer systems, making a thousand calculations and projections a second," Cross said.

"And we've just handed them C4I," Jaynes said.

"Calculated risk." Cross's voice was cool. "As I told you, there is a virus in that software. In sixty days, it crashes and takes their system down with it."

"The C4I operation was a mistake," Jaynes said. "For the record, I was opposed—"

Vail raised his hand. "Your objection is noted. It all seems to hinge on containing General Xing. I want you on top of this, Jon. Breaking something as hot as a palace coup in China would be a feather in the CIA's cap, and we sure as hell could use one. The president is being bombarded constantly—Congress, the military, the press—all telling him it's time to put us out to pasture. The Defense Department is arguing they can collect intelligence as well as we can—better. The president may be leaning that way, I'm afraid. Seems like I'm spending most of my time these days protecting my turf."

Cross sat forward in his chair. "Getting back to—"

Jaynes snorted in disgust. "Blanchard at Defense thinks it's all about special operations—send in the Green Berets. McHone's State Department guys are no threat; they're afraid to get their Guccis dirty."

If Cross was irritated at the interruption, he gave no sign. "We've known for a long time Hatchet is unhappy with what he sees as a softening of the Chinese hard-line," he said. "Now, with Hong Kong back in the fold, he has a lot more sources of revenue available to him. And, we know what he's buying, battlefield technology. It wouldn't be the first time China has been conquered from within. He could move before the end of the summer."

"Speaking of conquering from within, what do you make of this 'friend in Washington' business?" Vail asked.

"If Xing really does have an asset here in Washington, as this intercept suggests," Cross tapped the sheet of paper in front of him, "we have a lot bigger problem on our hands."

Vail said, "This needs watching, Jon."

"And we'll soon have a damn site better way of watching, true?" the director of Science and Technology asked.

Cross said, "The C4I software should be in Hatchet's hands in a week."

"And we'll be listening in real time?" Vail asked.

"If it works," Jaynes said.

DeLong interrupted, an edge in his voice. "It works. The software forces the computer to produce nonsinusoidal waveforms. We call them 'Walsh functions.' It's a newer version of the old Promis software. Data are broadcast directly to the Flint bird. We'll be able to hear everything Hatchet does, his weapons deployment, engagement strategies. Even his orders from Beijing. We have a lot of faith in that technology."

"I'm sure you do, Ray," Jaynes said. "Operations is 'wait-and-see' on that one. In spite of my misgivings, I have to say that if it works, it's a hell of a breakthrough. The only thing better would be to have a source inside the Ministry of State Security."

"That would be better," Cross said quietly.

Vail stood up. "The president has asked me to brief him and several members of his cabinet. They're very interested all of a sudden, so let's make this thing a priority. Keep me posted on the C4I situation. Thank you for coming down on short notice, Jon. We're adjourned." He walked out of the room.

DDO Jaynes rode with DeLong in the elevator to the seventh floor. Jaynes was angry. "Cross has the director in his pocket."

DeLong nodded. "I didn't notice Vail thanking *us* for coming down."

"That's because we don't work out of our palatial homes out in horse country."

"Something was definitely bothering our boy Cross this morning."

"There's a lot more to that C4I operation out in California than he's telling. There was a big flap at FBI yesterday. They accused the Agency of interfering in their investigation, impersonating an FBI agent. I hear they're going to call for a congressional hearing. Vail got involved; it was a hell of a mess. I know the president himself appointed Cross, but—"

"Gave him way too much leeway, in my opinion," DeLong said.

"The bastard is out of control."

"At least he's our bastard."

"Is he?"

The elevator doors slid open and the two CIA executives walked together down the blue-carpeted corridor.

★ ★ ★

Washington, D.C.

Song had been in agony the entire trip from San Francisco. A nasty mix of airline booze and painkillers still churned through his system. Jet lag, and three hours of sleep rudely interrupted by a call from the intelligence resident, Sun Shiliang, at the embassy, who demanded a meeting. He had longed to roll over and go back to sleep. But the resident was not a man you refused. Sun operated under diplomatic cover from the Chinese embassy, controlling a network of agents and Chinese intelligence officers spying in the American capitol. He was Song's conduit to the Ministry of State Security and famous for his temper when things went wrong. He did not like to send bad news to Beijing.

Song had ridden to the embassy crouched in the back of a laundry truck. His head had slammed painfully against the side of the truck as it bounced over a particularly huge pothole on Connecticut Avenue, and he had nearly passed out. The truck had let him off inside the compound, hidden from the CIA cameras outside the gate.

Had the rough ride started his wound bleeding again? He leaned back tiredly in the leather conference room chair and gingerly touched the bandage on his head. His fingers came away dry.

Sun Shiliang was speaking. "...it is clear that you must call in some favors?"

"Yes—yes, clear."

"Are you ill?" Sun asked.

"No, I am listening."

"Are you certain no one saw you make the software pickup?"

Song hesitated. "Software...no one." It was a dangerous lie.

"How were you injured? The man's eyes seemed to bore into Song's brain, ripping out the secrets hidden there.

Song drummed his fingers nervously on his knee. "I was attacked."

Shiliang slapped the table. "Why do you lie?"

Song jerked his head up at the sound. "Someone saw me. But it is being taken care of." Song told his story of the botched software drop as the intelligence resident sat glowering.

Sun stood up. "If you can't find the man who attacked you, if the security of this operation is compromised..." He shook his head, somberly considering Song's fate.

"I can assure you—"

Sun held up his hand for silence. "There is something more pressing at the moment." The resident scrawled on a slip of paper and pushed it across the table. He had written, "Bei Feng." In Chinese, the words meant, "north wind." It was the code name the Ministry of State Security had assigned to Song's top American agent. It was forbidden to speak the code name out loud inside the embassy walls. CIA bugs could be anywhere. "The Ministry wants to know if CIA has a mole in their headquarters. You are to make contact today."

"We all want that information, of course, but why the sudden urgency? I can't—"

The resident fixed him with a harsh stare.

"How—how much time do I have?" Song asked.

"I am telling you there is no time!" The resident's face reddened and he half rose from his chair. He sat down and went on in a softer tone. "You are a very persuasive man. That is how you achieved your present position, is it not? And we have provided you certain...leverage with this person."

"I will try, but I—"

"That is not what the Ministry wants to hear," Sun said sharply. "They want results."

Song ducked his head in acknowledgment. "They will have results."

"Squeeze him, crush him," Sun said. "Just get the information." The resident rose, bowed formally, and walked from the room.

★ ★ ★

Culpeper

The green Toyota pickup turned off of the highway onto a two-lane blacktop road that narrowed to a gravel track winding up the side of a hill through the lush, Virginia woodlands. As the pickup approached a steel gate, Smith pushed a button on a hand-held remote control. The gate swung open. Beyond it, the terrain was open, the timber and brush had been cleared. At the top of the hill sat a large, shake-roofed house, a barn, and several small outbuildings.

The pickup labored the last quarter mile up the narrow, dirt switchbacks and stopped behind the house next to a black Lincoln Town Car.

"He's probably out on the deck," Smith said.

The redwood deck surrounded three sides of the house. The hillside dropped sharply away beneath it, and thick brush covered the ground below. As Nyland walked, his practiced eye picked out several motion sensors hidden in the bushes. Down the hill to the east, he could see the gate and a long section of the road they had just traveled. Good fields of fire in all directions. The place was a fortress.

Jon Cross stepped through a set of French doors onto the deck as Nyland and Smith approached. He wore an immaculate gray suit, white shirt, and blue silk tie, knot loosened. On the carved wooden tray he carried were three bottles of Dinkelacker beer and frosted glasses. He looked tired, Nyland thought, but the concern in his eyes was unmistakable. "Anybody hurt?" he asked.

"Just the bad guys," Nyland said.

Cross sat the tray on a white wicker table. "I thought you both could use one of these," Cross said. "I know I could." He filled his glass and drank deeply. "Tommy Lin moved damn fast."

"He either followed me to the airport, or somebody leaked the flight number."

"Only Jacobs had that information. I trust him," Cross said.

"If you say so." Nyland told Cross of the pursuit from the air-port, Tommy Lin's intercepted cell phone conversation with

Song Zhenyo, and Smith recounted the destruction of the black Saab.

"Song has been behind this operation all along," Cross said. "That ties in with some things we talked about down at Langley this afternoon. Doug, you better hide your truck in the barn, and make sure all the alarms are on. Mr. Song is going to be very unhappy about all this."

After Smith had left, Cross lowered himself onto a chaise longue. "Let's forget Song Zhenyo for the moment." He sipped his beer. "Do you believe in love?" he asked.

Nyland sat down beside him. "Works for some people," he said cautiously.

"The kind of force that makes you do insane things, jeopardize your career? The kind of thing you believe in even when there's no earthly reason to?"

Cross was staring out at the Great Smoky Mountains to the west. Nyland studied his profile. In Iraq they had called his look, "the thousand-yard stare in a ten-yard room."

Nyland leaned forward in his chair, trying to read the man's expression. This was a Jon Cross he had never seen. But he knew little, he realized, of Cross's personal life. The man was in his late sixties, and had never married, dedicating all his energy to the CIA. He was rich, if you believed the rumors, an inheritance from his father. A solitary man.

On the job he was direct and decisive. Strike at the heart of the issue, get things done, that was Jon Cross. The man Nyland looked at now seemed old and tired, a sadness in his face Nyland had never seen before. Was it about the death of Jennifer Chin?

"I think it's time," Cross said, "I told you why I really brought you back." He drank the last of his beer and stared down into the glass. "Tuck, I need your help."

Nyland was immediately alert. The pleading tone was not Jon Cross. "We'll get Song Zhenyo," Nyland said. "I let him kill Jenny. I just sat there and watched him do it. I'm sorry—"

"No. There's—something else." Cross pulled a small box from his pocket. The lid was brocaded silk secured by a spear of bone.

"What I'm going to tell you has been a secret for more than forty years, kept between only two people. You will be the third." He held up his hand. "Don't interrupt. Hard enough as it is."

"I was posted to Burma after the war, my first overseas assignment. The Agency was brand new then, and we were still dealing with the old OSS networks. I ended up in Maymyo."

"Up in the highlands, east of Mandalay," Nyland said.

Cross nodded. "You were up there on a drug interdiction operation, as I recall. There was nothing like that going on when I was there; it was still very much a colonial outpost of the British Empire. Tidy brick buildings, neat, narrow little streets. There was a botanical garden there and an orchid house. That's where I met the Kingfisher."

Nyland's eyes were on the box in Cross's hand.

"Burma, this exotic, mystical place with elephants and tigers, flowers in the trees," Cross said. "All of us were on a great adventure in those days, fighting for freedom in a strange land. A schoolboy's dream. I bought the whole package.

"One night I went for a walk in the botanical gardens. It was clear, warm. I could smell the jasmine and tuberose. All of a sudden, I saw her. The memory is as clear as glass: a Chinese girl, young and slender in a blue silk dress. She was standing in the moonlight by the reflecting pool, staring down at the water. I got my nerve up and approached her. My Chinese was lousy. But she surprised me; she spoke English.

"She told me her name was Bao Qing. Her father was a Chinese diplomat stationed in Mandalay. I gave her my State Department cover story, and we walked around the gardens together, talking about nothing, showing each other the flowers, the orchid house—it sounds juvenile now, but—" Cross looked down at the box. "We fell in love that first night."

Nyland said nothing. A wind chime tinkled softly on the deck.

Finally, Cross spoke. "We spent a little over two weeks together, meeting each other secretly in the gardens, taking carriage rides. We both knew the risk was insane. There was a story around the embassy about an Englishman who fell for a Chinese girl. They told him it was forbidden. He didn't heed the warnings. One night at a party, he was abducted, drugged—both his hands surgically removed.

"Still, we kept meeting. I went down to Rangoon and bought her a going-away present, black market. Spent most of a month's paycheck on it. Ming Dynasty. I gave it to her on the night before she left. She—she gave herself to me that night."

"You never told her you were Agency?"

"Not until—later."

Nyland nodded toward the box. "The going-away present?"

Cross opened the box: a pin in the shape of a dragonfly. The wings, a delicate lattice of blue and silver, glowed iridescent in the sun. "It's inlaid with pieces of feather, from a bird called the Asian Kingfisher. Beautiful. You see them all over up in the highlands. I told her she reminded me of the bird when I first saw her, so slim and graceful standing by the water. She promised to keep it forever."

"But she sent it back," Nyland said.

"A week ago. I haven't been able to think of much else."

"How can you be sure she's...Have you kept in touch with her?"

"Off and on. And, I am sorry to say, it has not always been purely personal."

"My god, she's an agent," Nyland said.

Cross shook his head. "Not officially. She has given me a few things over the years, but the Agency knows nothing about her."

"That's a dangerous game," Nyland said.

"I contacted her this morning to tell her about Jenny's death."

"Why?"

"Jenny was her granddaughter," Cross said.

"Don't tell me you're Jenny's—"

Cross smiled and shook his head. "Her godfather. Her parents are both dead. I kept an eye on her as she was growing up. In her teens, Jenny looked exactly like her grandmother. She wore a blue silk dress at her high school graduation, her hair was long, down her back. The resemblance was—" he brushed a hand across his eyes.

"Forty years ago," Cross said, "Qing and I made a pact. We both knew we could never be together, but she told me that if there was ever a time she had to get out of China for any reason, she would send me this pin. Bao Qing and I told ourselves that if we couldn't live together, we would die together. Melodramatic stuff."

Nyland studied the dragonfly pin. The wings seemed to glow in the setting sun as if lit from within. "Does this mean the Kingfisher believes she's going to die?"

"Maybe she's found out about the coup, maybe she thinks she won't survive it. Maybe the MSS is on to her. Doug warned me email wasn't secure, but..."

"They could have intercepted it?"

"I don't know." Cross rubbed his hands over his eyes. "I only know that I promised to get her out."

Nyland turned the dragonfly pin over in his hand. "This is why you brought me back," he said quietly.

"This may sound ridiculous to you, but we pledged to be together at...at the end."

Nyland looked away, embarrassed at the intensity of emotion in the man's voice. The sun dipped behind the mountains and the light faded from the dragonfly's wings. The wind chimes had fallen silent.

★   ★   ★

Cross and Doug Smith had gone to bed hours before; the house was dark. Nyland leaned against the deck rail, listening to the crickets. He had promised Cross an answer in the morning, now only a few hours away.

Everything inside him rebelled against the idea of going after the Kingfisher. It was not the physical danger, he had faced much worse in his years as a SEAL and later in CIA special operations.

His victories, however, always seemed hollow in the face of his failures. His mother had trusted him to watch his younger sister, Lynn. He had failed, and she had died. The young Iraqi girl had died, shot dead before Nyland could react. And Jennifer Chin, Cross's godchild. She had turned toward him, beseeching him to save her. He had stood and watched her die. Three times, when others depended on him the most, he had failed. Three innocent people had died.

How could he put himself in that position again? Yet that was exactly what Jon Cross was asking him to do. The Kingfisher was nearly seventy, Cross had said. The journey was long and dangerous, there could be no guarantees of bringing her out alive.

He gripped the redwood rail with both hands and closed his eyes. If he should fail Jon Cross again and Bao Qing should die—who could live with that?

◄9►

Culpeper

The sun was just touching the crest of the Smokies as Jon Cross walked across the deck toward Nyland. A breeze blowing up the hillside flipped the hem of Cross's robe. He pulled it tighter around him. "Have you been out here all night?"

Nyland nodded. He leaned against the rail looking out across the mountains.

The wind chimes tinkled and fell silent. Cross's voice was strangely gentle: "I need your decision now."

"I let you down—more than once."

"At your worst, you're better than anybody we've got. You made that SEAL team in San Diego look like boy scouts. But I can't force you to go. I can give you a new identity, set you up in another country..."

Nyland shook his head.

Cross shivered in the morning breeze. He looked suddenly old, vulnerable. "You're the only chance she's got."

Nyland remembered the tenderness in the man's eyes as he talked about Bao Qing. He had seen that look in his mother's eyes when she spoke of his father. Love is a rare commodity in this world, she had told him. Worth saving. There was no choice, there never had been. Tuck held out his hand.

Cross's grip was surprisingly firm. "Thank you," he said.

★ ★ ★

Georgetown, Washington, D.C.

Song Zhenyo paced back and forth behind his rosewood desk, toying with a chrome letter opener. Tommy Lin sat in a straight-backed chair, eyes defiant. Song shook his head slowly, a bemused expression on his face. "You have compromised a major intelligence operation," he said softly. "Beijing is not happy."

Behind him, the open French doors let in dappled sunlight from the garden of his townhouse. Beds of white and yellow roses glowed in the afternoon light. His bodyguard stood, arms folded, near the wrought iron gate.

"You have shamed your country, shamed me," Song said quietly. "You let this man get away not once, but twice. You have jeopardized not only—"

"The American spy surprised me—as he did you."

Song stopped pacing and stared down at the seated man. "Be very careful," he said.

"And you, confidant to the president of the United States, you have not grown used to the decadent West?"

Song smashed his fist into Tommy Lin's nose. Lin toppled off his chair, hands cupped over his face. Blood trickled through his fingers. "You will not speak in this manner," Song whispered. He grabbed Lin roughly by the collar, dragged him through the French doors into the garden.

"Mr. Vasquez will teach you respect." The bodyguard grabbed Lin's arm and threw him against the brick wall. Song turned his back on the sounds of the beating and the grunts of pain. The roses were beautiful, he thought. He plucked a bright yellow bud and slipped it into his lapel.

He closed the French doors, sat down behind his desk, and leaned back in the chair. The C4I software would soon be in the hands of General Xing Wanpo, and he, Song Zhenyo, had made that happen. Now the general had the final piece of software needed to mold the antiquated People's Liberation Army into a high-tech fighting force, capable of focusing all its newly acquired weapons systems onto a single objective. An army able to launch the split-second attacks and counterattacks the computer-age battlefield demanded. China would be a military power second to none. The general would be extremely grateful when Song handed him the C4I software. And this was a man that was going places—he would take

Song Zhenyo with him. Song imagined the scene: the general smiling—impressed with Song's tale of risking capture by the FBI, his
courage and daring in the face of the enemy.

Life was going to be good, very good indeed, Song thought, as
soon as he corrected the one flaw in his otherwise perfect plan.
Thanks to Tommy Lin's stupidity, the man who had seen him kill
Jennifer Chin had gotten away. But he would be found, and he
would suffer before he died.

But first there was the matter of the spy in the Ministry of State
Security. The resident wanted answers today. Song picked up his
phone and dialed a Washington number.

Song's American agent, Bei Feng, answered on the first ring.

Song said, "Does the CIA have a mole in the MSS? I need your
answer today."

★　★　★

Culpeper

Nyland had gone upstairs to sleep and Smith was at work
downstairs. Cross, dressed now in chinos and a faded Harvard
sweatshirt, had the deck to himself. The sun touched the redwood
planks and the morning dew evaporated, sending up faint tendrils
of mist. He poured himself coffee, took a sip, and closed his eyes,
feeling the sun's warmth on his face.

At the distant sound of an engine, he opened his eyes. A silver-
colored Chevy Blazer wound its way up his dirt road, sun flashing
off its tinted windows. Cross recognized the car immediately and a
tingle of apprehension went through him. A personal visit from the
boss was rare—unheard of at this hour of the morning. Cross
pushed a hand-held remote button. A quarter of a mile away down
the hill, the gate swung open and the Blazer rolled through.

★　★　★

Billy Vail stepped out of the Blazer wearing an open-collared
shirt and jeans. "Took the day off to go fishing," he said.

"What kind of fish live on top of a mountain?"

"I'm allegedly down on the Rappahannock at my favorite hole."

The two men settled themselves on the deck. Vail sipped his coffee and looked out at the wooded hills. "Don't see how you get any work done. I'd be out here admiring the view. Almost makes you forget the Washington rat's nest." Vail put down his cup. "You don't ever forget, do you Jon?"

Cross smiled. "Even if I wanted to, those electronic tentacles downstairs wouldn't let me."

"I hope not. That man the FBI lost track of out in San Francisco yesterday, I assume he was one of yours, part of Task Force Seven?"

Cross nodded.

"Christ, keep him out of sight. They're raising hell clear up to the White House on this, claiming we obstructed justice."

"Interesting thing for them to say."

"I don't think I want to know any more about that operation," DCI Vail said.

"You approved it."

"I trust you, Jon." But the director did not meet his eyes.

"I assume we'll get around to the real subject of this fishing trip?"

The DCI pulled a cigar from his pocket. "Mind?" Cross shook his head. The two men sat in silence watching the smoke drift across the deck. Finally, Vail spoke: "I had an unusual meeting at the White House yesterday. They wanted a list of any assets we might have in the MSS, particularly the headquarters in Beijing."

"Why unusual?" Cross asked. "The possibility of a coup in China, the president might reasonably be concerned."

"True, but it's the personal interest that bothers me," Vail said. "It's out of character. The tone of the meeting was all wrong. They seemed almost—desperate. The president wants the list today."

Cross sipped his coffee. "Operations has all the files, why come to me? Is there something I don't know?"

"The question is, Jon, is there something I don't know?" He took a thoughtful pull on the cigar. "The CIA was penetrated by Chinese Intelligence in 1982. You found the mole. Nobody could ever figure out how."

"Larry Wu-Tai Chin tripped himself up. The rest was just details."

"It was a hell of a lot more than details. You always seemed to show up in the right place at the right time. Uncovering Chin made your career. There was some speculation at the time that you might have had some help from inside the Chinese Ministry of State Security—your own private source."

"So that's what this surprise visit is about?" Cross said.

"You know the Far East as well as anyone in the Agency, five tours over there. You meet people, you make connections. I have to cover all the bases, Jon."

"It's all in my file: every agent contact, every recruitment, the details of every network."

"You are a man who takes the initiative, Jon, the C4I project proves that. Sometimes you have to wonder what other initiatives..." Vail shook his head. "The president appointed you personally...He wants a payback. He wants anything you have about an agent inside the Ministry of State Security. And I don't think it's just about the coup business. It's—something personal.

"Some Agency people are a little nervous, and probably a little jealous, of the freedom your organization's been given. Operations people, especially."

"Robert Jaynes, especially." Cross leaned back in his chair. Jaynes, the deputy director of operations, would love to see him fail.

"The president wants a report. Task Force Seven's future is on the line here."

"And mine as well? We can't give him what we haven't got. By the end of next week the Chinese should have the C4I system up and running, loading in their data—and we'll be listening, reading it all. We're making progress, give him that."

The DCI sat down and snubbed out his cigar in his saucer. "I want the truth. Do you have any—private assets in the Chinese Intelligence community?"

Cross met his gaze with a level stare. "No," he said.

"I hope, for all our sakes, that you're telling the truth."

"Would you like some more coffee?" Cross asked.

"I have to get back. The fishing was lousy." The DCI stood up.

"A question before you go," Cross said. "What's your impression of Song Zhenyo?"

Vail ticked off the points on his fingers as he spoke. "Egotistical maniac. Damn good fund-raiser. Some people believe the money he brought in got the president reelected. Couple of senators, too. He's a White House regular. He'd like to think he's got the president in his pocket. Maybe he does." Vail paused. "Why do you ask?"

"We seem to be on the subject of China."

"Some of his money sources are questionable, but we've never linked him with their intelligence service."

"We've been wrong before," Cross said.

"Christ, don't remind me. Why all this interest in Song Zhenyo?"

"Innocent question."

Vail frowned. "You've never asked an innocent question in your life. Think about what I asked you. If you have a connection to Beijing that nobody knows about, and information is flowing, couldn't a person wonder if it's flowing both ways?"

"Director Vail," Cross said coldly, "are you making an accusation?"

The DCI smiled. "Innocent question."

The White House

The CIA director strolled beside President Jack Gardner in the Rose Garden. The sun had come out and the humidity was rising. The bushes beside the path hung heavy with blooms, their scent strong, almost stifling. The president picked a pale lavender bud and twirled it in his fingers as he walked. Vail knew the pattern well; the president would start when he was good and ready.

Like most who had held the nation's highest office, the president had aged visibly during his five years in the White House. His shoulders hunched forward now, as if shielding his body from a blow. The famous profile that some had compared to F.D.R. seemed diffused, weathered like stone.

"I value your counsel," the president said. "We spend too much time communicating through reports and aides and deputy assistants—I need a straight line of talk here, Billy."

"How can I help, Mr. President?"

"Tell me about your meeting with Jon Cross."

"He says we have no assets actually inside the Ministry of State Security. That kind of thing is mostly in the movies. The MSS is one of the most tightly controlled intelligence agencies on Earth, operating inside a controlled society."

"And you believe him?"

Vail stopped and examined a rose bush. His fingers brushed the soft pink petals. "There is nothing definite, but—"

"Tell me!"

The force of the president's outburst startled Vail. He drew his hand back as if pricked by a thorn. "Back in the early seventies, we learned a Chinese operative had penetrated the CIA. He fooled everybody for an embarrassingly long time. Jon Cross uncovered him. At the time, some of the old operations types grumbled that he was either the luckiest guesser alive, or he had an inside source."

"Which is it?" the president asked.

"He says all his agents were well documented in Agency files. We frown on private sources, you know. The suspicion is that information could well be flowing both ways. Otherwise, why keep it a secret?"

"You're saying Jon Cross could be working for the Chinese?"

"His record is spotless. He is the best Asia hand we have. He did ask me an interesting question this morning, however. He asked what I knew about Song Zhenyo."

The president looked across the lawn at the two secret service agents pacing warily back and forth, eyes moving over the grounds. One agent wiped sweat from his forehead with a white handkerchief. Almost like a signal, Vail thought.

"What did you tell him?" the president asked.

"What I know, which isn't much. Party bosses love him, the money he brings in. I know Song helped you get elected, but if you don't mind me saying so, I think he's an opportunist."

"Running for president means raising a hundred dollars a *second*, every hour of every day, did you know that?"

"I'm not judging anyone, Mr. President."

Gardner stared at the DCI for a long moment. "No, that isn't your style. Where are we on that C4I business?"

"We believe the Chinese have that software, or will very soon. Cross is saying by next week."

"Cross is saying?"

"The Agency is saying."

"The Chinese have no idea there is a trapdoor?" Gardner asked.

"No, to the best of my knowledge, Mr. President."

The president grunted an acknowledgment, turned, and walked slowly back toward the Oval Office. Vail followed a few steps behind. "Do you approve of the way Cross handled that operation?" the president asked.

"We wanted the Chinese agent to get away, but we didn't want to tell the FBI that. Cross had one of his people on site to—impede their progress. I'm not sure I approve—"

"You know," the president's tone was musing, "Song was out in San Francisco on a fund-raising tour at about that time."

"Yes, sir."

The president stopped before the bullet-proof glass doors leading to the Oval Office. "Billy, we've been talking—my staff and some of my cabinet. We—I believe we made a mistake authorizing Task Force Seven, giving Cross as much autonomy as we did."

"Desperate times require—" Vail said.

"I know the arguments. But Cross worries me, even the hint that he might be working with the Chinese. I want his operation closed down."

"He's a senior intelligence officer, just a couple of years from retirement."

"Close him down. Is that clear?"

Vail studied the president's face. He had known the man for nearly twenty years. They had run against each other for the U.S. Senate years ago. Vail had lost by a slim margin, but they had become friends in spite of their political differences. Vail noted again how strained the president looked. His face was a mask. Gardner's hand shook slightly as he reached for the door.

Vail laid his hand on the president's arm. "Mr. President, was closing down the task force your idea?"

"You're on dangerous ground, Billy."

"Is there something I should know?"

"Nothing I can tell you." President Gardner looked around the Oval Office. "They say the buck stops here. But they don't tell you it lands right on top of you."

"You may be getting bad counsel—"

"I've given you an order, do you understand?"

Their eyes locked. Then Vail looked away. "I understand, Mr. President."

★ ★ ★

Culpeper

Doug Smith looked up from his computer screen. "We have a little problem, Mr. Cross." His screen read: ACCESS DENIED.

"What can you do about it?"

The young intelligence officer was already typing furiously at the keyboard. "Give me fifteen minutes," he said.

Cross motioned Nyland toward the door. "Let's take a walk."

The night air was East Coast humid with a scent of pine. Nyland could see a few lights scattered in the valley below Jon Cross's house. A gibbous moon had risen, casting faint white light on the path. Cross lead the way to a small clearing above the house where the two men sat down on a log.

"About a year ago, the Agency began to focus more on the Far East, particularly China, so the president formed Task Force Seven. Our mission is to penetrate the Ministry of State Security. I was thought to have some expertise in that area, so they gave me control of the unit. I handpicked a certain number of people whom I thought were the best in the Agency."

"And nobody knew about your inside source?"

"It is extremely dangerous for Bao Qing and I to communicate.

She's only passed me information twice."

"She tipped you to a CIA mole back in the late seventies, you told me. What was the other one?"

"About a year ago, just before we initiated the C4I operation, she passed another message to me through—a third party. Overheard conversation was all it was, Qing's boss bragging to one of his agents about 'having a lock' on someone high up in the U.S. government, possibly even the White House. They had a very damaging film, something from the Vietnam era, that's all she heard. The agent had been given the code-name Bei Feng. It means 'north wind' in Mandarin."

"Did you believe it?" Nyland asked.

"I didn't until they started talking about forming a China task force. The odd thing about it was, all our work was to be focused on penetrating the MSS, and all our reports were to be sent directly to the president."

"This agent, Bei Feng, trying to find out how much you know about the Ministry of State Security?"

"Wanting to know, particularly, if we have an agent inside. The Chinese obviously suspect we do." Cross looked thoughtful. "That was precisely the question Billy Vail asked me yesterday afternoon."

"You think Vail is Bei Feng?"

"No, I think he's just following orders from the White House."

"You're not telling me the president—"

"The president's a spy? That works better in the movies. What you want is someone who has the president's ear, who can influence policy in a lot of little ways without causing alarm. The Chinese will always focus on the long game, a trade agreement, a shift in military strategy, intelligence priorities. Things that add up over time."

"So, who is it?"

Cross started to speak, then shook his head. "Speculative at the moment."

"The Kingfisher sending you the pin now—that couldn't be a coincidence?"

"She believes they're onto her. My guess is that Beijing is putting pressure on Bei Feng to find out who she is. I am certain the conduit of that pressure is Song Zhenyo. And since we did our job so well, uncovering Song..."

Nyland nodded. "We know the man's a spy and a killer."

"And a trusted advisor who helped raise money for the campaign," Cross said. "Gardner can't let that get out."

"Because he owes his presidency to Song's money. So the White House just closes us down?"

"They might have something a little more drastic in mind." Cross looked down across the valley where the lights twinkled faintly. A set of headlights moved along the main road and disappeared around a curve.

"What kind of weapons do you have out here?" Nyland asked.

Doug Smith stood waiting on the back porch as the two men approached. "It took a little longer than fifteen minutes, but I got back onto the network."

"What's the situation?" Cross asked.

"An order came down from DCI an hour ago to terminate our access. I got back on and managed to intercept a message that was supposed to go to the security detail."

"Message?"

"Ordering a team out here to pick us up. Somehow it didn't get through."

"You do good work," Cross said. "How much time do we have?"

"Probably several hours. There seems to be a major glitch in the Operations mainframe. It caught a virus." Smith smiled like a schoolboy.

"Remind me to give you a raise. I need to get in touch with some people immediately," Cross said. "Can we still get messages out?"

"Our system is still healthy; I designed it to operate independently of the Agency computers. We have better stuff, anyway. Plus, I hacked Bell Labs' satellite."

"Tuck, we'll be down in the strong room. There's an AR-15 up in my bedroom."

◄10►

"This is the president's direct order?" Billy Vail glowered at the man in the dark raincoat standing on his front porch. His visitor's face was shadowed by a wide-brimmed hat, his hands thrust in his pockets.

"Call him, if you want," the man code named Bei Feng said. "But I wouldn't advise it. All hell is breaking loose and he wants action, not rhetoric. And he wants it tonight."

"Why didn't he call me himself?"

The man on the porch allowed himself a brief smile. "Maybe you're not on the A-list anymore."

"I discussed Jon Cross's organization with him today—"

"We don't want a bureaucratic solution, Director Vail, we want action, as Churchill said, 'this day.'"

"What is the president asking me to do, kill him?" the CIA director asked.

"He's not *asking* you to do anything, he's telling you. Either you bring him in or I will."

"What will you do," Vail asked, "call in an air strike? Your own private hit squad? I assure you, we've already taken care of it. This ridiculous cloak-and-dagger encounter is unnecessary, and damned infuriating. Are we finished?"

"You have sent a team out there?"

"I already issued the—" The telephone on the hallway table interrupted. Vail stepped back inside and picked it up. "Yes. Go ahead." He frowned at the words he was hearing. "Nothing at all? What do you mean it's down? Did anything go out? Shit. I'm on my way." Vail hung up.

"Problem?" the man asked.

"Computer screw-up. It seems the message we sent to our

pickup team didn't get through. And now our whole communications system seems to be acting up."

"You're a fuck-up, Vail. I'm not too sure you're not in this with Cross. The president never would have appointed you if I'd had anything to say about it. But it's moot now. We're going to see some major housecleaning at CIA, starting at the top."

"If you want to get rid of the CIA so damn bad," Vail said wearily, "go ahead—tear it apart and stick the pieces up your ass for all I care. Or take it over yourself, that's what you really want, isn't it? Just out of curiosity, what is it they have on the president? Why is he so worried about agents in China?"

"Just fix your goddamn computer and get moving. I want Task Force Seven closed down." The man paused halfway down the front steps. "I want you to know I have a little contingency plan, just in case you don't follow through. But Billy, that would be a very bad idea—not to follow through."

"Whatever it is they have on you—whoever they are—this anarchy approach is not the answer."

Without a backward glance, the man named "north wind" walked away down the sidewalk.

★ ★ ★

Culpeper

Jon Cross sat back in his chair and rubbed his eyes. A good part of his plan was now in motion. It was nearly dawn. How much longer before Billy Vail's people came for him? There was still one more task. "Set up the email patch on your phantom line, Doug," he said.

There was one message waiting in Jenny's email box. Cross sent Doug upstairs to get a fresh pot of coffee, took down the Robert Browning volume, and began decoding Bao Qing's message:

POSSIBLE YOUR PRESIDENT COMPROMISED—PEOPLE'S AGENT BEI FENG. X-I-N-G SUSPECTS. NOTHING WILL STOP HIM. URGENT CONFIRM STRAWBERRY MARKET.

Tears filling his eyes, Jon Cross typed a reply:

STRAWBERRY MARKET CONFIRM MARCH 23.

March twenty-third. That gave him five days to get his team in position. The reference to the strawberry market, their old meeting place in Burma, was a code within a code. Bao Qing would be waiting at the Hauting temple in the Chinese city of Kunming, a location she and Cross had decided on years ago.

In the cold light of the computer screen, his face seemed drained of color. There were deep shadows under his eyes. "Bao Qing," he said softly.

He studied the message Bao Qing had risked her life to send. The president was compromised in some way by the agent Bei Feng. It confirmed Cross's suspicion that Gardner was acting out of desperation. It didn't take much imagination to conclude that Song Zhenyo was Bei Feng's control. What kind of hold did Song have on the president of the United States? Was it money, or was it something else?

The Kingfisher's message had mentioned General Xing Wanpo, saying, "nothing can stop him." She believed a coup attempt was inevitable. It was hard to imagine a China controlled by a madman like Xing Wanpo. Where would he strike? Taiwan, where the powerful Seventh Fleet patrolled, ships bristling with nuclear missiles and high-tech fighter-bombers? Or would he target the U.S. with his missiles? In either case, the world would be at war.

He glanced at the message again: XING SUSPECTS. Bao Qing was under suspicion. In his mind, he saw PLA soldiers smashing down her door, dragging her away. If she were arrested, there would be no lengthy trial. General Xing's brutal interrogators would torture every shred of information from her. Then throw her in an unmarked grave.

Cross logged onto Jenny Chin's email account. His pulse raced. "You have mail," the screen said. Bao was still in her office, monitoring her computer. Her message contained only the two digits: 29. He opened the Robert Browning volume. It was a page number he knew well.

When the two young lovers had met secretly near the strawberry market in Maymyo, they had read the Browning poems together, particularly one stanza in "Love Among the Ruins." Jon Cross still remembered the words by heart, and could recite them in English and Chinese:

> When I do come, she will speak not, she will stand,
> Either hand
> On my shoulder, give her eyes the first embrace
> Of my face,
> Ere we rush, ere we extinguish sight and speech
> Each on each.

Qing had gotten his message. She would be waiting. He slid the Browning volume back in his drawer. A discreet knock on the strong room door. "Come in, Doug, we have some overseas traffic to get out."

★　★　★

Hong Kong

Jon Cross's message crossed fifteen time zones in the blink of an eye. The computer on Martin Hausler's desk came to life, emitting a series of soft beeps. He paused by the door, dressed in his running clothes, ready for his after-work run. He sighed. The run would have to be postponed. He stepped back into his office and locked the door.

Hausler glanced at the on-screen clock. Just past 5:00 P.M. That made it three in the morning in Washington, D.C. Not the time to send a routine message. But then, Jon Cross never sent routine messages. Hausler tapped in his decryption code.

Hausler stared at the screen. "Holy shit." Plane reservations, contact schedule, it looked as if he would be missing tomorrow's budget meeting. He was being ordered back into the field. Hausler smiled. A break from the tedious world of marketing.

He was to meet two people, the message said, names not given. That meant someone he would know and recognize. Hausler's smile faded as he read the next line of his instructions. What in the hell was Jon Cross up to? Hausler was being sent to Kunming, the capital city of Yunnan Province, in far western China. He jotted a few notes, erased the screen, left his office, and headed up the stairs toward the indoor jogging track. He would run an extra mile tonight, he thought. If this was one of Cross's usual operations, Hausler thought, he would need all the conditioning he could get.

★ ★ ★

Beijing

Anne Hammersmith walked out of the communications center in the U.S. Embassy in Beijing, her head swimming with the implications of the message she had just received. Special assignment. Leave approved. Cover story was that she was going back to the States for emergency leave. Her dear mother, dead these past seven years, needed her back home in New Jersey. Reservations had already been made under a fictitious name on the morning flight for Rangoon. Jon Cross was putting her in the field with two other officers. One she would know on sight, the message had said, the other would give her a recognition code. Spy games.

The risks she had taken in the listening post in Xinjiang had paid off. She was through with routine technical assignments out of the embassy; she was going into the field for real. Her communications gear and laptop were stowed in her suitcase along with a new set of papers, a "shoe" in intelligence jargon. She would memorize the details of her new identity tonight, and tomorrow she would be on a plane to Burma.

★ ★ ★

Culpeper

Nyland lay in the brush overlooking the valley below Jon Cross's house. The moon was just above the horizon, a pale sliver in the dark sky. The sun would not be up for another hour. A lot could happen in an hour. What kind of force would they send for Jon Cross? A dozen men? They would not want to attract attention in this sleepy, rural countryside. One car, maybe, with a backup vehicle. Drive up to the gate, make a show, while the backup team moved in from behind.

He heard Jon Cross's voice in his headset: "What's the situation?"

"Quiet out here. I'm about a hundred yards due east of the house, above the creek."

"Director Vail just called. He had a visit tonight from what he called a 'high-level messenger.' Wouldn't tell me who it was. Checking to make sure Vail had ordered a team out to get us. While the guy was there, Vail got word that his computers had failed, the order hadn't gone out. The visitor was outraged, called Vail an idiot, said he would have to handle it himself. That pissed Billy off, so he called to warn me. This visitor of his has a 'special team,' a bunch of mercenaries he's hired to clean up his loose ends."

The sound of a car's engine drifted up from the valley below. "Hold on a minute," Nyland said. He swung the night scope around. A windowless van was moving slowly up the road, headlights out. As he watched, the vehicle stopped and several figures climbed out and began moving up the hillside, picking their way across the meadow. "Our friends have arrived," Nyland whispered.

"How many?" Cross asked.

"Six, plus the driver who seems to be staying with the van. I see two rifles, the rest have sidearms."

"Can you stop them? I've got a chopper coming, maybe twenty minutes."

"I can slow them down."

The mercenary team spread out in a loose file as they moved up the hillside. The last man in line, a stocky figure with a bandoleer of ammunition strapped across his chest, stopped to lean against a pine tree, readjusting his belt. Suddenly, his head snapped back and he was pulled out of sight behind the tree. Another went down a moment later: a hand covered his mouth, a hard blow to his temple. He dropped unconscious into the grass.

The leader, a tall, thin man in camouflage fatigues and beret, motioned for his men to join him at the fence. The moon had sunk below the horizon; the meadow was in near-total darkness. On the hill above, the team leader could barely make out the silhouette of a roof against the stars. Three of his team members knelt beside him at the fence. "Where the fuck is everybody?" he whispered.

"Shit if I know, Sarge. They were right behind us. Let's get the hell out of here."

"Christ, Jorge, get a hold of yourself. Stick together, keep your eyes open. Sons of bitches won't catch us asleep again."

The young, long-haired mercenary cocked his pistol. "Nobody sneakin' up on *my* ass."

The men crawled through the barbed wire fence, intent on their objective a hundred yards up the hill. Swede, the last man through the wire, snagged his pant leg on the rusty barbs and cursed softly, bending down to pull the cloth free. His eyes opened wide as a black apparition rose before him out of the grass. He had the flashing image of a pair of fierce eyes floating in the blackness before him, then a searing pain in his throat. Then nothing.

In an upstairs bedroom, Jon Cross was holding the Robert Browning poetry volume. He hesitated a moment, then stuffed it in his bag. This would be the last time he would see his beloved Culpeper house, he thought. He was under attack by his own government, or the twisted vestiges that remained. A government with a cancer inside—an agent of Chinese intelligence—calling the shots. He heard the crack of a gunshot outside and switched off the bedside lamp. Cross drew a 9mm from a belt holster and crept onto the balcony.

He heard the scuffle of boots on the gravel in the driveway, and ducked back as he saw a muzzle flash. The window behind him shattered. He crawled a few feet down the deck and eased his pistol over the edge. A shadowy figure creeping toward the house. He fired, heard a grunt of pain, and watched the man fall face down in the gravel.

Below him, the sound of smashing glass. The front porch light went out. Someone was pounding on the front door, kicking it with a boot. From the darkness at the edge of the driveway, Cross heard a staccato three-round burst. The AR-15. A scream of pain from the porch, then silence.

On the road below the house, a pair of headlights flashed on, and Cross saw a van accelerate back toward the highway. So much for combat discipline.

In the driveway, he heard the crunch of gravel and again raised his pistol. Two men walking slowly toward the house. A tall man in camouflage fatigues, hands raised above his head, moved reluctantly forward. Nyland held the AR-15 at his back.

The mercenary called "Sarge" was hanging upside down, his ankles tied to a rope looped over the balcony rail. His hands were tied behind his back, several strands of rope tightly circling his chest. He was panting for breath.

"It gets harder and harder to breathe," Nyland said. "But it takes a long time suffocate. Time's what we're short on, so I won't stay around to watch. One last chance to save your ass: who hired you?"

"Didn't say—"

Nyland pressed his fingers against the man's throat. Sarge convulsed and then slipped into unconsciousness. Nyland slapped his face with a sharp backhand blow. The man's eyes opened and he gasped in pain.

"Describe the man who paid you," Nyland said.

"Didn't see him. Smoked glass windows—limousine."

Nyland reached for him again.

"No, wait. License on the limo. Memorized it in case anything went bad."

"Everything has. Give it to me."

The mercenary leader mumbled a number. Jon Cross, who had been watching from the doorway, jotted in a small notebook. "Part of a sequence they issue the Executive Branch," Cross said. "The White House staff, members of the cabinet."

Nyland sliced the rope and the mercenary fell heavily onto the gravel. Nyland loosened the ropes binding the man's chest. "You just take it easy. You made the right choice. Somebody will come along and get you eventually." He dragged the man into the brush.

★　★　★

Doug Smith was waiting inside the strong room, a short-barreled shotgun across his lap. Nyland smiled as he entered. "Last line of defense?"

"This equipment is extremely valuable."

"Spoken like a true technocrat," Cross said. "Are you ready to go?"

"Yes, sir. I have my mobile system here in these two cases, computer, secure modem, and a satellite transponder."

"Get everything up to the barn and keep an eye out for the chopper."

Cross and Nyland walked outside together and stood looking out at the sunrise. Cross said, "None of those bastards are ever going to stand here and admire this view."

"What are you—" An unmarked, gray helicopter crested the hill and settled toward the parking lot, stirring dust and flattening the brush. The roar of its engine drowned out Nyland's question.

Cross held a metal cannister in his hand. "Hoped I'd never have to use this." He pulled the pin and threw the thermite grenade through the open glass doors. There was a flash of white light and a muffled boom from inside the house. Cross and Nyland ran for the helicopter.

Smoke curled from the eaves and drifted toward the helicopter as the two men buckled themselves in beside Doug Smith.

The chopper rose slowly out of the smoke and headed east, skimming the tops of the trees. When it had gone, a pair of red-tailed hawks glided above the hillside, looking down at the bodies of the men lying in the grass. They circled the house, avoiding the column of black smoke, and flew away to the west.

◄11►

The White House

The morning light through of the Oval Office windows cast gold highlights on President Gardner's white hair and deepened the lines on his face, giving him the appearance of an old lion at bay. He moved his shoulders as if shrugging off dead weight. "Billy, this crazy idea of yours—"

CIA Director Billy Vail stood nervously in front of Gardner's desk. "Mr. President, I apologize, but I have to ask. Did anyone on your staff say anything to you about sending a hit squad after Jon Cross last night?"

"What in hell's name are you talking about? Of course not—not to my knowledge."

Vail studied the president's face, gauging the anger in his eyes. The man was telling the truth. "In that case, I withdraw my resignation."

"I wasn't going to accept it anyway. What is going on, Billy?"

"I don't know. I got a call in the car on the way over here."

"From?" Gardner asked.

"The National Security Agency. I asked them to flag a certain email address. They've intercepted a series of messages."

"Whose?"

"The woman who made the C4I software drop, Jennifer Chin."

"Killed three days ago and she's sending email?"

"Exactly. Not just sending. She got a reply—from Beijing."

"Christ, who—"

"NSA doesn't know. The messages from this end were innocuous stuff about buying clothes and the price of groceries. The reply from Beijing contained a lot of numbers, too. Probably a cipher."

"Who's playing the part of the deceased Jennifer Chin?"

"Only one logical explanation. The whole C4I operation, including the drop that got her killed, was set up by Jon Cross."

"Where is Cross?" The president asked.

"His house was torched by an incendiary device last night. He's disappeared."

The president looked at his watch. "I'm scheduled to meet with a group of my advisors in an hour. I think under the circumstances we better get them in here now."

If the three men seated across the conference table from Vail and the president were bothered by the sudden change in meeting time, nothing showed on their faces. But for these men, Secretary of State Brian McHone, Secretary of Defense Charles Blanchard, and the president's Chief-of-Staff Fred Stevens, a poker face was a job requirement.

After Billy Vail told his story of the intercepted email, Charles Blanchard said, "That son of a bitch Cross is communicating with someone in the Chinese Intelligence?" He slumped in his chair. "Can this get any worse?"

"He denied it when I asked him yesterday," Vail said. "But there has always been a suspicion in the Agency that maybe he had a special private source, that some of his brilliant intuitive guesses weren't guesses at all."

"If there's always been a suspicion, why didn't you investigate the son of a bitch?" Blanchard asked.

"I'm not going to answer that," Vail said.

"Can NSA break the code?" President Gardner leaned forward, elbows propped on the arms of his chair.

"Two of the fastest computers in the world are working on it now. They've tried probably twenty million combinations since we sat down. They'll crack it," Vail said. "But all this leads me to a decision I find very distasteful."

"This whole goddam thing is distasteful," Blanchard said.

Vail ignored him. "If Jon Cross had an asset in the Chinese

government that he chose to keep secret from everyone at the Agency, there has to be a reason."

Secretary of Defense Blanchard smiled thinly. "Bastard was a mole," he said.

"We have to consider that. My job is to find out the truth. For Jon Cross's sake if not my own." He sat for a moment, his gaze moving around the table. "I don't want him hunted by a bunch of morons with ammo belts slung across their bellies. He deserves a fair hearing."

The president looked around the room. "Do we know anything about that, a hit squad?"

Fred Stevens, the chief of staff, said, "Sounds more like CIA tactics to me."

Secretary Blanchard sneered. "Better make sure those cowboys of yours are under control before you start accusing other people, Vail."

The president raised his hand for silence. "Billy, I want you to find Jon Cross."

"My first priority," Vail replied.

"Since we have you here, Billy," Blanchard said, "there is another man we're extremely interested in finding. What can you tell me about—" He flipped through a small notebook. "—Daniel Nyland?"

Vail said, "He goes by his middle name, 'Tuck.' He's one of Cross's people. A special operations type, former SEAL. He was fired from CIA for some foul-up in Iraq. Apparently, Cross brought him back against orders. He is probably what happened to the team of bumblers last night.

"It's a funny thing," Vail said. "When I talked to Jon Cross yesterday, he asked what I knew about Song Zhenyo. I asked why he wanted to know, he shrugged it off, called it an 'innocent question.' May I ask your interest in Tuck Nyland?"

Blanchard tucked a notebook in his pocket. "Innocent question," he said.

★ ★ ★

Langley

An hour after he got back to CIA headquarters, DCI Vail called an emergency meeting in the basement conference room. In spite of the usual banter between Robert Jaynes, the deputy director for operations, and Ray DeLong, the deputy director for Science and Technology, their faces were tense, mirroring the director's mood. Coffee was brought in. No one mentioned the missing Jon Cross.

The director ruffled a pile of papers in front of him, cleared his throat. The chit-chat around the table subsided. "Cross disappeared sometime last night."

Jaynes spoke softly, his Boston accent clipping the words. "About the time our computer system crashed?"

"Exactly. Christ, we depend on those damn machines—"

Ray DeLong interrupted: "Doug Smith's handiwork. We're trying to—"

Vail waved the comment away. "Yes, I'm sure it won't happen again, but the bottom line is, someone sent a team to Mr. Cross's house with the intention not of picking him up, but of killing him. They failed, apparently. There were no bodies in the ashes. I want your assurances that it wasn't the Agency."

DeLong shook his head.

Robert Jaynes said, "I'm not a fan of Cross, but—"

Vail said, "If it wasn't us, then that team was ordered by someone in the White House."

"I thought Nixon was dead," Jaynes remarked dryly.

DCI Vail sipped coffee from a monogrammed cup. "Maybe his ghost." Vail thought of his shadowy visitor from the night before. He had toyed with telling his top directors the man's identity, but had decided against it. The man was capable of co-opting Agency people, he knew. It would not be the first time the White House had used CIA officers for their own purposes.

"What would be the White House's interest in going after Jon Cross? A hit team, for chrissake." DeLong said.

Jaynes looked at the Science and Technology boss. "It seems obvious. Cross had something on somebody over there. And he's the kind who never lets go. It has something to do with his China connection, his agent."

"NSA has a partial decryption of Jennifer Chin's email," the Science and Technology director said. "Two words, appearing in both messages: strawberry market. Ring any bells?"

Jayne's eyes widened. "Maymyo. Little town up near the Burma-China border. Famous for its open-air strawberry market. You can smell the berries as you come up the road."

"Cross is meeting someone there? His agent from China, I assume," DeLong said.

Vail said, "I hate to say this, since Jon Cross is my friend, but I'll tell you what I told the president. We have to assume he's planning to defect. Maymyo could be the contact point."

Jaynes shook his head. "Cross isn't stupid. He knows email isn't secure. Maybe he just wants us to think he was headed for Burma."

"He's a goddamn defector, wherever he's headed," Vail said.

"Cross a double agent? I don't believe it." DeLong looked around the table. "Somebody trusted him enough to give him Task Force Seven."

"That someone was the president, at my urging I'll admit," Vail said. "But somebody in the White House is upset enough about Cross to send people out to kill him. It's all connected to the Chinese money man, Song Zhenyo. Who knows what kind of influence his kind of money could buy?"

"Enough to persuade the president to order a hit on an American intelligence officer?" Jaynes asked.

Vail shook his head. "Maybe not the president, but it seems likely that Song is running an agent somewhere in the White House."

"That's pretty frightening, but it's possible," DeLong said.

"Maybe Cross knows something about him that we don't."

"Director Vail," DeLong said, "if I could change the subject for a moment. I've been going over the C4I project, catching up, as it were. How do we know Cross didn't give them an unbugged version—without the virus? The perfect gift to your handlers, if you're a double agent."

"And arranged all the rest to cover it up?" Jaynes asked. "I have to admit it's possible. The only person who knew what was really in that C4I software was Jennifer Chin, who is conveniently dead. And the package is on its way to Beijing. I wonder if Jon Cross is delivering it himself."

DeLong slapped his hand on the table. "Cross engineered this whole thing!"

"I don't know, Ray." Vail sat back in his chair, deflated. "We have to find out—and find Jon Cross."

Jaynes glanced at his notes. "There was another interesting bit of information in the morning cables. Two people attached to Task Force Seven seem to be among the missing. Anne Hammersmith took an emergency medical leave to visit her mother who, unfortunately, died in 1991. Martin Hausler, who is under nonofficial cover in Hong Kong, left for a business meeting no one in his office seems to know about. We can't seem to find anybody who authorized either of these trips. They took off on their own."

"No, they didn't. Where were they really headed?"

"Hausler's the cleverer of the two. He chartered a private plane in Hong Kong, no flight plan. Disappeared. Ms. Hammersmith had fewer options leaving from Beijing. She flew to Jakarta, but her final destination was Yangon—we still call it Rangoon."

"So we're back to Burma." Vail stood up. "Use every asset we have in that country, every officer in that station. I have to know what the hell Jon Cross is trying to do. And let's pray it's not what I think it is. Meeting adjourned."

Beijing

Bao Qing, the woman Jon Cross had called Kingfisher, stood in the middle of her sparsely furnished living room. A bed, a chest of drawers, a large cupboard, a few chests and boxes, and sleeping mat in the corner. Not much to show for nearly thirty years of service to the Party.

She turned slowly, like a dancer, surveying the room. Her tears blurred the image of a small cloth bag near the door, holding all she would take with her. But she was leaving very little behind, she thought. She no longer considered China her country, not after all that had happened to her family. Her parents were dead, a joint suicide. One rainy night they had lain down in front of a freight train. It was the only escape they could see from the purges, the forced relocations—the murder and torture that had characterized Chairman Mao's Great Leap Forward. The police had forced her to look at the pictures.

She had been married briefly, a loveless union to a young PLA sergeant who had gone to serve on the Soviet border and never returned. The marriage produced one child, her daughter, Li, who grew up sullen and depressed, escaped to the United States in the sixties, and married an American. Qing heard very little from her daughter, except when Jennifer was born. Li sent several pictures of the new granddaughter, but the police confiscated them.

It was Jennifer, by then a nineteen-year-old college freshman, who broke the news of her parent's death. A car wreck on something called the James Lick Expressway.

With her only child dead, Bao Qing drew even farther into the world of espionage. She became the best code breaker in the MSS. She, like many in her country, tried not to think about living the lie: unquestioning allegiance to The Party. China was an emotional and a human desert. Always, she wore her public face.

She had survived by holding close the memory of Jon Cross, and their time in Burma. She remembered the look in his eyes as he handed her the blue dragonfly pin. They had kissed, made love later that night on a straw mat—her first time. It had been the most beautiful moment of her life.

It was fitting, she supposed, that he should be the one to deliver the news that her beloved granddaughter, Jenny, had been killed. A tearing sense of loneliness overcame her. In the darkest moments, her thoughts seemed always to return to the courtly American intelligence officer she had met so long ago in Burma.

Did she love Jon Cross? In a strange, bittersweet way she did, she was sure. Why else had his memory stayed with her for so long? It was the mention of the strawberry market in his email message that had stirred her memories. She sat down cross-legged on the floor by the window and closed her eyes.

They had walked together through the Maymyo's west gate and strolled amongst the strawberry vendor's stands. Jon had bought a thatched basket of the luscious berries and they had eaten them as they strolled. It had been almost dusk, a warm, golden glow in the air. Somewhere up on the hill a bagpiper, left over from the Gurkhas, played a strange, plaintive melody. "Danny Boy," Jon had told her. The scene was so unreal as to be overwhelming. To the young lovers, it seemed as if the world was standing still.

At dawn, as they said good-bye, a jungle cock had crowed, answering the village roosters. It was the last time she had seen Jon Cross's face. Bao Qing wept softly as the memory flooded over her. She could almost feel the warmth of his arms around her.

Was this the end? It was the end of everything in her life in Beijing. The short vacation she had asked for, and was grudgingly granted, would be one from which she could never return. She would go the city of Kunming in Yunnan province to the monastery where the monks would hide her, the place she and Cross had code named the "strawberry market."

And she would be bringing gifts—in the form of information. There was almost certainly a coup in the air in China. All of general Xing Wanpo's actions pointed to it. He was buying up high-technology equipment for long-range nuclear warheads, testing sophisticated new software, preparing his army for the twenty first century battlefield. He was violently opposed to the Politburo's decision to open the country to Western ideas. And he had friends in the top councils of government who agreed with him. They had formed a loose coalition, their forces building toward a coup. They had made the mistake of sending electronic communications to each other. Against orders, Bao Qing had decoded them.

She had also obtained a tape of a clandestine meeting in which General Xing had bragged he had control of the president of the United States. An MSS officer named Song Zhenyo had bought his way into the president's inner circle with funds provided by Chinese intelligence, and recruited a high-ranking agent called Bei Feng. This was information of the highest security classification in the Chinese government. To possess it without authorization would bring an immediate sentence of death. These were the gifts, each worth her life, that she would bring to Jon Cross.

She fought the negative thoughts rushing into her mind. General Xing Wanpo would become immediately suspicious when she didn't return from her "vacation," and unleash the might of the People's Liberation Army to find her.

The escape route was to be through Burma. But the country had been under military rule for the past fifteen years. How could Jon Cross hope to get past the army? He would have to cross the mountains of the Shan state, a savage place filled with heroin dealers and warring ethnic tribes. How could he hope to deliver on his promise, made so many years ago—to come and take her away?

She smiled at a sudden thought. She had been picturing him as the dashing officer with the rakish, black moustache who had charmed her forty years ago. She sat down, folded her legs into a full lotus position, and tried to imagine his face as an old man.

Still handsome, probably, with a high forehead and piercing brown eyes. Hair white now, shoulders stooped, perhaps. He could no longer come for her in person. But surely he would send others, young and strong, who would take her to him. They had to, there was no other place for her to go.

She focused her eyes on the blank wall, clearing her mind of all thought, and slipped into a deep, meditative state, oblivious to the noise and clamor of the world outside.

◀12▶

Langley

As the CIA's deputy director for operations, Robert Jaynes presided over an organization of more than six thousand people. It was operations the general public thought of when CIA was mentioned. Spies—cloaks and daggers. In reality, Robert Jaynes was more bureaucrat than secret agent. For all his twenty-seven years in the CIA, he had been a thorough, methodical public servant. A plodder, Jon Cross had called him. The brash ivy-leaguer had ridiculed him, saying, "With a little more personality, he could be an accountant."

Jaynes had taken it as a personal insult when the president decided to give Jon Cross Task Force Seven with its mandate to penetrate the Chinese Ministry of State Security. It was every intelligence officer's dream. Direct authorization from the president of the United States—do what it takes to get the job done. Free of Congressional oversight. That meant big budgets, the best personnel, and the freedom to develop whatever "sources and methods" were needed to crack the uncrackable intelligence targets inside Chinese Intelligence, the opportunity to do an intelligence officer's real job: bring home the secrets.

Technically, the task force should have been under Jaynes's control in the Operations Directorate. On paper, Jaynes outranked Jon Cross, but somehow it seemed the plodder had come out second-best again.

But, plodder or not, Robert Jaynes got the job done. The tortoise to Jon Cross's hare. And he was going to win this time. Because Jon Cross had finally gone too far. And it was given to Robert Jaynes to bring him down. It was his sworn duty, Jaynes thought. Cross was a double agent, a traitor. The evidence was overwhelming. His sudden disappearance was proof of his guilt.

What a wonderful irony that it would be he, Robert Jaynes, who would uncover the MSS agent—do the job Jon Cross had been given. And he now knew the name of the American intelligence officer the Chinese had co-opted. He wrote it on his yellow pad: Jon Cross.

Jaynes tapped a key on his PC and watched a document scroll out of the printer on his credenza. A numbered list with JAYNES TO-DO across the top. His ritual for starting an operation.

The technique was simple: accomplish each task in order, no deviations. At the end, you have a successful operation. Jaynes centered the paper on his desk and smoothed it with his hand. This was going to be extremely satisfying.

His office safe yielded a folder with SEVEN in red letters on the cover, his own private file on Task Force Seven. Inside was the usual collection of cables, memorandums, agent reports, and photographs—the fabric of intelligence work.

First, Burma.

His staff had provided a list of all Agency personnel in the area. The station in Rangoon would be able to provide only five people, but there were a number of officers in Chiang Mai, the CIA station in northern Thailand, that could be flown in, veterans of jungle operations in the Iron Triangle. Hardened men, whose business was tracking people down.

The old consulate in Mandalay had been closed in 1980, but, he noted, it was still owned by the U.S. Government. It was less than an hour's drive from Maymyo and the infamous strawberry market. A perfect base of operations for the team he was assembling. He was jotting notes, smiling faintly as he worked. A cup of coffee stood untouched at his elbow.

There were four photographs in his Seven file. All would be transmitted to his field team within the hour. Jaynes fanned them out on his desk, studying the faces. Tuck Nyland would be the one to watch in the field. Former SEAL, combat veteran trained in all the CIA's black arts. Jaynes remembered the afternoon of Nyland's disciplinary hearing when he had read the DCI's order terminating Tuck Nyland from the CIA, never to be reinstated. The look in the man's eyes still chilled him.

Anne Hammersmith was a question mark. Why was she part of Cross's operation? She was fluent in several Asian languages, including Mandarin. Her specialty was electronic communications. Perhaps Cross needed her for technical support. Jaynes made a note to contact the National Security Agency to request additional electronic surveillance along the China-Burma border.

Marty Hausler, according to his file, was a fifteen-year CIA veteran, having served in Afghanistan, El Salvador, and Bosnia, a decent, if mediocre, record. Why had Cross tapped him for membership in Task Force Seven? Most recently, Hausler had been operating under nonofficial cover in Beijing. Was he connected to the agent Cross had inside Chinese Intelligence? A note on the yellow pad: Hausler full background.

Jaynes laid the last photograph on top of the pile of papers. There were very few pictures of Jon Cross in existence, no formal portraits, only this grainy black-and-white taken perhaps fifteen years ago. Cross's hair was nearly white now, but the sharp, angular face had not, it seemed to Jaynes, aged much. Though Cross was no great friend, it still seemed strange to be sending his picture out to the hunters. Find this man. Bring him in. But it was very likely Cross was planning to defect. He must be stopped at any cost. Killed if necessary.

The next item on his list was Song Zhenyo, a Chinese intelligence officer, likely running an agent in the Executive Branch. And all the while funneling money into the president's election fund. Song had disappeared at the same time as Jon Cross. Were the two connected?

He pulled Cross's photograph toward him. A tall, wide-shouldered man wearing a rumpled khaki shirt, leaning against an Army truck, arms folded across his chest, aristocratic chin held high.

His old nemesis—but was this the face of a traitor? The image stared back at him as if daring him to guess the secrets. The answers lay behind that faintly mocking smile, Jaynes thought, and unless he wanted to be second-best all his life, he had better find Jon Cross.

There was one more item on his list. But all he had written was the letter X. There could be no paper trail to the cabinet-level officer who had called him a few hours ago. Jaynes had been shocked when the man had given his name.

Had the man on the phone been the spy they had talked about that morning in the basement conference room, the man who had dispatched a team of mercenaries to Jon Cross's home in Virginia?

Jaynes forced that thought out of his mind. There was no proof that the man was a spy. It was risky territory, he knew, but the benefits...There might be substantial benefits to cooperation, the man had said. Things were changing rapidly at the CIA, the future of the Agency was in doubt. There could be opportunities in the reorganization for a man willing to be a team player, to share information. A forward-looking man like Robert Jaynes might even find himself directing the Agency.

Jaynes first impulse had been to hang up the phone, but Director of Central Intelligence? Maybe it was time he took a few risks. Jaynes had tried to keep the excitement out of his voice: "What do you have in mind?"

★ ★ ★

Reston, Virginia

Bei Feng, the spy called "north wind," was not used to driving, certainly not in rush hour. But today he could not afford to be seen in his White House limo. He had taken his wife's Volvo station wagon, a lumbering but anonymous beast.

It had taken him nearly an hour to get past the capitol beltway and onto the Dulles toll road. Traffic thinned a little as he entered the rolling, open country near Reston. He glanced at his watch. Almost six o'clock. Song Zhenyo had said he would wait only ten minutes past the appointed hour. Do not be late, he had ordered in that shrill, irritating voice of his. Fuck him, Bei Feng thought. He swerved into the far left lane and urged the heavy wagon up toward eighty, ignoring the honk of an angry commuter. Where was the goddamn exit?

He rolled off the Herndon exit at two minutes past six o'clock. Eight minutes to find the roadside restaurant. Less than a mile from the toll road, he spotted a painted wooden billboard: The Kountry Kitchen. A grease and gravy place, he thought.

He pulled into the gravel parking lot and parked beside a dusty Chevrolet sedan with torn vinyl roof. A dirty-faced child played with a teddy bear in the back seat. In his rearview mirror, Bei Feng saw a pickup turn off the road and stop in a far corner of the lot. The pickup's lights flashed once.

Bei Feng smiled as he climbed into the pickup, glancing at Song's stained coveralls and baseball cap. The cap was tilted at a rakish angle in an attempt to conceal the bandage around his head.

Song said, "The embassy decided it was time for me to lose a little face."

"Very amusing. What the hell is this charade about?"

"I am going back to China, a plane from Dulles tonight. Until then, I stay out of sight." Song looked around as a car pulled up in front of the restaurant. A man and woman got out and walked in without looking at the pickup.

"I can't say I'm sorry to see you go," the agent said.

"Let us say I leave to fight on another front. I'll still be with you, even in China. I still have the film; it can still be given to CNN. You have betrayed your country's honor—and your own. There is probably someone out there right now photographing this meeting. You are a spy, Bei Feng. Even in America, they send such men to prison—for life."

"Listen, Song—"

"And when a man in your position falls, the president goes with him."

"If you came to threaten me again—"

"No threat. Compromise. I have to find the man who did this to me." Song laid his hand gingerly on the dirty bandage around his ear. "I believe he works for the CIA."

"He shot you?" Bei Feng pointed to the bandage.

"He...has some very compromising information about me. I want him very badly." Song clutched the steering wheel in both hands.

"Perhaps we can make a little—compromise. I would like very much to find that man myself."

"You are the government. The CIA works for you. What is the problem?"

"This is not Beijing." Bei Feng forced a smile. "This farmer costume, this sudden recall, you're in a lot of trouble. I believe you need my help."

"You mentioned a compromise?"

Bei Feng looked at Song's face, expressionless and unreadable in the fading light. The man could never be trusted, that was certain. But these were desperate times. The man Song wanted was Tuck Nyland, Bei Feng thought, the one who had singlehandedly wiped out Bei Feng's team of mercenaries. When they found the team leader, Sarge, dazed and covered with ashes near Cross's burnt-out house, he had said, "That's not a man you want after you."

Bei Feng had learned about Nyland only yesterday. It had been a risk to call Langley, he knew, but it was the operations people who had the real information. Sometimes, for a price, they were willing to share it.

The deputy director for operations, Robert Jaynes, had been cautious at first, looking for the *quid pro quo*. DCI Vail was obviously on his way out, Jaynes had said, a new DCI would have to be appointed soon...Bei Feng understood. He would give the appointment careful consideration, make his feelings known to the president. Not quite a promise, but enough to get Jaynes talking.

Jaynes offered a tidbit: would he be interested in the whereabouts of Jon Cross? The DDO knew about Bei Feng's attempt to assassinate Cross the night before at his Virginia home. He knew the man who had thwarted the attack, Tuck Nyland. The CIA was looking for both those men now, Jaynes said. He was in charge of the manhunt. The CIA man saved the best for last: Jon Cross was headed for Burma, Nyland with him. It was not clear whether Cross was defecting or trying to bring someone out of China. Keep me informed, I'll work on the director business, Bei Feng had said.

The old pickup's springs squeaked as Song shifted his weight nervously. "I'm waiting," he said.

Bei Feng let his breath out slowly, his decision made. "The man you want is Tuck Nyland. He is a very dangerous man, as you know.

He is a former Navy SEAL, and he works for a man named Jon Cross. We want both of these people as much as you do. When you get back to Beijing, tell your boss that these two people, and possibly two others, a man and a woman, are headed for Burma."

"For what reason?"

"Jon Cross may be defecting."

"Taking three people with him?"

"I am probably a fool to tell you, but possibly one of your people is going to defect. These three may be an extraction team. We cannot let them succeed—for both our sakes."

"You were going to withhold this information from me? That is dangerous and stupid."

"Are we in agreement?" Bei Feng persisted.

Song relaxed his grip on the steering wheel. "There is a term, 'unholy alliance.'"

"God help us," Bei Feng said softly.

The Kountry Kitchen had turned on a red neon sign in the window. Its light washed over the Volvo as it wheeled around in the parking lot and disappeared down the highway. Song leaned his head back on the seat. It had gone well. The resident would want an exact account of the meeting. Mentally, Song replayed his conversation with Bei Feng, fixing the details in his mind.

Why was the defector, Jon Cross, headed for Burma? It was difficult to imagine a more difficult route into China. Maybe Cross had a sense of history, Song thought. The old silk road connecting China and Burma was a centuries-old route for smugglers, traders, and spies.

He brushed dust off his coveralls and ground the pickup's starter. The engine caught, backfired, and died. He turned the key again: a click, and then silence. It was almost dark now, and the red light from the diner's sign washed over the pickup's rusty hood. He would have to call the embassy for a ride. He imagined the smirking face of the resident.

Song drew in a slow, ragged breath. To hell with the MSS. He would take his information directly to Xing Wanpo. The man was a demanding taskmaster, but he rewarded those who served him well. With the general's blessing, Song Zhenyo would soon be rid of broken-down pickups and back in a limousine where he so rightfully belonged.

Washington, D.C.

The C-130 was loaded and the cargo handlers had gone back inside. The plane sat alone behind a freight terminal at Reagan International Airport, engines rumbling softly, the cargo doors still open. The pilot and copilot kept themselves busy with the preflight checklist as an unmarked van pulled up beside the plane. Dark shapes climbed out and moved toward the cargo bay.

The hatch closed and the van pulled away. Clearance came quickly from the tower and the C-130 taxied onto the runway, engines revving in a crescendo of noise.

★ ★ ★

Tuck Nyland felt the vibration against his back as he strapped himself into the bulkhead seat. Beside him, Doug Smith was fumbling with the shoulder harness. "You don't get air sick, do you?" Nyland asked.

"Not as long as he can look at a computer screen," Jon Cross said. "Takes his mind off all that ocean below."

Smith smiled weakly. "You had to bring that up."

Cross laid a hand on Smith's shoulder, his look paternal. "You didn't have to go with us," he said. "But I'm glad you did."

Smith patted the aluminum case on his lap. "Where would you be without this?" Inside was a powerful laptop computer, transponder, and satellite encryption gear, all tucked neatly into foam dividers.

Cross nodded. "I would like to do a little more electronic eavesdropping on Jaynes, but we can't risk it. As it stands, there's no way he can connect us to this plane. Just a little air freight company that happens to be run by a very old friend, a pilot I worked with in Burma."

Like many officers in the clandestine services, Jon Cross had an escape package with false papers and two passports under different names, and the leather pouch under his seat was packed with hundred dollar bills. Being on the run cost money. His Task Force Seven accounts would be closed soon enough if Robert Jaynes had anything to say about it. Langley would believe the worst. And who could blame them? By now they probably knew that Cross had been in contact with someone in Beijing. And, as proof of his guilt, he had run.

They would use every resource to find him. He would have done the same. But there were three hounds on his trail, Cross thought. The Agency, in the person of Robert Jaynes, would be acting on the assumption that he had sold them out and was defecting with secrets gained from his access to the highest levels of intelligence. Song Zhenyo, aware now that Cross knew of his connection to Chinese Intelligence, would be under extreme pressure from the Ministry of State Security to silence him. And Tuck Nyland could place Song at the scene of Jennifer Chin's cold-blooded murder.

The American agent, Bei Feng, had already tried to kill him the night before, Cross thought—before Cross could unmask him, reveal whatever dirty secrets the Chinese had used to turn him to make him a traitor. A pack of three hounds. Maybe they would trip over each other.

After the plane leveled off, Cross leaned back against the web straps and closed his eyes. There had been very little time for sleep in the last twenty-four hours. They had checked into a motel in the Washington suburbs and spent the day on Doug Smith's portable communications gear monitoring the CIA's operation against them. The Agency apparently had no clue to their whereabouts. Then, as Nyland and Doug had dozed on the sagging motel bed, Cross made calls to a series of people on the other side of the world—old friends who owed him favors. Men who knew how to smuggle people across borders.

The plane bumped through a pocket of rough air and Cross opened his eyes to find Nyland watching him. In the shadows of the cargo hold, the man's eyes looked haunted. "I'm sorry to drag you into this, Tuck," Cross said.

"I know what the Kingfisher means to you."

"She started this whole thing, really. Even before she told me about the Chinese agent in the Executive branch, I had been thinking about—I don't know—my approaching mortality. The idea of bugging the C4I software kind of grew out of that. Use the technology to replace the aging human machinery."

"Still need people on the ground," Nyland said.

"Always will, but it won't be me. I hoped bringing you back, getting your career going again, would change things for you. Changed you into a fugitive."

"I've been on the run for a long time. It wasn't your doing."

On the other side of the crew compartment, Doug Smith was reading a computer magazine. Nyland leaned back in his seat, eyes closed. Cross smiled. Nyland had, with that magical ability of soldiers everywhere, gone to sleep.

But Nyland had not gone to sleep. He sat listening to the sound of the engines, remembering the dream. The last two nights it had come with maddening intensity: he was running across a wide, barren plain. His legs would scarcely move and he felt himself being pulled down. Faces before him, crying out to him: his little sister, Lynn, the sand and blood still clinging to her face, Jennifer Chin, eyes pleading, face a ghostly green in the night scope, and the little girl in the spider hole outside Baghdad, dress caked with blood. In the dream, he held out his hands out to them, but they seemed always out of reach. And in the distance, another figure crying out to him, surrounded by dark shapes, men with fists raised. In the strange logic of the dream, he was suddenly beside her, the both of them circled by the dark figures—always moving closer, choking off his air, killing him. He had woken each time struggling for breath, sweat running down his chest.

The drone of the C-130's engines was hypnotic. The corded muscles in Nyland's neck stood out as he forced his head back against the seat. Fighting sleep—fighting the dream.

◄13►

Doug Smith opened his eyes, alerted by the sudden change in the sound of the C-130's engines. He glanced at his watch. They had been in the air barely three hours. "What's going on?" he asked.

Nyland was looking out the window. "We have an escort."

"One over here, too," Cross said. "F-16."

The fighter kept pace just off of the C-130's wing, silhouetted against a field of stars. The cargo plane switched on its landing lights, illuminating the blue and white Air Force insignia on the fighter's fuselage. "I think your old friend sold us out."

"It wasn't my old friend," Cross said, "it was Bei Feng."

"Your pilot friend have any government contracts?" Nyland asked.

"A few. State Department, Defense," Cross said. He was staring out the window at the fighter plane. "Bei Feng...I think I know who he is. I didn't think he was clever enough to find us—stop us."

"He hasn't stopped us yet," Nyland said.

"No, he hasn't. I told my friend there would be two people on board. Our pilots didn't see how many got on, so there's still a chance."

"Bei Feng—who is he?"

Cross shook his head. "Need-to-know." He handed Nyland the leather money pouch. "Operating capital," he said. "Take the communication gear. Anne knows how to use it. Doug has programmed a couple of nasty little tricks into it. She'll understand."

"What happens to you and Doug?"

"They'll take us back to Washington, try to sweat something out of us."

"I can't let that happen," Nyland said.

"You can't fight the whole Air Force. The only hope we have—I have—is Bao Qing. She knows Song Zhenyo's connection to the White House, she knows about the coup. And she is living proof I haven't committed treason. You have to get her out, Tuck."

"I can't just let them drag you off the plane."

"When this plane lands, all I want them to find is Doug and me."

"You're sacrificing yourself."

"You'd do the same."

Nyland stared at Cross for a long moment. "I don't like it," he said. He got up and walked along the cavernous cargo bay, studying the bulkheads and peering at the pallets of cargo strapped to the metal decking. "There might be a way," he said.

The C130's tires screeched on the pavement as the big plane touched down and taxied to a stop at the dark end of the runway. The F-16s circled once, climbed into the night sky, and disappeared. The Air Force Security Police stood, weapons ready, as the cargo doors opened.

Rangoon, Burma

Anne Hammersmith was getting nervous. For the second night in a row, she had parked on this deserted road waiting for her contact. If he didn't show in the next few minutes, she would be out of the covert action business. Just as well, for then she could get out of this god-awful, depressing country. In the past hour, clouds had moved in from the ocean, obscuring the moon. The lights of the city shone faintly on the tall grass along the river. She watched a container ship moving up the river toward the Rangoon docks. It seemed to be gliding on a sea of grass. The smell of rotting vegetation was heavy in the air. She propped her elbow on the window sill and immediately felt moisture on her skin. A small animal of some kind rustled in the grass. She jerked her arm inside.

Where was her contact? What if he had been captured, betrayed her? Visions of a dank, dripping interrogation cell flashed into her mind. Strapped naked on a table—

"Eclipse."

Her code name!

"Oh, God!" The words came out of her mouth before she could stop them. She twisted in the seat trying to locate the voice. The man stood beside the rear fender of her car, the blind spot where policemen stood when they inspected a suspicious vehicle. She started to open her door, but felt the pressure of his hand against it. "Stay in the car." The man's voice sounded vaguely familiar.

He tossed a duffle bag in the back seat and slid in beside her. "My God, you scared me," Anne whispered. "I'm sorry—I realize the dome light—how did you—"

Then she saw his eyes.

Pale blue. She caught her breath. A lot of men had blue eyes, but together with the voice, the quick, insolent movements—it was the man from Camp Peary. "You don't remember me, do you?" she said.

He studied her face. "Should I?"

"It's nothing, but I think we met a few years ago at Camp Peary."

He looked at her without speaking. Was there a hint of a smile on his face?

Anne said, "You remember, I interrupted your training exercise."

"Officially, I wasn't there. You were running. You ran well, you just couldn't learn to keep out of restricted areas."

"We must have spent all of twenty seconds—" She shook her head and turned away to cover her embarrassment. How could she tell him his eyes had haunted her for almost ten years and that she had put off her boyfriend because he didn't measure up to a ghost, a ghost who now sat beside her?

"How did you get here?" she asked. God, what an inane question.

"Caught a ride up the river," he said.

His short, black hair was still wet. He wore a tight-fitting black sweater and cargo pants with a military style web belt, a pair of mud-caked running shoes. A deep, penetrating gaze, the pale eyes giving away nothing. A row of white scars, down each cheek, the kind fingernails make. A long-ago night of passion? Maybe she would ask him about the scars—later.

"I'm staying at the Strand."

"Room 214," Nyland said.

"That's right." She realized she had been holding her breath, and willed herself to relax. "So that's the correct response, and you know my code name, so I guess you're who you're supposed to be. Mr. Cross wanted me to contact him as soon as you got here. I have a satellite transponder in the trunk, do you—"

"He's not going to answer."

"What did you say?"

"Two nights ago, we flew out of Washington on a C-130. Two Air Force fighter planes forced us to land at Travis. They took him off the plane in handcuffs."

"They?'"

"Security Police from the base, acting under orders from the White House."

"Jesus Christ. The operation is off?"

"No." Nyland was looking out the window at the darkened field of grass around the car. "I'll fill you in. Let's go."

"By the way, do you have a name?"

"Tuck Nyland."

"I've always wondered." She wheeled the car onto the road toward Rangoon.

Nyland studied the woman as she drove. She handled the old car expertly, moving smoothly through the turns. Her bare arms, glowing with a faint sheen of sweat, rippled with muscle as she swung the wheel. She wore a sleeveless white blouse, and the thin fabric tightened across her breasts as she turned to glance out the rear window. So this was Jon Cross's high-tech communications wizard. He was surprised to find that he remembered their brief meeting at Camp Peary.

★ ★ ★

He had watched her approach along the trail through the woods. She had been wearing red jogging shorts and some kind of sport bra. She smiled at the sensual pleasure of the exercise, her face glistened with sweat.

He had been annoyed and amused at the same time. The group of agents he was training were all deep-cover, their faces never seen by the regular trainees at Camp Peary. In their assignments overseas, their very lives depended on anonymity. And a new recruit runs right into the middle of it. "I'm CIA," she had said. Right.

He put her out of his mind. There were more pressing problems. Cross had planned to run the operation from a fishing boat off of the Andaman Islands, but it was up to Nyland now. And he was responsible for three people—two of them women. The operation ahead seemed suddenly impossible. He closed his eyes and thought again of the SEAL's motto. The only easy day was yesterday.

And yesterday had been far from easy. He had managed to slip inside one of the packing crates before the Security Police came on board the cargo plane. There had been a tense hour of waiting after they took Cross and Doug Smith off in handcuffs. Nyland lay cramped in the darkness, back pressed against the rough wood of the crate, listening to the Travis SPs discussing what to do.

They had been ordered to remove two passengers and detain them for questioning. They had two men in custody. This was a civilian aircraft with a civilian pilot, a crusty old ex-Marine whose cargo manifest and flight documentation were in order. And he was hollering about their Gestapo tactics. There would be hell to pay if the guy decided to sue. They had sent the angry pilot on his way without bothering to search the plane.

During the long flight over the Pacific, Nyland had talked with the pilot, passing the time swapping Jon Cross stories. The man was a legend—and his current passenger, the pilot explained, was his heir apparent. It would be an honor to deliver him to the contact point. And if the Air Force butted in again, he would ram the bastards.

As the plane droned on across the ocean, Nyland had gone over and over the extraction plan in his head: the team would rendevous in Rangoon, travel north to Maymyo where they would arrange passage to China over the mountains to the city of Kunming.

The overland route from Maymyo to Kunming was twelve hundred miles of winding mountain roads with passes over nine thousand feet. It was a heavily used freight route and an infamous conduit for heroin. Contact with the Kingfisher would be in a small monastery outside of Kunming. Nyland would present the dragonfly pin as his bonafides. A third member of the team, who Cross would not name, would meet them in China.

The C-130 had landed at Port Blair airport in the Andaman Islands and was met by a dilapidated Chevy van for the two mile run to the beach. Without speaking, the driver, a heavyset man in a flowered shirt, carried the two bags down to a skiff waiting in the surf.

The skiff had taken Nyland out to a nondescript fishing trawler in the Andaman Sea. Some of the money from Cross's leather pouch bought the captain's assurances that the boat would be waiting off the Burmese coast when Nyland returned. A bit more had secured a small boat and scuba gear. A Japanese containership had unknowingly carried a passenger the last twenty-five miles up the Rangoon River.

Tuck and Anne were nearing the heart of the city now, theirs the only car moving along Strand Road. Nyland pointed at a passing billboard: "'Only when there is discipline will there be progress.' You believe that?"

Anne chuckled. "Here, it's heavy on discipline, light on progress."

"My father," Nyland said.

"My mother." Anne smiled at him; he looked away.

"This is the Strand," she said. The street in front of the hotel was deserted. A vintage Rolls Royce was parked near the entrance, behind it a dented '57 Chevy.

The Strand Hotel was a venerable Burmese landmark, and some of its faded glory from the days of British Empire had been restored. The columns had been replaced, a fresh coat of white paint applied to the facade. A Burmese doorman in a red uniform leaned, half dozing, against a huge potted palm near the entrance. Through the glass doors, the opulent lobby looked deserted. There was not much nightlife in this part of the city. Burma's repressive military government, run by the State Peace and Development Council, did not encourage such goings-on.

"Drive around the block, look things over?"

"Left, up there."

Anne circled the block and parked by a side door. Nyland led the way across the lobby to the elevators. A houseboy stood at the foot of the stairs, holding a stack of towels. As the two approached, he turned away and shuffled up the stairs.

Room 214 was furnished with worn-looking antiques—a marble-topped vanity, wicker chairs, and a four-poster bed. The wallpaper was a floral design in yellowing silk. French doors looked out on the street in front of the hotel. Nyland pushed back the lace curtains and stepped out onto a small balcony. The night air felt cool against his cheeks. The old Rolls and the Chevy still sat beside the curb.

"What's going to happen to Mr. Cross?" Anne stepped onto the balcony beside him.

"They'll try to force him to tell what he knows."

"Will he tell them—about us?"

Nyland's face was grim. "He would die before he did that."

"Who's in charge of this operation?"

"I am."

She rested a hip on the wrought iron rail. "You better start at the beginning, boss."

They talked for nearly an hour. He told her about the C4I software drop, Jenny's death, and sketched in the details of the operation. "We've got three days to get into China and back out."

"Who are we bringing out?"

"When the time's right, I'll put you in the picture."

She kept her eyes on his face, mesmerized by his voice. "You don't trust me?"

"This isn't high school. Have you ever been interrogated?"

She shook her head. "In training."

"If we're captured, you'll beg them to let you talk. The less you know..."

"What are our chances?" Anne asked.

"Not very good, but for Jon's sake, we have to try."

"He means a lot to you."

"He's never doubted me once."

"You doubted yourself?"

"You a shrink?"

She laid her hand on his arm. "It's just that we're in this together. We ought to get to know each other."

"That could be dangerous," Nyland said. Their eyes held for a long moment. Anne smiled. "Getting chilly out here."

Nyland held the French doors open and they stepped inside. "Since we're getting to know each other, what do you know about the other member of our little group?"

Anne said, "Our other man is setting up the China side. He has some very useful contacts there, I believe."

"Do you know this guy? Is he any good?" Nyland lifted the curtain and peered out the window.

"I'd say he's very good. He was under nonofficial cover in Beijing, has developed a couple of pretty valuable assets there. Actually, he and I are—friends."

"He have a name?"

"Marty Hausler."

"How good a friend is he?"

"What's that got to do with—"

"Because it gets in the way, you lose your objectivity."

"He wants me to marry him," Anne said.

"But you love your work."

"Now who's the shrink?"

Nyland said softly, "Love and work are a poor mix. You can't do either very well."

"Sounds like the voice of experience," Anne said.

Nyland kept his eyes on the street below. A car drove slowly past the hotel. A dog barked somewhere in the darkness. The silence in the room was heavy. In a few moments, the car reappeared. It stopped across the street and two men got out. Suits. Not Burmese.

Nyland stepped away from the window. "Car just stopped. Two men. Little late to be checking in."

She pointed toward the door. The knob was slowly turning.

The opposition had arrived. The two men on the street were backup—it was by the book. Nyland stepped behind the door. Anne stepped into the bathroom and closed the door. The toilet flushed.

The two men used the sound to cover their entrance. They stepped in quickly, pistols in their hands. The bathroom door opened. Anne, wearing only skimpy black panties, crossed her arms protectively over her breasts. "Get the hell out of here!"

The two men stared at her. "We need to do this very quietly," one of them said. His accent was Middle Eastern, Indian maybe, Nyland thought.

Nyland stepped up behind the two men. Anne was directly in their line of fire. He could take one, he realized, but not both. "I'm the one you want," he said.

The two men stepped apart, one covering Nyland. "Turn around, hands behind your head."

Nyland felt the cool metal of a pistol barrel against his neck. "No problem," he said.

"Over there, beside your boyfriend." A second man, standing behind Anne but farther back out of reach, by the sound of his voice. This one was American.

Anne's knees buckled and she fell backward. Instinctively, the man reached for her. She let herself go limp against him. Nyland felt the man behind him shift his stance. The pistol was no longer pressing against his neck. Tuck kicked back savagely. A grunt of pain, the sound of a gun hitting the floor.

Anne, suddenly revived, snaked her arm around the man's neck and shifted her weight forward. The man rose almost magically over her head and slammed onto the floor. As he struggled to rise, she kicked him in the face. He fell back silently, and a pool of blood formed around his head, staining the flowered blue carpet.

"Tuck, watch it!"

Nyland spun on his heel. The man he had kicked was raising his pistol. Nyland slapped it from his hand and punched him in the throat. The man fell beside his partner and lay still.

"Nice move," Anne said.

Nyland picked up the fallen man's gun, a stainless steel Ruger automatic, and shoved it into his waistband. "Nice diversion."

Five minutes later, the backup team crept into the room, stepping over their partner's bodies. Room 214 was empty, a night breeze lifted the curtain on the open window. They slid their pistols back into their holsters. "We are in the shit," one of them said.

◄14►

Maymyo, Burma

Nyland had chosen a veranda table at the Club Maymyo with a good view of the front door. He scanned each new arrival looking for a familiar face, a friend—or an enemy—who might remember. No one he recognized, but it had been ten years. He drained his club soda and motioned to the waiter for a refill. Would the gentleman be having dinner? Nyland shook his head. Tonight it was business.

Club Maymyo was a private club built originally for British officers during the Raj, and had changed very little over the years. The walls were paneled in teak, brass lanterns hung from the exposed beams on the ceiling, Burmese waiters moved among the tables, gold buttons gleaming on their starched white coats.

It had been an all-day bus trip from Rangoon, nearly nightfall before Tuck and Anne arrived in the small up-county town of Maymyo. The bus had been packed with Burmese nationals standing in the aisles with baskets and packages in their arms, talking incessantly. Tuck and Anne sat together on hard wooden benches at the rear of the bus. Their attackers of the night before were nowhere to be seen.

Tuck had bought a bottle of lemon soda at the first stop and shared it with Anne as the bus rolled north toward Mandalay. After a while, Anne had dozed, her head on Nyland's shoulder.

It had been years since Nyland had worked in Burma, but the sights and smells of the countryside had swept over him in a familiar wave. The gold spires of pagodas rose above the trees, ethereal and detached as he remembered. Monks in their maroon robes stood beside the road, the same bemused smiles on their faces. As if they were keeping a secret. The humid air carried a familiar scent, a mixture of decaying vegetation, diesel smoke, and incense.

Later, at Anne's insistence, he had shared some of his stories about the Burma days. He found it hard to talk about. He had been a young man then, building a career. But she encouraged him, listening attentively as she sipped her lemon soda. A faint smile played on her lips. Did she have a secret, too?

Ten years ago, the CIA had sent him, along with a small group of agents, to bring back information on the heroin trafficking along the Thai border. There were two ways to do it. You could search the jungled countryside with helicopters and study the infrared satellite images, or you could pay Thaung Lwin.

Thaung had controlled most of the heroin shipments out of Burma, nearly 60 percent of the world's supply, according to the analysts at Langley. Thaung was barely thirty when Nyland had first met him in a camp near the Thai border. He wore the trappings of his wealth proudly, the diamond rings and gold chains a bizarre compliment to his traditional *longyis*. Thaung Lwin had made a fortune in the drug trade, but he always wanted more. And he had information the CIA wanted. Nyland's orders from Langley had been clear: drug lord or not, pay him.

And so, a strange alliance had been formed. The CIA man and the drug merchant. It was a marriage of convenience, the kind of relationship that led much of the American media to charge that the CIA was in bed with heroin kingpins. The truth was, in this part of the world, money was exchanged for favors, for information. It was the drug merchants who had the information. It was not conspiracy, it was just business.

And so Nyland had come back to the Club Maymyo to talk business.

Anne had stayed with their hired car, parked a block away on a side street. Admittance to the club was a select affair. If your face was not known to the imposing guard at the steel shuttered gate, you were politely asked to leave. Ten years ago, Club Maymyo had been a popular watering hole for Agency types. Nyland had been a regular. The guard remembered.

Tuck sipped his club soda and stared out at the lush gardens surrounding the club. The other customers, most dressed formally in spite of the heat, all intent on their private conversations, sipped their gin and tonics and paid no attention to the lone man. It was not polite to take notice of strangers.

Still, Thaung Lwin's arrival caused a mild stir. He strolled regally through the front door, flanked by two large scowling men in starched khakis. Thaung wore his trademark white *longyis*. On his chest he had pinned four silver stars. General Thaung. His neck was festooned with a decidedly nontraditional collection of gold chains. Tuck was reminded of the actor Mister T, in the long-defunct *A-Team* television series.

Nyland stood up as the man approached his table. The two bowed ceremoniously. The locals, Nyland remembered, called Thaung by an unpronounceable Burmese nickname referring to the lethal white powder he dispensed to most of the civilized world. "The White Man," Tuck said.

Thaung smiled as he sat down and carefully arranged the folds of his *longyis*. "The reference is inaccurate. As you can see, I am a brown man." His eyes lit with a mischievous smile. "My old friend—what name are you using—Smith, Jones, it doesn't matter."

The two men ordered drinks, Thaung accepting only tea. Tuck inquired about Thaung's health, his mistresses, and the state of the government. It would never do to mention business so early in the evening.

"The State Peace and Development Council is made up mostly of old acquaintances of mine," Thaung said. "Doing the same business in a different stand, I believe the American saying goes."

"Your English is excellent," Tuck said. Let The White Man give the signal when it was time to get down to business.

The wait was not long: "Your station in Mandalay has been closed for some time now. How is it you come back?"

"I need a favor—for which I am willing to pay, of course."

"Of course. The question is, who will pay the most?"

Tuck lowered his glass, resting it on the white linen table cloth. "I don't understand."

"It seems that all of a sudden the hills are swarming with Americans wanting to buy information. A seller's market."

"These other Americans, who were they?"

"Smith, Jones, perhaps. They didn't give me their names, but they represent a certain American intelligence agency. I do not, however, think they were friends of yours."

"Why is that?"

"They offered me a large sum of money if I would tell them about two Americans looking for passage to China. Perhaps you know who they were?"

"What did you tell them?" Nyland sipped his club soda.

"That I would 'get back to them.' They seemed amused at that. But they were not amusing people. I would be very careful if I were you. Careful even of what you tell me." Thaung sipped his tea and motioned to his two bodyguards. "We have a history of business transactions, but I do not believe anyone would call us friends, agreed?"

It was a fair warning to a worthy adversary, a courtesy in remembrance of the early days—be careful. Thaung would sell him out in a heartbeat, Nyland thought, to a higher bidder.

"Your point?"

"If you are looking for a passage through the high country, it can be arranged, of course, but any trouble would be bad for business. My government friends down in Rangoon are always looking for ways to cause trouble for my—enterprises. I can't have them snooping around. And they would certainly do that if there was any unpleasantness with the Americans. They are not exactly welcome here." Thaung glanced around at the other customers, took a sip of his tea. "And my government employs many spies to keep an eye on the *hnakaung shay*." The words meant, "long-noses," Nyland knew. Burmese slang for Westerners.

"I appreciate your warning. But I still need your help," Tuck said.

"The strawberry market, the west end of town. You remember it? Meet me in two hours."

Tuck nodded.

"I advise you to conduct your business quickly and be gone. There are very bad people out in those mountains. I would hate to see harm come to any of my—assets." Thaung rose and walked out the door, bodyguards beside him.

★　★　★

Beijing

Song Zhenyo stood outside General Xing Wanpo's office struggling to keep his eyes open. He had managed only a few hours of sleep on the flight from Washington, D.C., and his wounded ear still throbbed beneath the bandage.

The general's door opened and a group of PLA officers filed out, faces grim. Song heard General Xing's voice from inside the office, a guttural shout: "Find the woman now—move!" The officers, two colonels and a major, broke into a shuffling trot, pathetic in their eagerness to appease the general. Song watched them pass. It would have been easy to laugh, but now it was his turn.

"The diplomat." General Xing spat out the word.

Song nodded his head slightly. Even the small movement sent a wave of pain through his head. He winced.

"Western clothes, Western shoes, even your eyeglasses reflect the decadent culture. You have been too long in America, Song Zhenyo." Xing stood up and walked around his desk. Without warning, his hand slammed against the side of Song's head. Song screamed in pain, his eyes rolling back in his head. His knees buckled and he fell to the carpet.

"Stand up," Xing said.

"Why do you strike me?" Song stumbled to his feet and wiped tears from his eyes.

"You are not in your comfortable Washington office any longer. You are at war. And the enemy is easily seen—the pathetic Americans you have been cuddling up to. What is their purpose? It is to undermine the will of China, to convert it to the obscenity of buying and selling. They wish to poison our culture. It will not happen as long as I am alive.

"Another enemy, not so easily seen, lives among us." Xing seemed about to say something else, but returned to his desk and sat down. "The Intelligence Ministry advises me that you have obtained certain leverage over a member of the American government. The agent you call Bei Feng."

Song nodded cautiously.

"And it is strong, this hold you have on him?"

"He was captured during the Vietnam war, interrogated by the NVA with the help of our intelligence officers. Those officers filmed the interrogation. He betrayed his own unit, many American soldiers died. He has tried to pass himself off as a hero. But he was a traitor. His career, his life, his honor, will be destroyed if the film is ever made public."

Xing chuckled. "Excellent. This agent of yours could be very important to me—to our country, depending on what you make of it." Xing stood up slowly. "I am told you have something for me?" The general's eyes were hidden in shadow. The lighting was a calculated effect; visitors faced the large south-facing window behind him, staring, as Song did now, directly into the sun.

"Yes, I—"

"Before you say anything more, you must understand that I have many enemies in this country. If you align yourself with me, they become your enemies as well. They are ruthless and would kill you with very little provocation." Xing laid both hands flat on the desk. "As would I."

Song opened a package bound with white tape and laid four small, rectangular boxes on the general's desk.

Xing picked them up carefully and turned them around in his hands. "The spoils of American technology. Now, we move forward. It is best that you have no further contact with the Intelligence Ministry; they are riddled with traitors and fools. Once you join me, there is no going back, do you understand?"

"What would be my choice?"

"I will ignore your insolence for the moment."

Song shifted his feet nervously. "There is something else I must tell you. Bei Feng informed me the CIA is looking for four people who they believe are going to attempt a border crossing from Burma into Yunnan Province."

Xing sat forward in his chair. "Have you told the MSS?"

Song shook his head.

"Coming to China for what purpose?"

"My source believes that either a senior CIA officer is planning to defect to China, or one of our people is trying to get out."

"He did not say which?"

Song shrugged his shoulders. "Only that they will try to enter China through Burma."

"When?" Xing asked.

"They may be here already. We have to stop them."

Xing smiled. "We? You have a personal interest in this?"

"One of them attacked me, did this to me." Song gestured toward the bandaged ear. "My career, my reputation have vanished. I was sent to meet Bei Feng dressed as a peasant, driving a pickup."

"I heard. Who is this man who shamed you?"

"His name is Nyland, he's CIA. He will probably be leading the operation into China. The senior officer I mentioned is Jon Cross. He is almost ready for retirement. He will not be fighting in the field."

"I know of Cross," Xing said. "And you are probably right, the field is not the senior commander's place. But he must field worthy adversaries."

The general smiled a wintry smile. "So, who will I send? You have hatred inside you. That is useful on occasion. Therefore, I will make you a proposition. Your career is ruined, at least in the eyes of the MSS. However, if you maintain contact with your American agent, and he provides me information I can use, there will be a place of honor for you in—our new government. And, I will give you a chance to put your hands on this CIA man, Nyland." Xing stood up. "Out of curiosity, did he cut you with a knife, shoot you?"

Song's cheeks reddened. "He—he tore it off."

"Your ear?"

"With his bare hands," Song said.

Xing chuckled. "This is a man we *both* want very much to meet." The spark of humor died abruptly, and a cold light came into Xing's eyes. "And we will meet him very soon, I think." General Xing stepped around his desk. Song cringed, but Xing merely bowed and extended his hand. "There is a secure telephone in the next office. You will call Bei Feng immediately."

Song felt the tension drain from him. The interview was over. Now everything depended on an American on the other side of the world.

★ ★ ★

Maymyo

The street behind Nyland was deserted. He wasn't being followed, he was certain. After his meeting with The White Man, Nyland had ducked into a small park near the Club Maymyo and hidden in the thick brush. No one had entered the park behind him. After several minutes, he had slipped out through a hedge and run down an alley to the next block. Only then did he turn toward his real destination.

His mind worked furiously as he hurried to meet Anne. The CIA was all over his operation. They had been waiting in Rangoon, and they had already gotten to The White Man in Maymyo. Had they tortured the information out of Jon Cross, or was there an inside source? He replayed in his mind the attack in Rangoon, remembering how Anne had led him off the balcony just before the backup team arrived. Yet she had fought well, kicking her attacker in the face, shouting a warning to Nyland.

What did he really know about Anne Hammersmith? She was handpicked by Cross, but people had switched loyalties before. And Hausler, their backup man in China, was her boyfriend. With Jon Cross a prisoner back in Washington, the CIA a step ahead of him at every turn, survival demanded he trust no one, least of all the corrupt heroin trafficer, Thaung.

He had arranged to meet Anne on a narrow side street three blocks from Club Maymyo. Nyland was halfway down the block when an aging, white Datsun rolled up beside him, bluish-gray exhaust drifting from the tailpipe. Anne called to him from the back seat, "Let's go, we've got company." As Nyland climbed in, she spoke to the driver in Burmese

The driver nodded enthusiastically. "Like movie!" He slammed the accelerator to the floor. A dark-colored sedan rounded the corner behind them. Their driver glanced in his mirror and spoke rapidly in Burmese.

Anne grabbed Nyland's arm. "He says that car back there has been driving around town all day, but mostly down by the strawberry market. Americans, he says, bad men."

"Does he have any ideas about losing them?" Marty asked.

"As a matter of fact, he does." As she spoke, the Datsun gathered speed, dodging its way around cyclos and pedestrians. Suddenly, the driver threw the wheel to the left, and the car darted into an impossibly narrow alley, scraping a fender on the brick wall on the way. An old woman on a bicycle rode slowly down the middle of the alley. The driver honked the horn and the woman scrambled into a doorway. As the Datsun crept by her, Tuck glanced over his shoulder. The sedan was stopped at the entrance to the alley, unable to negotiate the narrow space. Its high beams flashed and he could see a man climb over the hood and run toward them, silhouetted in the lights.

The Datsun surged forward, tires spinning on the cobblestones. Then they were out of the alley and racing along a side street. The driver was chattering happily in Burmese. "The locals call it 'mad husband alley,'" Anne translated.

"That was nobody's husband back there," Tuck said.

"I think we met some of their friends last night at the Strand Hotel."

"You're right. Tell him to let us out anywhere along here."

Anne handed the driver a sheaf of Burmese currency and spoke to him briefly. As the cab drove away, Tuck looked at her questioningly. "Told him to pick us up in two hours at the Candacraig," she said. "A guest house, famous local landmark."

"You set that poor cabbie up," Nyland said. "Our friends back in the alley are gonna find him, and beat that little tidbit out of him."

"That ought to buy us some time."

"You've become a hard case."

"Look at the company I've been keeping."

Nyland said, "The Agency has already gotten to The White Man, offered him money."

"Who knew we were going to contact him?"

"Jon Cross set it up; he told me about it on the plane. I don't know who else he told, but it had to be a damn short list."

"Why don't you just come out and say it?"

"You might sell me out, but I don't think you'd betray Jon Cross."

"Sell you out?" Anne said. "You arrogant bastard."

"Save your energy, we have a long way to go. There's no choice—we do this together. The White Man agreed to help us get into China. I told him we would pay double what the opposition offered. We set up another meeting. This time, you're going."

"You're testing me?"

Nyland's face was hard. "Call it what you like."

◄15►

Robert Jaynes's plodding determination had paid off. In an obscure footnote in his Seven files, he had found the name Thaung Lwin. The man was a regional military commander and a member of the newly formed State Peace and Development Council, most of whose members remained active in the drug trade. He was nicknamed, "The White Man."

General Thaung would be the man to see for safe conduct passage through Shan state and into China. He had had Agency dealings before, according to his file, but his loyalties remained for sale to the highest bidder. Such a man would undoubtedly be known to an experienced CIA officer like Jon Cross. Cross would need his services.

Robert Jaynes smiled. He had gotten to Thaung first. One of his field men, Donald Shenk, had flown his team into Burma from the CIA station in Chiang Mai, Thailand, and set up field headquarters in Mandalay. He had immediately contacted The White Man and made him an offer. If everything went well, Cross would contact Thaung, Shenk would move in, and the game would be over. Jaynes turned a fresh sheet on his yellow pad and jotted a note, Bonus for Shenk.

And Jon Cross would get life in prison. The deputy director of operations leaned back in his chair and let an image play in his mind: Jon Cross on the chain gang, in orange coveralls, swinging a sledgehammer.

But it was not about revenge, he told himself. Stopping Jon Cross was a matter of urgent national security. The man had been in clandestine contact with Chinese Intelligence for years, perhaps. And now he was headed for China—defecting, taking not only the C4I software, but information about CIA agents, codes, and operational details that could shift the balance of power in the world. But that was never going to happen because he, Robert Jaynes, was going to stop him.

He glanced at his computer clock. Shenk should be calling from Burma; he was three minutes overdue. The phone rang. "Yes, put him on," Jaynes said. "We've made contact with the subjects." Don Shenk's voice sounded strained.

"Excellent. Is there a problem?"

"Momentary, but we have it under control. Your information about the woman was accurate. I sent my people to the Strand Hotel down in Rangoon. She was with a man, probably Tuck Nyland, from the description you gave us."

"So you have those two?" Jaynes asked.

"Ah—no sir, they got away."

"That is not satisfactory."

"We found them in Maymyo."

"And rolled them up?"

"Well, no. They drove down an alley that was too narrow...Anyway, we have reason to believe they are still in Maymyo."

The hum of the long distance line filled a long silence before Jaynes spoke. "So you have nothing?"

"We know that Nyland is scheduled to meet Thaung again. We'll have the meeting place staked out. He won't get away again."

"There was no sign of Jon Cross?"

"He's probably too smart to show up in-country himself."

"Smart. Thank you for your most astute evaluation," Jaynes said. "I want all of them before they have a chance to get into China. Any means necessary." He hung up the phone and drew a red line through the words, Bonus for Shenk.

Jon Cross was probably too smart, Shenk had said. It would never do to underestimate him, Jaynes thought. The man had flown off in a C-130 from Washington, D.C., and, in spite of all the Jaynes's efforts to locate him, had simply disappeared. The plane had arrived in San Francisco two hours behind schedule, unloaded cargo, and taken off for Alaska. It had never arrived in Fairbanks. Jaynes studied the report again. What had happened to the missing two hours? Had the plane made an unscheduled stop? If so, Cross could have changed planes, could be anywhere.

Cross had his people in the field. He would be somewhere nearby, that was certain. And he would have to be in contact with them. That meant electronic communications. Jaynes made more notes: call the NSA. They would screen every signal to and from Burma.

Jaynes's red pen touched the *X* on his list. He scribbled a row of question marks beside it. A risky game, trading information with a powerful man like this. If things went wrong, he thought, it would be Robert Jaynes out in the cold. But the man had the president's ear, had persuaded him to form the China task force. He would remember his friends. And very soon the search would be on for a new Director of Central Intelligence.

He pushed a scrambler button on his phone, bypassing the Agency switchboard. *X* answered on the first ring. "I have some information for you," Jaynes said.

★ ★ ★

Falls Church, Virginia

Honeysuckle vines crawled up a wooden trellis in the front yard, their fragrant blossoms hiding the bars on the windows. If you knew where to look, you could spot the infrared sensors in the ivy behind the high chain-link fence. Otherwise, the two-story brick house looked like all the others along the residential street of this Washington suburb.

In the kitchen, the tall man known as Sarge was frying bacon and listening to talk radio. He nodded his head vigorously at the host recited another litany of liberal transgressions. "Shoot the bastards," Sarge chuckled as he cracked eggs into the pan. As they sizzled in the fat, he laid plates and silverware on two plastic trays. Housewife work, he thought. Waiting on those two upstairs like they were company.

In fact, they were prisoners. And it was time to go check on them. He carried the trays up the stairs. The old man was in the first bedroom, handcuffed to the cast iron bed frame. Sarge sat the breakfast tray on a night stand by the bed and slipped a Colt revolver from his belt holster. "Gonna toss you the key to those cuffs. Enjoy your breakfast, but you be damn careful. I'm gonna lock this door while I go feed your friend, and I don't wanna hear any noise, or I'm comin' back in here."

"The last time I saw you, you were hanging by your heels from my back porch," the old man said.

Sarge felt his cheeks redden. "On the other foot now, friend."

"Remember the man who cut you down?"

Sarge grimaced. The memory was painfully clear. The man had a serpent's icy stare. Sarge had been surprised that the man hadn't killed him.

The old man unlocked the handcuffs. "You better watch your back," he said.

Sarge cocked the revolver and walked to the window. "No way that son of a bitch knows where you are."

"Oh, you won't see him coming."

"Hurry up and eat, you're about to have company." Sarge backed out of the room, pistol in his hand.

★ ★ ★

Jon Cross looked with disgust at the greasy food. Eat, keep up your strength. Worry about cholesterol later, if there was a later. He buttered a slice of toast, laid a strip of bacon on it, and popped it in his mouth. It was the first meal since the Air Police took him off the plane at Travis two nights ago. You couldn't count the stale sweet rolls and coffee on the flight back to Washington.

He sniffed the mug of coffee. Whatever they were going to slip him was probably in there. He poured the coffee on the carpet behind an overstuffed chair in the corner. The dark blue shag absorbed it with hardly a trace.

He was lying on the bed, eyes closed when the door opened. He opened his eyes a slit: the dim outline of two men in suits. One, thin to the point of emaciation, carried a medical bag, the man behind him was tall, ramrod straight, with a shock of white hair.

The thin man opened his medical bag. "I suspect you're awake, Mister Cross."

Cross opened his eyes. "Feeling—dizzy."

Secretary of Defense Charles Blanchard curled his fingers around the cast-iron footrail of Cross's bed, the hint of a smile on his lips. "Game is over, Cross."

"I knew it was you, Blanchard, as soon as I saw the F-16s. Defense department doesn't deploy fighter planes for just anybody. I wonder what would happen if they knew they were helping a traitor? What do the Chinese have on you, Mr. Secretary? Something from Vietnam?"

Blanchard's knuckles went white on the cast-iron footrail and his smile faded. "You're going to tell us all about your agent in China. That person will know some things about me, some things that simply cannot see the light of day. Surely, you understand my position?" He motioned the doctor forward. "In deference to your long service to this country, we're first going to ask you politely. What happens after that is entirely up to you."

★　★　★

Maymyo

Thaung Lwin's car, a white Mercedes, was parked on a darkened street near the brick wall marking the west entrance to town. Thaung sat alone in the backseat, dressed in his camouflage fatigues, four stars pinned on each lapel. The driver had been instructed to return in an hour.

Across the street was the strawberry market where the CIA man, Shenk, waited with his team. Thaung smiled in the darkness. He would collect from both sides. Who knew what game the Americans were playing against each other, but it didn't matter. In this part of the world, his troops were the controlling force, and his money, gained from the sale of opium, insured that his rules were the only ones that mattered.

A flash of movement caught his eye near the brick archway. A figure walking toward the car, nearly hidden by the shadows of the trees. Shenk's people would have seen the figure as it passed through the gate, but they would wait until contact was made and Thaung gave the signal, time for him to conduct his business and receive his money. "Mister Smith" would be carrying cash in a suitcase, according to the arrangement they had made at Club Maymyo.

The back door opened and a tall, Caucasian woman slid into the seat beside him. She wore a heavy floral perfume. "Mister Smith has sent an emissary," Thaung said. "That was not our agreement."

"There's been a change of plans," the woman said. "Mister Smith is otherwise occupied tonight with some last-minute arrangements, but he asked me to tell you he will double the amount of money you agreed upon if you can provide an airplane by tomorrow morning. The old military strip near the teak mill. He was certain you would remember."

"I remember it well, but I do not like having conditions dictated to me."

"He said he is willing to double whatever the other side is offering, if you tell them nothing about this arrangement."

"That might be possible."

"He will be pleased," the woman said.

Thaung studied the woman. Red hair spilling over the collar of her white cotton dress. Pretty face. One of the group Shenk was looking for, he was sure. What kind of a price would she bring? Thaung slid his hand along her leg, pulling up the cotton dress. First things first.

"Since Mister Smith would like to renegotiate our arrangement," Thaung said, "perhaps sent you to—what is the phrase, 'sweeten the deal'?"

"I am just a messenger." The woman's breathing had quickened. She was afraid. Thaung smiled as he watched her breasts rise and fall against the thin fabric. Her nipples were erect. He slid his hand further up her leg. Plenty of time to signal Shenk and his team across the road.

"Don't touch me." She pushed his hand away.

"You are in my car, in my country. You are in no position to give orders." He cupped his hand over her breast and squeezed roughly.

She cried out, struggling against him, then relaxed, smiling weakly. "There's no reason to get rough."

"Much better." He began unbuttoning his pants. "First, a little taste, do you understand?" He felt the woman's fingers slide down his stomach and brush his penis. He closed his eyes and leaned back on the leather cushions. He felt his pants being slipped down around his knees and raised his thighs to ease the process. Her hand cupped his testicles, and he could feel the warmth of her breath on his now-erect member. He moaned softly.

"Just like a cock, only smaller," she said.

"What—" A flash of pain exploded in his groin. He felt her fingernails dig into his testicles, and he struggled to sit up. His legs were trapped by the trousers bunched around his knees.

"You may be the boss man around here, but there are some things that aren't for sale." She slammed her fist into his groin. The pain shot through his body, and he felt himself blacking out.

He fought against the pain as he struggled to pull up his trousers. The woman had slipped out of the car and disappeared into the darkness. He breathed heavily, his breath sounding ragged and harsh in the silence of the back seat. Blood from his injury darkened the fabric of his trousers. Tears of pain and humiliation ran down his cheeks. To hell with Shenk and his CIA cronies. He would find the woman and her cohorts himself. There was nowhere they could hide.

Don Shenk peered into the darkness across the street. What the hell was going on? Another fuck-up and Robert Jaynes would bust him back to a desk. But there had been no signal from Thaung since the woman had climbed into the car, and that had been the arrangement. Then, as Shenk watched, the woman climbed out of the car and walked quickly down the street. No sign of Thaung.

"Fuck him, let's get her," Shenk said.

His driver turned the key. Silence. He twisted it again. "Fuck."

"Go, she's getting away!"

The driver climbed out of the car and opened the hood. "Somebody cut the goddamn wires," he said. "Must have been her partner, crawled under the car—"

"Nyland. Jaynes told me to watch out for him." The woman in the white dress had passed under the brick arch and disappeared. Shenk leaned wearily against the fender. "We are in the shit," he said.

The jade merchant, U Khin, owned one of the most beautiful houses in Maymyo, a rambling Tudor surrounded by an acre of manicured gardens. The house was set well back from the road on a hillside overlooking the town. During the Raj, it had been the home of a General May, the British garrison commander for whom the town was named.

U Khin sat alone on his back veranda, his face half-lit in the light of the newly risen moon. To a casual watcher, it appeared he might be sleeping, but behind the hooded eyes, he was very much awake. The phone call had come an hour ago. The man on the phone had said there was a message from "John King." U Khin had not heard that name in nearly forty years. It was not his old friend's real name, he knew, but the CIA man had been insistent on maintaining his cover. John King must be nearly seventy by now, Khin thought, nearly as old as he. What could be the reason for the call?

Perhaps it had been a mistake to invite the mysterious caller to his home, but U Khin was curious about his old friend. Besides, there were the dogs, two Rotweillers who roamed the backyard freely. And the Uzi lying across his lap. Ample security.

"Alpha, Bravo. Come," he called. Silence from the darkened yard. He picked up the Uzi and chambered a round. A slight rustling sound to his right near the koi pond. He swung the barrel toward the sound. "Come out. Identify yourself."

"John King sends his regards." The voice came from behind, to his left.

U Khin turned slowly, his finger tightening on the Uzi's trigger. "Where are the dogs?"

Tuck Nyland stepped from behind Khin's chair and bowed to U Khin. "They aren't hurt."

"Impressive." Khin studied the tall man standing before him. He stood relaxed, but it was the stance of a jungle cat, able to spring without the least warning. There was world-weariness in his face, a coldness in his eyes. It was a look U Khin had seen only a few times before. "The kind of man John King would send." U Khin studied Nyland's face. "In ancient times, the Japanese had a name for men like you: *shinobi*. It means, 'stealer-in.' From the ideogram, they got the word, *ninjitsu*."

"Jon drew it for me one night on a cocktail napkin."

U Khin chuckled. "He is well?"

"He's in trouble. If there had been any choice, I never would have contacted you. He said that his troubles must not become yours."

"Yes, he would say that. You tell me stories, but what proof do you have that you represent my old friend?"

Nyland passed him a small silk brocade box. U Khin opened the cover slowly and stared at the dragonfly pin inside. "The King-fisher," he said softly. "I see those birds from time to time here in my garden. It has been a long time since I have seen this pin. The man who bought it was young and much in love. A forbidden love, and perhaps stronger because forbidden. The young are like that, do you agree?"

"I need your help."

"Yes, and I am certain you are in a hurry, the young always are. Let me have my memories. Did you know I loaned him some money to buy this pin?"

Nyland stood motionless, his dark clothing blending with the shadows.

"Where is my old friend? Of course you cannot say. I can guess, however. He has come for her; he always said he would. And you wish to travel to China, am I right?"

Nyland nodded.

"A very dangerous undertaking. You have likely been in contact with our beloved military commander, General Thaung?"

"He can't be trusted. He has been—"

"Purchased by a higher bidder, perhaps?" U Khin said. "He is a despicable, evil man, utterly without principal. Except for the principal of making money. He has been approached by the Chinese?"

"The Americans," Nyland said.

"A tangled web you weave. I read Shakespeare, you know."

"Will you help us?"

"What does John King offer in return?"

"I have money, but he said money would be an insult to your honor."

"He would be right. Honor. Such an outdated concept in our modern world. But the world has changed so much, I hardly recognize it anymore, yet still I am working, always trying to get more of what I already have plenty of. What makes a man do that?"

Nyland looked at him. "The waters of Earth cannot quench the spirit's thirst."

U Khin laughed, a dry cackle. "A *ninjitsu* and a philosopher. You have learned well from John King." U Khin rose slowly from the wicker rocking chair and motioned Nyland toward the house. "When do you want to go to China?"

"I would like to leave tonight."

"Do you expect me to be surprised?" Khin said. "I have had a lifetime of adventures that you could never dream of. I can put you on one of my cargo trucks within an hour. There is a special government sticker on the windshield. I have a business arrangement with our beloved general, Thaung Lwin, which, so far, he has chosen to honor. My trucks are never searched, and my people do not interfere in his opium operations.

"The roads over the mountains have become a thoroughfare for shipping of all kinds. You can even travel to China on a tourist visa. But I doubt that you are going as tourists. If you are going for the reason I suspect, there will be many allied against you. The problem will not be getting into China, the problem will be getting out."

◄16►

Beijing

The Chinese had practiced kung fu for over two thousand years. To honor the ancient Shaolin tradition, General Xing Wanpo had ordered a *dojo* built in his headquarters. Now, clad in the traditional black costume, he circled slowly around the polished wood floor of the training room, a long knife in each hand. His instructor moved with him, swinging a hardwood staff slowly from side to side. Like many martial artists, Xing Wanpo had started young. He had been a diligent student and, while still in his teens, had mastered the long pole and the butterfly knives of a style called Wing Chun. His teachers marveled at the ferocity of his spirit, how skillfully he swung the blades. As an adult, General Xing practiced daily with the razor-sharp knives.

The instructor whipped the long staff forward, a feint toward Xing's midsection. Xing spun around, his blades a blur of silver behind his opponent's suddenly unprotected back. The blade stopped a fraction of an inch from the black cotton of the man's uniform.

The two men stepped apart and bowed. "You let me win," Xing said. "Do not dishonor me again."

Xing walked toward Song Zhenyo who sat cross-legged on a straw mat against the wall. "The way of the sword is a spirit way," he said. He wiped sweat from his face. "You must be more than a soldier; you must be a man of war. And that is what my country needs at this perilous time. Men with the will and the spirit to destroy our enemies—men of war. Are you such a man, Song Zhenyo?"

"The weapons of war are many," Song kept his voice neutral.

"The path to peace is narrow."

Song nodded. Quoting Confucius, playing with swords, the man was living in a different century.

General Xing said, "You and I must train together some time, perhaps when your injury has healed."

Song bowed his head. "An honor."

"You have recruited the American secretary of defense—I am impressed. What does Secretary Blanchard have to say?" General Xing asked, buttoning his uniform.

"The CIA, as usual, has made a mess of things. Twice, it tried to catch Nyland and his woman friend. Once in Rangoon and again in Maymyo. They are in Shan State, on our border—coming our way."

"Does that frighten you?" Xing asked. "This is not the time for fear. There will be big changes in our country very soon. Your American connection is vital to us as our plans move forward. I can promise in the new China, you will not be riding around in pickup trucks."

Song could only nod his head.

"But I demand one thing in return," Xing said. "Your complete loyalty. Until death."

"Yes, I understand."

"You understand, but do you agree?" He picked up one of the butterfly knives and placed it in Song's hand. "Put the blade here, against my breast. Now I do the same." Xing raised his knife, staring into Song's eyes. "Do you swear on your ancestors?"

The man was caught in some warlord fantasy from the twelfth century. The realization hit Song like a physical blow. He remembered the sound of the steel blade whipping through the air, the shimmer of light on its mirrored surface. He felt the touch of the blade, just above his heart. "I swear my loyalty to you, General Xing." he said. Song grimaced inwardly. Now he was talking like a peasant.

"I know something the CIA fools do not," Xing said. "Nyland is coming to China to help a traitor escape. I know who that traitor is." He shot a warning glance toward the two armed soldiers standing at attention beside the door. "I will tell you the rest in my office. And we will call Bei Feng again. Your contact has only begun to help us."

★ ★ ★

Maymyo

Anne Hammersmith's hotel room was dark except for the faint glow of a laptop computer screen. The white cotton dress she had worn to meet Thaung Lwin lay discarded on the bed. She sat cross-legged on the floor in her underwear, fingers on the keyboard. The aluminum case Nyland had brought in his duffle bag sat open on the rug. Even with Doug Smith's instructions, it had taken nearly an hour to make sense of the laptop's complex programs.

The room she had rented, using her fake passport, was on an upper floor at the back of the building. It was a hotel frequented mostly by European tourists. Did the CIA—or General Thaung—have a way to check all the guests?

Faint starlight filtered through the window, muted by the lights of the town. Through the trees she could see the city's famous clock tower, a gift from Queen Victoria.

Nearly two in the morning. The moon would not rise for another hour. That would suit Nyland's nocturnal purposes, whatever they were. He had told her only that he would be back before three. But he had been gone for nearly two hours and she found herself growing anxious. Had he been hurt, captured?

No time for this schoolgirl foolishness, she told herself. It was time to put the computer online, to carry out Doug Smith's instructions. Did she dare? She got to her feet and walked to the window. Looking up at the faint web of stars, she imagined thousands of electronic signals criss-crossing the night sky: the National Security Agency monitoring its satellites, the massive computers searching countless transmissions, seeking key words. All looking for a signal from Doug Smith's computer.

But Smith had programmed the circuits to make the transmitter emulate a CIA station in southern Laos. Even if the Agency intercepted her calls, they would have a false location.

Smith had left instructions in a file on the laptop: the operations directorate of the CIA had a tactical net for the deputy director, providing instant access by satellite to his intelligence officers in the field. The net was heavily encrypted and supposedly uncrackable. Smith had written a program that could unravel its complex electronic web.

She stared at the computer. Showtime. Anne inserted a disk, per Smith's onscreen instructions, loaded the decryption program, and opened the satellite link. Numbers scrolled up the screen, then garbled strings of characters. The screen went dark for a moment then a group of numbers popped on the screen: radio frequencies. The program worked. She smiled as she keyed the frequencies into the communication program.

Pay dirt.

At 0040 hours local time, DDO Robert Jaynes had sent a message to his field people in Maymyo—highest priority. All personnel were to concentrate on the airports. A source had steered them in that direction. Anne smiled. A few hours before, she had had the "source," Thaung Lwin, by the balls—literally. Thaung had swallowed her disinformation about the airport.

Time for act 2.

Robert Jaynes was running a field operation from eight thousand miles away, dependent on the secure operations net. That net was about to collapse around his head, she thought. The trick was a simple one. The system was designed for short bursts of information, operational messages. Such a system would bog down if the encoder circuits were fed masses of data. Given enough, they would overload, and Jaynes's net would crash.

Hammersmith selected another disk from Smith's collection and slipped it into the floppy drive. Robert Jaynes was about to receive a message from the Laos CIA station. The disk contained reams of budget projections; a huge file, the equivalent of sixty-thousand typed pages. It would repeat itself endlessly until shut off.

Anne punched the Transmit key. Direct action against the enemy. Tuck Nyland would be proud.

Data poured into the network, thousands of pages a second. Robert Jaynes's super-secure operational network crashed in two minutes and twenty-eight seconds.

Beijing

"What is your report?" General Xing sat behind his desk eating a bowl of noodles. He did not offer his visitor a seat.

Song Zhenyo stood nervously in the center of the room feeling naked and exposed. His continued good fortune depended, he knew, on the Chinese general. He spoke carefully. "This time there is news. Bei Feng has been informed by the CIA that they think the people in question are seeking an airplane, to fly into China, I presume."

"Think? Presume? These things are without value in time of war."

"The CIA pursued them by car in Maymyo, but lost them."

"They cannot cross the border undetected. And if they do, we will be waiting at their destination."

"Their destination? May I presume to ask how—"

"You presume nothing!" Xing slammed the lacquered bowl down on his desk and went on in a softer voice. "I am surrounded by traitors. Including the person the Americans are coming to get." He motioned for Song to sit in a straight-backed chair beside his desk.

"What I am going to tell you now, you will tell no one, ever."

Song nodded, staring down at the top secret file Xing had taken from a drawer.

"The People's Liberation Army is the largest in the world. But we are ten or twenty years behind in technology. They call us a scrap-iron army. We must acquire these new weapons of war. Your acquiring this new C4I software is a large step in that direction. It is the key to targeting our nuclear arsenal. We will have it in operation in the next few days, I am told. Still, it will not be the technology that triumphs, it will be the people. Unfortunately, the people are much harder to control.

"One person in particular, a cryptographer, has been most helpful to me in developing secure means of communication in the field."

"Is this person—"

Xing slammed his fist onto the desk, upsetting a small jade Buddha. "The price of seeing is silence." He righted the jade figure and placed it carefully beside the top secret folder. "And that person," Xing went on, "was one of the few people able to listen to those communications. She heard messages she was not supposed to hear. She is very dangerous to us and to China.

"While you were talking to your spy, I received a message from the MSS. Only now do they tell me they have suspicions about this woman. She may have been in contact with the Americans by the email system. She has a granddaughter in San Francisco who may be working with the CIA."

Song nodded silently. A stirring of doubt fluttered in his stomach. A granddaughter in San Francisco. Was she the woman he had killed?

"The MSS tells me this morning that the woman has decided to take a vacation. They have gone to her home, contacted her family. She has disappeared."

"She is the one the Americans are coming for?"

"I am certain of it. I have not told the MSS of the Americans. I am selfish, I want them for myself." The expression on Xing's face was harsh.

"How will we find her?" Song asked.

"We will ask questions. We will get answers."

Maymyo

Anne Hammersmith was dozing in an overstuffed chair by her open window, the computer beside her, screen still glowing. She awoke to the gentle pressure of a hand on her shoulder and struggled to sit up. Nyland held a finger to his lips. "Pack your things, we have a ride to China."

She slid her arms around his neck. "I was afraid you'd gotten lost."

She felt his warmth against her, and caught the faint scent of incense. "Where the hell have you been?"

"I can see you stayed up worrying."

"Working late, give me a break." She stood up and stepped close to him. They were almost the same height. "You gonna tell me where you've been?"

"What have you got against wearing clothes?"

"What have you got against me?"

"Wrong time." He pushed her away.

"Will there be a right time?"

"We have an hour to catch our ride."

"Plenty of time." Her fingers traced the hard ridges of muscle on his stomach, lightly brushed the front of his trousers. "You don't trust me," she whispered. "Can't let yourself get in a vulnerable position? What if we got in a vulnerable position together?"

Nyland pulled her against him. She kissed him fiercely. "Let it go, Tuck, just let everything go."

"Anne—"

"Shut up."

They made love standing in the middle of the room. Anne's legs circled his hips, her arms locked around his neck. She moaned as he slipped inside her. His thrusts were slow and rhythmical at first, then harder and harder. His head was back, his eyes closed. Her thighs trembled and she cried, "Jesus, Tuck—now, now!"

He held her quietly for a long moment, and she could feel his legs shake. He carried her to the bed and gently laid her on the sheet. She stretched her arms above her head and smiled a lazy smile. "When you let go, you let go."

He lay down beside her, and when he finally spoke, his voice was barely a whisper: "I shouldn't have done that, but I—just lost it there..."

"Hey, there's two of us in this equation."

"We have to work together."

Anne laid her hand on his thigh. "I think we work together pretty goddam well."

"It's been a long time since I felt anything like that."

"Thank you, my friend. Maybe you've gone so long because you're afraid to let yourself feel. I think you're nursing an old hurt, Tucker. I saw it in your eyes back there at Camp Peary."

"That was ten years ago." Tuck turned away. Shutting down, she thought.

"Women notice those things."

"I don't know anything about women."

Anne smiled. "You don't? Then how do you explain this feeling I'm having right now?"

"You're a romantic."

"And you're not? On this mission, risking your life for your boss's old love?"

"Forget it," Tuck said.

"We'll talk about this later, on the way to China. And since you mentioned work..." Anne gestured toward the laptop computer. "I've been playing with the little toy you brought me."

Nyland listened as Anne explained her attack on Jayne's communication net.

"How long ago did it crash?" he asked.

"About an hour."

"They know we're onto them. That doesn't leave us much time."

"Did I do the wrong thing?" Anne asked.

"No, you did fine. We hit them, and we keep moving, that's the way to survive."

Anne brushed her hand gently along his thigh. "We—you and I— have to stop moving sometime. What happens then?"

Nyland pushed her hand away, put his hands behind his neck, and stared at the ceiling.

Anne kissed him on the cheek. "Come on, you've thought about it a little, admit it."

"I don't want to play games," Nyland said. "Maybe this is some kind of romantic fantasy for you, but "

"Tuck—"

"If I can't get the Kingfisher out of China, Jon Cross—none of us—have much of a future."

"Fine, let's talk about the *mission* if that's what you want. You don't speak a word of the language, you don't even know how to turn that computer on. I know you still probably don't trust me, but you better start learning. You need me, whether you realize it or not." She walked into the bathroom and slammed the door.

★ ★ ★

JOHN REED

Beijing

The interrogation cell was on the top floor of the general's headquarters, a windowless room with medieval-looking iron rings bolted into the walls. As Song entered behind General Xing a fetid odor assailed his nostrils. Sweat, feces, and the damp smell of stone. A man in his mid-sixties hung by frail wrists from the iron rings. He was naked and Song could see the burn marks that covered his body. His groin was a mass of purple bruises. Xing looked questioningly at the soldier who had opened the door. The man nodded toward the prisoner. "He has been given an injection. He will speak soon."

Xing knelt in front of the man, careful to protect his boots from the slime on the floor. He slapped the man's face. "Where has she gone? Where is your cousin?"

The man's eyes opened, a wide unnatural stare. "Kunming... monastery."

"There are a hundred monasteries in Kunming, which one?" Xing shouted

The man's body convulsed and he slumped against the wet stone. The guard prodded him with his rifle butt. "The injection was too strong," he said.

"The old man's heart—I told the doctor."

Xing spun to face the guard. "Bring the doctor to this room. And kill him."

★ ★ ★

Kunming, China

Poets called it the City of Eternal Spring. Its elevation, almost six thousand feet, put Kunming above the sweltering jungle heat, but the subtropical latitude shielded it from the bitter cold that often gripped China's northern provinces. The two million people who lived there were blessed with the best weather in China, some said.

To Bao Qing, the city had always been a sanctuary. She had spent her teenage years there, happy times with her mother and father, before the purges of Chairman Mao took them from her.

Now, she thought, it would provide sanctuary once again, the last on her journey out of China.

The Huating Temple, on the western hills above the city, had been built in the fourteenth century, and the years had turned its stone walls a soft blue-gray. Now, as Bao Qing strolled along a terrace outside the walls, she could feel the sun's first rays warm her face. In the valley below, traces of morning mist clung to the surface of Dianchi Lake, a few sailboats lay at anchor. The spectacular view had charmed visitors and locals for five hundred years. From a distance, the hills resembled the curves of a sleeping woman, her long hair flowing down to the lake. Up closer, they had a sinister look; many still believed they housed demons.

This spring morning, Bao Qing thought she could feel the demon's presence. She purposely turned her back on the snow-shrouded mountains behind her to the west, but she knew she would have to face them eventually. For beyond the mountains lay Burma, the way out—out of her life in China. The way was treacherous enough, but if General Xing Wanpo had found out where she had gone, escape would be impossible. Her life depended on the men Jon Cross was sending to get her out. She would say a prayer that he had chosen well.

With a last look at the shimmering surface of the lake below, she started up the winding path up to the monk's quarters. It was nearly half a mile from the temple, and never visited by tourists. The monks were old friends of her family and had taken her in without question, offering her a small guesthouse outside the walls. She would stay a day, possibly two. By then, she thought, she would either be on her way out of China, or be dead.

The camellias were in full bloom along the path, nestled amongst stands of eucalyptus and bamboo. The morning sun struck their blossoms and the soft pinks and whites of the petals seemed to tint the very air with an ethereal glow. This was the old China she had loved, timeless and serene. Where had those times gone? It seemed so distant, so different from the world of Bao Qing, chief cryptographer for the Ministry of State Security.

She reached in her pocket for a handkerchief and her fingers brushed the envelop there. The computer discs, smuggled out of the office in her underwear, contained computer codes, radio frequencies, the heart of General Xing's military network. And recorded conversations where the general had discussed his plans for a coup, named his coconspirators, all the while being reassured by the chief cryptographer that his communications were secure.

Xing was a warlord in the old style, interested only in conquest, heedless of the peasant population, the bloodbath that was sure to follow. He would welcome a chance to cross swords with the West. And now, Bao Qing realized, the means were within his grasp. The C4I software Song Zhenyo had brought into the country was the final link, interconnecting the modern, high-tech nuclear weapons and awesome manpower to form an unstoppable war machine. And Xing had made his alliances well, several members of the Central Committee were in on the plot with him.

The names of those conspirators on the Central Committee was a vital part of the information she was bringing to Jon Cross. Along with the message she had recorded two days before. It had come from the Chinese Embassy in Washington, D.C., and concerned Song Zhenyo. Though he had been successful in acquiring some top-secret computer software, the message said, there had been trouble. Song had killed a woman in San Francisco, and someone had seen him do it. His cover had been compromised. Bao Qing had cried as she read the message. She knew whom he had killed in San Francisco. Someone else would be needed to run his agent, Bei Feng, the Embassy said. Song was being recalled.

The message noted Song's arrival time at the Ministry of State Security headquarters in Beijing, but he had never shown up. He had joined Xing in his coup attempt, she would bet on it, and the price of admission had been the C4I software.

The monastery was quiet as she approached the front gate. The monks were at meditation. The cottage they had given her was smaller than her living room in Beijing, with only a straw mat and a water basin for furnishings. She lit red joss sticks for luck, and sat down cross-legged facing the wall. She relaxed her muscles but her mind would not clear, an image of Jon Cross insinuated itself: a handsome young man, barely more than a boy, walking beside her in the botanical garden in Maymyo, feeding her strawberries from the market, laughing as the juice dripped down her chin. Bending toward her, kissing her lips. The juice was red and sweet. And later...

Her cheeks felt warm in the cool air of the monastery cell. This was no place to entertain such thoughts. Her window looked out into a manicured garden where a path wound its way among brightly blooming rhododendrons. Several monks in their saffron robes walked, heads bowed, across the ancient stones. She would see Jon Cross in less than a week, if things went as planned. She tried to imagine what that meeting would be like. They were old now, would the flame still burn? Qing blushed again. From the tingling sensation she felt, she was certain that it still burned for her.

The promise they had made to each other so many years ago was one she would keep, even if it was the last thing she did on Earth.

◄17►

China-Burma Border

The freight truck looked no different from the dozens of others grinding their way up the mountain toward the Chinese border. It was a tough old Mercedes Benz, body dented and covered with dust, veteran of a hundred such crossings. The driver shifted to a lower gear and turned up the heater. He had climbed to nearly two thousand meters, and the air was noticeably colder.

He could almost make the run in his sleep, he thought. But there would be no sleeping tonight, not with the cargo he carried. The sticker on his windshield had always gotten him through the checkpoint, but what if someone had found out about his two passengers? Who would feed his family after the border guards killed him? He had seen a driver killed just the week before. A truck had been pulled out of the line and searched, the driver beaten. As he passed the checkpoint, he had heard a burst of machine gun fire and watched his rearview mirror as the soldiers tossed the man's body into a ditch.

Now, the familiar cluster of buildings marking the border checkpoint was just a hundred yards ahead. Spotlights glared on the steel barricade. Three other trucks waited in line. He pulled up behind them, letting his engine idle. A dozen soldiers, rifles slung over their shoulders, milled around the checkpoint eyeing the waiting trucks. Twice the usual number. Did they know about his two American passengers? He pulled a rumpled cigarette from his pocket, lit it, and drew the harsh smoke deep into his lungs. In a few minutes he would know the answer.

★ ★ ★

Nyland tightened his arm around Anne's shoulders as the truck slowed. "Welcome to China," he said.

"They just wave us through, right?"

"So the man said."

Tuck and Anne lay huddled together in the freezing darkness, wrapped in two thin blankets the driver had given them. They had made the journey from Maymyo hidden in an empty packing crate in the back of the truck.

Anne was listening to the voices outside. "Asking him to show his papers," she translated. "Burmese army guys."

Nyland felt her shiver beside him, and for a moment was back in the spider hole outside Baghdad, remembering the little Iraqi girl, the feel of her dead body pressing against him. He touched Anne's face gently with his fingertips. She put her hand over his as they waited in the darkness.

The pistol he had taken from their attackers at the Strand Hotel in Rangoon was a 9mm Barretta. Fifteen-round clip. Not much against the soldiers outside, but if they opened the back of the truck, a few of them would pay the price. He worked the slide, chambering a round.

Finally, after what seemed an eternity, the truck began to move. Nyland lowered the Baretta. "Only eight hundred miles to go," he said.

Anne moved closer to him and slid her arms around his waist. "Once again, we have a little time on our hands," she said. "Talk to me."

"About what?"

"Do you always have to be so damned obtuse? Tell me your sorrows."

Nyland pulled her closer but he said nothing.

"It's a line from an old folksong."

They snuggled closer and he felt himself relax into the warmth of her body. "My sorrows..."

★   ★   ★

As the old Mercedes truck rumbled across the mountains of western China, Anne and Tuck made love with a slow, delicious intensity, hands and mouths exploring each other's bodies in the darkness. Afterward, they slept.

Nyland woke first. Anne's head lay across his chest. He stroked her hair and she snuggled closer. He smiled to himself in the darkness. For the first time in a week, there had been no nightmares.

Her voice was slurred with sleep. "Where are we?"

"That's what I was wondering."

Her fingers traced his lips in the darkness. "You're smiling, you horny devil."

"I wish I could see the look in your eyes."

"What do you think you'd see?" she asked.

"I—think we're out of the mountains, probably about halfway there."

"He withdraws, or is that some kind of metaphor?"

"I was thinking about Jon Cross."

"That's flattering."

"Not a game, Anne. His life, and ours, are on the line here."

"I know that. How did you meet him?"

"I was in the SEALs. Sometimes we ran some joint operations with the CIA. We were just coming off a training cycle in San Diego. And there was a warning order waiting. We saddled up and off we went. To Peru. A Marxist terrorist group called Shining Path trying to overthrow the government."

"Operation Snowbird," Anne said.

"This was the operation before Snowbird. We went in, freed some hostages. I took the point, made the grab. Team took down about thirty of the guerrillas. Afterward, there was a debrief on the ship. Cross was in the back of the room, nobody introduced him. It was supposed to be all Navy types. I glanced at him a couple times as I gave my after-action report. He had a look to him—calm, cold—hard to describe. He stared at me the whole time, got on my nerves. I finished my debrief and sat down. A few minutes later, I looked around and he was gone. I asked the Lieutenant who's the civilian. There was no civilian here tonight, he said. You didn't see anybody."

Anne sat up and leaned her back against the rough wooden crate. "Did you hear from him again?"

"I'm talking too much."

"That's what you do when you trust somebody, you tell them things. Relax, Tuck."

Nyland said nothing for a long moment. "After Peru, we came back to Coronado. I signed out, headed off-post, and I noticed a car was following me. The training kicked in. I was carrying a .44 mag in a holster under the seat. I pulled off the road and got set to put whoever it was away."

"You'd shoot a civilian?"

"Look, I'm—after all the training, you respond automatically. I thought maybe it was a carjacking. I had a nice little Alpha convertible at the time. I shut off my lights. The guy behind me shut off his. I was out of the car and in the brush in a second. I worked my way up to the car, stuck the .44 in the driver's window. And there sat Jon Cross. He just smiled. And you know what he said?"

"What?"

Nyland chuckled in the darkness. "'Satisfactory.' Kind of pissed me off. In the SEALs there is no satisfactory. There is the absolute best, or nothing at all."

"What did you do?"

"I had a head of steam up by then. Who was this fucking civilian to be following me around? 'You almost got yourself killed,' I said. I heard a click from inside the car and I knew what it was in an instant, and I almost fired. But Cross was still smiling. And there, lying across his lap, pointed straight at my family jewels was a Remington 870 pump shotgun, a SEAL weapon. Three-inch magnum shells. It would have torn through that car door, and ripped me in half.

"Cross said, 'So did you,' and he was right. If I had fired, his reflexes would have touched off the trigger on that shotgun. The man was balls to the wall."

"He knew just how to impress you," Anne said. "He did the same thing to me, not with a shotgun, but he told me how much my contributions to the Agency meant. He knew my file by rote, dates,

assignments, efficiency reports. He seemed to focus his whole attention on my life."

"He does that, makes you feel like the most important person in
the world."

"And there he is with a shotgun pointed at your crotch."

"I asked if he always went hunting with a shotgun. He said it
depended on the game. I asked him, still kind of pissed off, what the
goddam game was. He said, 'You.' He invited me to get in his car. We
put away our hardware and I got in."

"And he gave you his recruiting pitch?"

"Damndest thing. He said my CO had told him I was the best he
had. Very complimentary, but I wasn't going to be sold on any flat-
tery suck-up bullshit and Cross knew it. For me, the SEALs were the
best; there was no big leagues above that, sure as hell not in CIA.

"He said something about how would I like to play in a different league, and at that very instant, two red dots appeared on the
front of my shirt. Not one, two. Two laser sights trained on my
heart. Two shooters out there somewhere. I still don't know how he
did it, maybe a hidden microphone, a second car following. I'm usually pretty good at spotting that kind of thing. But I saw nothing.
Maybe it was a different league."

"He went to a lot of trouble to impress you."

"I can tell you it was starting to work. Here was this old guy sitting there calm as a duffer, and I was staring down at those two red
dots on my shirt. Then he said kind of offhandly, 'Satisfactory,
gentlemen,' and the red spots disappeared. I never saw a microphone, or a sign of the snipers outside, though the cars that went by
were shining on the shoulder in front of us. I can tell you that Cross
certainly had my attention."

"Like he planned."

"I got the feeling, and I had it many times over the next few
years, that Cross was somehow reading the script a few pages ahead,
he knew what was going to happen. He knew things about me that
I didn't know."

"Like what?

"You don't really want to hear all this," Nyland said.

Anne jabbed an elbow in his ribs and he went on, "He said I needed to belong to something, but that I really didn't want to be close to other people. He knew that I was afraid of that. I wasn't afraid of dying, being killed, that's part of SEAL territory, I suppose. But I was afraid of putting myself close to people who could hurt me in a different way."

Anne kissed him on the cheek. "I'd say he knows you pretty damn well."

★ ★ ★

Dali, Yunnan Province, China

The sky to the east was just beginning to lighten above the jagged mountains. The heavy truck slowed as it moved off the highway toward a cluster of frame buildings lit by small lanterns in the windows, the Chinese equivalent of a truck stop. Food was available, sleeping mats for rent. Dali was the traditional overnight stop on the Burma Road, but they would not be stopping long tonight, the driver thought, not with the cargo he was carrying.

The driver pulled past several others parked in front of the buildings and stopped five hundred yards farther up the road. He raised the cargo door and watched his passengers climb down. The man walked into the darkness across the road. The woman approached him. "Where are we?" she asked in Chinese.

"Dali. Very famous vacation place. But you are not on vacation."

"I would not call seven hours in the back of a truck with two blankets and a bowl of noodles a vacation. How much farther?"

"Kunming, twelve hours." The driver switched on a small flashlight. Its beam cast a weak yellow glow on the muddy road. He felt an iron grip on his arm and the flashlight was plucked from his fingers.

"Tell him no signals," Nyland said.

Anne translated and the driver spoke rapidly, shaking his head. "He wasn't signaling. The light was to show me the bathroom, which I take is out there in the bushes. He is loyal to U Khin, he says, and he is in as much danger as we are if we're discovered."

"How much longer?"

"He says we'll be in Kunming by late this afternoon."

The driver spoke again. Anne nodded her head. "There is food in the little restaurant back there. He'll bring it. We stay out of sight."

Nyland nodded and the driver trotted away down the road. The dark shapes of trees were just beginning to materialize beside the road. "My turn," Anne said, and walked into the bushes.

★ ★ ★

She returned to find Nyland sitting on the truck's running board, looking deep in thought. "A penny," she said.

Nyland said, "Thinking about Bao Qing. She and Jon—it's kind of a love story. I'll tell you some time."

"A love story? Tell me now."

He shook his head. "She'll be waiting at the Huating monastery about four miles south of town on Dianchi Lake. Jon showed me the satellite photographs. There's a terrace on the east side. She will be there tonight at nine. She'll wait an hour."

"What if you don't show up?"

"If I don't show, that means I'm dead. You're the fallback, same place, tomorrow night."

"Does this mean you've decided to trust me?"

Nyland was looking down at the roadway. He idly tossed a pebble into the bushes.

"Tuck, are we ever going to talk about Marty Hausler?"

"Your boyfriend? Forget about him."

"Cross gave me a number and a contact schedule."

"I don't care; it's too risky," Nyland said. "The Agency's been all over us since we hit Burma. We don't know whose side Hausler's on."

"Jon Cross sent him, for Christ's sake. We don't have a hell of a lot of friends in China."

"Damn few, I'll grant you. Your Burmese friend, General Thaung, will be in touch with his counterparts in Kunming by now.

God only knows what they might have waiting for us. We can't trust that truck driver—anybody for that matter."

"You would never have mentioned Marty if I hadn't brought him up, would you?" Anne stood close in the darkness looking up at Nyland's face. "We have to call him. He's part of this operation; Cross set it up that way."

"It's a different game now. We've got enough leaks as it is."

"We'll talk about this."

"I imagine we will."

The two climbed back into their hiding place in the truck beneath a pile of machinery crates. The sun was just coming over the mountains as the truck pulled back onto the Burma road.

★ ★ ★

Langley

"It was a beautiful trick," the young computer engineer said. "They overloaded the decryption circuits and the net started cycling back on itself—"

"Save me the rave notices," Robert Jaynes said. "Are you certain it was Doug Smith?"

"The system is pretty much hackerproof. Doug's the only guy outside our design team that knew this particular chink in our armor, and the only guy with the access codes."

"We're back online?"

"Yes, sir. But we have to assume we're compromised."

"Well, change the goddamn system, change the goddamn codes. I'm in the middle of a very sensitive operation here. And part of it involves locating Doug Smith. We do that, and we've got Cross. Do you have any idea where this jamming signal came from?"

"Somewhere in Southeast Asia. This guy can imitate anybody—electronically. We're working with Naval Intelligence in the area. They have certain jamming capabilities. They're trying to block his transmissions. We'll find him, sir, it's just a matter of time."

"Let me know immediately." Jaynes didn't look up as the young man left his office. That son of a bitch Cross had gotten ahead again. He no doubt knew about Shenk's team looking for him in Burma. Jaynes had been unable to talk to Don Shenk for the past twelve hours. Tuck Nyland and the woman could be anywhere by now. But one thing was certain, they were headed for China.

Jaynes made new notes on his yellow pad. "Cross defecting?" That was looking less likely. He was somewhere, probably in a boat off shore, issuing orders to his field team. Otherwise, he would already be in China and lost to the CIA forever.

If he wasn't defecting, that meant he was sending his team to bring someone out. But why be so secretive? What was the agent bringing out that was so important? Why not just turn her over to the American government? Either way, Cross was operating on his own, without Agency sanction, and that was a treasonable offense. The way to figure Jon Cross's game was to find him and ask him.

The scrambler phone on his desk buzzed. "Jaynes. Yes, I understand there is a security risk here. Put me through."

Don Shenk's voice echoed hollowly over the scrambled circuit from Burma. "No contact to report," he said. "Didn't get your regular transmission."

"We had a little trouble with the net. We're back online, but we have to be very careful about what we say, understood?"

"Roger. Subjects have presumably left the country. The White Man's mounting a major blocking operation. Helicopters, two companies of infantry, a truck convoy headed up to—headed east. If anybody is crazy enough to try coming back into the country, we'll have him."

Jaynes severed the connection. He thought of his conversation with the secretary of defense. Find Cross, Charles Blanchard had said, and there's a new office waiting for you on the seventh floor at Langley. Jaynes leaned back in his chair, imagining a walnut door with a shiny brass plaque: Robert Jaynes, Director of Central Intelligence. If Cross got away, he could kiss the plaque good-bye, he thought.

But whatever Jon Cross was up to, he couldn't hide forever. He had to break silence sometime to communicate with his in-country team. And NSA was monitoring every satellite for his transmissions. The White Man's troops were sealing off the border. There was no way out of China now. If they came back through Burma, they would end up right in his lap. Jaynes allowed himself a brief mental image of Jon Cross being dragged away in handcuffs. Very satisfactory.

He studied his notes again, a thought nagging at his methodical mind. A loose end. The missing two hours on Cross's flight from Washington to San Francisco. Had there been mechanical problems? What if the plane had landed somewhere and Cross had gotten off?

Another note on the pad: call FAA—flight plans?

Jaynes's pencil wandered across the note pad doodling, creating a maze of lines. He remembered a book he had read, describing the world of espionage as a "wilderness of mirrors." Jon Cross was lost in the wilderness. What had happened during those missing two hours?

★ ★ ★

Falls Church

Jon Cross opened his eyes. A vague shape loomed above him, outlined in the glare of the ceiling light. Charles Blanchard bent closer, bringing with him the odor of breath mints and sweat. Cross closed his eyes.

"You're a clever man, pretending to drink your coffee like that," Blanchard whispered. "'Fool me once, shame on you. Fool me twice, shame on me.'"

Cross moaned softly, eyes still closed. Both his wrists were handcuffed to the bed. He had caught a glimpse of the doctor as he raised a hypodermic needle. The guard called Sarge was standing at the foot of the bed. Make it convincing. He opened his eyes and let a trail of saliva run down his chin. "What...do you want?"

"The goddamn truth!" Blanchard drew back his hand and slapped Cross viciously across the face.

Cross gasped for breath, a gurgling sound escaped from his throat.

Blanchard raised his fist. "Cut the fucking act."

"Hey!" Sarge grabbed Blanchard's arm. "The old guy's hand-cuffed—"

"Don't you ever touch me! We'd have them all if you and your cohorts had done your job. Get the other one, move."

★ ★ ★

Doug Smith stumbled into the room, prodded by Sarge's gun. His eyes were wide with fear. Sarge cocked his pistol and held it to Smith's temple.

"Cross, I'm going to give you five seconds to tell me about Song Zhenyo," Blanchard said. "One...two..."

"Wait." Cross's voice was weak, barely audible. "He works for Chinese intelligence. Tell your man to put the gun down."

Blanchard nodded to Sarge and he lowered his gun. "Now, let's talk about Chinese intelligence. They tell me you're the resident expert. And I have heard that you have some inside information. I want to know about your Chinese agent. You were headed for the Far East to bring him out, weren't you?"

Cross shook his head wearily. "You have a vivid imagination."

"We can't afford—I can't afford—to have that agent telling what he knows," Blanchard said.

"That's what agents are supposed to do."

"Gentlemen, give us a moment, please," Blanchard said. Sarge holstered his gun and escorted Doug Smith out of the room. The doctor packed up his bag and followed.

After they had left, Blanchard said, "Our problem is finding Song Zhenyo."

"*Your* problem is finding Zhenyo."

"Since you probably know already, I'll tell you that he is in pos-session of some—damaging information about me."

"Information that you betrayed your country. Why did you do it? Money—what do they have on you?"

"What difference does it make? They'll hang me for espionage."

"That's how the game is played," Cross said.

"Song's disappeared, I assume gone back to China. He has shared his information with their government. Now if there were to be a defector from the MSS who knows—"

"That you're Bei Feng. That you sold your country out."

"I can't allow that defector to—"

Cross interrupted. "Even if there were such a defector, Doug and I are locked up here. How are we going to do anything about getting him out?"

"Where is Tuck Nyland?" Blanchard asked.

"No idea."

"Is he in China?"

"Tired...very tired." Cross closed his eyes.

Blanchard slapped him. "Nyland is bringing that agent out, isn't he?"

"Nyland is working for Robert Jaynes."

"What?"

"Ask Jaynes." Cross stared at Blanchard, cold hatred in his eyes.

"I'll do that, and if it turns out you're lying to me—" Blanchard stalked out of the room.

Sarge sat at the foot of Doug Smith's bed smoking a cigarette. "That old bastard scares the shit out of me," Sarge said.

"An old man, handcuffed to the bed?" There was contempt in Smith's voice.

Sarge snuffed out his cigarette in an empty coffee cup on the night stand. "They got a tiger up at the National Zoo, been there twenty years at least. That cat will lay there on the other side of that moat and just look at you, never blink. There's no doubt in your mind what he's thinking. That's the kind of look your friend has. I wouldn't want to be Blanchard if he ever got loose."

"How long are you going to keep us here?"

"Until Blanchard gets what he wants. And he will, one way or the other."

"Blanchard didn't have to hit him."

"Gotta agree with you. No way to treat an old guy. I was into a lot of dirty business in 'Nam, but that was war. I almost got into it with Blanchard..." He shrugged. "You gotta make a living."

"You can't let him torture Mr. Cross; he's an old man."

"Out of my hands. I just cook the grub and watch the perimeter. Gets kind of boring, really. Don't even have a TV. Just that damn computer. What am I supposed to do, get on the Internet? You know anything about that computer stuff?"

Smith turned slowly from the window. "You have a computer with a modem?" he asked.

"Downstairs."

Smith said, "I know a little bit about that stuff."

◄18►

Kunming

The helicopter, a French-built Harbin Z-9, sped low across Dianchi Lake, its rotors churning the surface. General Xing Wanpo spoke into his headset, "General Thaung, I had no choice but to send up those fighters. Tell your people not to be alarmed; you are in no danger from us. But you understand this American death squad must be stopped?"

Xing switched off the radio and glanced at Song Zhenyo. "He will help us. The fool appreciates the tanks and guns I've been sending him. Even gunboats for his pathetic navy. Without them, the rebels would overthrow his government in a week. Burma is a very corrupt country, Song Zhenyo. That will not happen in China.

"That city down there was once called the City of Spring. Now it is a city of drugs, all brought in from Burma."

"Yet we still do business with them," Song said.

"Sometimes we sacrifice for the greater good, for our country." Xing bent closer. "If Bao Qing escapes to the West, our revolution—our country—is doomed, you understand?"

Song nodded. "She knows what you are planning."

"More than that. She has taken our honor."

Song smiled weakly. "Yes, honor." Xing had talked about honor during most of the three-hour flight from Beijing. He was a man of dreams, he had proclaimed. And his dream was of a return to the old China, one without decadent Western influence. China's honor must be restored.

Billboards in Beijing sported garish advertisements for Nike and Diet Pepsi, the ubiquitous blue-gray and green People's uniforms had been replaced by the colors and fashions of the West.

Short skirts and high heels. Chinese women parading themselves on the street. It was sickening.

There would be purges, Xing said—not those helpful to the revolution, of course. He had laid his hand on Song's arm. Not those with valuable intelligence connections to the West. In the new order, Song would be a general.

At first, Xing's plot to overthrow the government had seemed preposterous. But as the general went on about the PLA units under his control, his nuclear arsenal, upgraded with the new technology he had bought—and stolen—from the West, it had almost begun to seem plausible. And Song had chosen to ride the tiger. There was no way to dismount.

A few miles west of the city, the square, gray buildings of a military base came into view. As the general's chopper settled onto the landing pad, a jeep and two open trucks filled with soldiers sped toward it across the tarmac.

General Xing jumped from the helicopter, leaving Song to clamber out on his own, head tucked down to avoid the whirling rotors. The general threw a perfunctory salute at the colonel who stood at rigid attention beside his jeep. "Your people will concentrate on monasteries and temples. I have reason to believe she is hiding in one of them."

"General, there are a thousand—"

"Search them all. You are looking for two Americans, a man and a woman. The woman has red hair. That should not be too difficult."

"Many tourists this time of year—" The colonel caught Xing's look and went on hurriedly. "We will find them, General."

"I want all aircraft mobilized. Now!"

"General, what about my regional commander?"

"Tell him nothing. This is a national emergency, you act on my authority only."

The general's crisply pressed uniform jacket flapped in the rotor wash, outlining the muscles of his chest and shoulders. He stood a head taller than the colonel, and his presence was formidable. To oppose him seemed unthinkable. The colonel shrugged his shoulders and moved toward his jeep.

Xing had seized control. And Song was now a "general" in his army. His ear still throbbed with pain—the infection was spreading. Was it worth it just to get back at the man who had disfigured him? The general was walking back toward the helicopter. Too late to worry about it now.

As the helicopter rose off the pad, Xing said, "There are only a few roads into Burma. We will cover every one, search every vehicle if we have to. We have tight control on the Laotian border, but I don't think they will try to go that way, or to Vietnam. I think the Americans had enough of Vietnam." The general allowed himself a thin smile. "You and I will lead the hunt from the air, General Song. How do you like the sound of that, General Song Zhenyo?"

"I am proud to hold that rank."

"You must fight for what you believe in. Do you believe in me—in our cause?"

"Of course, General Xing."

A dozen helicopters now flew in formation beside the general's chopper. But how could you spot one woman in a city of a million people, Song wondered. An insane task, as insane as overthrowing the People's Republic of China. And he was part of the insanity now, Song realized. If the woman got out of the country, the coup was finished, and "General" Song Zhenyo along with it. He raised a pair of binoculars and scanned the rooftops passing below.

The afternoon light, filtered through the dusty warehouse window, touched Anne Hammersmith's high cheekbones and glowed softly on her red hair. Her eyes opened. She sat up and swept the hair back from her face. The dust from the grain sacks around her tickled her nose and she fought the impulse to sneeze. All she needed.

She peeked over the pile of sacks. The driver who had brought them into China sat on the running board of his truck, smoking a cigarette. The driver had offered to take them to a safe house in Kunming, but Nyland had assured him that they would manage on their own. She and Nyland had left the warehouse, but Anne had snuck back in and hidden in a storage loft beneath the rafters. Keep an eye on the driver, Nyland had said.

She had kept watch of the man, but he had done nothing but sit waiting for his truck to be loaded for the haul back to Burma. Nyland had warned her not to trust the man. Maybe he had been wrong. He was wrong about Hausler, she thought, and she had told him so.

She had been surprised at how strongly he had objected to contacting Marty Hausler. Was he jealous? She smiled at the thought. Nyland had been adamant, staring at her in that cold way of his. Their survival depended on security. And there had been too many breaches already—the Strand Hotel, The White Man. The operation was full of holes. Somebody had leaked something.

An hour ago, Nyland had gone to Hauting temple where Bao Qing was waiting. She glanced at her watch. The truck convoy was scheduled to leave for Burma at eleven. Nyland had three hours. His orders then had been clear: if he didn't make it, she was to get on the truck and leave China, forget the twenty-four hour fall-back plan, forget Marty Hausler.

Though she had said nothing at the time, Anne had known she could not leave without Nyland. Her feelings for him had grown over the past few days. They had talked for hours in the back of the truck, and she had felt him open up to her, slowly begin to trust her. He had told her of the murdered Iraqi girl—how he had lain next to her dead body in the spider hole, and the death of his little sister, his feelings of helplessness.

His voice had been barely a whisper, and she leaned closer to catch his words. "It always seemed that everything depended on me. And I always let people down."

"I don't think you let anybody down. There was nothing—"

"But the pain of it. I—I'm afraid of feeling it again."

She had cradled his head against her breast then, and after a while felt his shoulders began to shake. And finally, his tears came. She had wiped them away with the corner of the blanket, and clung to him fiercely as if to protect him from the pain. The memory of it now, the closeness she had felt between them, brought the sting of tears to her own eyes. It was the kind of thing that could grow into love, she thought, if you weren't careful.

But there was more to her feelings about Tuck Nyland. Something about the depth of his commitment to the operation. She had always laughed at the idea of causes. Patriotic nonsense. A job was a job. But for Nyland and Jon Cross, it was—no better words—a mission, something she suddenly longed to be part of.

She rolled onto her stomach and peered over the sacks. Forklifts moved about the warehouse, loading pallets of equipment on the waiting trucks. The main doors were open, letting in the fading afternoon light. The driver squatted near the doorway now, eating a bowl of rice.

A Chinese army truck roared up to the door and half a dozen soldiers leaped out. The driver dropped his rice bowl, leaped to his feet, and ran. The soldiers caught him at the door, and one struck him savagely in the stomach with his rifle butt. All activity in the warehouse had stopped. The workers stood open-mouthed, watching as the soldiers beat the driver.

The soldiers began shouting orders, rounding up the warehouse workers. Which trucks had come in from Burma? Where were the drivers? Asking about Americans. No one knew anything. Anne and Tuck's driver lay unconscious on the warehouse floor, blood pooling around his head. Their way out of China had just been closed.

Anne tore off a piece of her T-shirt and hung it in the dusty window. The emergency signal. She slid backward over the sacks of grain and lowered herself to the warehouse floor. Nyland wouldn't like it, but their only hope now was Marty Hausler.

Bao Qing walked along a flagstone terrace set into the hillside below the Huating temple. The sun had set over the western hills and the light was fading from the calm surface of Dianchi Lake, turning it a deep, cobalt blue. As the dark green leaves of the camellias along the terrace melted into the dusk, their pink and white blossoms seemed suspended in air. Bao Qing sat down on a bench near the wall and gazed at the flowers. How ethereal they seemed, unconnected to the world.

It was almost dark. Jon Cross's people could arrive at any time. There was no way to turn them back, no way to tell them she had changed her mind. It was the helicopters that had done it. She had seen them all afternoon, buzzing like dragonflies over the surface of the lake and circling in the hills. Several times they had flown over the temple, hovering for a moment over the very terrace where she now sat. It was Xing Wanpo, she was certain. He had found out where she had gone. Perhaps someone had talked. Xing was notorious for his interrogation techniques. She forced her mind not to dwell on that subject. She could not risk the lives of the people Jon Cross was sending to her. Enough people had suffered on her behalf.

It was nearly dark now, and deep shadows enveloped the ancient walls of the temple. She smiled grimly. Her worries about the safety of her rescuers had been for nothing. The men weren't coming. Perhaps they were already in the hands of general Xing. She rose, and with a last look down at the lake, walked up toward the monastery.

Three steps up the path she froze. There on the step above lay a single camellia blossom. From the darkness beside the path came a man's voice: "*Wo zai zher.*" The Chinese words meant, "I am here." She turned toward the sound, staring into the thick foliage, but could see no one.

"And I am here," she said in English. "Show yourself."

A tall man, dressed in black, stepped soundlessly onto the path. He picked up the camellia blossom, handed it to her and bowed slightly. Bao Qing cupped the blossom in her hand, studying the man. There were scars on both his cheeks, long white marks that looked like some kind of tribal markings. His eyes were fixed on her, a hint of a smile on his face. There was a fire in them that reminded her of another American she had met so many years ago. His muscles were tense, the energy in him seemed barely contained. A soldier, a fighter, but someone who would leave a flower on the path.

"My name is Tucker Nyland," the man said

"I am Bao Qing."

"The Kingfisher."

"Do you speak the language?" she asked in Mandarin.

He shook his head. "You have heard my entire vocabulary." He held out a small, silk brocade box.

"I know what it is. But I must tell you, I cannot go back with you."

"Then why did you meet me here?"

"There are soldiers everywhere and helicopters searching the city all day, you must have seen them. It is too dangerous for you. Enough people have suffered because of me. Go, please. And take— take that with you."

"I can't do that."

"Go now. The soldiers have been here once. The monks lied to protect me, but the soldiers will be back."

"Where will you go?"

"I don't know," she said. There were tears in her eyes.

"Please take this." Nyland opened the box and laid the blue dragonfly on her palm.

Bao Qing brushed her fingers over the iridescent blue wings. The feathers felt silky to her touch. Their color had not faded over the years. "No, let the memories be enough."

"The helicopters, is it General Xing?"

"You know of him?"

"We believe he is planning to take over the government. Someone has to stop him before he tears this country—your homeland— apart. That someone is you." Nyland stepped back into the bushes and returned with a small cloth bag. "I have your things, including the computer discs. You have to come with me."

"You were in my room?"

"No one saw me."

Headlights flared on the highway below and Bao Qing heard the sound of a truck's engine laboring up the grade, then shouts and the sound of running feet. She felt a powerful arm around her waist. Her feet left the ground and she was being carried through the darkness. She felt an odd sensation of floating. The man, even carrying his burden, made almost no sound as he ran.

Below, on the road, another set of headlights appeared. More soldiers moving toward the monastery. She heard the roar of a helicopter overhead and saw the glare of its searchlight throwing a bright cone of light on the hillside.

As the circle of light moved up the hill toward them, Nyland set her down and crouched beneath a tree. More voices nearby, shouting in Chinese. "They have found a car back up the road," she whispered.

"One I borrowed," Nyland said.

"This way—and I prefer my own two feet." Bao moved down the hillside at a surprising pace, Nyland jogging behind. She paused beside a stone wall. "Where is the car?" she asked.

"Down there, just past the end of the wall. Stay here." The darkness swallowed Nyland's form.

Bao Qing pressed her back against the wall, clutching her canvas bag to her breast. The helicopter hovered over the monastery on the hill above her. She could hear the soldiers working their way through the brush. They seemed to be moving away. There might still be a chance to escape. Strange. A few moments before she had been saying she would not go. Nyland was having none of it. The man's power and assurance had energized her.

Nyland returned in less than five minutes, carrying an AK-47 in his hand. "They left two men with the car. Probably thought we could never reach it." He held her hand, guiding her along the wall.

They stepped over two still forms beside the road, the soldiers left to guard the car. "Are they dead?"

"One is. The other will be out for a while." Nyland helped her into the passenger's seat of a dilapidated sedan and handed her the assault rifle. "Know how to use this?"

Bao nodded. She drew back the bolt, chambered a round, flipped the selector to full automatic, and laid the barrel over the seat back.

Nyland smiled as he swung the car onto the road. The woman must be all of seventy, but she handled the heavy rifle with casual assurance. He glanced in the mirror. The helicopter moved slowly across the brush-covered hillside behind him. A streak of fire shot from the underbelly of the chopper and the hillside erupted in smoke and flames. Pieces of smoldering debris bounced off the roof of the car.

Nyland glanced behind him. "He doesn't even have a target, he's firing blind with his own troops right under him."

"That is Xing Wanpo," Bao said. "Such things do not bother him."

The car rounded a curve and Nyland switched on the lights. A military jeep raced past, but Nyland saw its brake lights flash. It was turning around. Bao leaned over the seat and fired a deafening burst from the AK-47 through the rear window. The jeep's headlights receded. "There, by the stone arch, turn left."

The car slid in the gravel and righted itself on the narrow lane. Nyland glanced in the mirror. Only darkness. They had lost their pursuers.

It took nearly half an hour to reach the trucking warehouse on the north side of town. Nyland drove slowly down the darkened street past the warehouse. Something was wrong. The place should be a beehive of activity. Where were the warehouse workers, the drivers? Lights were on inside the warehouse and Nyland could see trucks and forklifts standing idle. There, behind the dusty loft window where Anne had hidden, hung a scrap of white cloth. Her signal: stay away.

Then he saw the two military jeeps parked beside the warehouse. Their escape route had been discovered. Bao Qing crouched low in the seat. "What is wrong?" she whispered.

"My friend isn't here," Nyland said. "We're on our own."

◀19▶

Kunming

By nightfall, General Xing Wanpo had abandoned his helicopter in favor of his newly acquired command and control vehicle. The C2V had been stolen from a shipment destined for the Fourth Infantry Division at Fort Hood, Texas. The U. S. Army markings had been painted over and the vehicle's forward hatch now sported a cluster of yellow stars on a field of red. General Xing, seated inside at the command console, was marking on a computer screen with an electronic stylus.

Song Zhenyo sat beside the general, his face bathed in the pale glow of the screens. The console had a futuristic look to it; digital readouts and computer screens displayed a constant stream of images, messages from the general's outlying units. The Americans called it an all-source analysis system. Electronic circles and arrows appeared on a computer map as Xing moved the stylus. "We concentrate on this area, along the border," he said. "I want to move troops here...and here. Now, I send this to my field commanders." Xing tapped a key on the computer console. "As soon as the C4I system is in place, every unit, army, navy, and air force will have this information in an instant."

"The new replaces the old." Song studied the monitor before him.

"No, we remember and we honor the old," Xing said. "But a warrior uses every weapon at his command, including common sense. We concentrated on supply convoys from Burma. That is the logical method of entry. Most of the trucks go to the freight terminal district here." He pointed to the screen. "That is where we found the driver who brought the Americans."

"And they will try to escape the same way?" Song asked.

"When they come to meet their ride to the border, we will be waiting. Nyland is yours. A spoil of war."

"He killed two men at the monastery—right under our noses. I don't see how he could have escaped."

"Is that fear in your voice? He is human. He bleeds; he can be killed. That pleasure I reserve for you. And you will enjoy it soon. We'll be at the freight terminal in five minutes."

A red dot glowed on the communications screen, and Xing scowled as he recognized the number flashing below it: the idiots from the PLA counterintelligence branch in Beijing. Always the last to know—anything. Xing flipped a switch. "Go ahead, Beijing."

A metallic voice on the speaker above his head: "General, we have intercepted a telephone call that may be of interest to you."

"I am very busy."

"We have been watching an officer, a colonel in the intelligence liaison's office, for some time now. He is suspected of being in touch with the American CIA."

"Well, arrest him. Why bother me with this"

"The officer's name is Liu Yin. He received a telephone call about an hour ago, spoke to someone in English, a woman with an American accent."

"What did she say, this American?"

"The man who made the intercept speaks no English."

"Was the call recorded?"

The voice was faint, hesitant. "There—was no time."

"Enough of your incompetence. Where is Colonel Liu now?"

"Not far from you." The intelligence man recited a Kunming address. Xing tapped his driver's shoulder. "Hauncheng Street?"

The driver nodded.

"Go!" Xing shouted.

The driver stomped the right brake pedal, and the C2V pivoted abruptly, its steel tracks tearing chunks of concrete from the roadway. Several cars skidded off the road, horns blaring, as the huge vehicle sped by.

As the command vehicle roared back toward town, Xing sat, hands cupped over his earphones listening intently. "Yes, that is what he is doing. We will handle it." Xing took off the headset. To Song, he said, "The area around Highway 20 near the Laotian border has been placed under martial law. A battalion of troops has closed the highway."

"Under whose order?" Song asked.

"Colonel Liu Yin."

"He is trying to block their escape that way?"

General Xing repeated his conversation with the intelligence ministry. "A lesson in tactics, General Song. He is not blocking their escape, he is covering it. His soldiers will allow the vehicle to pass, keeping out the local police. He is helping his CIA friends escape. Nyland will not be back to the warehouse. Colonel Liu has arranged a different escape route. They are going south. They probably got through before we got the roadblocks in place." He punched several buttons on his keyboard and a map appeared on the screen. "There is only one main road south to Laos. Even with a two-hour head start, it is still a long way to the border. Colonel Liu will tell us exactly where to look." The C2V sped through the dark streets of Kunming, scattering cars and cyclos with its raucous horn.

The C2V's maneuver threw Marty Hausler off guard. He heard the roar of its engine and the clatter of its tracks on the pavement as it spun around in front of him. His first thought was that he had been discovered. His second was that the armored vehicle was trying to run him down. The vehicle raced down the center of the street, klaxon blaring. Marty cursed and swung the wheel sharply. The car bounced through the rocks and grass along the shoulder and lurched to a stop, the engine dead. "What the hell was that?" Marty asked.

Anne pulled herself upright in the seat and ran a hand through her hair. "That was a very angry general headed in exactly the wrong direction."

"How do we know this?"

"That was a third-generation command and control vehicle

owned by the U.S. Army. There are only four of them in the world. Three are in Fort Hood, Texas. The fourth one just ran us off the road. Xing was testing it out in the northern provinces last week. I happened to be listening to his conversations."

"He was headed for the freight terminal district." Marty said. "Looks like he changed his mind."

"That terminal is going to be crawling with troops. We have to warn Nyland."

Marty ground the starter, and after a moment it caught. He slipped the car in gear and eased out the clutch. The vehicle lurched forward with a loud scraping noise. A red light flashed on the dash. "Oil pan's punctured," he said.

"The warehouse is at least a mile, can we make it?"

Marty stepped on the gas. "Have to," he said.

Nyland lay on the flat tin roof of a shack across the street from the warehouse. The soldiers had moved their jeeps inside and hidden themselves behind the wooden pallets and crates stacked beside the doors. A few workers moved slowly around the warehouse, pretending to work, glancing nervously at the hidden soldiers.

And where was Anne? Had they discovered her hiding place in the loft? The warning flag she had left in the window was undisturbed, but Nyland felt fear tighten his stomach. What if she was being interrogated, tortured? He remembered the soft warmth of her next to him in the truck, the feel of her body entwined with his as they made love in the hotel room in Maymyo.

But the fear was different this time. Anne was no fragile soul needing his protection, not like his sister, or the little girl in Iraq. She was a trained intelligence officer, a professional. No one had forced her to go on this mission. He remembered how quickly and forcefully she had moved against her attacker in the Strand Hotel, disabling him with a kick to the head. A woman who could take care of herself. No, the fear was something different, not the paralyzing ache of being responsible, always being to blame. It was, he suddenly realized, a sharp, aching fear of losing someone precious to you. A fear that no amount of training could overcome. Was he in love with Anne Hammersmith, he wondered?

The sound of a car's engine roaring at full throttle caught his attention. The soldiers across the street had heard it too. They raised their heads cautiously over the stacks of pallets, rifles trained down the street. The car itself appeared a moment later, careening toward the warehouse, flames erupting from beneath its hood. It scraped the side of a parked truck, tilted on two wheels, and crashed through the wooden wall of the warehouse, exploding in a ball of fire.

The soldiers scrambled to escape as flames leaped up the walls. A burning timber fell across an army truck igniting its gas tank. The explosion threw several of the soldiers onto the floor.

From the corner of his eye, Nyland caught a flash of movement in an alley to his right. Two people running toward him. Anne with another man who could only be Marty Hausler. Nyland slid off the roof and dropped into the muddy alley in front of them. "Quite an entrance," he said.

"You, too," Anne smiled. "Diversion was Marty's idea. Rag in the gas tank, jam the throttle."

"Elementary physics," Marty said.

"Appreciate it." Nyland was staring at Hausler. To Anne, he said, "I thought we talked about this."

"Tuck, will you stop being the goddamn Lone Ranger? Marty is trying to help save our asses here."

Nyland put his hands on her shoulders. "You're right. I got a little crazy there, thought they had you."

There were tears in Anne's eyes. "...thought they had *you*, Tucker." She sat down her aluminum case and threw her arms around him.

Nyland pulled her close, cradling her head gently in his hand.

"They'll have us all if we don't get the fuck out of here," Hausler said. As the three Americans ran down the sidewalk, their shadows raced before them, stark black in the reddish glow of the fire. The wail of sirens was growing louder.

★ ★ ★

Nyland threw open the back door of his stolen car. Bao Qing pushed aside her blanket and stared at him. In her hand was a lethal-looking knife. "Who are these people?" she asked.

"Anne, Marty, meet the Kingfisher."

Anne climbed in back beside Bao Qing, Hausler took the front passenger's seat. As he drove, Nyland recounted his escape from the monastery with Bao Qing. "General Xing must be getting desperate. The PLA is all over this goddamn place. I counted fifteen choppers in the air at one point."

"He was firing air-to-ground rockets on his own troops at the monastery," Bao Qing said. "Dangerous man. Insane."

Anne laid her hand on Qing's arm. "Are you OK?"

"I didn't want to come, too much risk for all of you. He persuaded me," Bao Qing said. "Picked me up like a child, most undignified." She chuckled. "Very strong man."

Nyland said, "Either we take you back or we don't go."

"Things are starting to look like we don't go," Anne said. "General Xing has the whole damn city covered. Obviously, our ride back to Burma is canceled."

"There is one piece of good news, Tuck," Marty said. "We got in touch with an old friend of mine from Afghanistan, Colonel Liu Yin."

Bao Qing threw him a sharp glance. "That man is known to the MSS. They believe he is in contact with your CIA."

"They're right," Hausler said. "He agreed to help us get out of the country.

Nyland asked, "Help us how?"

"He sent the order to mobilize troops down along the Laotian border, make it look like we're headed that way."

"Will General Xing buy that?" Nyland asked.

"We better hope he does."

"I've got a plan." Anne opened her aluminum case. "This worked once, maybe it will work again." She opened the cover of Doug Smith's computer. "I intercepted the general's radio traffic a few weeks ago. Smith has the same software on his machine." Anne turned on the laptop and hit a series of keys. "Tuck, can you find a road that goes uphill? I need a little elevation to give me some line-of-sight."

"Turn right up ahead, go west," Bao Qing said. She looked at Anne's computer screen and shook her head. "Xing is now using the digital system in the C2V. It is back-ciphered, never repeats in the same order. You cannot intercept him without the decoding protocol."

"Where would I get something like that?"

Bao smiled. "I wrote it."

★ ★ ★

It was nearly ten o'clock when Nyland parked the car on a deserted road in the western hills above Kunming in China's Yunnan Province. The lights of the city spread out before them, subdued and warm, like an old tapestry. Missing were the brightly lit high rises and glaring sheets of neon that marked American cities. But that would soon change, Nyland knew. Driving through the city, he had seen the massive modernization effort the Chinese had begun, tearing down the historic old city, putting up a shiny, modern facade. The new China, he thought ruefully, how many had there been?

Anne and Bao Qing sat in the back seat, heads bent over the computer screen that was now connected to Anne's radio receiver. The computer was reading the discs Bao Qing had brought from the intelligence ministry. Tuck and Marty walked away from the car, leaving the women to their technical discussions.

Hausler bent to pick up a small stone and hurled it away into the darkness.

"Anne tells me you were against contacting me," Marty said.

"I saw no reason to take the risk."

"We're all taking a risk here. Colonel Liu set up a diversion, bought us a few hours. Probably risked his life doing it."

"You're Anne's boyfriend?" Nyland kept his voice even.

"I want to marry her, if it's any of your business."

"So you want to look good in front of her."

"Look, Nyland, you need my help whether you want it or not. What's between Anne and me has nothing to do with it."

Nyland shrugged his shoulders. "Whatever you say." Why did he feel this sudden animosity toward Hausler? The man was only trying to help. And he was right, whatever he and Anne had going was his business. Nyland thought of the way Anne had hugged him: thought they had you. Crying, touching his face. Nyland had seen the quick flash of anger in Hausler's eyes. Anne's presence hung between them. Which one did she favor? He pushed the thought from his mind. The kind of schoolyard thinking that got you killed.

"I managed to steal an AK," Nyland said. "It's in the trunk. We can bust a few road blocks if we have to, even travel overland. I've done it before. But one thing is certain. I'm going to deliver Kingfisher to Jon Cross if I have to carry her on my back. And we're gonna make it. Believe that, Marty. Anything, or anybody, that gets in my way...."

Hausler nodded and walked away without speaking. His thoughts, too, were on Anne as he stood looking out over the lights of Kunming. You would have to be blind to miss the signs of affection that passed between her and Nyland. And to miss Nyland's hostility toward him.

What had happened on the long trip from Burma? Anne had said only that Nyland really knew his way around in the field. She told him about the attack in the hotel room in Rangoon, what an effective team the two had been. Her eyes had been glowing with excitement. A little girl in the big world of espionage, an eager student with a very experienced teacher. What else had Nyland taught her, Hausler wondered.

Below, a revolving beacon caught his eye. It was situated on what appeared to be a small control tower, and nearby, a twin string of blue lights. Runway lights. Anne's shout from the car interrupted the thought growing within him.

"We intercepted the bastard," she said. "Come and listen."

★ ★ ★

Kunming

Song Zhenyo's shirt was splattered with blood. His fists were clenched, there was a glint of madness in his eyes. He screamed at the man tied in the chair. "You are lying, Colonel Liu!" He smashed his fist into the man's face. "Where are the Americans going—which way?"

General Xing grabbed Song's arm. "Don't kill him—yet."

Colonel Liu spat out blood and bits of broken teeth. "Please, no more. Highway 23, toward Laos. They think you will be looking for them on the Burma Road." Liu's head sank onto his chest.

General Xing's voice was strangely gentle. "What have you told the CIA about me?"

Liu shook his head. His eyes were nearly swollen shut. He turned toward the sound of Xing's voice. "No CIA—helping a friend."

"Now you will help me." Xing motioned to an enlisted man standing near the front door. The man brought a military radio in a green canvas case. Xing cut the ropes from Liu's wrists. "Call your field commander, tell him to hold the Americans—on my order. Release them only to General Song."

Liu's voice gained strength as he spoke, relaying Xing's orders. "You will tell no one, understand?" There was a crackling of static, and an affirmative reply. The microphone dropped from his hands.

Xing snorted derisively. "Excellent."

Song turned his back on the prisoner and whispered to Xing, "You ordered them to release the Americans to me? You aren't going?"

"You will go in my place. I've have been away from Beijing too long. The Central Military Commission will demand an explanation as it is. Besides, our great operation will commence very soon, there is much planning to do. But we cannot act while Bao Qing and these Americans are still running around free. You are in command now, General. What are you going to do?"

"He knows more than he is telling. He can lead us to Nyland." Song slapped the man across the face, knocking him to the floor. "Where is he?"

"He will tell us everything eventually," Xing said.

As he lay on the floor, Liu Yin could feel the pain receding. The drug he had taken was starting to work. The powerful poison would kill him in minutes, a painless death, he had been told. Unlike life, he thought. The figures of the two men swam before his eyes, but they no longer mattered. He had relayed the cover story he and Martin Hausler had concocted, sold the general on the Laos route. Perhaps Hausler and his friends would still be able to escape.

Now, in the last moments of his life, he smiled. Long ago, in Afghanistan, Marty Hausler had saved his life. The debt had been paid. The figures of the two men moved closer. He raised his head and smiled, watching their faces fade into blackness.

◄20►

Falls Church

Sarge dozed in the overstuffed chair in front of the computer, snoring softly. Doug Smith leaned slowly over the sleeping man and laid his fingers on the keyboard.

Sarge had polished off an entire six-pack of Rolling Rock while surfing the Internet under Smith's tutelage. The young computer expert had shown him how to find websites about weapons, mercenaries, and finally, naked women. Sarge had been a fast learner. The beers had disappeared at an increasing rate as he scrolled through the lurid scenes of sex and debauchery, hardly mindful of the prisoner he was supposed to be guarding.

"Look at that, little buddy, all these women *shave*. Never had me a woman who..." Sarge had sunk back into his chair and closed his eyes.

Since they had been taken prisoner, Doug Smith had almost gotten to like the man. The hostage syndrome. Though Smith had nothing in common with the fifty-year-old soldier of fortune, he had come to see him as honorable underneath the bluff, beery exterior. Sarge's name, he learned, was Bill Wiley.

Over the past two days, Sarge had grown increasingly angry at Charles Blanchard's treatment of Jon Cross. Cross had been deprived of sleep, given drugs, and beaten by Blanchard, who seemed to be growing more desperate by the hour as Cross refused to talk.

Earlier that evening, Sarge had allowed Doug a few moments alone with Cross while he went to prepare supper. As soon as Sarge had left the room, Cross opened his eyes and smiled crookedly at Smith, wincing at the pain from his split lip. He had seemed confused and disoriented as Smith sat down on the bed beside him.

Smith whispered, "I don't know if you can understand me, but there is a computer here, with a modem."

Cross, hands still cuffed to the iron bed rail, motioned with his head for Smith to bend closer. In a surprisingly clear voice, he whispered, "Room is bugged. Get a message to Nyland. He has to know that Blanchard is a double agent working for the Chinese. That way, somebody knows—somebody we can trust—in case Blanchard tries to cover all this up by killing you and me. I'm sorry I dragged you into all this, Doug. I had no right."

Smith shook his head. "I'm a grown-up, I knew the risks."

"You have to get a message to Langley. I don't want to tell Jaynes where we are, but if we don't..."

"Blanchard will kill us both," Smith whispered.

Cross's eyes had been closed when Sarge came with the food. Doug had been sitting on the bed, gently wiping dried blood off Cross's face. Sarge snorted in disgust. "Son of a bitch had no call to work the old man over like that. I'm supposed to keep him awake, but hell, let him sleep. Blanchard ain't coming back tonight."

Now, Smith worked furiously at the computer as Sarge slept in the chair beside him. It was nearly two in the morning, but he had never felt more alive. His fingers flew over the keys, sending lines of computer code along the mysterious back channels that were the domain of hackers and spies. He left a message on a server in Germany that he knew his laptop would automatically retrieve when Anne Hammersmith turned it on, assuming Nyland had gotten it to her.

The second step was to contact Robert Jaynes. Sarge had unwittingly given him an idea earlier in the evening when he had casually mentioned that Blanchard used the computer to communicate with the White House. He was probably using the EX-10 system, a network that included the CIA. It hadn't taken Smith long to hack into the secure White House network and send his message to Robert Jaynes.

★   ★   ★

Langley

Robert Jaynes called an emergency meeting at 2:00 A.M. He stood at the head of the long mahogany table, a satellite photograph in his hand. A computer sat on the table beside him, its screen glowing white. George DeLong of Science and Technology, and Scott Brader of counterintelligence were unloading papers from their briefcases. "Thank you for coming at such short notice."

"What's the urgency?" Brader asked.

"The satellite's picking up a lot of troop movement along the Laotian border. The Chinese Tenth Ranger Group is closing off the whole area. I'm guessing it involves Jon Cross."

"So they're trying to block this agent of his?" DeLong asked.

"They would hardly mobilize to keep him from getting in," Brader said.

DeLong tapped a pencil on the table. "Doesn't that mean he's on our side?"

Brader shook his head. "He's disappeared. That's *de facto* evidence—"

A red light on Jaynes's telephone flashed. He snatched up the receiver. "Patch it through." As he hung up the phone and switched on his computer, a string of letters appeared on the screen: URGENT: Have you briefed Blanchard?

Jaynes typed on the screen: Where are you?

Don't know. Blanchard has us. Tell the president.

Jaynes and the others stared at the monitor. Jaynes typed, Why believe you? An answer: Blanchard agent for China MSS. Blackmailed by Song Zhenyo. Wants China agent killed to cover himself.

Jaynes typed, Chinese have closed the Laotian border. How are you bringing your agent out? The screen stayed blank. He typed again: Are you defecting?

The response came a moment later: Contact FBI and White House.

Send—the message disappeared abruptly, leaving the screen glowing white.

"He got cut off," Brader said. "Send what? Help?"

"It's all disinformation," DeLong said.

Brader nodded. "Cross is just using Smith's little computer tricks to throw us off while he smuggles that agent out."

"Buying time."

Jaynes held up his hand for silence. He was buying time as well, regaining his composure, keeping his face expressionless as his mind raced. Relax, he told himself. No one could connect him with Charles Blanchard, the *X* on his to-do list. "All right," he said finally. "Let's think this through. If Cross—assuming that was him—was going over the Chinese, why take the risk of contacting us?"

"Send us on the wrong track?" DeLong asked.

"Let's assume for a minute Cross was being straight with us. Blanchard has him, Blanchard is being run by the Chinese—we're supposed to go to the president with this?" Jaynes asked. "That his secretary of defense is working for the Chinese?"

DeLong said, "Play right into Cross's hands, jam ourselves up?"

"I say we tell the DCI and let him call the FBI, the Justice Department. Let them handle this career-limiting bullshit," Brader said.

Jaynes leaned back in the soft leather chair. "Cross used to say the principal job of the CIA was covering its own ass. It looks like we're well on our way to proving him right."

Brader was not to be dissuaded. "Cross tells us this preposterous tale about Blanchard 'having' him? The secretary of defense holding him hostage? We're supposed to believe this shit?"

The phone rang. Jaynes snatched it up and listened intently: "You're certain? Thank you." Jaynes replaced the receiver. "Perhaps we should believe this shit, as you call it. Cross was using the EX-10 network just now."

DeLong laid his gold pen on the table, a stunned look on his face. "That's a local White House network. Cross is in Washington!"

Jaynes's hands trembled slightly on the latches of his briefcase, but his voice was calm. "Is he?"

Falls Church

Doug Smith felt the pistol jab his ribs, and reached for the computer's power switch. "You just stay absolutely still, little buddy." Sarge stood up unsteadily, gripping Smith's arm. "You're a clever little son of a bitch, I'll give you that."

"I was just surfing the net, like—" Smith said.

Sarge tightened his grip, twisting Smith's arm painfully. "You sent a message to somebody, you better tell me who."

"Nobody, just fooling around."

"Sorry, little buddy." Sarge smashed the pistol barrel against Smith's temple.

★ ★ ★

Kunming

Nyland and Hausler lay side by side in the tall grass. The runway lights cast a bluish glow on Nyland's cheek as he scanned the hangars across the tarmac.

The two men had lain silently for the past twenty minutes, watching the small airport put itself to bed. There were two military police jeeps and an armored car stationed by the access road. Perhaps half-a-dozen PLA soldiers had set up a makeshift checkpoint a hundred yards down the road outside the entrance gate. The rest of the airport was enclosed by a high chain link fence. Several cars were parked by the terminal building, caretaker staff.

A flashing strobe on the control tower revealed a row of small planes on a concrete apron. An aging passenger jet was parked in front of a hangar nearby. Marty was studying the small planes.

"I like the little four-seater, second from the end," he said. "Air Force trainer, looks like."

"How much time do you need?" Nyland asked.

"Ten minutes, at least. To fire the damn thing up, get a little oil pressure, taxi down to the south end of the runway. Assuming Anne and Bao Qing get there, hell, it might even work."

"How bad do you need the runway lights?"

"They'd be handy. What did you have in mind?"

"A little fireworks. Main thing is to get Anne and Bao on board. If I don't show up, get the hell out of here."

"You don't think Anne would let me leave you here?"

"Kingfisher is our priority." Nyland picked up the AK-47. "Keep your eye on those transformers, the pole just to the right of the terminal." He ran across the runway.

From where he lay, Marty could see Nyland's muzzle flashes in the hangar's doorway. The explosion on the power pole plunged the airport into darkness. The soldiers near the gate were shouting and Marty heard the roar of the armored car's engine. The .50 caliber machine gun on the turret was their biggest threat, he knew. How could Nyland knock it out with a rifle? There was no time to think about that.

Marty ran toward the trainer and pulled away the wheel chocks. An explosion behind him lit up the runway. One of the engines on the passenger jet had burst into flames. A second later, the fuel tanks blew, sending pieces of sheet metal into the air. Marty felt the pressure of the explosion against his eardrums. He cranked the engine.

Fire had spread to the hangars and somewhere a siren began to wail. A jeep raced along the apron, red light flashing. Suddenly, the driver toppled from his seat and his body bounced onto the pavement. The jeep careened off the apron and crashed into the chain link fence. Nyland's aim had been good.

Marty watched his gauges. Oil pressure and engine temperature climbing slowly. There was no time for a decent preflight, just get the goddamn thing in the air. He eased the throttle forward and taxied out onto the darkened runway. Navigating by moonlight, he taxied toward the south end of the runway. The light of the flames behind him cast a grotesque shadow of the plane before him. Too much light. If the armored car spotted him, the plane would be torn to pieces by its heavy machine gun.

Anne and Bao Qing ran toward the plane and scrambled into the rear seat. Anne gripped Marty's shoulder. "Where's Tuck?"

"He's coming." Marty's voice was tight.

It was hard to tell what was happening at the terminal building. The fire seemed to be spreading. Several small planes were burning. Marty could see figures waving their arms, motioning to a fire truck. The armored car had joined the cluster of vehicles on the periphery of the fire and Hausler could see soldiers climbing from the rear hatch, raising their weapons and firing at the roof of the control tower. No one was looking toward the south end of the runway where the trainer sat, propeller spinning. Nyland had created a hell of diversion, Hausler thought, now where was he?

Marty looked at his watch. Five minutes.

Anne reached over the back seat and clutched Marty's shoulder. "We can't leave him."

"In another couple of minutes, they're going to figure out what's going on. They'll have air cover in here, those gunships we've been seeing all day. If we wait, they'll blow us out of the sky. Our only chance is to get out now, head for the mountains, stay under the radar."

"Armored car, coming this way," Bao Qing said.

The armored vehicle had turned from the flaming buildings and was lumbering toward them. Marty's hand was on the throttle, but he hesitated. There wasn't time to get airborne before the heavy machine gun tore the plane to pieces. "Get out, run," he shouted.

But the armored car had changed direction, rumbling into a slow turn, pointing the .50 caliber back at the soldiers near the hangers. A stream of tracers burst from the weapon, tearing into the group of soldiers. Several collapsed on the pavement, the rest dived behind the fire truck.

"It's Nyland," Anne shouted. "He stole their armored car!" Marty shoved the plane's throttle forward.

Nyland jumped off the armored car and raced toward the plane. Anne held the door open as he threw himself in. She clutched his hand as the plane gathered speed. Several soldiers had crawled from beneath the fire truck and were shooting at the small plane. A side window exploded and Anne wrapped her arm protectively around Bao Qing. Nyland crawled out on the strut and fired a burst over the top of the cabin. The plane was gaining speed. "Get back inside," Marty shouted. "We're almost out of runway." He grunted in pain and the Cessna slewed sideways.

Nyland dropped back into his seat and slammed the cabin door. "Shut it down!"

"Too late for that," Marty said.

He hauled the stick back, the nose wheel lifted off the runway, and the plane was airborne. A second later, the chain link fence flashed beneath them. As the plane gained altitude, the light from the flames faded behind them.

"Where are you hit?" Nyland asked.

"My back. Nothing serious. Seat cushion took most of it."

"First aid kit back here," Anne said. "Let me put a compress on it."

Marty nodded, sweat beading on his face. She slid a gauze pad between his back and the seat cushion. "Tape should hold it in place until we get down."

"If we get down," Marty said.

"Press your back against the seat. It's the best we can do for now."

Marty banked the plane toward the west and set the autopilot. Below them a string of headlights wound through the darkness toward the mountains.

Marty nodded at the scene below. "Our navigation system."

"Follow the highway?" Anne said.

"It's all we have," Nyland said.

◂21▸

Robert Jaynes had been awake for nearly twenty-four hours, most of it spent working at his desk. He had not even bothered to take off his suit jacket. His only concession to comfort had been to loosen the knot on his red silk necktie. He was making notes on his yellow pad: Options regarding *X*. Jaynes was only now recovering from the shock of seeing Charles Blanchard's name on his computer screen at the emergency meeting. Had the secretary of defense really kidnaped Jon Cross? If so, his special informant at CIA, Robert Jaynes's, had certainly aided and abetted.

Jaynes's list of options was short. He could distance himself from Blanchard. There was no evidence linking the two, a few telephone calls on a scrambled phone. No one could prove he passed unauthorized intelligence information. However, if Blanchard was holding Cross prisoner, he had crossed the line. Such an act could earn him a death sentence, along with anyone else he chose to implicate. Option two: join forces with Blanchard, try to round up Nyland and the Chinese agent, keep everything quiet, protecting Blanchard from his blackmailers. There were major shakeups coming in American intelligence. Charles Blanchard would owe him. The payoff would be the DCI's job, his career would be made.

Jaynes scrawled a note on his yellow pad and bowed his head, eyes closed. He had made his decision. He had written "...conscience asks the question, 'Is it right?'" Martin Luther King's words had been running through his head all night, along with thoughts of his Irish Catholic father and his constant sermons about duty and country. Had he been a religious man, Jaynes thought, this would be a good time to pray.

But it was time to put away his selfish desires, his impossible dream of a CIA directorship. It was time to act for the good of the country, not the good of Robert Jaynes. He had to bring down Charles Blanchard.

All ninety-six stations on the White House's EX-10 network were in the Washington area, the computer people had told him, but they didn't have exact locations. But was Cross really in Washington? Doug Smith, his computer wizard, could have planted a false electronic trail. Cross could be anywhere.

He had been wrong about Jon Cross, had let his personal feelings get in the way of ferreting out the truth. He had dishonored his family name and now, he must put it right, whatever the cost...

Jaynes's eyes blinked shut for a moment, and he felt his head droop with fatigue. No. Stay with it. Concentrate. Jaynes remembered the missing two hours on Cross's C-130 flight. Suppose someone had ordered the plane to land or forced it down somehow. Force meant armed aircraft, fighter planes. And who but the White House had that kind of power? Somebody like, say, the secretary of state.

Cross had asked that the FBI be called in. That didn't sound like Jon Cross. He usually had little good to say about the agency. But if Cross were telling the truth, and the White House was involved in some kind of kidnaping plot, it would have to be handled by the FBI.

Jaynes flipped through his Rolodex and dialed a number. FBI Special Agent Edward Dwyer came on the line. "Didn't expect to hear from you people." His voice was chilly.

"I have something to run by you. Could we meet somewhere?"

"What's wrong with my office?"

"You'll understand when we talk," Jaynes said.

"Tonight. Nine o'clock, Key Bridge Marriott. I'll wear my trench coat." Dwyer hung up.

Wearily, Jaynes returned to his list. The next item was Laos. The CIA station there was still reporting Chinese border forces on alert. The satellite cameras showed unusual troop movement along Highway 23, the main road from Kunming to the Laotian border. All the Agency analysts argued for Laos as the likely escape route. It made more operational sense, they reasoned. It was the most direct route.

Burma was too much of a gamble. The road to the China-Burmese border was long and tortuous. It would be very easy for the Chinese to block. Yet Cross's team had made it in, gotten past Jaynes's people, past the Burmese army. And breaking out the same way, no matter how impossible it seemed, was the kind of thing a wild man like Nyland might do.

Jaynes glanced at his watch. It was almost noon. The middle of the night in Western China. His head had begun to throb. Maybe Cross's team had gone to ground for the night. Maybe they were already out of the country. They would have had to sprout wings, and—

Wings.

He tossed his pen aside and pawed through a pile of personnel folders he had ordered from the records section. He flipped through Hausler's file. There, under special qualifications: Martin Hausler was a certified pilot, qualified for multi-engine and rotor-wing aircraft.

Jaynes studied the large-scale map of Burma on his bulletin board. A quick calculation told him that even in a single-engine plane, it was less than a two-hour flight to the Burmese border. They could already be out of China. He reached for the phone.

A faint buzzing in his ear, then Don Shenk's voice from Maymyo: "I was about to call you. We may have—"

Jaynes interrupted, "I think Nyland is headed your way by airplane. Hausler is a pilot."

"Information may be too late," Shenk said. "I just talked to The White Man; there's bad news—or good news, depending on your point of view. Chinese fighter planes have been flying along the border most of the night, which means they think he's coming this way. But the border patrol just reported a small plane crash near a Burmese village called Mong Yu, just across the Chinese border."

"Have they searched the wreckage? Did anybody survive?"

"Hard to tell," Shenk said. "There was a fireball—down in a canyon. They can't go in until daylight."

"Get up there and secure that crash site. Use whatever influence you have with The White Man; pay him if you have to. The

sun will be coming up in about three hours. I want a report."
Jaynes hung up.

Good news or bad news, depending on your point of view. If
Nyland and his team had crashed in a canyon, most of Robert
Jaynes's problems would be over, he thought. Jon Cross's sleeper
agent would be dead, and all that remained would be to locate
Cross, himself. And he would do it all by the book, no half-assed
kidnaping schemes. He would call Charles Blanchard at home later,
ask him point blank about Cross—startle the truth out of him. He
set the alarm on his wristwatch, lay down on the leather sofa by the
window, and went to sleep.

★ ★ ★

Yunnan Province, China

The air force base at Jiang Cheng sat on a high plateau in the
mountains ten miles from the Laotian border. The morning sun was
just touching the radar dishes on the mountaintop above the runway. The small cluster of hangars, barracks, and maintenance buildings were the only sign of habitation on the barren plateau. The base,
unlike many such remote facilities, was scrupulously neat. Garrison
troops swept the compound daily with straw brooms, paying special
attention to a cement block building behind a barbed wire fence
near the main runway, reserved for visiting brass. The base commander had alerted everyone about the general arriving from Kunming, called a full formation to meet his helicopter the night before.
Song Zhenyo, acting on orders from General Xing, himself.

Soldiers pushing their straw brooms took special care of the
dirt path leading up to the fence, raising industrious clouds of dust.
They stopped and came to attention as the base commander
approached. Two guards stood outside the entrance, the first light
of dawn glinting on their bayonets.

Then, as if on some prearranged signal, General Song made his
entrance. He wore a rumpled field uniform, there was a white bandage wrapped around his head. One of the guards fought to suppress
a smile.

The colonel commanding the remote air field was a seasoned veteran. He stood at rigid attention as Song Zhenyo approached. Without preamble, Song said, "Two of your SU-27s flew a mission last night. Why was I not informed?"

"I have no such orders. The garrison commander in Kunming called me. We were to search the border area for a small plane. One of the fighters located it for a moment on radar, but it was flying low in a deep canyon near the Burmese border. We lost it. The fighters returned just before dawn. I am happy to render the general any assistance possible." The colonel's voice was rigidly formal.

"This small plane, is it the same one that was stolen from Kunming?" Song asked.

"We assume so. There are no flights at night over the mountains. A small plane at low altitude...suicide."

"Did the plane cross the border?"

"It is possible. But surely the Burmese army would have spotted them. All the airfields in Shan State are heavily guarded. There would be no place to land."

"Have my helicopter refueled. I am leaving immediately. I will deal with you later," Song said. He turned and walked toward his command helicopter where the pilot stood holding the door open.

Yunnan Province

The mountains along China's western border were desolate, forbidding. Only a scattering of pine forests broke the monotony of the barren highlands. Some of the peaks rose to ten thousand feet, eternally capped with snow. Few roads ran through the region.

Highway 3, the Burma Road, appeared below Song's helicopter as a thin gray line winding its way through the canyons. Shadows from the puffy clouds drifted over the ground in the early morning sunlight. A beautiful morning, and, for the first time in many days, Song felt a growing sense of optimism. He was on the hunt, and the forces of the PLA were at his disposal. Nyland could not escape such a force. Song fingered the silver star on the collar of his fatigues and remembered the fear in the base commander's eyes as he stood at rigid attention. Fear of Song Zhenyo. General Xing had returned to Beijing the day before to make final preparation for his coup—he had discussed it openly with his newest general. He had made it clear that everything depended on finding Bao Qing before she escaped to the West.

Just before he boarded his plane, Xing had gripped Song's arm roughly, a maniacal light in his eyes. His voice was a cold whisper: "The hour is very near. I will not tolerate failure."

Song had heard Xing's voice in his dreams.

He trained his binoculars on the road. Even at this early hour of the morning, traffic was heavy, mostly covered trucks and vans snaking their way toward the border. And somewhere down there was Tuck Nyland, the man who had mutilated him. Had he made it into Burma? Song was flying near the spot where Nyland's small plane had last been seen by the Chinese fighters.

The pilot tapped Song on the shoulder and pointed to a headset hanging on the console. "The Burmese general," he said.

Song pressed the headphone against his good ear and spoke into the microphone. "Thaung Lwin, you have done General Xing many favors in the past. Now, on the general's behalf, I must ask for one more."

"I assume you are looking for a certain aircraft?" Thaung said.

"What do you know about this certain aircraft?"

"I am aware that your fighter planes were flying near our border most of the night, but I doubt that you are planning an invasion. When I heard of this rogue aircraft, I thought—"

"What did you hear?" Song pressed the earphone closer.

"We've found the plane. It went down in a canyon about five miles over the border."

"Was anyone—"

"My soldiers rappeled down to the crash site—here is the curious thing—no bodies in the wreckage."

"How is that possible? Did they survive, escape into the mountains?"

"No one survived that crash, General Song. What wasn't burned was scattered down the canyon."

"There were four people in that plane."

"And you know their identities?" Thaung asked.

"It is imperative that I find them if they are still alive."

"It is imperative that *we* find them. They are, after all, in *my* country."

"I would like permission to cross the border, meet you at your headquarters. We need to work together—it is vital."

There was a faint crackle of static on the radio, then Thaung said, "Follow the highway across the border. Our helicopters will escort you to Maymyo." Song switched off the radio, leaned back in the seat, and rubbed his eyes. Where had his quarry gone?

The pilot looked questioningly at Song. Burma? Song nodded. The helicopter banked sharply and raced toward the border.

★   ★   ★

China-Burma Border

Anne Hammersmith laid small branches on the fire and fanned the flames with her hand. To the east, the horizon was just beginning to lighten. No smoke, Nyland had warned her. As soon as there was light, the planes and helicopters would be back looking for them. But the bitter cold mountain air had crept through her thin clothing and she shivered as she put her feet close to the fire. The purple silk scarf she wore loosely tied around her neck provided little warmth, but there was no reason to completely give up your femininity just because you were out in the boondocks.

Bao Qing lay sleeping on a bed of pine needles nearby, a survival blanket tucked around her. Its silver metallic coating reflected the morning light on her face, softening the lines. She looked almost childlike in repose, Anne thought.

Their campsite was just below the crest of a ridge, hidden in a deep stand of pine trees. In the canyon below, she could see the highway, the Burma Road, winding its way westward. A small collection of huts and several army trucks marked the checkpoint—the spot where China became Burma. At least a dozen soldiers milled around the checkpoint. Several more were setting up a heavy machine gun in the rocks above the road. Could it have been yesterday they had passed that checkpoint on their way into China? This was the third day, she thought, that Tuck Nyland had been in her life. How many more did they have left?

He was somewhere down there now, looking for a way out. The troops were on full alert. She wanted to shout at him down the mountain: be careful.

He had been gone for nearly an hour, and Anne had never felt so alone. The silence of the forest was profound. She imagined ghosts in every shadow. At times like this it was easy to see how legends of the abominable snowman stayed alive. She felt tears sting her eyes, and wiped them away angrily. She had wanted to be in the field, and now, goddamn it, that was exactly where she was. Better tend to business.

The batteries in her computer were dangerously low, and the cold wasn't helping. She unzipped her rucksack, pulled out the battery pack, and placed it inside her jacket, shivering as the cold metal touched her breasts.

Bao Qing shifted slightly, trying to get comfortable on her bed of pine boughs. The woman had never once complained, except when Nyland picked her up and carried her. She had stopped to catch her breath, her face looked haggard in the moonlight. She was not a child, she protested as he swept her into his arms. They had followed a pack trail nearly five miles, mostly uphill, from the spot on the highway where Hausler had landed the plane.

They were all looking like hell, Anne thought. Lucky to survive this long night. And they owed a lot to Marty Hausler. The man was a gifted pilot. Guided only by the light of the moon, he had set the plane down in the middle of the Burma Road. As soon as Nyland, Anne and Qing had climbed out, he spun the plane around and raced back down the highway. A truck had rounded the corner, catching the onrushing plane in its headlights. The driver had veered into the ditch just as Marty lifted off.

The plane circled to the west and disappeared in the night sky. The driver pulled back on the road and continued his journey. There would be tales to tell when he got to his destination.

Nyland had found the trail near the highway and they had started to walk, stumbling in places where the trees were thick and the moonlight could not penetrate. The moon had set just after three, Anne remembered. It was then they had camped in the forest to wait for dawn.

Now it was dawn, where the hell was Nyland?

She started at a small sound behind her, and turned, hand pressed against her mouth. Nyland stood in the shadows, the limp form of a small animal in his hand. "Is that breakfast?" she said.

"Rabbit." He knelt down in the pine needles and pulled a black commando knife from his boot. Anne watched him skin and gut the rabbit, his movements quick and exact. He laid the carcass aside and began sharpening a small stick. "I have a fondness for rabbit." Bao Qing sat up and rubbed her hands together over the fire.

"How are you feeling? Did you get enough rest?" Nyland said. He jabbed the sharpened stick in the ground, suspending the rabbit carcass over the flames.

"Fussing is not necessary."

Nyland wiped his bloody hands on his pants leg. "Save your energy, we have a long way to go."

The rabbit cooked quickly and Nyland divided the carcass with his knife, handing out the portions to Anne and Bao Qing.

Bao chewed on a drumstick and smiled approvingly. "You have proven that you are a determined man. Jon made a good decision sending you. And you, too." She nodded toward Anne. "Very good with all your new American technology. The new ways compliment the old. The two of you compliment each other. Do you love this man?"

Anne made a choking sound in her throat. "What kind of a question is that? There isn't time to worry about that kind of thing."

"Always time for that kind of thing. Maybe that is all the time there is. That is what Jon told me many years ago. Even in the middle of a war, we found the time—you don't want to hear an old woman's private business. But, if you want my advice, take the time."

Anne looked up. Nyland was watching her. "What?" she said.

"You have rabbit grease around your mouth."

"And you smell bad." She smiled. "So much for love talk." She stood up and motioned for Nyland to follow her. They walked slowly up the ridge. "Do you have a plan to get us out of here?"

"You think Bao Qing is...?" Nyland asked.

"What she doesn't know, she can't tell anybody."

"You're learning."

"You're teaching me," she said. "You put your whole heart into everything you do, that's one thing you've taught me. I seem to have spent a lot of my time trying to figure what I could get out of this job, instead of what I could give. And I appreciate you treating me like an equal." She took his hand. "There seems to be a reasonable chance that none of us will get back alive, but I just want you to know—"

Nyland shook his head. "Anne, please don't."

"No declarations of undying love here, I just wanted you to know that you don't have to worry about me. And you don't have to take care of me. And nobody expects you to." Their eyes locked and he bent forward to kiss her gently on the lips.

She smiled. "So what's your plan?"

"The old and the new," he said. "Your computer has got to find Marty, assuming he got out of the plane all right. We're just across the border. The little town he was headed for is about twenty miles farther.

"The highway makes a tight switchback about a mile from here, over that ridge." He pointed west. "There is a boulder hanging partway out over the roadway. The grade is steep and you have to slow down to a crawl to get around it."

"So you just kind of drop in on somebody? Like in the movies?"

"I want a covered truck of some kind, military possibly. I wouldn't mind a little more firepower. The AK is down to about ten rounds."

They walked together back to the campfire. Qing was finishing her breakfast with obvious relish. "Did you shoot the poor little rabbit?" she asked. There was a smile on her face.

"Knife," Nyland said.

"Rabbits are very fast, often get away." She winked at Nyland.

Anne reached inside her shirt and pulled out the battery pack. "Warmer now," she said.

"Who wouldn't be?" Nyland said.

Bao Qing looked on with interest as Anne set up the computer and the satellite transceiver. "Digital phasing array. Better than ours," she said.

"Yes, it is, but not much good without batteries. We're down to about 20 percent according to the meter. A couple more shots is all we've got."

The blank computer screen glowed faintly in the dim light beneath the trees. "Come on, baby," Anne whispered. Suddenly, the screen flashed to life and she gasped in surprise. "Somebody is trying to send us a message."

She struck a series of keys. "That goddamn Doug Smith is really good."

"Are you gonna let the laymen in on this?" Nyland said.

"He got hold of a computer somewhere. Set up an automatic activation program that triggers this computer whenever it accesses the satellite. It looks like he routed this through a computer somewhere in Germany. This man is a serious hacker."

"What's the message?"

"Read it for yourself."

Nyland stared at the screen: PRISONERS. HOUSE IN DC LOCATION UNK. HONEYSUCKLES AND FIRE SIRENS. BLANCHARD INTERROGATING JC.

"Blanchard. That miserable son of a bitch. Anne, can you get a message to Robert Jaynes?"

"If the batteries hold out."

"Tell him he's looking for a safe house with honeysuckles growing somewhere nearby, a place that's near a fire station."

"Jaynes isn't exactly on our side," Anne said.

"Blanchard will kill Jon and Doug both. He'll have to, to save his own ass."

Bao Qing laid her hand on Anne's arm. "It is true. Blanchard is a Chinese agent. Run by MSS for five years. They have a film of him—an interrogation in Vietnam. He told them where his unit was landing. Betrayed his country. That was the hold they had on him."

"Blanchard won the Medal of Honor," Anne said.

Bao Qing made a sour face. "No honor in that man."

"Blanchard has been privy to the absolute top level CIA briefings. And he's been feeding it to China?"

"He knew about the C4I software," Bao said.

"What did he know?" Nyland's tone was sharp.

She looked at him quizzically. "Song Zhenyo planned to steal it."

"Using Jennifer Chin. You knew about Jenny's involvement?"

"I do not believe my granddaughter betrayed the United States."

"She didn't. I wish I could tell you more."

"I understand. Perhaps when we get out of this." Qing patted his hand in a motherly gesture.

"Tuck, tell me we are going to get out of this," Anne said.

"Can you get a message to Jaynes without revealing where we are?" Nyland asked.

Anne spread her arms in a shrug that encompassed the unbroken rows of mountains around her. "I don't *know* where the hell we are." She bent over the keyboard.

The message flashed over the blind circuits Doug Smith had programmed into his computer, mirroring the electronic signature of the CIA station in Thailand. "Done," Anne said. "I hope it's enough to let him find the house. And I routed it into Jaynes's supposedly top security tactical network. That will get his attention."

"Now, can you find Marty?" Nyland asked.

Anne slipped a disk into the computer, hit a series of keys, and an aerial photograph appeared on the screen. "There's Highway 3." She rolled the computer's track ball with her thumb. "This is the meeting point, Mong Yu. He could be anywhere between there and the border."

"What if his GPS tracker isn't working?"

"Then we pray. Wait—there he is." A faint blue dot appeared at the top of the screen. "Looks like he's on a ridge above the highway, about a mile from the meeting point."

"He made it," Nyland said.

"The dot isn't moving. He's probably holed up."

"How do we know he's alive?" Nyland asked.

"If he had gone down with the plane, the tracker would have been destroyed. We know where he is, all we have to do is get to him." Her fingers faltered on the keyboard. She was crying.

Nyland put his hand on her shoulder. She pushed it away, stood up, and walked up the hillside. He shrugged helplessly at Bao Qing.

"She has to make up her mind," Qing said. "It is very difficult for her. Your best plan now is keep quiet. But you know what I think?"

Nyland shrugged.

"She will choose you."

"What makes you think so?"

"You two look at each other while eating the rabbit—like making love." Qing hummed softly to herself as she folded her blanket.

◄22►

Drivers hauling freight over the Burma Road called it Come Back Rock. Five miles past the checkpoint, on the Burma side, a boulder hung over the road, marking a turn so sharp you met yourself "coming back." The army truck grinding its way up the mountain was barely moving as it rounded the turn beneath the overhanging boulder. The driver felt a thump on the cab roof. Had a rock fallen? He leaned his head out window and looked into the muzzle of an AK-47. He shouted a warning to his seat mate and stepped on the gas.

The soldier in the passenger's seat fired a short burst through the cab roof. The noise was deafening in the small space. The driver's door flew open, an arm reached in and dragged the driver out. The soldier was bringing up his rifle again as a bullet tore into him. He pitched backward out of the cab.

Nyland dragged the two bodies to the edge of the highway and pushed them over the steep bank. He grabbed the driver's rifle and jumped behind the wheel. The truck ground away up the hill and there was only silence at Come Back Rock.

It took Nyland nearly ten minutes to reach the spot where Anne waited with Bao Qing. They had simply walked over the ridge, while the road wound several tortuous miles around the hill. The meeting point was marked by a fallen tree that lay beside the road, split open by lightening. A Burmese army truck was parked beside the tree. Two soldiers stood on the shoulder, rifles aimed at Anne and Bao Qing.

The soldiers waved their arms, motioning Nyland over. He stepped on the gas, sending the truck straight toward them. The soldiers raised their rifles and fired. Nyland's windshield exploded. The truck was gaining momentum on the downgrade. If he was going to jump, it would have to be soon.

As he jumped, he caught a glimpse of Anne pulling Bao Qing down into the ditch. One of the soldiers screamed as Nyland's bumper caught him, and carried him over the edge of the cliff. The truck disappeared down the canyon and Nyland could hear it crashing through the trees.

The second soldier had rolled into the ditch and was firing blindly in Anne's direction. Nyland climbed to his feet and walked toward him, firing the AK-47 from the hip. The soldier's weapon clicked on empty. He threw up his hands and stepped out into the road.

Anne and Bao Qing rose from behind the lightning-torn tree. "Do you always stand up and walk right into bullets?" Anne asked.

"He was shooting at you. Are you—"

"She is fine and so am I," Bao Qing cut in. "What now?"

"Let's go find Marty," Nyland said. He motioned the Burmese soldier forward and the man took a few tentative steps, raising his hands higher. "Anne, tell him we'd like a ride to Maymyo."

Marty could feel a warm rivulet of blood running down his back as he sat beneath a pine tree. The makeshift bandage he had fashioned of parachute cloth was soaked with blood. The bullet wound was superficial, he knew, but the loss of blood was serious. The plan, born out of desperation in Kunming, had worked up to this point. He could hear the sound of trucks on the highway just over the hill. If his calculations were right, Mong Yu, a mountain village that was to be the rendevous point, lay just beyond.

He had set the plane's autopilot, and gone out the door at fifteen hundred feet, the GPS tracker zipped in an inside coat pocket.

The plane had crashed and exploded a few miles away in a rugged canyon off the highway. He had seen the flames just before his parachute drifted below the ridge line.

He landed in total darkness on a rocky hillside, and the impact tore loose the bandage Anne had rigged for him on the plane. Strips of nylon torn from his chute had stopped the bleeding, and he was able to get a few fitful hours of sleep in a thick grove of trees near his landing site, wrapped in the chute's remnants.

At daylight, he had headed south crossing a series of steep ridges and narrow canyons until he had finally caught the distant sounds of the trucks on Highway 3. He and Nyland had agreed to meet at dusk on the eastern side of Mong Yu. Here the highway ran level and there was a gravel turnout where drivers often stopped to rest before the long trip over the border into China.

He leaned back against his tree and pulled the GPS device out of his coat pocket. It resembled a cheap portable radio, and would cause no undue notice if he were captured. The device had one purpose: to broadcast its position in code to a satellite. A receiver, reading the coded frequency, could locate the tracker to within one meter, anywhere on earth. In Kunming, Anne had shown him how it worked, and he tried to imagine her, bent over the laptop watching the small blinking blue dot on an electronic map.

Can you see me, Anne? Here I am. He grinned crookedly and held up the tracker toward the sun, but grimaced at the pain in his back. Maybe Anne was dead, he thought, and there was no one tracking his position. Except the entire armed forces of Burma. On his way south he had seen several military helicopters pass overhead, flying toward the crash sight. But it would take them a while to figure out that no one was in the plane. He had buried the remnants of the parachute, and picked his way carefully over the rocks, leaving no trail to follow. It would take the bastards a while to untangle this mystery.

The authorities would be concentrating their search around the crash sight. If he could remain hidden until dark, and if Nyland did manage to get Anne and the Kingfisher across the border and make it here to the rendevous point, there might still be a chance. But

Nyland would have to get his hands on some kind of vehicle—assuming he was still alive.

Tuck Nyland had proven himself a resourceful man. It was no wonder Anne admired him so much. Hausler had seen the looks they exchanged when they thought he wasn't looking. Maybe they had already become lovers. He had a fleeting image of them making love in the back of the truck—a tangle of arms and legs. He closed his eyes for a moment. It was just past midday. Perhaps he would rest a here a while, then cross the last ridge to the highway later in the afternoon.

A shout, somewhere below him in the trees: he opened his eyes. There were three of them, Burmese army from their uniforms. They were running toward him up the hill. Though they were in rifle range, the soldiers kept their weapons slung over their shoulders, apparently confident of capturing him alive. He jumped to his feet, the pain of his wound forgotten. He must lead the soldiers away from the rendevous point, protect Anne and the others.

He ran up the hill, putting distance between himself and the soldiers. He glanced over his shoulder. One of the men had moved out in front of the others, and seemed to be gaining ground. He was smiling, confident of overtaking his enemy.

Hausler lengthened his stride, his legs pumping smoothly as he raced through the forest. The sound of his pursuers footsteps faded behind him, and he heard the man shout to his companions. A rifle shot tore bark off a tree above his head. He ran faster, dodging between the trees without breaking stride. The long hours of training were paying off. And he had another advantage, he thought; he was running for his life.

★ ★ ★

Maymyo

General Thaung Lwin, wearing a starched camouflage uniform with four black stars on each collar, stood alone on the tarmac as the Chinese Z-9B helicopter settled on the pad and a man in a rumpled PLA uniform climbed out. The man looked like hell, Lwin thought: eyes bloodshot, face unshaven, a filthy bandage around his head. The man cringed below the whirling blades, clutching his coat around him as he ran. So this was Song Zhenyo, emissary of the mighty General Xing.

Thaung brought up his hand in a casual salute as the man walked toward him. Song ignored it. "Have you found them?"

"Welcome to Myanmar, General."

"I am Song Zhenyo."

"Your face is known to me," Thaung said. "Known to many who follow American politics. I am surprised to find you here instead of Washington, D.C. There is concern as to your whereabouts, according to the news."

Song glared at him. "The reporters say what they are told to say."

"They say there is a reward on your head." The White Man smiled.

"The airplane—"

"We have confirmed there was no one on board when it crashed. They must have parachuted. We are searching the area around the crash. I will be notified immediately when they are found."

Song shook his head. "It is hard to believe all four people parachuted from that plane."

"I assure you, that is what happened."

"Can you take me to the site?" Song asked.

"What would be the use? My soldiers are very familiar with those mountains. They will find them if anyone can. Why do you find the parachute theory hard to believe? These Americans are trained CIA agents. They have slipped past us a number of times already."

"There is something I must tell you," Song said. "One of the people on that plane was a Chinese woman, an old woman, nearly seventy. I don't think she jumped out of the plane. The pilot must have landed somewhere, dropped his passengers off, then flown the plane across the border."

Thaung considered it. "The pilot jumped, and let the plane fly until it crashed. Possible."

"How far could it fly?" Song asked.

"With the wind drafts up in the mountains, I think not very far."

"They will find only one man near the crash site."

"The others, then, are crossing the border on foot? A difficult and foolish adventure."

Song said, "What choice do they have? They must reach their CIA friends here in Burma."

"Strange that their CIA *friends* have offered me a large sum of money to help capture them."

"And you have helped them?"

"The Americans have offered me money, but there are other things. Is it true, Song, that you have the ear of the Americans, as the media says?"

"I may have certain—contacts." Song said.

Thaung motioned with his arm, and his staff car, a dusty Ford sedan, rolled toward them. When the two men were seated inside, Thaung said, "It would be extremely helpful if we had a little bargaining power with them. I believe these people we seek are very important to the U.S. Government. When we capture them, we find ourselves in an extremely strong negotiating position." He produced a cell phone from his inside pocket. "Call your—contacts—now."

"No." Song pushed the phone away. "These people are *mine*. The security of my country is at stake here. We will not give these people to the Americans."

"No one is talking about *giving* them to the Americans," Thaung said. "We will extract a great price for their return, the lifting of the trade embargo, for instance."

"No." Song's eyes blazed with anger.

"Consider your situation: Shan State is very large and very treacherous. Even my soldiers do not venture into every region. You have one helicopter, I have three divisions. So we must ask...who has the best chance of finding these people?"

"I agree we must cooperate, but these people are mine!"

"My men are capable fighters, but they do not give me connection to the White House. If you truly have Washington's ear, Song, perhaps you can let them know we are interested in doing business. Is that agreeable to you?" He held out the cell phone.

Song glanced at it. "Latest digital technology—from China. I see Burma is advancing into the new millennium."

"My country is called Myanmar now." Thaung's voice was cold.

★ ★ ★

Langley

Robert Jaynes had made a religion of records and files. He had even worked in records as a junior officer twenty years ago. He nodded to the clerk on duty inside a wire kiosk at the entrance to the dimly lit basement room. The man looked vaguely familiar. It was the same man who had presided over the area twenty years ago. His hair was white now, and his shoulders were hunched. "Harris? Still at it?" The man nodded as Jaynes presented his ID badge and signed the register.

A walk into the narrow rows of shelves stacked with dusty boxes of files was a walk back in time, to an era where the recording instruments were typewriters and pencils. The agency had an ongoing project of computerizing all the old files, but it would take another ten years even by the most generous estimate. Meanwhile, there was no alternative to searching the stacks by hand.

Jaynes pulled several files from dusty cardboard boxes stacked beneath a metal staircase, sat at a Formica-topped table and started to read.

He worked through the afternoon. Occasionally, he would make a note on his yellow pad, get up and search the long, dark rows of documents, select another yellowed folder, and return to his seat.

Jaynes knew that the first rule in intelligence was never underestimate your opponent. If Jon Cross had sent a team into China, he would certainly have a plan to get them out. At first, Jaynes had thought his plan was The White Man. That was logical. But that had been a ruse. The team had never intended to use The White Man. But somehow they had gotten over the border while a full alert was in place. That meant they had help.

Jaynes turned the yellowing pages slowly, studying each one. Jon Cross's first posting had been to Burma just after WWII. What had happened forty years ago? Had some old friendship been established that Cross might now bring back to life? The answer, if it could be found at all, lay somewhere in the dusty stacks of paper in front of him.

He found it at ten minutes after seven that evening, in a file labeled, "Economic Development and Postwar Reconstruction," a footnote in an agent report concerning a young jade merchant living in Maymyo.

★ ★ ★

The Burma Road

The Burmese army truck slowed. It had taken nearly two hours over the winding rutted road to reach the gravel turnout, their meeting place with Marty. The driver's hand edged toward the door handle. Anne, crouched behind him under the canvas cover of the truck, prodded him roughly with the barrel of the AK-47. He put his hands back on the wheel.

Nyland sat beside her, cradling Bao Qing's head in his lap. Her voice was faint, nearly drowned out by the roaring of the truck's engine. Nyland bent closer as she spoke. "I said, you are a very resourceful man, Mister Nyland, but I am afraid we really have no chance of getting out of this country alive."

"You can't give up now. Think about Jon Cross." Nyland slipped off his coat and draped it over her shoulders. "We didn't come all this way for nothing." Her face was even more haggard that before, Nyland thought. The last twelve hours would have been hard on anyone, let alone a seventy-year-old woman. Though he had said nothing, he had thought of the hopelessness of their situation. Half the country looking for them. Marty waiting somewhere, wounded, assuming he hadn't been captured.

He patted her shoulder. "You rest now."

Anne spoke to the driver again and the truck turned off the highway.

"Tell him to park over there, at the edge of the gravel." Nyland lifted the canvas flap on the back of the truck. It was near dusk, and he could see the turnout was crowded with trucks, all waiting for the blockage to clear. Several had ignited small hibachis and were preparing food on the ground beside their trucks.

Branches scraped along the canvas as the truck backed into the brush. It rolled to a stop half hidden in the foliage. "Let me have your scarf, Nyland said. He parted the canvas cautiously, leaned out and draped the scarf across the domed canvas top. The purple silk glowed softly in the fading light. He studied the brushy hillside for a moment, but could make out no sign of Marty.

"He's out there, Tuck," Anne said.

"We'll give him ten minutes. If he's there, he'll come down. If he isn't, we'll make a run back to Maymyo, and hope the little battle up on the mountain will divert everybody's attention."

The driver spoke in Chinese, an agitated tone in his voice.

"He has to go to the toilet," Anne translated.

Bao Qing rose on one elbow from the bed of the truck and said something in Chinese to the driver. He nodded his head and sat silently, hands on the steering wheel.

"What did you tell him?" Nyland asked.

Anne chuckled. "She told him I was a madwoman American who would blow off his testicles if he moved."

"She was probably right." Nyland raised the canvas flap and studied the brushy hillside behind the truck. No sign of movement. "Tell him to start the engine," he said. He jumped over the tailgate and disappeared into the brush.

Nyland moved slowly up the hill in the growing darkness. Behind him, on the highway, drivers were turning on their lights as they began the long climb up to the border. His position was extremely vulnerable, he realized. He had left the rifle behind, no way to use it without alerting the soldiers milling around the rest stop below. And anyone waiting in the trees at the top of the hill would have a clear line of sight as he climbed.

So many things could have gone wrong since they had plotted Marty's position on the GPS early that morning. He could have been killed or captured and forced to lead the soldiers to the rest of his party. And, though Hausler had flown them across the border, had been wounded in the process, suspicion stuck in Nyland's mind. Could Marty Hausler be trusted?

Nyland stopped near the crest of the hill and slowly turned a full circle. If Hausler were anywhere near, he would have seen Nyland's approach and given a signal. The only sound was the rumble of trucks on the highway below. Tuck glanced nervously down at the gravel parking lot. Several army trucks and APCs had pulled off the highway and sat, engines idling, near the truck where Anne and Bao Qing were hidden. If anyone got curious, strolled over to bum a cigarette, it would all be over.

Nyland studied the brushy hillside again. The wind had died, and he could hear no sound. Give it another minute, then break the news to Anne. Marty hadn't made it. A small night bird flitted past and landed on a branch nearby. Tuck followed the movement. The bird rose suddenly with a squawk of alarm and flew away into the gathering darkness. The branch wiggled slowly back and forth. Nyland crept closer, knife ready.

"Tuck?" Hausler's voice was faint. "...thought it was the bad guys..." He lay on his back beneath the tree, arms flung out at his sides. His shirt was soaked with blood, his face was pale in the dim light, sweat matted his hair and dripped down his cheeks.

Nyland lifted him gently and wiped the sweat from his face. "Did they spot you?"

"Three soldiers—tried to chase me down. Lost 'em back there somewhere." Marty closed his eyes and drew in a ragged breath.

Nyland laid his hand on Hausler's feverish brow. "Hang on, Marty. Just hang on." The man had very nearly given his life to protect his comrades. There could be no question of his loyalty now. Nyland lifted Hausler onto his shoulders in a fireman's carry and scrambled back down the hill.

◄23►

Washington, D.C.

The dining room at the Key Bridge Marriot, with its muted pastel walls and dark wood accents, was designed to convey class, but the effect was a bland anonymity. It looked no different from dozens of others scattered around the country and the world. The same could be said for the two men in business suits having dinner in a back booth. Both had gray hair, carefully barbered. Nothing remarkable about their appearance. They could be salesmen or CEOs.

They chatted casually, but a close observer would have noticed the attention they paid to their surroundings, checking entrances and exits, scrutinizing waiters as they passed, glancing at the faces of the other customers.

Special Agent Edward Dwyer brushed his lips with his napkin and smiled at the CIA man across from him. "The veal was excellent. Goes down a lot easier than this story of yours."

"There are a lot of things I can't tell you, but I hope you understand my position," Robert Jaynes said. "Bottom line is, I need your help."

"Let me see if I can summarize your position. You believe the secretary of defense is working for the Chinese, and he's holding two of your people hostage, whose names you cannot give me. The proof you offer is a message from these nameless people that you admit could have come from anywhere. And you need the Bureau's help finding him. Maybe you should be telling this story to the *Enquirer*. I imagine they pay a little better."

Dwyer shook his head as the waiter offered him coffee. Jaynes nodded and the man refilled his cup.

Jaynes added sugar and sipped gingerly. "I know you're pissed about the business out in San Francisco, but that was not my operation. I would have handled it differently. I've always been one to cooperate with the Bureau, you know that."

"Oh, certainly."

"Let me lay some cards on the table. The man who did set up the C4I software exchange is the same man Blanchard is holding hostage."

"A man you cannot name."

"Correct."

"A woman got killed in that exchange. Someone interfered with my agents, and the killer got away. You're telling me the CIA—or this nameless man—engineered the whole thing?"

"Its more complicated than that. This man, whom we believe Blanchard is holding prisoner, has the key to all of this. The White House operates a special computer network—"

Dwyer interrupted, "I'm familiar with the EX-10 system. There's a terminal in the director's office."

"The place Blanchard is holding our people has an onsite EX-10 terminal. Two hours ago," Jaynes bent closer and lowered his voice. "I got word from another source that it's near a fire station and there are honeysuckles around the place."

"And you got this hot tip from where?"

Jaynes looked away. How could he tell the FBI man the message had probably come from somewhere in China? "Will you at least check this out? If we can find the house, we can likely find a lot of answers to your San Francisco case."

"You could give me a lot of those answers yourself, if you wanted to."

"There may not be a lot of time. Blanchard is feeling the pressure here. He knows he's stepped over the line."

"The White House will have to be informed," Dwyer said. "We're talking about a member of the president's cabinet here. We can't afford mistakes. And the Bureau is not about to start snooping around their secure communications system without telling them."

"Do what you need to, but will you help me?"

"You made a fool of us in San Francisco, sending that bogus

agent in to spring your guy. Your people broke Federal laws—a dozen of them, including obstruction of justice. We can't just ignore that."

"That wasn't me—not my idea."

"Whose was it? I wasted a lot of time and manpower on that investigation. And, CIA was actively conspiring to jam us up. A lot of laws were broken, not that such niceties bother the mighty Central Intelligence Agency."

"Do you want me to get down on my knees? This thing is bigger than some goddamn interagency bickering."

"And what do you get out of this?" Dwyer asked.

"If I'm lucky, I get to stay out of jail."

"And why would you be worrying about going to jail?" Dwyer was suddenly alert. "Are you leaving something out?"

"I'm just trying to do my job here."

Dwyer stared at him a moment, then folded his napkin and laid it on the table. "There are almost a hundred computer stations on the EX-10 network, but three-quarters of them are in offices downtown, a long way from fire stations and honeysuckles. I'll make a couple of calls. If I get the go-ahead, we should be able to locate the one you're looking for before morning."

"One more favor," Jaynes said.

Dwyer looked at him questioningly.

"When you go in, I want to be there."

Dwyer stood up. "We'll see," he said.

As Jaynes drove back toward Langley and the CIA headquarters, he thought again about Jon Cross and his China operation. A highly placed source in Chinese intelligence would certainly know about Charles Blanchard's life as a spy. Blanchard would be desperate to get to that source and keep him quiet, his career and his life were at stake. And Jon Cross held the key. Cross must be nearly seventy, Jaynes thought. How long could he survive the modern arsenal of truth drugs and torture?

On a whim, he dialed Blanchard's cell phone number. Surprisingly, the man answered.

"Blanchard." He sounded out of breath.

"Sorry to bother you at this late hour, but you asked me to keep you up to date. We think Jon Cross's team is in China, and they're trying to bring an agent out. Sorry to say, I don't have any word on where Cross might be."

Blanchard laughed. "A pretty elusive guy, all right. It seems he just got on that C-130 and disappeared. Look, I've gotta let you go, I'm in the middle of something here—"

"No problem, I just wanted to update you."

Blanchard mumbled something unintelligible, and Jaynes pressed the receiver closer against his ear. Over the sound of Blanchard's labored breathing, a fire siren was faint but unmistakable. Then the line went dead.

Hurriedly, Jaynes dialed another number.

"This is Dwyer."

"I just talked to Blanchard. I heard a fire siren in the background. He's at the safe house now! And I know he has our people."

"You know something you didn't know before?"

"I may regret it, but I have to let you in on this. Blanchard knows what kind of plane our man was on when he took off from Washington. We briefed the White House that he had gone, but at the time, CIA didn't *know* what kind of plane he was on. Blanchard just now mentioned a C-130. Confirms what I thought all along, he grabbed our man off that plane. We need to know where that safe house is!"

"Where are you now?"

"G.W. Parkway."

"Take the Glebe Road exit. That's your shortest route to Falls Church."

"You found the house?"

"The Attorney General talked to the president. He gave us the go-ahead. We rousted a very surprised computer programmer out of bed a few minutes ago. He narrowed it down for us." Dwyer read off an address.

"I know Fulton Street," Jaynes said. "I live a couple miles from there."

"Fine, but keep out of my people's way. They'll be easy to recognize. They're the ones in the spiffy blue flack jackets."

★ ★ ★

Maymyo

U Khin's house was built in the Tudor style with brick and exposed timbers. You could see the lights of Maymyo from the second-floor balcony. The house seemed out of place, a colonial artifact against the backdrop of soft, green jungle foliage. Its terraced gardens and flagstone patios were surrounded by an ornamental iron fence, now rusted and overgrown by tropical vines. The real security devices were harder to see. Thin wires carrying a lethal electric current ran along the fence, motion detectors nestled in the thick foliage. The carved teak door was reinforced with steel. Two Dobermans silently prowled the grounds, moving in and out of the shadows like ghosts.

The three men who walked along the upper balcony, however, openly advertised their presence. They carried assault rifles and side arms and walked slowly back and forth, eyes sweeping the long gravel drive and the surrounding grounds. The guards were new. U Khin had flown them in from the jade mines in Hpakan the day after he arranged passage for Tuck Nyland into China.

Helping Nyland had been a risk, one that could upset the fragile truce with General Thaung Lwin. And the general was not a man to upset. It could be bad for business—and for your health.

U Khin sat in his ground floor study behind a mahogany desk, absently stroking a small, jade elephant. The carving, like many artifacts in the ornate room, dated from the fifth century.

The last rays of sun through the window struck the figurine and it glowed a luminous green against the blue and purple irises in a porcelain vase on the desk. All colors in nature were in harmony, Khin thought. Only man's intervention brought discord. He closed his eyes and inhaled the flowers' delicate scent. There had been a time long ago when he would have whiled away the afternoon in such sensual meditation, but today other thoughts crowded his mind.

There had been a skirmish on the highway near the border. A number of Karen rebels had been killed, and several government soldiers wounded. This could be the start of the long-predicted rebel assault. Traffic had been stalled for hours on Highway 3, making many of his deliveries late.

But there was another problem of much more immediate concern. Something had obviously gone wrong with Nyland's operation. The Chinese army had been stopping and searching all vehicles as they crossed the border, including U Khin's delivery trucks. All army units in Shan State had been placed on full alert. U Khin had seen several helicopters pass over his house, headed toward the mountains. His drivers brought back stories of long military convoys moving along the roads near the border. General Thaung was looking for someone. It had to be the man who called himself "Nyland."

Where was the young CIA man who had made such a ghostly appearance on his patio a few nights ago? There had been no word from the driver in whose truck the two Americans had crossed into China. Had the driver been detained—interrogated? If that had happened, the trail might very soon lead back to U Khin.

General Thaung was a powerful figure, Khin thought, but his hold on the region was tenuous. His continued prosperity—his life—depended on the Chinese military, the weapons and supplies they provided him. If he learned of U Khin's treachery, that he was helping the Americans against the Chinese, Thaung would destroy him without mercy.

Nothing could be gained, he thought, by worrying. And, as always, he had a business to run. He lifted a pile of shipping documents and orders out of his desk drawer and picked up the phone. He worked steadily for nearly two hours, arranging shipments, confirming orders, settling minor dispute among his workers up north in the jade mines.

Finally, he laid down his pen and rubbed his eyes in weariness. His housekeeper knocked discreetly. "Visitors," she said.

The housekeeper stepped back to admit General Thaung and a Chinese man U Khin did not recognize. The general, wearing a white silk suit and red satin shirt, bowed deeply as the two men shook hands. "It is past the hour for calling, U Khin, and I apologize, however, there is a question I must ask, if you will indulge me?"

"And your friend?"

"A visitor from China," Thaung said.

U Khin shook the Chinese man's hand, noting the bandage around his head. "I hope your injury is not serious," he said.

"No, not serious," the man replied.

U Khin could hear the dogs barking behind the house, perhaps aroused by the visitors' arrival. "Would you like some tea?" he asked, motioning for the two men to sit. Neither seemed to notice the dogs barking.

"Let me get to the point," Thaung said. "My friend and I are very interested in a group of Americans who we believe may have crossed the border recently—perhaps last night."

"The border is open," U Khin said.

"The border is closed, on my order. These Americans are enemy agents. Surely you have heard the army is on alert?"

"What does all this have to do with me?" U Khin asked. "You and I have an agreement, long standing. The free pursuit of—commerce."

Thaung replied, "These people have been particularly difficult to locate. This leads me to believe they may have friends in this country, friends who might assist them in certain illegal acts."

"You come to my house to accuse me?" U Khin asked.

"Your trucks make many trips back and forth on the Burma Road. They are not regularly inspected at the checkpoints."

"Until today. Lwin, I assure you that I value our mutual cooperation highly. Why would I do anything to jeopardize it? How would it profit me to do so?"

"Profit, that is what we all pursue, is it not?" Thaung's gesture included the opulent furnishings of the room. "I can assure you, if these Americans who we now believe to be in Myanmar, are allowed to escape, our alliance with the People's Republic," he nodded toward the Chinese man, "will be upset. Profits will diminish greatly.

If that were to happen, those responsible would pay a terrible price. Do you still maintain that you know nothing about these people?"

"I am a jade merchant, nothing more."

"Oh, you are much more. Like me, you pursue many interests. Take care that these interests do not interfere with your—profits. If you hear anything of these Americans you will inform me immediately. To do otherwise would be considered an act of treason. Our long-standing friendship, I am afraid, would not shield you in that eventuality. Good night." General Thaung and the Chinese man walked out the door without looking back.

U Khin stepped out onto the rear patio. The dogs had fallen silent. The searchlights shown on the rows of bushes and flowers. A small fountain burbled in the warm night air. A guard stood near the side gate, his rifle slung across his shoulder. "Everything is secure," the man said. "The dogs were barking at your visitors."

U Khin studied the dark shapes of the bushes along the fence. It was easy to imagine them as human forms. Getting tired. He nodded to the guard and walked back to his study.

There, beside the mahogany desk, stood Tuck Nyland.

Nyland drank the strong, black tea gratefully. U Khin lifted the pot, but Nyland shook his head. "Our position is a difficult one," U Khin said. "General Thaung is closing his net. The military is on alert, there will be checkpoints on every road."

"I have a man wounded, and a seventy-year-old woman. We need your help. I don't like it, but there's no choice."

"You and your friends should be safe here until morning. General Thaung has only his suspicions."

"The old woman upstairs is very important to Jon—King."

"I know who she is. Her name is Bao Qing. She lived here in Maymyo many years ago with her father and mother. I suspect she has become a very important person in China. Many people want her back. They will do anything to see that she doesn't get out of the country."

"If you can get us to Rangoon, I will pay you—"

"There is talk of a bounty for your capture. Half a million American dollars."

Nyland stared at U Khin. "Why don't you turn us in?"

"There is little honor in the world today. Let us preserve what we can." U Khin lit a small pipe and drew deeply. The bowl was carved in the shape of a cobra, the eyes were small diamonds. Khin stared at Nyland through the smoke. "You, too, are a man of honor. You could have escaped at any time. You do not do this for any reward. Why do you sacrifice yourself?"

Nyland shrugged. "I owe Jon a debt."

"I owe him as well, though I doubt that you would understand. He has kept my belief in—there are no English words—the spirit of man. It is difficult for me to explain." The two men sat in silence, U Khin smoking his pipe and looking out the window at the darkened garden. Finally, he said, "There is a way."

★   ★   ★

Falls Church

"Nothing personal, son, but you have to understand you have definitely jammed me up." Sarge jabbed the revolver into Doug Smith's back, pushing him out onto the patio. A tall, wooden fence enclosed the backyard, its weathered boards a pale gray in the moonlight. He was going to die in this yard, Smith thought, his last picture of the world a wooden fence and a gibbous moon. He felt tears sting his cheeks. The smell of honeysuckle was overpowering.

Sarge jabbed him again with the pistol. "Over there by the tree."

"You can't just shoot me." Doug Smith's voice trembled slightly.

"The boss has left me the dirty work, as usual. Just be glad he didn't kill your friend. Guess he still wants to use him as a bargaining chip."

"Where did they go?"

"You think they'd tell me? After I let you get on that computer? The boss was sweatin' bullets there, yelling about the feds rolling us up. Hell, I thought we were the feds. I can tell you one goddamn thing, I am through with this bullshit. If it was up to me, I'd probably just knock you on the head and get the hell out of here, but since you can identify me—and the boss—and I still need that one last paycheck..." Sarge shrugged his shoulders and raised the pistol.

"No, please. I won't say anything." Smith stared up at the sky and tensed his shoulders.

The sniper's bullet made a sound like an ax hitting a side of beef. Sarge fell without a sound. Blood spurted from the hole above his right ear as he lay crumpled on the grass.

The FBI men jumped down from the fence and ran toward Smith, who stumbled dizzily across the lawn. "Who's in the house?" one whispered.

"Nobody. Blanchard and Cross are gone." Smith, a dazed expression on his face, clutched the FBI man's arm. "I'm still alive."

★ ★ ★

An FBI agent in a dark blue windbreaker wiped blood off Smith's shirt as he sat shivering in a kitchen chair. Robert Jaynes and Edward Dwyer waited as the young man collected his thoughts. "Jon Cross was alive," Smith said. "But he was unconscious, drugged. Blanchard carried him out to the car. I have no idea where they went."

"Describe the car," Dwyer said.

"Never saw it. Is Sarge dead?"

"He was going to kill you."

"He thought he was being a good soldier, like the rest of us."

"No, he wasn't like the rest of us. He was working for a man who is selling out his country to the enemy."

"So you killed him?"

"What kind of a game do you think we're in here, son?" Dwyer asked.

Smith closed his eyes and took a deep breath. "His name was Bill Wiley. He came from Charleston, West Virginia. He could have given you information."

"He has a point," Jaynes said.

"My agent saved his life," Dwyer said. "I don't need this second-guessing shit." He walked out of the room.

Jaynes squatted on the floor in front of Doug Smith's chair and spoke quietly. "Can you reach Tuck Nyland?"

Smith nodded. "With the right equipment."

Jaynes helped him to his feet. "We're going back to Langley."

★ ★ ★

Maymyo

Song Zhenyo swallowed another of the pills Thaung had given him and sipped from a water bottle. Whatever was in the pills, they seemed to dull the throbbing pain in his ear, and, though it was nearly four in the morning, he felt unnaturally alert. No cars had turned off of the highway onto the narrow road leading up to U Khin's estate in the last six hours, but still he sat waiting. The car General Thaung had given him was an old Datsun, fenders rusted, bumpers dented and scratched. Not much of a step up from the rusted pickup they had given him in Washington, D.C.

He shifted his legs in the cramped front seat and took another sip of water. He had had some difficulty persuading Thaung to give him the car and let him stake out the house. It was pointless. U Khin had too much to lose, Thaung had told him, by helping the Americans escape. Thaung had threatened the jade merchant with death. He may have helped them over the border into China, but there was no way for them to get back to his house undetected, and he would surely have turned them in if they had. Song had been forced to tell Thaung the embarrassing story of losing his ear to the CIA man, Nyland. Thaung had laughed, but had agreed to let him have the car. A personal vendetta he could understand.

The stimulants coursing through Song Zhenyo's blood had put him in a vicious mood. His fingers clenched on the steering wheel of the old Datsun and he imagined sinking them into Tuck Nyland's neck, slowly squeezing the life out of him. Nyland's tongue would flop out of his mouth, his eyes would bulge out of his head—Song released his grip on the wheel. A car was coming down the road, headlights sending shafts of light through the trees.

Song crouched down in the front seat. From the Datsun, hidden in the trees beside the road, he had a clear view of the car as it rolled past. A late model Jaguar sedan, maroon or black. He could make out the driver's form, but the rear windows were heavily tinted, showing as opaque black squares as the car went by.

This was it! U Khin was sneaking the Americans away. Song reached for the ignition key, but paused at the faint sound of another car's engine. In a moment, it, too, passed Song's vantage point. This car was an American sedan, driving slowly with only its parking lights on. Clearly trying to avoid being seen by the Jaguar. Who was this? Song could see the dim outlines of four men in the car. The CIA team Thaung had mentioned?

Song's first impulse was to follow the procession, but some instinct made him hesitate. If Nyland and the rest were in U Khin's house, what better plan than a decoy to draw away any possible watchers? Apparently, the ruse had worked. The CIA team was following the Jaguar. Song glanced at his watch. Another hour until daylight. He had come this far, he would wait and watch.

Fifteen minutes later, three jeeps and an armored personnel carrier turned into U Khin's driveway. The vehicles slowed to a crawl, their headlights off, as they moved up the long gravel drive. So, Thaung had not believed in U Khin's innocence after all. He wanted the Americans for himself. General Xing would not be happy when he found out.

Song crept out of the car and snuck through the brush toward U Khin's house. A warning shout, followed by the dry chatter of automatic weapons fire. Song dropped to the ground beneath a banana tree and watched as the soldiers moved toward the house, firing an occasional burst at the second floor balcony. The fire was immediately returned by the guards. It was difficult to follow the course of the battle from his vantage point, but it looked as if the soldiers were slowly encircling the house.

Silently, he begged the soldiers: don't kill Nyland. Save him for me.

◄24►

Nyland was awake in an instant. It was the silence that had roused him. The jungle had a certain pulse at night, a symphony of small cries and rustlings the ear became used to. When the symphony stopped, it always meant danger. He had fallen asleep fully clothed on a sofa in one of U Khin's upstairs bedrooms. Anne and Bao Qing were asleep in a bed in the corner, Marty in a bedroom down the hall.

Nyland snatched up the AK-47 and crept to the window. Two guards stood at the balcony rail looking down at the darkened garden. One shouted something in Burmese. There was an answering shout from the garden below. The challenge was obvious.

Nyland heard the brush of a footstep on the carpet behind him and spun around, raising the assault rifle. U Khin stood in the middle of the bedroom holding an automatic shotgun. "It's Thaung Lwin. He has come to settle his accounts. He warned me—"

"It's Bao Qing he wants."

U Khin nodded. "He must please his Chinese masters, or there's no more guns and airplanes, markets for his heroin. And you have embarrassed him, made him lose much face. If he lets you escape, his honor will be destroyed." U Khin peered out the window. "His soldiers are demanding entrance. Time for you to leave."

"We can hold them off." Nyland turned to the window and raised the AK.

"No. Thaung had insulted me and my house. We will make him answer for it. It is no longer your affair. Leave now!"

A burst of automatic weapons fire shattered the window and Nyland pulled the old man to the floor. "I'll take the south window," he said. "You stay here."

Anne and Bao Qing were climbing out of bed. "Tuck, where are you?" Anne whispered.

"Get Qing and Marty downstairs."

Nyland smashed the glass with the barrel of the AK and fired a burst down into the garden. Return fire chipped the wooden beams beside the window and sprayed broken glass into the room.

The fire from the soldiers was growing more intense, but U Khin's guards were using their second floor position to good advantage, pouring fire down into the garden. Nyland emptied his magazine twice, picking his targets as the soldiers moved toward the house. It was only a matter of time, Nyland knew, before the house would be overrun.

Nyland heard the boom of the shotgun to his left. U Khin reloaded the weapon and stepped to the French doors.

"What the hell are you doing?" Nyland shouted.

"Go! Give my best to Jon Cross. I knew his real name all the time. Don't tell him." He shook his head and smiled. "Silly spy games." U Khin pushed the shotgun's muzzle out the door and fired both barrels at the soldiers below. Nyland heard the screams of the men torn by the shotgun's blast.

The soldiers below were quick to retaliate. The explosion blew out the French doors and threw Nyland back across the bed. He stumbled to his feet, ears still ringing from the explosion. The heavy mattress was all that saved his life, he realized. He had heard the signature 'whump' of the grenade launcher and was diving for cover when the round struck. The French doors where U Khin had been standing were gone, glass and splinters of wood littered the carpet. There was no sign of the old warrior.

From the balcony, Nyland heard the scream of one of the guards as he toppled over the rail to the garden below. There was nothing he could do for Jon Cross's old friend now. Nyland ran for the door.

★   ★   ★

Mandalay, Burma

Through decades of civil strife and rebel insurrections, the Burma Railroad had always run on time. But the departure of the morning train from Mandalay to Rangoon was a tumultuous affair. The train station, its stiff, British columns and facades coated with the dust of passing ox carts and pedicabs, overlooked a swirling mob of humanity. People laden with bags and packages jostled each other as they climbed into the waiting cars; street vendors circulated with baskets of food, shouting for the customer's attention. At the head of the train, the old diesel engines rumbled steadily, sending a column of black smoke into the already dusty air.

The train offered only two classes: upper and lower. Ten of the waiting cars were designated lower. The eleventh contained, within its teak-paneled walls, a time capsule from the days of British rule. The car was divided into a sleeping compartment, a kitchen, and a parlor. A dining table, covered with a stiff, white linen cloth, was set with bone china. The silverware was heavy and solid, each piece engraved with the initials, BRR. The Burma Railroad was a journey into the past.

The porter assigned to the executive car, an old Burmese man who doubled as cook and valet, had served the railroad for nearly twenty years. He began his set-up ritual each morning at five. This morning, he had been met by a Burmese man who seemed to simply materialize out of the early morning darkness. They had exchanged a few words and a thick envelope of American dollars.

The porter had been asked to prepare the car, then leave it unlocked and make himself disappear. Tell no one. The tickets were in order, but he noticed the names were not filled in. The man had scrawled a name and address on the tickets and left the porter counting his money in the predawn darkness.

The porter had hurried through his routines of laying out linens, stocking food and liquor in the galley, and polishing the brass fittings in the car, and was smiling as he stepped off the executive car just after 6:00 A.M. He would not be traveling to Rangoon today; there would be plenty of time to contemplate spending the money the man had given him.

The request that he leave the passengers to their own devices was not unusual. Many people preferred privacy on the twelve-hour run to Rangoon. But the size of his tip was most unusual—nearly four month's pay, he calculated. Enough to erase any thought of telling the soldiers patrolling the depot about his mysterious passenger.

Perhaps he would surprise his family, buy something special for supper at the market, pork, or fresh fish. They would eat well for the whole summer on the sheaf of American greenbacks he carried in his pocket.

He had not seen the people who would be traveling in the executive car. In this part of the world, many people found it necessary to remain secretive about their business. He hoped the passengers, whoever they were, had a pleasant trip to Rangoon.

For Don Shenk, it was a rare occasion; he had just finished talking to his boss in Langley, and there was a smile on his face. The two things seldom went together. Robert Jaynes always wanted more, better, faster. Nothing was ever good enough for Mr. Meticulous. But this time, Shenk had behaved just like his boss. It had earned him a rare word of praise.

All CIA operations in Burma had been put on hold until Tuck Nyland and the Chinese agent could be located. So, Shenk had played it by the book. He had his team covering every possible avenue of travel out of northern Burma. His routine surveillance of the railroad station in Mandalay had paid off.

The officer stationed there had been watching people board the 7:00 A.M. train to Rangoon when he spotted a Chinese man trotting along the platform. Song Zhenyo's picture had been widely circulated after his disappearance from Washington, D.C. There had even been a memorandum from the DCI urging all personnel to be on the lookout. Burris had gotten a good look at his face as he climbed aboard. The injured ear described in the memo was now partially concealed by a wide-brimmed straw hat.

Burris, the only one of Shenk's men who spoke Burmese, had chosen not to get on the train, but went to talk to the railroad officials. He had uncovered an unusual bit of information. The porter who usually traveled in the special executive car at the rear of the train had taken the day off. He had been smiling when he left, the station master said. He'd been paid off.

Who rented the executive car? Burris had asked. The rental forms were useless, an illegible signature scrawled above a non-existent address. The stationmaster had mentioned that the car was often reserved for a jade merchant named U Khin.

Burris had been watching as the train pulled out of the station. The curtains in the executive car were tightly closed.

Shenk, after hearing Burris's report, came to the obvious conclusion. Tuck Nyland and the Chinese agent were on the train. He had called Jaynes immediately and the man had sounded almost happy. He congratulated Shenk on his team's excellent work, and asked for an update on the firefight at U Khin's house. U Khin and two of his bodyguards had been killed by The White Man's soldiers. A cook and two house boys had been found cowering in the kitchen. No sign of Nyland.

But the deputy director of operations had been only half-listening. Put it in your report, Jaynes had told him. The priority was stopping the train and capturing the Chinese agent. This agent was privy to the inner workings of the MSS. It would be the intelligence coup of the century. Though the DDO didn't say it, the implication was clear; the credit would go to Robert Jaynes. If the agent got away, was killed, or recaptured by the Chinese, it would be Shenk's fault.

And that had damn near happened. It was fortunate, Shenk thought, that he had not been called on to explain the details of the previous night's fiasco. His report would not mention how he and three of his men had followed a maroon Jaguar for nearly three hours before realizing it was a decoy. Now, thanks to Burris's sharp eye, they were back in the game.

Much of the CIA's operation in Burma, aside from developing assets within the government, involved interdiction of the drug trade. Their primary weapon in that effort was the helicopter. Shenk had spent many hours flying over Shan state searching out poppy fields and supply trails. The planes were supplied by a private company called Burma Air International. BAI was a proprietary company of the Central Intelligence Agency. It owned one helicopter, a Vietnam–era Huey. It no longer sported machine guns and grenade launchers, and it had been repainted a muddy shade of gray, but it was still a Huey, and it still flew.

It was after 9:00 A.M. when Shenk, Burris, and three other officers climbed aboard the chopper. The train had gotten a two-hour head start, but there was only one way it could go. Burris had learned that the train made a regular stop at Pyinmana, about halfway to Rangoon. The chopper could reach that spot easily in an hour. They would set down on the tracks, block the train, and Nyland would be theirs.

All five CIA men carried M-16s, their field jacket pockets bulged with extra clips. They would not be outsmarted by Tuck Nyland again. Try not to kill anybody, Jaynes had said, but, whatever you do, stop them.

◄25►

South of Mandalay

The jungle sliding past the train's window had an almost hypnotic effect. Occasionally, a mist-shrouded canyon would flash by, offering a brief glimpse into the timeless serenity of the back country. As the train moved farther south toward Rangoon, Nyland had seen the brilliant green of rice fields and caught the damp, musty scent of the stagnant water where they grew. He had thought immediately of Sacramento, the rice fields there.

The memories were bitter. After his sister's death, his mother had been despondent. Then one day she had packed an overnight bag, saying she was going to "get help." But she simply disappeared. Driven away, the young boy was sure, by his terrible failure to protect his little sister. He had gone to live with an aunt and uncle in Sacramento who didn't seem to want him, either.

The rice fields had been his escape. He had ridden his bike for miles past fields like these. Riding until he collapsed from exhaustion, running away from his memories.

The train's executive car was laid out with the sleeping room in front, dining parlor in the middle, and kitchen in the rear. Nyland and Hausler sat on velvet sofas in the dining parlor, staring out the window, each lost in their own thoughts. Anne and Bao Qing were sleeping in the forward compartment on a four-poster bed, cocooned in nineteenth-century opulence.

More cultivated fields rolled by, some being plowed by oxen. Nothing had changed in Burma, it seemed, for a hundred years. But the almost surreal calm of the countryside was an illusion. Burma was in the grip of a brutal military dictatorship.

The ruling junta had earned an international reputation for brutality during their long fight with the rebel bands in the hills, and the viciousness they often directed against their own people. The United States had blocked all investments in the country until the human-rights record improved. No one believed that would happen anytime soon.

The junta held the county in an iron grip, with informants everywhere. The government soldiers had proven their ruthlessness the night before, he thought, killing the old man U Khin.

There was an army arrayed against them, Nyland thought. Alone, he could probably evade the soldiers, but three other people were depending on him, trusting him—with their lives. He laid his head on the seat cushion and closed his eyes. The fear was never far from the surface. He would fail—others would die. He remembered the face of Jennifer Chin, eyes pleading for his help. And the lifeless body of his sister lying in the sand.

The hand on his shoulder startled him.

"You having bad dreams?" Marty asked.

Sweat dripped down Nyland's face. He wiped it away with his hand. "Dozed off—didn't realize..."

"You deserve a little rest. I'll keep watch."

"Can't afford to sleep now."

Marty shrugged and sat down across the aisle. "Don't really know how to thank you," he said.

"You would have done the same."

"I'd like to think so, but I'm not so sure. I'm not really a brave guy, Nyland, not one of those Special Operations killer-types."

Nyland smiled. "Like me?"

Hausler said, "Hey, no disrespect, I owe you my life. But it's obvious you're a different breed of cat. And that's why Anne is so attracted to you. There's nothing I can do about that." There was bitterness in his voice.

"She's probably better off with you."

"Why? Safety and stability? Good, gray Marty?"

"What's wrong with that?" Nyland stared out at the passing landscape. The train had moved into heavy forest again, and trees pressed close to the tracks.

"Safety and stability—shit." Hausler threw a glance at Nyland.

"None of us are gonna get out of this anyway."

"We'll make it, Marty." But the longer they stayed on the train, the more time Thaung Lwin—and Jaynes's CIA team—had to find them.

"Haven't seen any planes," Marty said. "That's a good sign. But I don't—"

"Relax. Keep your eyes open. Be ready for the bastards when they come," Nyland said.

"Right. You hungry?" Marty stood up and walked into the kitchen. His back wound had been treated and bandaged by U Khin's housekeeper, but he still moved slowly, holding himself stiffly erect. How would he react in a firefight, Nyland wondered.

Hausler lifted the lid off a large, copper skillet. "Breakfast's ready," he said. "Little something I found in the refrigerator. Rice and pork and some kind of vegetables. Burma stir-fry special."

The door to the sleeping compartment opened. "Smells great, but can I have bacon and eggs?" Anne asked. She smiled at Nyland. "Nap, bath, fresh clip of ammo. I'm a new woman." Slung across her back was a short-barreled MP-5 machine gun borrowed from the arsenal in U Khin's house. Nyland watched her as she walked toward him. The sling passed between her breasts, emphasizing their fullness. Nyland smiled. She caught his look and shook her head slightly. She nodded warningly toward Marty.

Bao Qing stepped through the door behind her, took in the scene before her, and smiled. "She is a warrior princess, yes?"

Nyland grimaced. "You're a matchmaker, Qing."

"She wears her purple scarf for you."

"Qing, you have one hell of an imagination." Anne unslung the MP-5 and opened the laptop computer. "We have, courtesy of the Burma Railroad, a full charge on our batteries. Tuck, I don't want to be a complainer, but maybe you would be so kind as to tell us what the hell the plan is? I'm assuming Jon Cross was supposed to meet us at the coast. He's in Washington, a prisoner."

"There's a fishing boat waiting in the Andaman Sea, about ten miles out."

"I hope you paid him well."

"Twice the going rate. He said he'd wait three days."

"How do you know he won't just keep the money and sail away?" Marty asked.

"He's an old friend of Jon's," Nyland said. "Anyway, I had no choice but to trust him."

"That's comforting," Anne said. "Speaking of trust, when were you planning to tell us all this?"

"Less you know—"

"Right. This is bullshit. Why don't you just come out and say it. You don't trust any of us."

Bao Qing laid her hand on Nyland's shoulder. "Any of us here could have betrayed you anytime, but we fight together, we come a long ways. We will make it the same way—together. But it is much your pride. Women are weak, can't depend on them?"

Nyland looked out the window, said nothing.

"Is that how you feel, Tuck?" Anne asked. Her cheeks flushed with anger. "It's not security you're worried about, it's your macho pride."

"All right, if you want the goddamn truth, I am worried about—security. But it doesn't matter too much now."

"And why is that?" Anne asked.

"It's still a hell of a long way to the coast. If they find out we're on this train, we're sitting ducks."

"So this is the famous SEAL spirit? We quit?"

"We do the best we can. You can't expect any more—" Nyland's voice was a whisper.

"And we concentrate on survival, right?" Marty said. "And that means we need a little nourishment." He dished the food onto the bone china plates and sat them on the table.

The four sat themselves around the table to eat. The tension of the moment was broken. Marty said, "After we get out of the country, where do we go?"

"Maybe Thailand," Nyland said.

"And after that?" Marty asked. He was looking at Anne.

She shrugged. "Let's see how we do."

"We have to talk to Robert Jaynes." Nyland gestured toward the computer. "Will that thing work on a moving train?"

Anne picked up an embossed silver fork and began to eat one-handed as she tuned the transponder. "We'll find out."

★ ★ ★

Langley

Though he was operating on very little sleep, and his headache was working its way into a migraine, Robert Jaynes was smiling as he walked into the CIA communications center. The endgame was unfolding before him. Don Shenk and his team in Burma had located Nyland and the Chinese agent on the train. They should have them within the hour. The FBI had mounted a full-fledged manhunt for Charles Blanchard and Jon Cross. It was simply a matter of time.

Jon Cross had been the key to the operation, Jaynes thought, but he was almost irrelevant now. With Nyland and the Chinese agent almost in the bag, Cross, if he survived, would be sent to prison. Jaynes would get the credit for stopping him. Blanchard was the only dark cloud on the horizon. If he were taken alive, he would likely try to implicate Jaynes in his double agent's game, conspiracy to commit espionage. A life sentence.

If he were taken alive. Something to consider.

Jaynes greeted the communications officer with a forced smile and a slap on the back. "Going to be a good day," he said. When he finally had Nyland and the Chinese agent in hand, it might even be true.

Jaynes had just finished pouring his coffee when the call came on the secure tactical net. Had Don Shenk rolled up Nyland and his group? He sat the cup down and rushed to the console.

The voice on the speaker was firm, commanding: "This is Nyland. I want a deal."

"He's on a transponder, we're trying to locate—"

Jaynes motioned the technician to silence. "What kind of a

deal?" he asked.

"Where is Jon Cross?"

"He's OK."

"Does Blanchard still have him?"

"We found the safe house, thanks to you. Blanchard and Cross were gone. The FBI is full-court on this. He won't get away."

"Nothing happens to Jon Cross. No trigger-happy FBI agents. And you let him go. No charges."

"And in return?"

"You get an agent who knows the Ministry of State Security inside out. You'll be a hero, Jaynes."

"How do you know I won't get this agent anyway?"

"You've tried three times. Three strikes."

"What's that noise in the background, Nyland? Where are you?" Jaynes looked at the technician. The man shook his head. No trace established.

"Deal?"

"Ah—yes. Deal. Cross, when we find him, goes free, you deliver the agent. Where do we—"

"I'll contact you in twenty-four hours." The connection went dead.

Jaynes looked at the communications officer. "What did that noise sound like to you?"

"Sounded like they were in some kind of truck, a train, maybe."

A train. Don Shenk's intelligence had been right on the money. His chopper would outrun the train any minute now. And Nyland's deal would be meaningless. Jon Cross was on his own. Jaynes picked up his coffee cup. It was going to be a good day.

Burma

The train began to slow. Anne reached for the machine gun. "What the hell is happening?"

"Pyinmana. Scheduled stop, according to U Khin. Probably ten, fifteen minutes." Nyland closed the velvet drapes.

Marty was watching the left side. "Lot of people getting off. Looks pretty normal. A few soldiers in the crowd, but nobody seems to be paying us much attention." The car was lit by the soft glow of cut-glass sconces attached to carved mahogany paneling. Without a view of the outside world it could be 1850, Nyland thought.

Bao Qing sat beside him on the velvet sofa. "This bargain you make with the CIA, you didn't ask me?"

"First we get Jon Cross out, then we worry about the other part of the deal."

Bao Qing smiled. "You perhaps have lied to this man Jaynes?"

"After so many years, you and Jon belong together. I'm going to make that happen, whoever I have to lie to."

Song Zhenyo pressed the receiver tight against his good ear. The din of the Pyinmana train station and the steady rumble of the diesel locomotive made conversation almost impossible. "I told you where they are! How long?" he shouted over the noise. "Yes, good-bye." The troops were on their way. Thaung had assured him that he would have soldiers at the station in the next few minutes. There might be time for one more phone call. He clicked the receiver impatiently and finally the overseas operator came on the line.

The passengers in the forward cars had all returned to their seats. It had been twenty minutes, but still the train had not moved. A few were looking at each other questioningly, but any thought of complaining was quickly stifled as an army truck loaded with soldiers rolled onto the platform. An officer jumped from the cab and ran toward the engine, shouting orders over his shoulders.

His soldiers fanned out and crept toward the rear of the train. A few of the braver passengers scrambled off the train and ran toward the jungle, leaving the others cowering in their seats. They had seen the soldiers in action before. They scarcely noticed the Chinese man following the soldiers.

Song Zhenyo caught the last man in the line, wrenched his rifle from his hand, and clubbed him viciously in the throat. Song chambered a round and crept forward.

★   ★   ★

Nyland opened the side door and peered down the tracks. The Burmese soldiers were twenty yards away, edging toward the executive car, rifles ready. Nyland bolted the mahogany door. Marty looked at him questioningly.

"Lock and load," Nyland said.

◄26►

Pyinmana, Burma

Outside the executive car, the shouts of the soldiers were getting louder. Several were pounding on the rear door. Anne saw Nyland raise the AK-47. Marty was crouched on the sofa in the sitting room peering through a slit in the curtain. She pushed Bao Qing down beneath the table and picked up the MP-5.

There was silence for a moment, and her breathing sounded loud in her ears.

A burst of machine gun fire exploded through the dining car window, showering glass across the table. Marty fired a burst in return and bullets tore through the thin walls of the car, splintering the carved mahogany panels and shattering the glass fixtures on the walls.

Nyland fired through the door and heard screams outside. "Marty, get this goddamn train moving, I'll catch up." He threw the door open and jumped from the car, his AK spraying a steady hail of bullets. The group of soldiers outside, taken by surprise at the suddenness of his assault, crumpled onto the cinders beside the track. Marty was firing out of the shattered window and he accounted for several more who peeked their heads around the row of cars. He fired another quick burst, kicked away the broken glass and clambered out onto the roof.

Anne pulled Bao Qing back into the sleeping car and pushed her beneath the bed. Using the butt of her machine gun, she knocked out the glass in the small window above the bed. Immediately, a hail of fire poured through the opening.

Suddenly, the firing stopped. She heard more shouting, voices raised above the screams of passengers. Cautiously, she peered out the shattered window. A Burmese army officer was arguing with a man in wide-brimmed straw hat. She caught a few words in

Chinese: "...take them alive."

At the rear of the train, she could see a tangle of arms and legs. Soldiers were wrestling with Nyland. Several held his arms and legs. One slammed a rifle butt into his stomach, and he doubled over. He got one hand free and slashed viciously at the man holding his arms. Blood spouted from the man's nose and he screamed in pain, releasing his grip. For a moment, it looked like Nyland was going to break free, but more soldiers joined the fray, urged forward by the officer that stood beneath Anne's window. She jabbed the muzzle of the machine gun out the window and shouted in Chinese, "Call off your men! Let him go."

The officer looked up in amazement. He shouted a warning and raised his pistol. Anne shot him. The machine gun bucked against her shoulder and the man toppled backwards, his face a mask of blood. He lay still on the cinders.

The man with the straw hat had disappeared.

Then the train began to move. Anne ran to the rear door. Nyland had shrugged off the last of his attackers and was limping toward the moving train. She held out her hand as he swung aboard. The train was gathering momentum. Several soldiers ran along the tracks firing at the retreating car. Anne returned their fire one-handed, leaning out of the doorway.

"No," Nyland said, "Save your ammunition."

"Are you hurt?"

"Ankle twisted." He took a breath and grimaced in pain. "Bao Qing?"

"She's fine, I stashed her under the bed. Your rib—is it broken?"

"Don't know. How did they find us?"

"There was a taller man, Chinese, talking to the Burmese captain I shot. I didn't see his face from my position. He sounded like he was giving orders."

"Song Zhenyo. I would bet he's still on the train." He grasped an iron ladder outside the rear door, his tattered shirt flapping in the wind.

★ ★ ★

"Where the hell are you going?"

"Marty's up in the engine. Have to let him know—" Nyland stumbled as stepped onto the ladder, his face contorted with pain.

"Get back in here, I'll go." Anne swung the machine gun over her shoulder and climbed up the ladder.

The train was traveling at full speed now, jungle flashing past on both sides of the tracks. Anne crawled slowly along the swaying line of cars, nearly suffocated by the plume of diesel smoke blowing over her. The smoke shifted suddenly as the train rounded a bend, and she sat back on her knees, panting for breath. Then she saw the gray helicopter.

Anne scrambled into the cab beside Marty. "Company," she said.

Hausler took his eyes off the engineer for a moment to look where she was pointing. A Huey, the letters BAI painted on the fuselage, flew slowly above the jungle canopy, keeping pace with the train. "Company, all right," Marty said. "Our own goddamn people."

Anne said, "Jaynes had us nailed all along. He had no intention of making a deal."

The chopper swung in front of the train and hovered just above the tracks. The engineer pulled the throttle back, and the train began to slow. "A little game of chicken," Marty said. "You know that one?" He jabbed the muzzle of his rifle into the man's ribs. The engineer, eyes bulging with fear, shoved the throttle forward.

The helicopter moved off the tracks, giving the three men crouched in its open doorway a clear field of fire as the train passed. Marty saw the winking muzzle flashes as bullets tore through the windshield and ricocheted inside the cab. The engineer jumped from his seat and was reaching for the sliding steel door when the bullets hit him. His hand left a smear of blood on the black metal as he fell from the train. The helicopter was directly above them now. Marty held his AK out the window and fired blindly up at the sound. The noise of the chopper receded. It was climbing.

Marty pushed the throttle forward. The diesel engine growled in response and the train slowly picked up speed. "Hold the goddamn thing wide open," he shouted.

Anne gripped the throttle. "What the hell are you doing?" she said. "There are at least four people in that chopper. You move outside this cab, and you're—"

"Nyland's back there."

"This isn't the time to play hero. We have to make those assholes think we're all up here in the engine."

Marty leaned cautiously out the door. "They already know somebody's in the executive car, they're right above it." As Marty watched, two men jumped from the helicopter's skids onto the top of the executive car. He fired a quick burst and both men dropped to their stomachs. He pulled the trigger again: a dry click. "Shit." A bullet struck the cab's iron roof and he dodged back inside. "That was my last clip."

Anne held the throttle open with one hand, with the other she handed him the MP-5. "I've got a couple left," she said.

Bullets rang against the steel roof and ricocheted off the engine. A choking, black smoke poured from the engine, filling the cab. Diesel fuel splashed across the bullet-pocked windscreen, covering Anne and Marty with a hot, sticky film.

"We're fucked here, Annie, I'm sorry."

"Not your fault. If I'd listened to Nyland," she said, "you'd still be back in Kunming, and you'd be safe."

"I love you, Anne." Hausler put his arm around her shoulder and kissed her. "I know it's too late, but—"

She gently laid her fingers on his lips. "Haven't got us yet."

But the smoke was getting thicker, the engine's gauges were swinging wildly, red lights flashing on the console. The train began to slow.

Nyland crouched beside Bao Qing in the sleeping compartment, shielding her with his body. He could feel the train slowing down. There was no more firing from the front of the train. Had the bastards killed Anne and Marty? "Get under the bed," he said. "I'll come back for you."

"Look out!" she shouted.

Nyland spun around, reaching for the AK. Two men stood in the doorway, rifles trained on him. "Give it up, Nyland," the short one said. "We want you alive."

Bao Qing sat on the bed beside him, her hand on his shoulder. No way to get her out of the line of fire. He dropped the assault rifle on the blanket and raised his hands.

The pickup operation took only a few minutes. The helicopter landed on the tracks in front of the stopped train. A few of the terrified passengers jumped off and disappeared into the jungle, but most remained crouched on the floor in the passenger cars, peering cautiously over the window sills as the Americans threw their captives into the helicopter and took off.

As the chopper climbed above the jungle, a man climbed painfully out from beneath the executive car. His clothes were torn and blackened from his desperate ride clinging to the rods beneath the car. He rubbed his arms, trying to ease the cramps from his death grip on the cold iron. His wide-brimmed hat had fallen off far back up the tracks. The bandage around his ear was black with soot.

There was pure hatred in Song Zhenyo's eyes as he watched the gray helicopter disappear to the east toward the Thai border.

Washington, D.C.

A faint light...concentric circles of red and green. Pain pounding behind the eyelids. Good—still alive to feel pain. Jon Cross opened his eyes. Shadows moving across the white fabric of the head liner above him. Backseat of a car—blanket wrapped tightly around him. He struggled against the soft fabric. Arms too weak to move. He closed his eyes and forced himself to relax. He had survived, and he hadn't told Blanchard where Nyland was or about Bao Qing. His symptoms told him Blanchard had given him a truth drug called Christmas, the latest addition the CIA's chemical arsenal. It was named for the red and green flashes the victim sees when regaining consciousness. The drug would wear off in a few minutes, Cross knew, once you saw the flashes.

Slowly, the images came back. Blanchard talking to Sarge as he dragged Cross into the car: "Smith has done enough damage. Just get rid of him." Then Blanchard had plunged a needle into Cross's arm. They were going to kill Doug! Cross had struggled briefly before the drug hit him and the world tilted on its side. His last conscious image had been the car's head liner, a white blur above him in the dimly lit garage. And the smell of honeysuckle.

Cross slowly opened and closed his fists, forcing circulation back into them. He was still alive. And he had beaten Blanchard. In spite of the drugs and the beatings, Cross had revealed nothing about Bao Qing, about where Nyland was taking her. Blanchard was desperate, he knew, to find her and kill her before she could tell the world her secret—that the secretary of defense was an agent of Chinese Intelligence, a traitor.

As Cross's eyes came back into focus, he could see a series of streetlights move by above him. Then the car slowed, and he heard horns honking. Stalled in traffic. The pungent odor of diesel smoke filled the back seat, and Cross could hear the roar of an engine. Bus, probably, or a heavy truck.

Cross raised his head off of the seat and was punished with a wave of nausea. He closed his eyes again and lay still, waiting for it to pass. He had caught a glimpse of Blanchard's head and shoulders in the front seat before the nausea hit. And something else. Lying on the carpet under the passenger's seat was the hypodermic needle Blanchard had jabbed into his arm. Cross's head was beginning to clear. He reached slowly and closed his fingers around the syringe. The car still had not moved, and the sound of idling engines and horns was now joined by angry shouts and the distant sound of a siren. Washington gridlock.

★ ★ ★

Blanchard pounded on the horn, adding to the clamor. He glanced in his mirror. Cars were backing up behind him, clouds of exhaust hung in the air. Then Cross's face appeared, blocking out the scene. Blanchard felt a needle prick the skin behind his ear.

"It's Christmas, Blanchard, your favorite drug," Cross said. "Keep your hands on the wheel or I put it straight into your brain. Now, I'm going to tell you exactly what to do."

Blanchard stared straight ahead, hands gripping the wheel. Christmas was meant to be injected into a muscle. A shot straight into the brain would cause instant respiratory failure—death. "Whatever you say, Jon, just be careful." The bus in front of him started to move. Blanchard put the car in gear and inched forward with the traffic. His car phone rang. He glanced at it cradled on the console beside his seat. It rang again.

"Answer it." Cross's thumb was on the plunger.

The secretary of defense picked up the phone. "This is Blanchard. My God, what do you expect me to do?" He glanced at Cross's image in the mirror. "Look, this is not a good time—"

Cross snatched the phone from his hand. The caller's voice was faint in his ear: "...very simple. CIA has them. You control the CIA and I control you. I want those people back. Once they're out of the country, into Thailand, it will be very difficult. There isn't any time..."

Cross muffled the receiver against his chest. "Tell him you'll handle it. And ask him where he is." He handed the phone back to Blanchard.

Blanchard said, "Yes, I'm here. I'll call the DCI—I'll call the president. But you realize there aren't any guarantees—yes, of course. Where are you?" Blanchard listened for a moment and then hung up the phone.

"Be very careful with your answer." Cross eased the tip of the needle into Blanchard's skin. "That was Song Zhenyo?"

"Yes."

"Where is he?"

"Burma. The town was Pin—something, Pinmata?"

"Pyinmana," Cross said. Nyland had made it halfway to Rangoon, but now the CIA had Bao Qing. Jaynes had pulled off the intelligence coup of his career, capturing an enemy intelligence officer who possessed all the secrets—if she could be made to talk. Qing's interrogation would come next, sleep deprivation, truth drugs. Torments she could not survive at her age. His thumb trembled on the plunger.

Blanchard's eyes widened as he saw Cross's expression in the mirror. "What are you going to do with me?"

"Don't tempt me. Right now, you're a bargaining chip. The federal penitentiary system will treat you well, once you get used to the culture. You just relax and let it happen."

"I can't go to prison. You might as well kill me right now."

"You don't deserve a decent killing. You betrayed your country. And I don't think it's the first time."

"Don't know what the hell you're talking about."

"You want to tell somebody, don't you Blanchard? You've kept it inside you all these years, ever since Vietnam. You were a prisoner of war. Medal of Honor. The world thinks you're a war hero. But you aren't—are you, Charlie?"

Blanchard stared at Cross in the rear view mirror. Tears ran down his face. "I couldn't help it. They were..."

"What did the Chinese have? What did they have?"

"A film. The North Vietnamese used some Chinese interrogators. Experts. They beat me, put electrodes on my—God help me, I told them."

"Told them what?" Cross asked.

"My unit. Where their LZ was."

"And the NVA was waiting."

"Those guys were coming back for *me*. And I betrayed them. Two companies of United States Marines—massacred. And you know what I got? I got an extra bowl of rice and a piece of fish."

"The Chinese held onto the film?" Cross asked.

"Until I was tapped for secretary of defense. A plain old U.S. senator wouldn't do them enough good, I guess."

"Even one who got elected on his war record?"

"Everything I stood for—all a lie." Blanchard pulled to the curb and cut the engine. "That's the end of it. Are you satisfied, Cross?"

"Not quite. Call Robert Jaynes."

"But he's—"

"Tell him you'll make a deal. Me for the Chinese agent. Tell him to meet you at Rock Creek Park, the Connecticut Avenue entrance. And bring Doug Smith."

"He'll never—"

"Do it!"

Blanchard talked for less than a minute with Robert Jaynes. He hung up and looked at Cross in the mirror. "He said he'll be there. Ten o'clock tonight."

"Satisfactory." Cross jabbed the needle into Blanchard's shoulder.

Blanchard stared at him in horror. "You said—"

"I lied."

Blanchard slumped across the steering wheel, eyes closed. The Christmas drug, injected into a muscle, would keep him immobilized for several hours. But he would wake up with nothing worse than a pounding headache, the kind Cross was feeling now. Cross slid out the back door and walked unsteadily away across the Safeway parking lot.

◀27▶

Burma

It had finally happened. The CIA had won. Nyland sat with his back against the helicopter's cold metal bulkhead, eyes closed. He could not bring himself to look at Anne and the others. He had failed. And now, they would pay the price. The helicopter banked sharply right and Nyland braced his arm against the seat. The door of the chopper was open, a yawning abyss threatening to grab him and hurl him to oblivion. Maybe that would be the best, he thought.

Then, below him, he saw the jungle, a dark green carpet, broken by a shining strand of water. The Sittang River.

He was suddenly alert. The Sittang was a way out.

It opened into the Andaman Sea less than twenty miles downstream. They might still be able to meet the trawler. But once the chopper crossed the mountains into Thailand and reached the CIA base at Chiang Mai, there would be no hope of escape.

The guard next to Hausler held an M-16 across his lap. He was looking out the cabin door. The leader, who Nyland had heard called Shenk, was in the copilot's seat, talking on the radio. Nyland could not hear his words over the roar of the engine. Shenk was the one who had searched them, confiscated the computer equipment. He had taken the Kingfisher pin and shoved it in his pocket without a glance.

The two CIA men who had broken into the executive car and captured Nyland and Bao Qing sat in the rear of the chopper, rifles ready. They were good soldiers, Nyland thought, but their position was a mistake. If they were forced to fire, they would be aiming directly at the pilot. This was a group who had little experience guarding prisoners, Nyland thought. There were four armed guards in the cabin, the two in the rear, one seated between Marty and Anne on the right side near the door, and another between Nyland and Bao Qing who lay across several seats behind the pilot.

Nyland caught Anne's eye across the cabin and inclined his head toward the door. She nodded. She had seen the river, too. Marty sat forward in his seat, casually stretching his legs. He was ready.

Bao Qing opened her eyes and sat up slowly. The guards glanced at the frail old woman, but paid little attention as she slid her hand into her coat pocket. Nyland noted the furtive movement, and remembered the deadly fighting knife she had brandished in Kunming. He watched in fascination as she leaned slowly toward the pilot. Nyland tensed. Marty had seen the movement, too. It was now or never.

Shenk switched off the radio and turned around in his seat, glancing at his prisoners. Bao Qing froze, her hand in her pocket.

Shenk pulled the Kingfisher pin from its silk box and studied it. "Pick up a little Burma souvenir for your girlfriend?"

"Fuck you," Nyland said.

"Tough *hombre* we got here. Keep your little trinket, Nyland. Where you're going, I don't think they wear a lot of jewelry." He tossed the pin over his shoulder.

The dragonfly seemed to hang suspended in the air. Flashes of blue and silver glinted in the afternoon sun, drawing the eyes of the passengers. Nyland snatched it out of the air.

The guard beside him reached for Bao Qing, but he was a second late. Her hand flashed forward, drawing the razor-sharp blade across the pilot's throat. Blood spurted into his lap. The helicopter lurched to the right, throwing the guard beside Nyland off balance. Nyland spun the man across the cabin, sent him crashing into the two guards seated in the rear.

The chopper tilted sharply as the pilot fought for control. His hand clutched the wound on his neck trying to staunch the flow of blood. In the copilot's seat, Shenk was shouting into the radio.

Marty and Anne struggled with the guard sitting between them. His M-16 went off, sending a stream of bullets across the cabin. Nyland threw his body across Bao Qing, sending them both to the floor. The guard struck Marty a vicious blow across the face with his rifle butt. Anne grabbed his arm in a lock and pushed him toward the door. He screamed as he plunged through the opening and disappeared.

In the copilot's seat, White shouted into the radio, "Our position is—" Nyland lunged forward, locking his fingers around the man's throat, cutting off the sentence. He punched the man savagely at the base of his skull and Shenk slumped forward, unconscious.

The cabin was in chaos: Marty and Anne were fighting the three remaining guards. Hands and elbows flew. It was impossible to bring a weapon into play in the close confines of the chopper. Nyland lifted Bao Qing back into her seat and clipped a shoulder harness around her. "Stay up here," he shouted, and plunged into the brawl.

The melee was short-lived. As Bao Qing watched, the pilot's eyes rolled back in his head and his hand slipped off the stick. The chopper began to turn slowly on its axis. The jungle canopy was rising toward them. Bao Qing clung to the seat and closed her eyes.

As the chopper dropped into the thick canopy of foliage, the rotors slammed into the trees and disintegrated in a burst of flying metal. When the Huey finally came to rest, jammed against the trunk of a huge teak, the mangled hull was twenty feet above the ground. The smell of fuel was overwhelming.

Nyland was the first to stagger to his feet. One of the guards lay unconscious against the rear bulkhead, the other two were reaching for their weapons. Nyland kicked one in the face, the other dodged toward the side door, now tilted crazily toward the ground. Marty rose to his knees behind the man and shoved him out. He bounced off a heavy branch, fell to the ground and lay sprawled on his back, his neck twisted at an unnatural angle.

"Anne?" Nyland yelled.

"Here," she said. Her clothes were soaked in jet fuel, her hair plastered against her head.

Nyland unfastened Bao Qing's shoulder harness and cradled her in his arms. Her eyes blinked open and she smiled. "I take it we are alive."

He shook his head. "You don't like the ride, just cut the pilot's throat."

Bao Qing sniffed the fuel-laden air. "This helicopter will explode very soon," she said.

Marty was rigging a rappel line, tying a long nylon rope to the chopper's landing strut. Anne slid down first, the MP-5 machine gun slung across her back. Marty followed and held the rope steady as Nyland stepped off the strut with Bao Qing clinging to his neck, a guard's M-16 in his free hand.

The pain in Nyland's ribs ripped through him like fire. He wrapped his legs around the rope and hung for a moment, sweat dripping down his forehead.

"Tuck?" Bao said anxiously.

"I'm OK. Hang on, we're going down."

The four were fifty yards away, pushing their way through the thick foliage, when the Huey exploded.

★   ★   ★

Washington, D.C.

Robert Jaynes's minivan rolled into a turnout at the edge of Rock Creek Park, and stopped in the shadows beneath a stand of maple trees. Jaynes climbed out and stood beside the door. He wore a dark windbreaker over his white shirt and tie; his wool slacks were sharply creased. "Come on out where he can see you," Jaynes said. "'Bring Smith along.' He was pretty adamant about that. I don't have the slightest idea why."

Doug Smith, dressed in jeans and an MIT sweatshirt, climbed out and stood beside him. The night air in the park was clean and fresh, tinted with the musk of spring blossoms. The sound of traffic on Connecticut Avenue was muted by the dense foliage. The rushing noise of the cars blended with the gentle murmur of Rock Creek.

Jaynes had followed directions from the secretary of defense, and brought along Cross's computer expert, Doug Smith—though that request made no sense. Bring Smith. Be on time and tell absolutely no one, Blanchard had said. Jaynes had followed only half the instructions. He was on time, but a backup team waited out of sight back down the road. Now it was up to Blanchard to fulfill his part of the bargain, and bring in Jon Cross.

Blanchard had chosen the spot well, Jaynes thought as he looked around at the dark forest. The only light came from a street-light a hundred yards away, filtered through the branches of the trees. Half-a-dozen trails led off into the park, it would be impossible to cover them all. Whoever waited out there in the darkness had every advantage. Jaynes reached inside his jacket and loosened the Glock automatic in its holster.

Smith said, "Nervous?"

Jaynes ignored him and glanced at his watch. The secretary of defense was late and, in truth, Jaynes was having second thoughts. Was this some kind of trick? Why would Blanchard, a fugitive from the FBI, take such a risk? His career, his life, was finished. What could he hope to gain by trading Jon Cross for the Chinese agent? But the biggest question was why would he want Doug Smith along? All this clandestine meeting business—it seemed more like something Cross would do. Jaynes felt a sudden chill in the warm, spring evening.

"You're sure Cross was unconscious when Blanchard loaded him in the car?" he asked.

"They dragged him into the garage wrapped in a blanket. He'd been through a lot. Drugs, sleep deprivation, he was barely coherent. You don't have to be afraid of him."

"I'm not afraid of Jon Cross." The words came out louder than Jaynes had intended.

"Sure you are. Blanchard is, too, that's why he treated Jon so badly. I'd like to get my hands on that son of a bitch." Smith paced beside the car.

"Forget the vendetta crap. This is about Jon Cross. Blanchard has him; I want him. He has a hell of lot of things to answer for. He was running a Chinese agent on his own, maybe even giving our secrets to China. He broke the law interfering with the FBI, and he tried to leave the country. Even if this Blanchard kidnaping thing happened the way he said it did, there are a hell of a lot of questions unanswered. Cross has been making up his own rules for years. It's my duty to bring him to account. You keep your mouth shut; let me do the talking."

"How dumb are you people?" Doug Smith said. "Jon Cross is not a traitor; he's the best intelligence officer you have. He should get a medal if anything."

"This is a team effort. There's no place anymore for his private wars," Jaynes said.

"We've seen what your team efforts have accomplished. CIA is on the verge of going out of business. The defense department is ready to take over the whole Agency."

"I'm not going to debate policy with a computer programmer."

The voice came from the darkness behind the car: "Not even one who beat your whole system?" John Cross's familiar, mocking tone was unmistakable.

Jaynes jerked the pistol from his coat as he spun around. "I was halfway expecting you, Jon. Where's Blanchard?"

Cross stepped out of the darkness. "I came to offer you a deal."

Jaynes raised the gun. "You're in no position to make any kind of deal." He released the safety. "Now where the hell is Blanchard?"

"I want you to let Nyland and Doug go. No charges, clean slate. You get Blanchard in exchange. And I think you want him badly, Robert."

"No!" Smith shouted. "He doesn't have Nyland. The Agency helicopter he was on disappeared—crashed somewhere near the Thai border."

"Nyland and—the others?" Cross stared at Robert Jaynes.

Smith shrugged. "Nobody knows."

"That was a costly mistake, you little bastard." Jaynes said.

Cross smiled slowly. "If Nyland got away again, which is very likely, it would seem you have no cards to play."

"One or two." Jaynes held the Glock steady as he unclipped a radio from his belt.

Smith threw himself at Jaynes, sending them both to the ground. Jayne's pistol clattered across the blacktop. He threw a punch at Smith's head and Smith fell back clutching his nose. Jaynes stumbled to his feet.

Cross held the pistol. "You put your faith in technology, Robert. You don't pay enough attention to the people. That's the fundamental difference between us. Now Doug and I are going to disappear. You are going to call off your dogs while we do so."

"And why is that?" Jaynes asked.

"Because you want the output of that C4I software."

"Excuse me, but we already have it. We should be hearing the Chinese military communications in a few days."

"You'll be hearing nothing without the little software trigger that Doug has devised. He could explain it, but neither of us could understand the explanation."

Smith wiped blood from his nose. "There is a timed sequence of commands that must be fed to the satellite, otherwise, the trapdoor stays closed."

"And you planned to keep this a secret?"

"Insurance," Cross said. "I want your promise that you won't come after us. You'll have your technology and I'll have—my life. Give us three days to get clear. If nothing happens, we give you the software trigger."

Jaynes leaned tiredly against the car's fender. "Even if I did trust you, I don't have that kind of authority."

"Get it."

"You were running an agent on your own, weren't you? Nyland has him?"

"I doubt you'll find either of them, but you'll get every bit of intelligence my agent has to deliver. The kind of information that can make your career, Robert. I never planned to withhold anything. All I want is to be left alone."

"What if I say no?"

"Then I will kill you where you stand."

Jaynes held his hands in front of him. "No, wait. You'll give me the key to the trapdoor?"

"Do we have a deal?"

"Where is Blanchard?"

"Georgetown. In the Safeway parking lot on M street. Look for a green Ford Taurus, and a very dizzy secretary of defense. One more thing, we'll need an airplane."

Jaynes nodded. "An airplane." There was resignation in his voice. "Just out of curiosity, did they turn you, Jon?"

"No."

"You wouldn't have shot me—?"

"Yes," Cross said.

He and Smith stepped into the darkness and disappeared.

◄28►

Burma

Song Zhenyo had stolen a Burmese Army helicopter. It was a Chinese Z-11, a light observation aircraft nicknamed, *Squirrel*. Song had evoked the name of General Thaung to no avail, offered the Burmese Army captain a wad of bhat, and finally, in desperation, had shoved the muzzle of a 9 mm pistol into the man's stomach. There could be no going back now.

Song's Burmese pilot spoke a little Chinese and no English, but Song had managed to direct him west, toward the Thai border—the direction the gray chopper had gone. The Huey was faster, and had perhaps a half-hour head start, but for Song there was no other choice. Nyland must be hunted down. How many times had he slipped away? Song had been standing less than ten feet from Nyland. A squad of soldiers had surrounded him, yet, somehow he had escaped. Only to be swept up a few minutes later by the Americans in the gray chopper. It didn't take a genius to realize they were CIA. It was also obvious that they were taking their captives to Thailand, probably to the CIA station in Chiang Mai.

His chances of catching the gray Huey were slim, Song knew. It was a little over an hour flight to the Thai border. His Burmese pilot would not cross it, and what if he did? Song was one man against the whole station.

Charles Blanchard had agreed to help him, to intervene with the CIA and the White House, but could he be counted on? He had sounded frightened on the telephone, starting to crack. Had Song pushed him too far?

It was just after noon when the Chinese observation helicopter crossed the Sittang River. Below, a motley collection of fishing boats and barges drifted on the slow-moving brown water. The river was not as big as the Irrawaddy, but it still served, Song knew, as a major route for commerce along Burma's western valleys.

The pilot shouted something in Burmese and pointed ahead. There, rising out of the jungle foliage, was a column of black smoke. As the pilot circled above the site, Song brought up his binoculars. Only a few flames flickered amidst the twisted wreckage of the chopper, but the trunks of nearby trees were scorched, attesting to the fierceness of the blaze. A part of the fuselage had not been burned and he could make out the BAI logo.

Two bodies lay on the forest floor and a third hung over a limb below the charred chassis. He adjusted the focus. All three were men, and all wore black jump suits. Nyland had been wearing khaki trousers. Beyond the burned area, the triple canopy jungle completely hid the forest floor. If there had been survivors, they could be anywhere in the dense forest below.

No, they would not get away with the trick twice. The staged plane crash on the Chinese border had created enough confusion to allow Nyland to slip through The White Man's net. Had he tried it again? There were at least five armed men on the helicopter, how could Nyland have overcome them all? But the site of the crash was too good to be a coincidence, less than a mile from the river. The jungle canopy spread unbroken in all directions. To the east, Song could see the mountains that marked the Thai border. A mile away was the Sittang River, a shining ribbon cutting through the trees. The only route through the impenetrable forest

Maybe Nyland had somehow forced the chopper down, planning to work his way back to the river, perhaps steal a boat. The river opened into the Andaman Ocean a few miles downstream. He could lose himself among the hundreds of nondescript craft making their way up and down the river. Once Nyland reached the ocean, he and Bao Qing would be gone, and with them, any chance of Song's survival.

Or did Nyland's body, and those of his three companions lie somewhere below, charred beyond recognition? There was no place to set the helicopter down. Song jabbed the pilot's shoulder and motioned for him to fly west, back to the river.

For the next half-hour, the helicopter worked its way down the Sittang River at tree-top level, checking the boats. A few were motorized, but most were small fishing boats, paddled by hand. A raft, made of teak logs floated slowly along, a thatched hut in the center. A primitive delivery system that predated the British occupation. Several people sat on the logs and one man stood in the rear, holding a long steering oar. They waved at the helicopter.

Twice, Song thought he saw his prey, but each time, the binoculars revealed only fishermen. The pilot said something in Burmese and pointed at his fuel gauge. It hovered just above empty.

Song pointed to himself, then toward the ground. "Can you put me down somewhere along the river?"

Several minutes later, the chopper settled over a muddy clearing at the bank of the river. A group of fishermen and laborers lounged on a crude log dock smoking. They rose and melted into the forest at the arrival of the military helicopter.

Tied to the dock was an open aluminum boat with a rusty outboard motor. A tangle of fishing nets and equipment lay in the bottom beneath the plank seats, a Styrofoam bumper hung over the side on a yellow plastic rope. Song climbed on board and pushed off as the helicopter rose above the trees and disappeared to the north. The sun had dropped below the trees and long shadows reached across the river. It would be dark soon. He would have to rig a light of some kind, keep going. He fumbled with the starting rope, his hands clumsy in their urgency. The motor finally caught on the fourth try. Song steered the craft out into the current and twisted the throttle open.

Wyn Gyi, the log raft's pilot, clutched his steering oar and peered into the darkness ahead where his two brothers crouched with lighted torches at the forward edge of the raft. His older brother shouted a warning from the starboard side and Wyn swung the lever. This was madness. You did not take a sixty-foot raft of logs down the river at night. Even in broad daylight it was a difficult task avoiding the shifting sandbars and negotiating the hairpin turns in the channel. But the Americans had left him no choice. Keep going, the American woman had told him. Her Burmese wasn't good, but her meaning was clear, backed up by the guns the American men carried. One, the tall one who helped the old Chinese woman onto the raft, had such a wild, dangerous look in his eye that Wyn Gyi had hastened to follow his orders.

Several hours before, Gyi had watched a gray helicopter fly over the river and then, a few moments later, had seen the column of smoke rising from the jungle. These people had somehow survived the crash; their clothes reeked of jet fuel. There was no doubt they were running from the government soldiers. That made harboring them an insane risk.

The four passengers had hidden themselves in the thatched hut in the middle of the raft just before Wyn saw a second helicopter come down the river, flying low, obviously searching for someone. Such flights were common here, where the rebels and the government soldiers often traded shots. It all meant trouble, Gyi thought, and he and his family wanted no part of it. There would be good money when the raft of logs made it to Rangoon. Nothing must happen to the raft.

But now its very existence was endangered by the American's order to float downstream in the dark, with only two torches to light the way. Several times, Wyn had been tempted to jump overboard and swim to shore. But he could see the big American lying in the doorway of the hut, his rifle aimed in Gyi's direction. And besides, you did not desert your family, or risk losing your livelihood. So the raft floated on downstream.

They were near the delta now, Wyn knew, where the channel would widen. He whispered prayers into the hot night air that the foreigners would leave his raft soon, and that the army would never find out that he had helped them escape.

Another shout from his brother, and he felt the raft grind against a sandbar. The stern began to swing out into the current as he fought the steering oar. Suddenly, the two Americans appeared on deck, picked up long poles and ran toward the forward edge of the raft. Both men pushed their poles into the soft bottom and strained against the force of the current. Slowly, the huge mass of logs slid off the sandbar and swung back into the channel. Wyn waved his arm in thanks. The two men disappeared back into the hut.

★ ★ ★

Nyland lay on his stomach in the doorway of the hut, taking his turn on watch. The others were asleep. He could hear Marty's steady breathing behind him. He deserved a rest. Though he hadn't complained, it was easy to tell the wound in his back was bothering him. Nyland glanced around at the dim forms of the two women. Just then, Anne rose on one elbow and touched a button on her wrist watch, sending a faint, greenish glow over the thatched walls. Her face and arms were streaked with dirt, her hair matted with sweat. Her shirt had been torn and charred in the helicopter crash, but there was a strange serenity in her eyes as she looked at Nyland.

The two crept outside the hut and sat together on the rough logs. He slipped his arm around her shoulder. The Burmese men slept on a small platform at the forward edge of the raft, exhausted after the long night of fighting the river. The two torches that were their navigation lights still flickered on bamboo poles at the forward edge of the raft.

"What if our ship's not there, and we can't make it to Thailand?" Anne asked.

"I have some contacts in Malaysia. Pinang."

"The idea of defeat never enters your mind does it?"

"You'd be surprised."

"No, I admire you for that. I gave up a bunch of times. But what about Bao Qing? How much farther can she—"

"I promised Jon Cross I'd bring her out."

"You're a strange man, Tuck. All this code of honor bullshit."

"It doesn't matter."

"I'm sorry." She laid her hand on his arm. "I want to understand, I want you to—let me in. This isn't some goddamn John

Wayne thing. You have feelings, you hurt, you're afraid sometimes. You can tell me."

"I'm afraid all the time."

"You're the bravest man I've known, does that sound melodramatic? I didn't mean it to. But you have risked your life a dozen times for all of us. You saved Marty's life up in Maymyo, you didn't have to do that."

"He means a lot to you."

"We were—lovers."

"You love him?" Nyland asked.

"That's not the same thing. We were kind of drifting apart, as they say. He wanted more. I wanted—" She looked out at the dark water.

He studied her face. "You wanted what?"

Her voice was a whisper. "I wanted—someone like you."

The silence widened.

"I—still do," Anne rolled onto her side, facing him. "I guess I'm finally starting to understand who you are, what drives you. Up until a week ago, my biggest dream was getting to the next pay grade, and maybe finding a decent guy. Is that a bourgeois idea or what?"

"The American Dream," Nyland said.

"But you put your whole soul into bringing Bao Qing back, risked your life a dozen times. I need something like that—something to live for, not just something to work for. The two of us can have that together, Tuck."

Nyland looked at her, started to speak, but said nothing. After a moment, she crawled back into the hut. He wanted to call after her, but what was there to say? There was no way to know if they had a future, even a day. At dawn there would be planes in the air, armed patrols on all the roads, probably gunboats searching the river and the delta. The raft wouldn't be hard to spot.

Nyland could smell the salt on the night air, mingled with the faint scent of flowers and the musty smell of the jungle along the bank. The river was growing wider as the raft of logs moved into the delta.

The fear was returning. He must protect Bao Qing, and all the secrets she carried. And Marty, who had risked his life to bring them this far. But the worst fear was not having a future—of not having Anne.

Nyland stood up and walked to the forward edge of the raft. The sky was just beginning to lighten and he could see the darker shadows of the jungle on either side. The channel was now at least half-a-mile wide.

Behind him, Nyland heard the faint sound of an outboard motor. A boat approaching from upriver. The motor raced at full throttle. This was no early morning fishing expedition. Then Nyland caught the white flash of spray from the bow's wake. The boat was headed directly at him.

The M-16 he had salvaged from the chopper lay on the log beside him. He snatched it up and fired a three-shot burst at the boat's waterline. The boat veered to the side, and the driver cut the throttle. The Burmese crew, wakened by the shots and the roar of the motor, dived behind their sleeping platform seeking cover. The old man was reaching for the steering oar when a bullet struck him and he toppled into the brown water. The other three dived in and swam toward shore.

Nyland lay on his stomach hidden behind the sleeping platform as Marty crawled up beside him, cradling his rifle in the crook of his arms. "Hundred yards off the starboard beam. One man."

"What kind of maniac—"

"Remember the guy in the straw hat Anne saw when they stopped the train? I saw him again, just as the CIA chopper was lifting off, standing beside the train, shaking his fist. Song Zhenyo. Somehow he followed us."

The log raft was drifting closer to the shore and there were reeds in the water now. Marty pointed toward the bank. "This little firefight brought us some company."

Another boat was moving toward them. A searchlight flared on its bow, bathing the raft in a hard white light. Nyland raised his rifle and fired. The searchlight went out. Anne, clutching her machine gun, crawled toward the two men. "River patrol," she said. "They're radioing our position to Lwin Thaung's troops right now, I bet."

"Fire at the water line. Shoot and move," Nyland commanded.

She fired a quick burst from the MP-5, then ran toward the thatched hut.

Nyland tossed Marty the M-16. "Cover her," he said.

Marty fired a quick burst at the patrol boat. When he looked up, Nyland was stripping off his shirt. "What the hell are you doing?"

"Going for a swim." Nyland dived into the muddy water.

★ ★ ★

There was sporadic firing from the patrol boat now, but they were unsure of their target. The log raft lay low in the water and was nearly invisible in the half-light of dawn. It would not take them long to call in reinforcements.

The boat moved closer and a voice from a loudspeaker shouted a command in Burmese. "They want us to identify ourselves," Anne said. She lay behind the sleeping platform, her arm protectively around Bao Qing. A machine gun on the patrol boat opened fire and she watched the hut's thatched roof fly apart.

"They don't know where we are," she said.

"It won't take them long to figure it out," Marty said.

The boat idled toward them cautiously, and the loudspeaker crackled again: surrender. There were muzzle flashes from the mangrove swamp along the banks now, the sound of gunfire. A foot patrol had been alerted by the noise.

The raft was drifting slowly toward midstream. Marty crawled to the rear of the raft and sliced at the ropes with his knife. A large log floated free and bobbed in the water beside the raft.

"Can you swim?" Marty asked. Bao Qing nodded. To Anne, he said, "Hold onto the log, paddle for the other bank. I'm gonna try to hold up this patrol boat. Nyland is over there somewhere, he'll find you."

"No, we stay together."

"That will get us all killed. Move! Before it gets any lighter."

"Marty, I—"

"Don't make this any harder."

She squeezed his hand gently; there were tears in her eyes. The two women slipped into the water.

The log was a dim shape in front of them, riding low in the dark water. As they paddled toward it, Anne could see the patrol boat moving closer. The crew had stopped firing, apparently uncertain of their target. Suddenly, Marty jumped to his feet. His M-16 bucked in his hand as he poured fire into the boat. Its fuel tank erupted in flames and the boat listed heavily to port.

The crew, surprised by the sudden assault, but now sure of their target, immediately returned fire. Marty ran forward, away from Anne and Bao Qing.

Anne could barely make out his running form outlined by the flames from the patrol boat. He was firing from the hip as he ran. The boat was listing badly, water only inches from the port gunnel. Several of the soldiers had jumped overboard and were flailing in the water, but two more knelt in the bow, firing at the raft. Marty reached the end of the raft and turned to face them. He had used the last of his ammunition, Anne realized.

When the soldier's bullets hit him, he threw up his arms, fell back onto the logs and lay still. Anne laid her cheek against the rough bark and wept.

Nyland's head broke the surface without a ripple. His pale eyes scanned the dark water. The aluminum outboard drifted near the far bank, a hundred yards away. A figure, face indistinguishable in the predawn darkness, crouched in the stern. It had to be Song Zhenyo. The man who had worked his way inside the White House, gotten a strangle hold on the top man in the president's cabinet. The man who had calmly pulled a pistol from his pocket and shot Jennifer Chin. Nyland swam toward the boat, each stroke sending stabs of pain through his chest.

The SEAL training was coming back. Chief Thompson shouting: do it when you can't, do it when you can't. The words revolved in his head like a mantra as he swam.

When he surfaced again, the boat was only yards away. Song Zhenyo was staring across the river, his attention on the firefight. Nyland took a breath and slipped beneath the water.

Song Zhenyo strained to see in the darkness. The patrol boat's searchlight had given him a brief glimpse of the people on the teak raft. It was his quarry, no doubt, but they were well armed and it would have been suicide to approach the raft directly over open water. Now it looked as though the Burmese patrol boat was about to do his job for him. He saw muzzle flashes from the raft, and return flashes from the patrol boat. It was difficult to follow the progress of the fight, a ragged series of shots punctuated by shouts over the patrol boat's loudspeaker. Then the voice fell silent and the firing stopped.

The light was gradually increasing in the eastern sky, casting a faint, pink reflection on the slow-moving water. Song could see no one on the raft. The Burmese patrol boat floated nearby, listing severely to starboard. Movement caught Song's eye farther out in the channel. A floating log, and two figures in the water. Bao Qing and the American woman. He twisted the outboard's throttle, sending the boat racing out into the channel.

As he closed on the floating log, Song saw the red-haired woman straddling it, furiously working the slide of a short-barreled machine gun. Her expression told the story. The weapon was jammed.

He cut the throttle and stood up in the boat, leveling his AK-47 at the woman. He could see the old Chinese woman clinging to the log, her face just above the water. Bao Qing, the espionage agent. Song Zhenyo smiled, for once forgetting the pain of his festering ear. This was a prize he had worked hard for. Returning this woman to China would make him a hero.

"Throw your gun in the water," he said. The red-haired woman scowled, but didn't move. "Now!" Song's boat drifted closer to the log. "Bring the old woman here." Song held the AK-47 on his hip.

Bao Qing stared at him impassively. Song raised the rifle, his finger tightening on the trigger. The boat tilted crazily. He caught a fleeting impression of an arm rising ghost-like from the water, a savage, grinning face. He felt a hand grip his ankle, then he was in the water.

★ ★ ★

Nyland released Song's ankle, groped blindly in the murky water, and caught hold of his shirt. Song's fingers clawed at Nyland's eyes, forcing him to loosen his grip. Both men bobbed to the surface at the same time, gasping for air. Nyland grabbed Song's arm and pulled him back under. As the two men struggled, Nyland saw the man's face dimly before him in the dark water, lips twisted into a grimace of rage. Suddenly, a sharp pain jabbed through Nyland's groin. The force of the kick was lessened by the water, but it doubled Nyland over in pain. Song rose to the surface.

The need for air was screaming in Nyland's head, but he swam toward Song and drove a sword hand into the man's solar plexus. Song's body went limp and he sank back into the water, floating beside Nyland, his mouth gaping open. A thin trail of bubbles escaped into the murky water and trailed toward the surface. Nyland swam behind the man and slipped an arm around his neck.

Song struggled desperately, his arms reaching, seeking his tormentor. His bandage had come undone and floated around his head like pale kelp. A sharp pain jabbed across Nyland's arm and a thin ribbon of blood drifted in the water around the two men's heads.

Song had a knife. With his free hand, Nyland reached for Song's wrist and twisted it savagely. The knife disappeared down into the watery blackness.

Nyland scissor-kicked to the surface for air, his arm still locked around Song's neck. He took a deep breath and sank back under. Song's struggles were growing weaker. A column of bubbles drifted out of his mouth and rose toward the surface. His form went limp. Still Nyland kept his grip, ignoring the scream in his brain—air.

Song's body hung lifeless in his arms, but still Nyland did not release his hold. Raw, animal instincts gripped him. Then, the scene in the spider hole in Baghdad flashed before his eyes. He forced himself to relax. Keep Song alive.

His responsibility. Must not fail again.

He kicked his way to the surface and grabbed the keel of the aluminum boat. Anne's face lit up in a smile as she reached for his hand. Together, they dragged Song into the boat. He opened his eyes and coughed.

"I thought you were going to kill him," Anne said.

"I was." Nyland grabbed Song's arm and sat him up. "Where are the rest of your people? You didn't come after us alone."

Song stared at Nyland, a mix of fear and hatred in his eyes. "I came alone—almost made it." He coughed again, bringing up a foul mixture of salt water and bile. "Why didn't you kill me?"

"You have a lot to tell us."

"Who is 'us?' CIA wants you dead. You are as much an outcast as I am."

"What the CIA does with you is their business. But you're gonna stay alive long enough to tell them about Bei Feng—and clear Jon Cross's name."

◄29►

With four people on board, the aluminum boat rode low in the water, barely making headway as the small outboard chugged its way across the water. Song sat in the bow, his arms draped over the side of the boat. Anne and Qing shared a plank seat amidships. Anne kept the MP-5 trained on the prisoner. Nyland sat in the stern, his hand on the tiller, ignoring Song's glare of hatred. The swells were gentle and there was almost no breeze. The sky was blossoming into a tapestry of reds and golds.

"There's the trawler," Nyland said. "Another mile."

Nyland could see its dark shape ahead, riding on the swells and let himself relax. The trawler could blend into the fleet of fishing boats and they would disappear. He gasped in pain as Bao Qing tightened makeshift bandages around his ribs, and then the knife slash on his arm. "You're gonna turn me into a damn mummy," he said, pushing her hand away.

"You have to learn to let somebody take care of you for a change."

The explosion behind them was a dull boom. A geyser of water erupted twenty yards off the port side. "Gunboat," Nyland said. "Closing fast."

The deck gun boomed again, and this time the shell exploded to starboard. The boat planed across the water, sending a wide, white wake over the smooth surface of the ocean. It was a Houdong Class patrol boat flying the Burmese flag. A solitary figure stood on the forward deck behind the twenty-millimeter. "General Xing," Anne said.

Song struggled to sit up, waving his arm at the gunboat. Anne shoved him down. The gunboat slowed, its bow settling back into the water. Nyland could see several Burmese soldiers on the rail. General Xing swung the gun toward the small aluminum craft. A voice on a loudspeaker: "You are prisoners of the People's Republic of China. Stop your engine."

Anne fired a short burst from the MP-5 and saw a sailor pitch forward over the rail. The gunboat was less than a hundred yards away now. The loudspeaker amplified Xing's laugh across the water. "You have a brave crew, Mr. Nyland, but you are outgunned. Stop your engine."

Anne raised the machine gun, fired a single round, and the pilot house window shattered. Xing dodged behind the deck gun's steel plate.

"Save your ammunition," Nyland said.

"Yeah. That was my last fucking bullet."

The report from the deck gun was deafening. The shell exploded off their stern, drenching them. Waves lapped over the stern and the aluminum boat wallowed helplessly, rocking with the swells.

The gunboat loomed over the small outboard now, blocking the sun. Two Burmese soldiers stood at the rail, rifles trained on the boat. "Stop your engine! It is over." Xing's voice was harsh and mechanical over the loudspeaker. "I have no wish to kill you."

Nyland felt a sudden weariness overcome him. Xing was right; it was over. A SEAL never surrenders: the words rang hollow in his mind. Nyland looked at Anne and Bao Qing huddled together on the seat and, for the second time in two days, raised his hands.

The gunboat's crew attached lines to the aluminum boat and threw a rope ladder over the side. Anne and Bao Qing were first to board. As they stepped onto the gunboat, one of the soldiers urged them below, prodding them with his rifle. Song Zhenyo stood up in the aluminum boat and reached for the ladder. Xing leaned over the rail and shouted, "No! You stay. And contemplate your failure."

He studied Nyland for a moment. "The warrior. Please come aboard. I have something special in mind for you."

The aft deck of the gunboat was small, scarcely fifteen by ten, the size of a living room, surrounded by ammunition lockers and gun mounts bolted to the steel planking along the rail. Xing and Nyland faced each another, both stripped to the waist. Xing was several inches shorter than Nyland, but the muscles on his chest and shoulders stood out in stark relief in the early morning light. "You know Wing Chun style, Mr. Nyland?"

Nyland nodded. The primary weapons were butterfly knives and a wooden staff. The style was named after the woman who invented it, Lim Wing Chun.

Nyland had proven himself a true warrior, Xing had explained, and thus had earned the honor of meeting the general face-to-face. The gunboat's crew had been instructed to stay forward, out of sight of the rear deck. General Xing reserved for himself the pleasure of killing this most persistent of his enemies.

There was little hope of escape, Nyland realized, even if he bested the man. The crew was unlikely to release their valuable prisoners. The only faint hope lay in the fact that Xing had come after them alone. He had commandeered the Burmese ship and it's crew, apparently without notifying the Burmese army, or the PLA. There were no reenforcements coming. Bao Qing held the secret of his coup attempt, something he dared share with no one.

There were two soldiers guarding Anne and Bao Qing in the cabin below. The odds were nearly hopeless. But there had been no choice but to accept Xing's taunting challenge.

Xing's nostrils flared like an animal's as he turned the butterfly knives over in his hands. The blades were the length of a small machete, with curving steel hand guards. White silk scarves trailed from the handles. When Xing attacked, Nyland knew, the scarves would whirl around the knives, confusing the eye of the defender.

Nyland held a long, hardwood staff, the other principal weapon of the Wing Chun style. Not as impressive as the flashing knives, but in the hands of an expert, a terrifying weapon. The pole was seven feet long, an inch-and-half in diameter. It took great strength in the wrists and arms to use the pole effectively, but it allowed long-range thrusting strikes that could reach inside the deadly, flashing blades. Nyland held the staff in a relaxed, two handed grip, stepping automatically into a deep horse stance. The deck rolled gently beneath his feet as the boat rode the swells. He kept his breathing slow and steady, concentrating on the knives in Xing's hands, trying to ignore the pain in his ribs and ankle. If he and the others were to survive, he would have to defeat the man quickly; he had no strength for a prolonged fight.

Xing glided forward, quick and graceful as cat, the butterfly knives held straight up before him. Nyland jabbed the staff at Xing's throat, felt the shock of a downward parry, and jumped to the side, pulling the staff back.

"You are very fast," Xing said. He caught the staff on the edge of his blade and pushed it aside. The silk scarves swirled around the shining steel in a blur.

Again, Xing stepped in, and a blade passed inches from Nyland's face. He parried the thrust, but his back was against the steel railing. He pivoted suddenly and spun the long staff in a sweeping arc a foot above the steel planking. The pole caught Xing behind the knees and he dropped to the deck.

He rolled to his feet in an instant, rage burning in his eyes. But his advance was slower this time, Nyland noticed, more cautious. He was favoring his right leg. Suddenly, he leaped forward, the butterfly knives a blur amidst the swirl of the silk scarves. Nyland parried right and left, backing slowly toward the port rail. There was a trickle of blood down his arm; one of the blades had grazed his shoulder. He felt himself growing dizzy. Have to end it soon.

Nyland feinted toward Xing's stomach, reversed the pole suddenly and sent it whipping down at Xing's head. The butterfly knives came up in an X block, catching the full force of staff. The boat rolled to starboard on the swells, and Xing stumbled backward. He was no sailor, Nyland realized. The gunboat righted itself and Xing stumbled again.

In the instant Xing was off balance, Nyland leaped, turned in the air, and snapped a kick at Xing's chest. Nyland's foot struck Xing over his heart. Tuck felt the man's ribs break beneath his heel.

Xing's eyes rolled back in his head, he staggered drunkenly and fell face down on the steel deck. The kick had ruptured his heart, and killed him instantly. The butterfly knives skittered across the deck and over the side.

An explosion sent a painful wave of pressure against Nyland's ears. For a moment, he thought the deck gun had fired again. The gunboat listed heavily astern, the deck gun angled toward the sky. Smoke and flames poured from the cabin and the bow tilted higher. The explosion had come from below decks—where the soldiers had taken Anne and Bao Qing.

Nyland threw the wooden staff aside and struggled up the slanting deck toward the cabin door. It burst open before he could reach it, and one of the soldiers ran toward the rail, intent only on saving himself. A moment later, Anne and Bao Qing stumbled out, coughing in the cloud of acrid smoke surrounding them. Bao Qing's knife was clenched in her hand, the blade covered with blood.

"What the hell happened?" Nyland shouted.

"Guards weren't paying attention—watching the fight." Anne's face was smeared with soot, a trickle of blood ran down her cheek. "Qing's idea to grenade the engine room."

"They never learn to take women seriously," Qing said. She folded the knife and slid it in her pocket. Flames were leaping out of the cabin windows behind her and black smoke billowed into the sky.

Nyland shook his head. "Mistake you don't make twice."

"You're getting there," Anne said.

Nyland held the ladder as the two women clambered into the aluminum boat. Song Zhenyo was fumbling with the tow rope. Bao Qing pulled out her knife. "Sit," she said in Chinese. He sat down in the bow, eyes downcast as the two women climbed into the boat.

Nyland was halfway down the ladder when the fuel tanks exploded, ripping the vessel open. The blast threw him backward into the water.

★ ★ ★

Nyland's head broke the surface and he felt hands tugging at his arms, lifting him from the water. He opened his eyes and took a ragged breath. Anne was cradling his head in her lap. The gunboat had disappeared beneath the waves. Burning oil spread on the water, the black smoke rising in the tropical sky.

"You're OK," Anne said. More a statement than a question. There were tears in her eyes.

He struggled to sit up. "Have to—"

She laid her hand gently on his shoulder. "The trawler's spotted us, they're coming in. We have time now." She bent forward and kissed him.

Nyland closed his eyes, felt the warmth of Anne's body against him. The sound of water lapping against the hull, the cry of a sea bird. Time now—all the time in the world.

After a while, the flames burned themselves out and the last of the smoke drifted away. The sea was empty and silent as the sun rose.

◄30►

Jon Cross held Bao Qing's elbow as they walked down the wide flagstone steps into the terrace. A blue and silver dragonfly pin gleamed on her kimono. At the bottom of the steps, Cross released her arm and bowed to her, a courtly gesture, curiously out of time. But the whole place was out of time, Nyland thought. The worn stone bench where he sat was elaborately carved. Winged satyrs cavorting with nymphs.

The house was on a small island in the Andaman Ocean, three hundred miles off the southern coast of Thailand. It was owned by a shadowy Thai businessman who owed a debt to Jon Cross.

The house had been built at the turn of the century by a Dutch shipping magnate who was really more of a pirate. The estate had been named Kakana in honor of the Thai girl he had taken as his mistress. Tropical flowers and trees covered the windward side of the island, surrounding the house, concealing it from scrutiny. Here on the flagstone terrace, there was little sign of the twentieth century.

The island's population at the moment numbered five. Doug Smith had set up residence in a small study on the top floor overlooking the ocean to the west. He had been hard at work for the past month upgrading his communications system. Security was even tighter now, all the codes and encryption systems had been replaced.

Tuck Nyland and Anne Hammersmith had chosen a small guest cottage above the main house. The stucco walls were painted white, a potted orchid sat next to the white wicker bed. The bamboo curtains were rolled up to let in the westerly breezes. They made love most mornings, a delicious, languid affair that often lasted until noon.

Jon Cross and Bao Qing had taken the master bedroom in the main house, a huge space with mahogany beams in the ceiling, a floor of teak planks fastened with hardwood pegs. They usually retired early.

The five had been in residence for nearly three months. During that time, when news of Xing's death in the Andaman Sea came out, people came forward to testify about the plot to overthrow the government—chief among them the relatives and friends of the people he had tortured and killed. China had been thrown into turmoil as the government struggled to smash the coup, and weed out and punish Xing's co-conspirators. Half-a-dozen PLA generals had been thrown in prison. Two members of the Central Committee were publicly executed.

The crash of the C4I system—after only sixty days in operation—set China's military back, even by conservative estimate, at least ten years. Many of their high-tech weapons systems sat useless, their screens dark. Units were forced to communicate by telephone. The Ministry of State Security, in a state of near panic after Bao Qing's defection, rushed to change their codes and recall hundreds of agents stationed abroad.

The two months the C4I system was in operation, the trapdoor functioning just as promised, provided the CIA with a mountain of data about the inner workings of the MSS and the People's Liberation Army. It was a priceless intelligence coup, but, like many successful intelligence operations, one the media and the public would never hear about.

Through Doug Smith's untraceable satellite links, Cross had been in regular contact with the CIA. At first, Billy Vail, the director of Central Intelligence, had tried to talk him into coming back to Washington. With Robert Jaynes under indictment for conspiracy, the Operations Directorate was up for grabs. A new task force was being put together—counterterrorism—was Cross interested? But, as the weeks passed, and Cross politely refused his offers, the DCI had ceased to ask. He would have to be content with the flow of information from the C4I software, and debriefings from the Chinese agent Jon Cross had code named "Browning."

Congress had launched an investigation into President Gardner's fund-raising activities, focusing primarily on the role of Song

Zhenyo. Though the president had denied any knowledge of Song's connection to Chinese intelligence, it was clear from evidence provided by Agent Browning that the Chinese had played a key role in financing Gardner's reelection.

He had sold out the Oval Office, he told the CIA director, for thirty pieces of silver. Facing the almost certain threat of impeachment, Jack Gardner had resigned as president of the United States, the second man in U.S. history to do so. Vice President Wilson Alexander had been sworn in as president the following day.

Vail had forwarded the new president's congratulations and his thanks for unmasking Charles Blanchard. There were reports that a film, reportedly of a POW interrogation in Vietnam—featuring Blanchard—had surfaced at CNN. Bootleg copies were in heavy demand. Vail added a somber footnote: the secretary of defense had committed suicide in his cell, less than a week before the start of his trial for treason.

Song Zhenyo was undergoing intensive debriefing, Vail said. The man's ear had healed, but he now sported a shapeless pink lump on the side of his head, which he had tried to cover by letting his hair grow. His interrogators, Director Vail had noted wryly, were using a powerful truth drug called Christmas.

And the SEAL Tommy Thompson had gotten his other stripe. He was now Master Chief Petty Officer Thompson.

Cross walked with Bao Qing to the bench where Nyland sat. "Doug just got a message from the sub. They're about ten miles off shore. Chief Thompson says his SEALs are anxious to meet you."

Nyland stood up. "Better not keep the Navy waiting."

"Pickup time is nineteen-hundred hours. You don't have to go right this minute," Cross said.

"Yes he does," Bao Qing said. "He is a young man with a purpose."

"And I am an old one, with none?" Cross smiled at her.

"Our purpose is what it has always been, to be together." She turned to lay her hand on Nyland's arm. "She's waiting down on the beach. You had better go."

"Just out of curiosity," Nyland said, "did you know about Anne—about our meeting at Camp Peary?"

Cross smiled. "Sources and methods."

Bao Qing shrugged her shoulders. "Don't look at me."

Nyland laid his hand over hers. "Take care of—" His voice broke and he fell silent.

Cross frowned. "Are we going to chit-chat all day? The Navy's waiting."

Nyland shouldered his duffle bag and walked down the stone steps toward the water.

Anne sat on the white sand, staring out at the ocean. The sun was just settling into the waves. She stood up as Nyland approached. He slid his arm around her waist and kissed her. She bumped him playfully with her hip.

"You're looking pretty fit," he said.

"Thanks to you and your insane training regimen. If anybody told me I would be swimming five miles a day, I would have—"

"It paid off, though?"

"Are you talking about our sex life?"

Nyland chuckled. "Fringe benefit."

"Always the romantic."

"Just heard from the sub. Contact time one hour." Gentle rollers moved across the water toward them and slid with a gentle hiss onto the beach. Nyland shielded his eyes from the sun and squinted out to sea. Somewhere out there, aboard a U.S. Navy attack submarine, Master Chief Thompson and his SEAL team waited.

Nyland pulled Anne closer to him. "Our little stint in paradise is over—for the moment," he said quietly.

"Paradise is what you do, not where you are," she said. She tucked her short-cropped, red hair into the hood of her wet suit. "Let's do it."

The two shouldered their rucksacks and waded into the surf.

THE END

ABOUT THE AUTHOR

John Reed served as an Army Intelligence officer at Fort Bragg, North Carolina, Vietnam, and other overseas postings. His poetry has appeared in numerous literary magazines in the United States and Canada. *The Kingfisher's Call* is his second novel. Reed lives and writes in Eugene, Oregon.